Antonio Sandoval

Free Rider
Antonio Sandoval

2012 Second printing
by Antonio Sandoval

This book is dedicated to the Police Officers I have known and had the honor to work with, who like myself had their faults, did their job, made their mistakes and not always received credit when it was due. When we made mistakes, we stood alone. We were not always friends, but when faced with danger, we stood together and I always had your back. I think always of those of you that I left behind, those that have passed on and most of all those who still carry on bravely for the rest of us.

When faced with a life and death physical confrontation, you will react and survive according to the value of your training and the diligence of your practice. In the absence of practice, you will survive according to Chance, Fortune, or the Mercy of your attacker. *Quotes of a Kempo Master.*

Introduction

She heard the loud crack of the pistol shot and almost lost her grip on the reins as she started up the small rise. Her horse topped the rise just when she reached down to grip the pommel and went on at a full gallop for only a moment longer before he stumbled...Time went into slow motion. She felt herself flying through the air and thought only to cover her face and duck into an almost fetal position out of fear. She closed her eyes and felt the ground hit her shoulders and the middle of her back and realized she was still conscious and looking directly up at the sky. She felt herself breathe and was amazed that the fall hadn't knocked the breath out of her, then she remembered with a start---she had been trying to get away from the men who had shot at her.

Chapter One

The two women walked along the storefronts in the midmorning sun. They looked enough alike to be twins except for their age difference and their style of clothing. The older more mature woman could easily be in her mid thirties and her companion in her teens or early twenties. Wearing light colored jeans and a light blue short sleeved shirt, her hair in a loose pony tail, tied with a bandanna, open slightly at the neck, she listened almost absentmindedly while the younger woman talked and gestured with her hands. Her blue gray eyes appeared more gray than blue in light of the morning sun.

She looked over at the younger woman occasionally, but her even featured face was almost free of emotion, her thoughts seemingly drifting in another place. Her young companion, wearing blue jeans and a collarless short sleeved knit shirt, barely out of her teens, hair flowing loosely over her shoulders, continued to carry on the one way conversation. Her full hips and long shapely legs filled the jeans tightly just as her round soft shoulders and breasts filled her otherwise loose top.

Both women, tall and similar of physique, showed the close family relationship, except that the older woman was somewhat slimmer, slightly taller, with the softness of the younger woman gone from her face. The light brown western boots made them both taller and they weren't unnoticed as they walked casually, almost carefree along the busy but uncrowded sidewalk. Most of the men, young and older on this sunny street in Holbrook, Arizona, took the time to look and admire the striking good looks and beauty of both women.

Five men standing on a side street next to their custom bikes had seen them too and followed their progress along the sidewalk, staring at them openly as they came their way. They had arrived the night before after traveling south from Montana into Colorado, then to Denver, southwest on U.S. 285 to avoid the busier Interstate 25 and the higher number of trooper patrols.

The rest of the large group of riders had gone west past Joseph city and past Winslow and more of them south to Show Low, spreading their numbers around a larger area, so not to draw any more attention than necessary.

"Hey brother, look at that will you?" one of the men told his companion.

"Take it easy," his companion cautioned. "Those two are not just reg'lar broads. Some big shit kicker with a rifle or a wheel gun might be waitin' for 'em down the street in his truck."

"Jinx, you're full of shit," he said. "They're just another couple of good lookin' bitches."

"Brooks, I'm tellin' you man, you don't want to mess with those two. They look like they belong to some cowboy with big bucks who won't take no shit." Jinx replied.

"I'm just gonna talk to them. This is Holbrook; just another Arizona hick town. You worried or something?" he asked.

Brooks walked away from the group and approached the sidewalk directly across the street where the women were still walking in his direction. Jinx shook his head, shrugged, then followed. The thought of some big cowboy or rancher with a bad temper waiting for the women didn't intimidate Brooks in the least, especially after firing down several glasses of Southern Comfort.

It was nothing that stirred any worry in either of the two men, except that Jinx was cautious. The younger woman stopped and looked in their direction and smiled; the other woman didn't look, even when the two men crossed the street to lean against a building in front of them and leered at them, especially at the older woman, as they walked by.

My plan was to ride from Kenai, Alaska, into Canada then along the Cassiar Highway into British Columbia then into Seattle, Washington. I was going to wait until early June when it would be getting a little warmer and the roads clear all the way through Canada, but I hadn't been pinned down to any kind of schedule since I retired the second time four years ago. The opportunity to make the trip came up a little sooner than I expected, so I decided to take a chance and leave early.

The roads would be icy in most of Alaska until late May or early June but there was a chance they would be clear most of the way through Canada and at the other end of the road closer to Seattle. "Breakup," as the spring thaw in Alaska is called, begins in late April and early May but it's still cold and even where the highway surfaces seem clear, there is the black ice, which of course you can't see. It can cause the most unbelievable spinouts with any kind vehicle.

It would be getting warmer and even hot the farther South I traveled, so the plan was to trailer the bike south until I reached clear roads. I may have made a risky decision to leave the first week of May and as it turned out it was still wet and muddy most of the last six hundred miles. There wasn't enough clear road most of the way until I reached Watson Lake, in Canada; past that point the road got worse but I continued south on the Cassiar Highway and entered the states through Washington.

I wanted to ride along some of the old routes, following U.S. 395 along the Washington, Idaho border all the way to Reno, Nevada and south on U.S. 95 to Las Vegas. From Las Vegas I would head south to Kingman and then east so I could see the desert, it would be a great ride and I could take all the time I needed if I found an interesting place to stop. I could pick up the old Route 66, now Highway 40, then cross the desert and head into the mountains to Flagstaff, then travel south toward Albuquerque.

I was doing well following the inland route on the way to Reno but I broke a shock bolt on the swing arm and I had to head east to Utah to find a place to repair it. I had to limp in on the remaining shock for almost two hundred miles on Highway 20 until I reached Caldwell, Utah. It didn't look like I was going to get anyone there to take out the broken stub of the bolt in less than a week, but a customer and friend of the service manager offered to help me fix it.

The ride from there heading west into California was hot and the highway was busier than I wanted it to be. I stayed on Highway 20 until it intersected with 395 again and rode through part of the dry plains of eastern California and into the California desert into a bright orange sunset that streaked through the clouds in long bars of orange and yellow gold streams.

It was one of those sunsets that seem to light up the sky, the clouds and the distant rolling hills of the desert with rising flames from the falling sun. Sagebrush and Greasewood and a few small green plants with small blossoms can be seen a little closer to the road, but in the distance only the darkening landscape and the dying embers of the seemingly burning hills are seen on the horizon.

Nothing seems to grow very large except cactus in the hot California and Arizona desert sun. The flowers open only in the cooling afternoon, and then close again to save energy for the approaching heat of the next day. I had traveled these same roads many years ago at least once a year when I was on leave and still in the Navy. Route 66 has long since been replaced by Interstate 40 and a lot of the traffic seems to be on the upper northern route on U.S. 84 or farther south on Route 80 through Phoenix, which was just a gas stop in the 60's when I traveled through there many years past.

I listened carefully, as always to the thumping and clicking of the new engine on the Harley Davidson frame and the familiar and pleasing smell of the hot metal. I wanted an individual bike which was put together the way I wanted it, so I looked for several years and finally settled on a 99 Harley Softail frame. I remembered riding a bike much older than this, sometime in the last century it seems, when I was 15 years old.

The frame had been what I was looking for to build the custom bike I wanted. After stripping it down and replacing the swing arm, which would take the larger rear tire, it started to look pretty good. After reshaping the tanks, adding new fork tubes, new wheels, new bars and controls and a new 100 cube engine, it started to look like the nice custom bike I had expected it to be. The big difference was and would continue to be, that I could insure it as a Harley.

My thoughts returned to the present to listen to the big engine rumbling softly then a little more loudly across the flats starting into the gentle climbs of the Northern Arizona desert. It gets cold in the plains and deserts at night, and being desert, most would think that it's warm or hot and muggy at night, but it isn't. It begins cooling rapidly when the sun begins to set and continues to get colder during the night.

There isn't a lot of plant life except scrub willow bushes and some weeds in the wet season until you reach the mountains, and in this area of the highway there was even less. Heading out of the higher altitude of Flagstaff going east to Holbrook, the highway is long, mostly flat and hot by day and cold at night.

I wanted to find a place to stop before it got too dark to set up some sort of camp and not trespass on someone's ranch. I started looking for any turnout that didn't have a fence cutting it off from the highway; that, at least would tell me that it wasn't owned land. I passed up a lot of possible camp sites until I saw the fence lines that were farther from the highway. It may have been an area where there was more road right of way that hadn't been used to widen the highway yet and with luck, not private land.

I made a stop in an old cattle gate turnoff in the road, so I could be out of traffic, and shucked into my old leather jacket, took my time zipping the coat closed and carefully pulled on my chaps. The chaps helped a lot, but it still got a little cold in the back until I was sitting on the bike going down the road. The engine heat rising up next to my legs might help if I might decide to go on farther before I found a site to stop.

It was farther along Interstate 40 that I pulled through the old gate over a cattle grate and followed the rutted, old and probably long unused cattle access road a short distance from the highway.

This part of the trip was what the whole ride had been about; stopping somewhere along the desert plain and pulling off the road to camp and make notes of the terrain and the geography of the area. The large sand mound that was between my camp and the highway would shield me from view of any passing traffic and any light from my fire would be reflected into the desert away from the highway and not likely to be seen.

While scouting some firewood, sticks and shrubs to start a fire, I thought back to other times when I had camped like this, long before I had a motorcycle, that is. Camping had always been a lonely, rough and sometimes tiring experience at best. It is cold, rough, and without comfort and always lonely; but for me, there was much about each one that had been worth doing and it was something I should have done years ago. If I had stopped just a little earlier, I could have enjoyed more of the brilliant light show of red, gold, then blue and purple colors that the sun made as it settled into the long flat horizon.

It was getting dark now, so I picked up more sticks and broken off branches from the willow scrub, Greasewood and Creosote while I could still move around in the coming darkness. The sunset had already settled into the darker blue and purple streaks with a very small amount of clouds just on the horizon.

I loved the smell of the air, with a little sage and some faint fragrance of flowers. It was cooler now and flowers could be seen here and there that would have been closed earlier and they wouldn't be open for very long; they would close again when the temperature reached freezing. There was no other sound but the slight movement of the air around me from a slight breeze.

I had a pot to make some cinnamon tea and some water in a small canteen; the last of the Alaska water. I covered the bike after I set the kickstand on a flat stone and settled back on my still rolled up sleeping bag that I had set against a rock. The sand here was soft and it felt good on my legs and was good to sit on. I just hoped there weren't too many critters crawling around waiting to get up on my legs.

I shouldn't have to worry much about snakes during the night if I hadn't seen any of them yet, but I was sure there would be spiders. Snakes would be more likely to be out during the cooling period before it got too cold for them to move, but they would be nearer piles of rocks or shrubs to keep cool during the heat of the day. After that, they would, I hoped, just stay put and not try to crawl under my warm sleeping bag.

This seemed like a good camp, protected from view of the highway and the view extended out into the desert plain marked with dry washes and an occasional arroyo. I couldn't see the highway and I was far enough off the road so the light from my fire shouldn't be seen behind the large mound between me and the highway.

It wasn't going to be the standard camp out of a Western novel with a piece of hemp rope around my sleeping bag to keep out the snakes and critters, though I might be wishing I had a rope to use before the night was over. I was going to be on the ground close to the fire and I was hoping that the heat and the flame would keep the critters away.

I started to feel the uncomfortable tightness in my head and the almost dizzy tiredness that I recognized as my blood pressure rising just before I decided to stop for the night. I had never taken medication for it until four years ago when I started feeling chest pains. I had avoided any prescribed medication after reading about the side effects and a growing tolerance which led to increases in dosages. This time I had no choice; it was either medication or a heart attack.

I was hoping that a large part of the drowsiness was more a condition of Narcolepsy, which was the reason I couldn't stay awake if I sat or remained standing in one place too long. During the years I was an active police officer, I had found myself intolerably sleepy many times in the Police cruiser. If I stopped and didn't get out and walk around instead of just sitting in the car, I could be asleep in minutes. There were times when I just fell asleep sitting there and I actively tried to wake but I couldn't. It was like being trapped in a wall of dark smothering clouds, or like being in a closed room with no exit.

That's what I was feeling now, except that now after all these years of being fully retired; I didn't have to stay awake. So here I sat watching what was left of the sunset and letting my thoughts take me back to the days of my childhood, a warm stove and the smells of home. It had been a long way down the road since childhood and a long time since I had been an active Police Officer.

As a Police officer I had actively worked at having to be alert all the time and looking at every one and everything with suspicion, and always expecting trouble. I missed the job almost every day even after fifteen years, but I had lost most of the tension and stress that I had almost every day of the job. The many years after retirement had softened my short temper and impatience and sometimes even let me sleep at night.

Chapter Two

It had been a long ride to this place in the desert, far from home and yet nowhere and it had been a great ride so far. Now I was just tired and felt like I could fall asleep; I was feeling at ease and grateful that it had been uneventful so far. There had been no problems with the bike after the broken shock bolt that I had to fix in Caldwell and gas and rest stops the rest of the way had been as frequent as I needed them to be.

I had been able to conceal the bike at every rest stop and motel so far. It's great having a nice custom ride, but it's another thing keeping the curious and careless at a distance from the bike. The nicer the paint job and the more radiant the chrome, the more need for greasy, scratchy, nosy little fingers to reach, just to touch and rub the paint.

Most of the physical requirements of police offices were changing long before I retired. The height and weight standards were removed and new applicants could be short, fat, female, tall or weak, most of the time in the same package. If any of the new candidates couldn't fight to make difficult arrests, it didn't matter. If they couldn't or wouldn't do it, their partner or someone else would be expected to or they would back down in the absence of someone willing to do it.

Ironically, the capable officer was the one who got in trouble if he failed to make a difficult arrest rather than the one who lacked the attributes or the desire to do it. If he could do it, he was expected to, and the one who stood back and watched out of fear, reluctance or lack of desire, wasn't ever called out on it.

One night while working on the graveyard shift, 11 P.M. to 7 A.M., I drew one of the guys from the 8P.M. to 4A.M. shift as a partner for the first part of my shift. I had never worked with Franklin Stearns and I didn't know much about him, except that he was considered one of the new breed of officers that know everything and have a new way of handling police work. He was cautious with his conversation with me and I knew that he was testing me when he told me about an encounter with "Big John," also known as "Boy".

"A few of us went to a disturbance and he was coming out of the bar when we got there. He just said, come on motherfuckers, take me if you can!"

"You should have arrested him," I said.

"What would you do?" he asked me. "Would you try to arrest him and get beat up?"

"Yes, I would have arrested him," I answered.

"It wasn't worth it, we let him go," he said.

"Then all of you are in the wrong job," I told him. "If you can't handle a tough arrest that may get you into a fight, I can understand. It means you have to call for backup. But if you won't make an arrest with or without help, then you're in the wrong line of work."

"What was I supposed to do?" He asked. "He could beat the shit out of all of us."

"I would do my job. I would have arrested him, with or without help," I answered.

"Well, that's easy for you to say. What if he beats the shit out of you and whoever's with you?" he asked sarcastically.

"So he'll beat the shit out of me, and when I see him again, he'll have it to do again and he'll have to check in bushes and under cars for the rest of his life until I arrest him and take him to jail," I said. "If I don't get it done alone, I'll do it with help, but he will be arrested."

"Why?" he asked. "Is it worth it?"

"That's the job. You're obligated to the people who called in the complaint, whether or not they're entitled to your protection is not for you to decide. If you can't do the job with what you have, you call for help; if you won't do it, with or without help, then you're in the wrong job and it's dereliction of duty. Besides, if you let him go, someone else will have it to do and may get hurt or killed in the process. If you try and you can't get it done, the rest of us will understand and when the call comes in for backup, we'll come and help you arrest him," I told him.

"Haven't you ever been scared?" he asked.

"Being scared is not the same as being a coward," I said. "You can be scared shitless and still do your job."

He still didn't believe me or he felt I was just boasting and I'm sure he hated me for calling him a coward.

"Well, it's easy for you to say," he said.

"I don't care if you believe me or not. I can and will do my job," I told him. "Hey, but you aren't alone. There are a lot more out there like you that can't or won't fight when they have to and they're getting paid for it, so you may as well too, but sooner or later it'll catch up with you. You'd better get out before it gets out that you're a coward and before you get someone else hurt or killed that ends up having to do your job for you."

It was one of those conversations where he was asking me a hypothetical question based on something that had happened to him but he wasn't going to let me know what it was until he had an answer from me. As it turned out, they had run into John on the same night about 30 minutes before I did, just a few days before our conversation. I had to go to the north side of town and arrest John, out of my patrol area, just after they let him go.

We were short of officers because of the high incidence of calls most of the week and especially that night. Big John had left "The Depot," a downbeat bar on the "South Side" and gone to the "Staircase," in midtown after he had backed down Franklin and his friends. He was walking down the long foyer to leave just as we arrived. He must have thought that just because he had already backed down three officers, he was going to shoulder right past me and my partner.

I grabbed his arm when he tried to shoulder check me and spun him face first into the brick wall of the walkway just as he reached me. He hit the wall and I reached down and pulled his legs out from under him, dragging his face down the brick wall and into the floor. He hit the floor hard and so quickly that my partner had tripped over his extended legs and landed on top of him.

I reacted so quickly and with such force, that I had him handcuffed behind his back and started dragging him out to our car with my partner hanging on to one of his arms trying to keep his balance. What got me to thinking about it afterward was that John knew me and had seemed to be friendly when I saw him in the Gym.

Most guys I knew would talk to me and see if I would use discretion in their favor if they got in trouble. However, I always suspected that he held it against me that I had arrested and roughed up his older brother several years before, even though they didn't like each other.

I never had any illusions that my dedication to training would increase the odds in my favor in a fight or a firearms encounter. It could easily have been me that walked into the bank the day Ben Hollis and his partner walked right into the muzzle of a 44 Magnum. Of course, they'd taken no precautions. They'd driven right into the parking lot and walked into the bank in plain sight like they were on a bank errand or another false alarm or making a stop for donuts instead of the real thing. They lived because the robber wasn't prepared to shoot a cop. Instead he took a hostage, even though he had no possibility of escape and was shot and killed in an abandoned house where he tried to make a stand.

They hadn't followed the tactical procedure we had taught. Maybe because they didn't believe in what we were doing, or they resented that we thought we knew the best way to do it. But even by following procedure, I might have approached the bank carefully, concealed the car, sneaked up to check inside the bank to see if everyone inside was behaving like everything was Ok, then gone in and had a gun stuck in my face too.

Such is the unpredictable nature of the job of Policing. Unlike them though, I would have done everything just the way we taught them to answer alarms and therefore I would've decreased the odds of failure and being caught unaware.

I didn't know at the time I stopped at the cattle gate way out here in the middle of the Arizona desert that I was about to get into the fight of my life. I couldn't have known how I would react after the years of training that I constantly and consistently had put myself through in a lifetime of preparing myself for the worst scenario, or if I would even react after having been retired for fifteen years.

Reacting to a fight or to a sudden attack was something I convinced myself that I had to do all the time. I may not have always reacted quickly enough or correctly, but I had made the decision many years before, to prepare myself for the worst possible situation that could happen at any time. I had prepared myself continually, day to day over all the years so I could beat the odds; but that was while I was still an active Police Officer.

I had to make it a point each day of my life as a police officer not to become complacent, or careless or overconfident. If I had been blindsided, it wouldn't have been because I wasn't prepared each day. I tried not to dwell on the possibility that someday I would be looking into a gun muzzle and be in a life and death situation that I could lose. I had reminded myself of that possibility when I trained, when I worked and each time I responded to an assigned call, or when I initiated a contact.

There had always been the close calls. Guns were drawn and I was prepared, but each time it had ended without a shooting. I had been in countless disturbances with all manner of troublemakers, family disturbances, robbery or fugitive arrests and car chases, but none had ever escalated into an actual shooting. The worst happens and we made mistakes. Most of the time we survived out of sheer dumb luck, but as a civilian and retired now for almost fifteen years; I could likely and very easily, be caught off guard.

I had worked hard to change my attitude after I retired so I could work around teachers and students without making everyone apprehensive when I looked at them with the usual steely eyed stare of the eternally suspicious and curious cop. I had to try to forget that I had fought at least three times a night two to three times a week for most of my career. I had thought each day of the possibility of a life and death encounter and always tried to prepare myself mentally and physically for it. That was all gone now; I had long since retired and the memory had faded a little more each day, except in my nightmares.

Another event was taking place west of my camp earlier the same day where I had passed a farm Road about five miles back along the highway. I had barely seen the sign, which was a little farther off the road than usual, had considered stopping there, but the spot I was looking for as a camp would be farther from the road, sheltered by rocks or mounds, if I could find one.

Two young women on horseback were riding along a fence line near a road, the access road to a ranch ten miles south. From their appearance and close resemblance, they could have been twins except for their choice of clothes and the apparent difference in their ages. They were enjoying the very warm and almost hot day and weren't in any hurry. They had ridden farther from the ranch before this, were on familiar ground and without a clue that their life could change as suddenly as the shift of the light desert breeze.

The younger one was a little softer looking, with longer blonde brown hair halfway down her back that flowed like it was wild, laughed a lot and made a lot of gestures when she talked. She still had the soft features of high school youthfulness on her face and arms. The older woman's shorter well kept slightly lighter hair flowed gently around her more mature face when she turned to talk to her companion. Both were dressed for riding, with western hats, boots and long sleeve shirts and riding jeans. The horses walked along slowly and to any observer, they would have appeared to be gentle or tired horses, content to walk slowly in the midday sun.

"You can not just walk up to strangers and start a conversation," the older woman said, emphasizing *you can not,* to get her meaning across. "Those men looked mean and a little wild. They aren't like the guys you know around here, or even like the guys I knew at school in California."

"What could they do right in the middle of town? We were just talking anyway. What harm can that be?" she asked.

"You just don't get it do you? Those men are not high school boys or even college age young men; they are much older and dirty and they look like motorcycle bums. Respectable men don't approach high school age girls and start a conversation and ask them to go sight seeing on a motorcycle."

"I'm not a baby. Besides, this is Holbrook! What can happen out here?" the younger woman replied.

"You could try to be with young men who are your age," she said.

"There aren't any young guys here, except Toby and Hank and a few Indian boys who hang around town; most of the young guys work way out on their ranches or leave for school and only come back in the summer, if at all."

Her attention shifted from their conversation to the sound of motors and loud pipes coming from the highway. A large group of motorcycles was heading west from the direction of Holbrook. Five of them slowed down and one of them pulled over to the right side of the highway, close to the fence and stopped off the pavement in the hard packed dirt and gravel. The older woman saw them too and she recognized them as the men her younger companion had talked to in town.

There was no doubt they recognized them on the horses when they slowed down and stopped next to the fence. She started to say something as the younger woman turned her horse in the direction of the fence, swung down off the horse, handed her the reins and her hat and started walking to the fence.

"Don't go over there!" she shouted.

It was too late. She was already at the fence and talking to one of the men. She watched helplessly as the younger woman went to the fence, ducked down to go between the wires while one of the men held them apart, walked with him to one of the motorcycles and seated herself on the bike behind him as he started it. She sat her horse and helplessly watched them pull out, going in the direction of Winslow.

Three of the men waited and watched her for several minutes while they talked to each other. She thought they were going to leave too, but they got off the motorcycles and while one of them held the wires, the other two went through the fence. She became frightened then and reined the horse to the left to leave.

"Where you goin' pretty lady?" the one in the lead said when she reined the horse and he started to turn. "Wait bitch!" he yelled as they started toward her.

The horse hadn't yet turned completely when she saw that the man in the lead had a pistol in his hand.

"Stop or I'll shoot you, you dumb bitch!" he yelled.

She had already turned the horse and kicked her heals back. He jumped into a run quickly and she glanced over her shoulder to see that the other horse was following at a gallop. She heard the loud crack of the pistol shot and almost lost her grip on the reins as the horse started up the small rise. Time went into slow motion and she realized she was completely off the horse and headed for the ground.

The horse had topped the rise at a full gallop just as she reached down to grip the pommel and she felt herself flying through the air. She thought only to cover her face and ducked her head down into a fetal position out of reflex, causing her to make a half somersault.

She closed her eyes and felt the ground slam against her shoulders and the middle of her back and realized she was still conscious and looking directly up at the sky. The reaction of fear and ducking her head to her knees had saved her life. She felt herself breathe and was amazed that the fall hadn't knocked the breath out of her, then remembered with a start that she had been trying to get away from the men who had shot at her.

She sat up quickly, looked around for the horses and saw them running away from her. She glanced back and didn't see anyone coming over the rise, so she stood up and started walking quickly in the direction the horses went.

She didn't dare call to them for fear the men would know she had fallen off and was now on foot. She looked back again and saw the men coming over the rise at a run. There were rocks and boulders on a low hill to her left and the ground dropped lower on the other side. She headed for the rocks thinking she could hide there or go down the other side of the hill and hide in one of the dry washes that crossed toward the road in the direction she had been going.

The ranch where they had ridden from was about ten miles north in the direction of the foothills. It was an impossible distance to walk at this time of day and it was getting hotter now that it was the middle of the day. They had started back in the direction of the ranch just before seeing the motorcycles and hadn't been worried about the distance on horseback, with water in the canteens and the road back to the ranch only a short distance away.

She reached the rocks and started through the openings between them headed for the high ground ahead. She looked back again and could see that the men had stopped and were turning to go back to the highway. It didn't matter; it was too far and without water she could be in trouble in a matter of a few minutes, so she couldn't go directly to the ranch.

She thought she could go in the direction of Joseph City, which was a distance of about ten miles or she could keep the highway in sight and try to get help from a passing motorist. The going was hot and difficult, but she continued to walk east while keeping a short distance from the highway. She crossed arroyos and dry washes and skirted around mounds and piles of rocks at times then took a chance and headed back to the highway. There had been an occasional car or truck going by and there was still a chance she could get one of them to stop.

She thought she heard the sound of an engine and prepared herself to go through the wire quickly so she could get out to the highway and wave someone down. She was almost at the fence when she saw the source of the engine noise; it was the three men on motorcycles. She choked back her fear and turned and ran away from the fence toward one of the arroyos in the distance. She fell down twice and the panic was growing in her as she struggled to get up each time to put more distance between herself and the fence.

She chanced a look back just as she reached the lip of the arroyo and saw that the motorcycles were stopped at the side of the road. The men didn't follow her. Each time she looked back she could see that they were still there looking in her direction. She found a low spot on the lip of the gully and went down into the arroyo.

She was exhausted, thirsty and beginning to feel ill and dizzy from the heat. Early May in Arizona in this area of the desert is bearable only if one can get under cover during the hottest part of the day. The engines of the motorcycles sounded in the distance as they left. She walked out of the gully and watched as they disappeared in the distance in the direction of Winslow.

Her earlier apprehensions turned nearly into panic, she couldn't go near the highway or in the direction of Holbrook; they would come to check on her again and find her closer to the highway and she wouldn't be able to get away the next time. It was past noon and the sun was making shadows on the east side of the bank when she went back into the arroyo and sat in the small amount of shade from the embankment behind her. She awoke in the late afternoon in a feeling of disorientation and didn't remember that she had removed the new boots to ease her painfully swollen feet.

She wasn't sure where she was and the lack of water was making her vision blur and she was beginning to lose her balance when she walked. She followed the arroyo back to the highway until it became shallow and she was walking on open ground again. It wasn't as hot anymore so she kept walking westward toward where she had lost the horses, all the while keeping the fence to her left. She wasn't sure where the road was anymore but the sun was in front of her as she walked. She didn't know she had fallen into the shallow arroyo and rolled into the bottom of it.

Chapter Three

I had traveled down through a small corner of California to Reno, Nevada, south to Las Vegas and then headed east through Kingman and Flagstaff, Arizona. It had been many years ago that I had traveled these same roads when I was on leave and still in the Navy, but they still seemed familiar. I stayed at older Motels because they probably wouldn't know that I would later park the bike inside the room so no one could vandalize it or fool around with it. I left early enough each morning to get the bike out of the Motel room before anyone was awake.

I hadn't fallen asleep yet. I just sat there looking to the west. It didn't feel like I was looking west, but I knew it had to be, because the sun was setting behind the range of long low hills. It was a beautiful sight, watching the sky change color, darkening with dark blues and purples with the last of the sunset. I could feel the cold approaching from the other side behind me, almost as if the retreating sun was drawing the cold towards the darkness of cooling sands.

This was Thursday in the second week of May. I had crossed the Arizona State line day before yesterday. I had propped up my motorcycle cover like a tent in case the air was moist during the night then slid my bag under it and lay there just trying to shut out the immense silence so I could sleep. I decided that I would pick up and tidy up my camp in the morning and not worry about it until then.

Sounds were coming from somewhere in the direction of the Highway, but the large mound I had used for a shield from the road where I thought it was coming from, deflected and disbursed the sound. I wasn't sure how far it was or with any certainty where it was coming from. I walked around the mound to look in the direction of the highway, but I wasn't going to use my flashlight until I got close enough to the noise to see where it was coming from. At first I heard some brush snapping and I thought it might be an animal of some kind. This was surely Coyote country, but a Coyote wouldn't be making any sounds.

I stopped and listened before moving any closer to where I thought I had heard the sound. It sounded like a gasp and choking, then panting like someone who is straining to lift something heavy. I was going by sound only now and I couldn't see anything in the dimming light of the sunset from the direction of the highway. I pointed the flashlight in the direction of the sounds and walked on the right side of the road that led back to the highway.

I couldn't see what it was that was making the noise, but I could see a shallow wash and shadows made by the beam of my flashlight. I walked to the edge of it and with the light of the flashlight; I could see someone in the bottom of the wash lying face down. It looked like a young girl with long hair, barefoot and wearing a long sleeved light colored denim shirt and blue Jeans. The denim shirt was dusty and torn in several places and hanging over her jeans.

I skidded on my heels with my left hand behind me down to where she was lying in the dust and weeds. She was moaning softly when I reached out to touch her and she didn't respond or protest when I pulled her over by her shoulder to look at her face. Her clothes and face were dusty but she didn't seem to be injured other than some good sunburn. I sat her up and squatted down in front of her so I could lift her and put her over my shoulder.

It wasn't as easy as it should have been, even though she seemed to weigh no more than 140 pounds. She wasn't a small woman and I had a little difficulty getting her into a position where I could lift her. I got her over my shoulders in a Fireman carry and crawled on my hands and knees, with some occasional traction with my toes. I was totally exhausted and I was beginning to see spots by the time I got out of the wash. I stayed on my knees with her still draped over my shoulders for a few breaths, and then I stood up and carried her the short distance back to my camp.

It was getting colder, but I managed to clean her face with a small towel from my pack and some warm water and managed to get a little water into her mouth. Her lips were parched and she felt hot to the touch. She seemed to be unconscious or drugged, but I couldn't smell any liquor. I could see now while I was cleaning her face that she had pretty even features and she was older than I first thought her to be. I pulled some socks over her bruised and slightly burned feet after I cleaned them, then propped her up and managed to put her into my sleeping bag.

I didn't know what else I could do with her until I could find out what condition she was in. I checked her eyes and they seemed to be dilated and slow to respond, but that may have been only because she wasn't awake. She moaned softly a couple of times, so I left her alone for the time being. I didn't think it would hurt to put something cold on her face after a while, so I wet the small towel and waved it around to cool it and applied it to her face. That got a response; she gasped and coughed and opened her large blue eyes, but she didn't say anything. I had never seen anyone who had been exposed to the sun, then afterwards left in the cold, so I had no idea what condition she was in.

When she started moaning, I gave her some more water and got some of it down her throat, but it started her gagging and she seemed about to vomit. I turned her to one side and held her but she didn't gag out the water. Ordinarily, I wouldn't have given water to someone unconscious or sick, but she had to have been dehydrated from being out in the desert sun.

I gave her some more water, which she swallowed, then she drooled a little of it out the side of her mouth. There were few items in my bag, but I had thought to bring along a little sunburn remedy, which I had already put on her feet, so now I put some on her face and forehead, then not knowing what else to do, I let her lie back.

Thinking that she may have been beat up or may have some internal injuries, I pulled open the sleeping bag and opened her dusty shirt and pulled up the knit shirt under it to check for bruising on her stomach. She didn't seem to have any injuries and was starting to shiver so I buttoned her back up and pulled the cover of the sleeping bag over her. I watched her until she stopped shivering and seemed to be sleeping quietly and breathing evenly. There hadn't been any traffic at all since I stopped before dark and I hadn't seen or heard any traffic at all since, so there wouldn't be any use trying to flag anyone down for help.

She moaned and tossed and turned a couple of times, shivered, then seemed to fall asleep mumbling something. I woke her again after a little while and got her to swallow some warm tea. After a couple of swallows of it, she gagged, so I turned her on her side so she wouldn't get it all over my sleeping bag. I took off my jacket and chaps and placed my blanket over my shoulders and leaned back against the motorcycle to watch her for a while before I relaxed.

I didn't know I could fall into a deep sleep camped out with only a blanket, but I did and sometime before morning light, I woke up startled and slightly disoriented. I came out of my daze suddenly when I heard a commotion coming from the other side of the mound; then I remembered why I was asleep in my blanket and not in my sleeping bag.

A feeling of dread washed over me as my senses came quickly into focus and thought that this was going to be real trouble. I looked over to where the woman should have been in my sleeping bag and saw with a start that she wasn't there. I was still trying to think and move at the same time when I heard the scream from the other side of the mound. I slid the blanket off my shoulders and started around the mound in the semidarkness to see if I could see where the noise was coming from.

When I got far enough around the mound, I could see her on the ground surrounded by at least eight men. Even in the very dim light I could see that they were dressed in the various biker garbs, mostly leather and some of them had bandanas on their heads.

I kept moving to get closer to them as I reached to my left side under my sweater for my pistol, a Smith/Wesson 45 automatic that I had taken to carrying again after I crossed the border out of Canada. The stainless steel model 645; the first of the .45 caliber double action semi automatics that Smith and Wesson made, had been my choice instead of the smaller caliber 9MM pistol.

A worry started to grow in me now that it was too shiny and could be seen before I could surprise them, or that it wasn't shiny enough and wouldn't be seen as a definite threat when they did see it. As Murphy's Law applied, had I been carrying my black Colt 45 instead, I may not have been seen before I was close enough to have them covered.

True to course, the worst of my long thought out recurring concerns over the years, happened. One of them did something I had always feared deep down all those years I was a cop; that whoever I was facing would react with deadly action before I was set and had the advantage of surprise. Some of them must have seen the glint of light off the barrel slide in the very dim but growing light of the sun about to rise behind them, and they reacted.

The man directly across the circle from me had something in his hand that looked like a large shiny revolver and he pointed it right at me. Three of the others on my side of the circle were scrambling sideways to get out of the line of fire just as he brought it into line. I knew that I was in his sights and I didn't have time to think or choose a tactic. Even as I jumped to my left and rolled to get out of his line of fire, I could almost feel where the bullets would hit when he opened fire.

The bright flash blinded me and I heard a popping sound like a dry limb breaking almost against my right ear just as I heard the blast from the pistol. Unlike the movies where countless rounds are fired by both sides and no one is ever hit, this was the real world. Even if I had fired before he did; I realized I would have been shot if I hadn't dived for the ground. Jumping and rolling to get out of his sights had more than likely kept me from being shot, at least from his first attempt.

I jammed my shoulder when I rolled and knew I had lost my pistol when I rolled back the other way onto my belly. With a scramble of boots and the sound of leather, they were all running in the direction of the highway. I didn't know right away that one of them had tripped over the woman on the ground.

I got up from the ground with the dread that she had been shot and I started to walk in her direction, when I saw one of the bikers getting up from the ground just beyond her. He looked like he was pawing under his jacket for a gun. I looked around quickly for my pistol, which I probably wouldn't have been able to see anyway in the poor light, and then charged him in near panic in a low crouch, hoping to hit him before he turned around.

He was already up and facing me with something in his right hand but I reached him in time. I slapped it to the right with my left hand, caught the barrel in my right hand, then clasped my left hand over the barrel in a baseball grip with both hands just the way I had practiced so many years ago. He countered my move to raise his arm by trying to pull his arm down, which was what I had hoped he would do. I dropped to my right knee quickly and twisted down suddenly and felt fingers snap when I pulled the pistol almost to the ground, but he still hadn't released it.

He screamed and yelled, "yow!!.... you son of a bitch!"

I jerked the pistol back up to force him to release it and it came out of his grip suddenly, but not the way it was supposed to. It flew over my right shoulder and fell to the ground with a thud somewhere behind me. He fell backward and I fell to my right knee in front of him.

He scrambled to his feet faster than I could move to stand up and kicked at my face. I deflected the kick to the left with my left hand and punched him hard in the groin with my right fist just as his heavy booted foot touched the ground. My fist hit bone with a shock of pain going up into my shoulder.

"Unhnn!" he moaned.

I stood up quickly and felt a huge blow on the top of my head. He fell to the ground almost face first saying, "ohhh," in a painful groan.

I realized that I had stood up so fast after I punched him, that his chin had struck me on the top of the head and I had gone down to my knees again. There was a flash in my eyes then almost a blackout as I fought dizziness to get back on my feet. A thought went through my mind that this was not the way I should be fighting after all those years of training; you were supposed to hit what you struck at and they were supposed to fall when they were hit.

He was already on his feet and he jabbed a long punch at me with his left while I was still in a crouch. I deflected the punch to the left with my left hand and grasped his left wrist, then grabbed his muscled arm just above the elbow with my right hand, made a smooth pivot on my left foot and kicked him hard just behind the leg above the ankle when he tried to pull back his arm from the end of his punch. My instep hit the back of his leg and it felt like I had tried to leg sweep a tree stump, his leg gave, but it wasn't a complete sweep. His body jerked back when he lost his balance and he seemed about to fall backwards, but he stayed on his feet.

He backhanded me with his left hand just as he regained his balance and it caught me on the left temple just over my left eye. I felt the shock and I couldn't see out of that eye for the moment. He shifted position and punched a wide looping punch with his right hand. I was falling off balance to my right; otherwise his punch would have hit me square on the jaw. As it was, it glanced off my shoulder and off the top of my head and he yelled again in pain when his right hand hit my head. It was enough force to knock me the rest of the way off my feet.

I fell on my right shoulder and I felt shooting darts of pain in a shoulder already stiff with arthritis. I rolled when I hit the ground and felt something metallic in the middle of my chest. I heard gasping breathing close to me and realized that the woman was kneeling close to where I fell. She would be close enough and in the line of fire if he had found his pistol. I knew I didn't have time to push her away out of danger, so I just reached for the lump under my chest. As soon as I touched it, I knew it was a large revolver and I knew it wasn't my pistol.

I grabbed it and rolled backward to my left onto my left elbow. Engines were starting in the distance and I was startled that only seconds had passed and they were pulling out to head down the highway. I was consciously fighting not to be distracted by the sound of engines and the woman too close to be out of the line of fire. In a clear realization that everything was happening too quickly, I saw that he was standing with his feet apart and starting to raise his left arm to point.

I was on my left hip and left elbow with my right shoulder slightly higher, holding the large revolver in my right hand. If it was my pistol he held, the safety would be off and it would fire when he pulled back on the trigger, unless he had moved the safety after he picked it up. I had no way of knowing in the dark if it was a double action or single action revolver that I held now.

All I could tell from the size and feel of the pistol in my hand was that it was large and heavy. I had a flash of thought that it might be a single action Ruger or an older Casul. I reached up and placed the butt of the pistol in my left hand, pulled the hammer back with my right thumb and gripped tightly with both hands to steady it.

There was a bright flash and the loud clap of sound close to my left ear and I knew it for the sound of a large caliber bullet going by. I pulled the trigger and with a bright flash from the muzzle, the pistol bucked in my hand.

He jerked back and landed flat on his back as if kicked by a mule. His legs were up and bent at the knees and they stayed that way for what seemed a long time, although it was only seconds at most. I watched so amazed at the position of his legs, that I didn't think to fire again, even though I was conscious of pulling the hammer back a second time.

Chapter Four

Years ago, I had come upon the realization after years of practicing combination attacks of punches and kicks and trying to be faster with each practice, that time seemed to slow down and I seemed to be the only one moving or perceiving the passage of time. I seemed to be moving faster than he was, because for me, time had slowed down.

For a small moment in time, except for my movement and my perception of time; he seemed to be barely moving. There was time to think now and experience the slowness of time and I realized that it was only because I was alive and he was no longer moving. He still had gotten the drop on me and fired first, but he had missed, I hadn't.

Now as I watched the man's legs relax and fall to the ground, my thoughts came rapidly to the present with the realization that someone may be finally and irreversibly dead. The woman was still kneeling on the ground moaning, her head forward and looking at the ground in front of her as if she was having trouble breathing. I got up painfully and looked for my pistol.

It had fallen out of his hand and the hammer was still back. I lowered the hammer on his pistol and pushed it under my belt and picked up my own. I lowered the hammer out of the firing position by toggling the safety lever down and up, then pulled up my sweater with my left hand and guided my pistol into the holster on my left hip.

Cops in the movies are always right and they always shoot straight. When the heroes fight, they all know Karate and fights go on for half an hour if it is against the main bad guy. If I had ever had to fight more than a couple of minutes against anyone, other than in a Karate match, years ago in the ring; I wouldn't have made it through the first round. I went up against my friend Chris Gallegos in Denver at the old Santa Fe Theater in 1980 in a three round Karate match. The rounds were only 2 minutes long because it was a demonstration and not a scheduled sanctioned match. The first two minutes were uneventful and went by swiftly.

The second round seemed much longer because he must have decided that I was doing too well and turned it into a real match. I was fighting back totally in the defensive and barely keeping from being knocked out until I connected with a good left and a solid roundhouse to his head. He didn't seem effected, but he backed off a little and I made it through the round. I remembered that now and I realized that I had been holding my breath as I fought. I heard myself draw in deeply and loudly, now that I was consciously remembering to take a breath.

My friend Larry, who was also my Captain, had commented about the quick defensive moves I was able to make in a confrontation. He watched as a student in my Karate class had asked me a question, kicked a low kick at me followed by a high kick at my face. He had seen me block it before it hit me.

"It was a good thing you had the presence of mind to realize you were going to be kicked in the face and you were able to block it," he said.

"Truthfully, I didn't know I was going to be kicked in the face; I didn't have time to realize what he was going to do. It was just reaction to an attack after seeing it over and over in practice."

Another time he had made the Joking comment that I had moved so quickly and deceptively to hit someone in the booking room at the Police Department jail, that it didn't look like I had moved at all. The subject I had been booking had fallen down as if struck, which was exactly what he would have claimed later in his court hearing or in a lawsuit.

"Goddamn that Maxwell. He's so fast, he hit that guy and knocked him down from all the way across the room and he didn't even have to move," Larry had said laughing when he saw the guy fall down as he was watching it on the monitor in the Desk Sergeant's office.

I knew he had meant it as a joke at the time and it was more than likely that he had made the comment to belittle my conditioning efforts by making the statement. No matter how much I devoted to my workouts; it didn't give me any more ability or speed than anyone else. He had faked being hit and it was obvious that it would have been impossible for me to have hit him from ten feet away.

However, the Internal Investigations Captain was convinced that I had because Larry had said I was faster than the eye could see. He didn't know that Larry didn't believe his own statements more than half the time. He was used to telling so many made up war stories about what he or others had done, that he sometimes believed his own lies. Most of the time he couldn't remember which ones were lies, or who had actually done what he said; and it was his way of changing the story from a joking comment about my ability into an opportunity to get me in trouble.

It started an investigation that would at the very least get me suspended. At worst it could get me charged with assault and get me fired. When he found out I was being investigated for it, he tried to convince the Internal Affairs Captain that I may have hit him and that he should look into it. The captain was convinced that he could make the charges stick, even after looking at the film from the Video monitor.

The film clearly showed that I was too far away and I hadn't even made a move to hit him. Most of the time when a cop had charges made against him, he was too scared to protest the charges and any decision that might be made against him was just a matter of course. It was safer to accept the charges and just take a couple days suspension, rather than risk getting fired, even if the charges were false.

Captain Paul Perea had been a Captain a long time. He made his promotions during a time that it was impossible to get advanced without the support of the administration. He was a Captain before I joined the Police Department and now I was a veteran of 12 years. He had been a Police officer before, during and after the changes from the "old guard" to the new.

He was a cop when being a cop meant fighting bare handed or with a baton and you took your licks and handed them out. He knew how it used to be and probably used a little extra force himself on more than one occasion or he wouldn't have remained a cop during those early years. So, if I had "roughed up" a prisoner, he should have known the difference.

I sat in the office watching the video recording with him and asked, "Does that look like I was close enough to hit him?"

He replied, "Well, maybe you hit him before he got on camera and he just reacted."

"If I did, then it's not on film, so it didn't happen, did it? Besides, it would have to be the longest delayed reaction to being hit that I ever saw."

He had just realized how stupid his reaching statement had been and he knew that he had blown his case.

"There's no need to get smart about it," He said. "No one is saying you hit him."

"So, just what is this meeting about then?" I asked.

"A charge has been made, so it has to be investigated."

"I would think that I would have the same right to due process as any common criminal; that is, informed of some charges and being represented by counsel whether or not there is probable cause," I said.

"No charges have been made, so there's no cause for you to be insubordinate," he said forcefully.

"So if there are no charges, and according to your own statement, no one is saying I did anything wrong; just what am I doing here?" I had asked quietly.

He just sat there behind the desk looking at me for a couple of minutes, then said, "That's all for now."

He knew I had just made him look stupid and he was smart enough to let it go. The investigation ended and not even a comment was made to me, or an apology for having accused me in the first place. Maybe he still believed it and decided he just couldn't pull off a conviction if I was going to take a stand against it. I wasn't willing to make any damaging statements, so it was dropped, but the accusation still carried the possibility that I had, and the paper trail was made. Even though unproved, unsubstantiated and false, in my case; it constituted a pattern of behavior as far as they were concerned and could even substantiate charges made at any future date.

Chapter Five

I looked at the woman now and could see she wasn't dressed as she would have been, had she been keeping company with the roughly dressed bunch of bikers. It wouldn't have been unusual, although now I didn't believe that she would have been with them by choice; she could dress any way she wanted to and sit behind a biker if she chose to, but it didn't fit. I was thinking that it was more likely they had been trying to take her by force and she had escaped and they had tried to catch her and hadn't succeeded until now.

She was too clean except for the newly acquired desert dust; she had healthy skin that was sunburned but not sunburned enough had she been on the road on a bike for any time at all. Except for the dust and sand on her face and being slightly sunburned and with torn and dusty clothing from being on the ground; she could have been someone on vacation or some rancher's daughter home from school for the summer.

She was wearing jeans and at a glance they looked like Levis or wranglers, not faded, but new looking and not dark blue like unwashed jeans off the shelf. She was wearing a white knit pullover shirt under the light colored denim shirt, like the ones that look like underwear, but without buttons at the neck. She had no rings or wristwatch that I could see and long hair, maybe light brown or blond in the light.

"But how did she get here and how did she lose her shoes?" I thought out loud.

She wasn't moaning anymore, but she was still bent forward looking at the ground. I knelt in front of her and took hold of her shoulders and held her away to try to make her look at me.

"Who are you?" I asked. "What were you doing with those bikers?"

She didn't respond.

"You're safe now. Talk to me; those men are gone now, but they may come back at any time. Why were they after you?" I asked her.

She still didn't respond, she just glared at me with a dull expression on her face as if dumbstruck or in shock. Looking at her in the growing light, I could see that she was not just a pretty woman; she was movie star beautiful, with the almost perfect features of a model that doesn't need makeup. I couldn't tell if she was afraid, in shock, or just not certain if I was one of the bikers she had just been trying to escape.

We were at least three hundred feet or so from the highway and my bike was another hundred feet around the other side of the mound, so I didn't figure she would go anywhere. I could jog to my bike and be back here before she was able to go anywhere in her almost bare feet. I was more or less already packed and loaded and it wouldn't take me long to pack the rest of my gear, start up and roll back here.

I found my flashlight and I used it to look around for empty casings from my pistol in the growing light. I only found one; he had only fired once with my pistol. I didn't know how this was going to turn out if I reported it to the authorities at Holbrook or in the next town, if there was a Trooper there. I was already thinking that I didn't want to leave anything around that could be traced back to me.

I had gone through Winslow pretty late in the afternoon yesterday before stopping here just before it had gotten too dark to go on. I was somewhere between Winslow and Holbrook; Holbrook being closer and maybe a better choice to report what had happened if I chose to. I had no idea which direction this bunch had come from or where they had picked up this young woman, who seemed to be in her late twenties or early thirties.

I couldn't remember how many bikers I saw in the circle around her before all hell broke loose, even though I had made a mental picture of about eight of them. I hadn't seen the motorcycles where they had been parked close to the highway and I didn't think I would have been able to see them from where I camped even if I had looked that way in the low light. I must have been dead asleep to have missed their arrival. Looking in the direction of the highway, I could see what looked like a lone motorcycle in the growing light.

She didn't seem aware that anything had happened to her, so I left her where she was with her back to the biker on the ground. I kept glancing back to make sure she didn't move. I was without a clue what any of them or their bikes looked like and I didn't even know which way they had gone. This was far enough off the road that the dead man shouldn't be found easily, but there was a bike to dispose of. I didn't think she would be much help even if I could ask her, so I dragged him for a distance past the mound and over one ditch to the next wash.

There was soft sand everywhere, so I rolled him into the ditch and pointed the beam of my flashlight at him. The bullet had passed completely through after hitting him in the stomach, leaving a large explosive wound in his back. I pushed sand around him until it looked level, and then I walked around and picked up some rocks and brush to cover him up the rest of the way and dragged the area with brush to wipe out the tracks. I covered him with enough sand and rocks that he wouldn't be dug up by critters any time soon, and when they did; it was far enough from the highway that it wouldn't be noticed.

I walked back to where I had left her and walked behind her and tried picking her up by gripping both her arms above the elbow. It didn't work; she was heavier than she looked. I got in front of her again and put her right arm over my shoulder and reached across her chest with my right arm and stood up with her. She stayed on her feet so I shifted around and kept her right arm behind my neck and my left arm behind her and held her by the waist. I realized that she was as tall as me even in her bare feet, as I guided her in the direction I wanted her to go. I took her around the mound to my camp and sat her against the rock I had leaned on the night before.

I took my ground tarp out of my pack and set his pistol on my pack. She didn't look like she was going anywhere, so I took the time to walk to the road to check the bike that was left. The keys were in the ignition below and on the left side of the seat. It was a clean looking custom bike, with an extra elaborate custom paint job, in blue, with lines and flames. It started easily, so I kicked it into gear and started back in the direction of my camp.

I looked at her as I went past and saw that she seemed unaware of the sounds of the motorcycle, so I continued up the low hill. It traveled easily up the hill and I followed a small arroyo until I could see a low spot where I could cross it. I crossed a couple more low ditches and stopped to look back toward the road, which was now obscured to my vision by the small hill I had just gone over.

An arroyo just off to my left, that was about ten feet deep with a way into it where the wall had collapsed, looked like a good place to bury the bike. I rolled down into it and headed to the opposite wall where the bank was its highest. I propped it against the wall, covered it with my tarp then found a way up the side of the arroyo above the bike. I stomped around on the arroyo wall until the wall collapsed over the bike. After the dust settled I could see that it covered it well and since it was not at the bottom of the arroyo; it wasn't likely to be washed up, unless it was a real deluge of rain and water.

It hadn't taken me too much time yet, so I took the time to sweep out the tracks of the bike in the soft sand layer over the hard packed dirt. It took no more time than it would have taken to just walk back to my bike. Now I just had a woman in shock on my hands and I didn't even know if she could tell anyone what had happened. Whatever the reason was that she decided to crawl out of my sleeping bag and get caught on that side of the mound, it had saved my life. If they had found me when they found her; I would be the one in shock right now, or dead.

I put my leather jacket on her and I pulled another pair of socks over her feet. She must have lost the other pair of socks between here and where she had been caught by the bikers. It was lighter out now so I took another look at the dead man's pistol. It was a large blue revolver of very large caliber; one of those 454 Casul's, with two spent casings in it.

It was double action after all, but I didn't have the time to look it over with him pointing my own gun at me. I hadn't been willing to take the chance, so I had pulled the hammer back and fired in single action. The added factor of one or two broken fingers from having the pistol twisted out his hands, made him have to fire left handed and may have kept me from getting shot.

I stuck the pistol in my pack for the time being and shook out a bandanna from my bag and tied it around her head so her hair wouldn't be flying everywhere and attract attention. I had already tied my larger bag behind the backrest on top the small luggage rack. She didn't respond or protest while I guided her over to the bike and with difficulty lifted her left leg over the seat and propped her up against the backrest.

I held her against the sissy bar and raised my leg up high to clear the seat and tank without scratching it with my boot. I reached back and placed both her arms around my waist before I hit the starter and balanced the bike to head down the road to the highway. I accelerated when I reached the pavement, made a left turn and went east in the direction of Joseph City and Holbrook.

This was the second week of May on a Friday morning and already late spring to early summer, so there should have been traffic and activity from the ranches in the area. We were north of the Apache reservation and west of the Navajo reservations and I should have been seeing travelers starting to move on the highway. Everything in my range of vision looked different now; it was getting lighter and I was seeing a lot of things I hadn't noticed before today that were close to the road.

Yesterday I was looking into the distance at the hills, the mountains and the distant landscape without a worry as I traveled down the highway. Now I was noticing the smaller plants, noting crossroads and checking for a possible ambush behind every clump, rock and mound that I could see. There wasn't any traffic yet and it must be about six o'clock in the morning. This was just a guess, because I hadn't wanted to attract attention out on the road by flashing my Rolex, so I had stored it with some other things in my bag when I had started on this Run.

Suddenly I was feeling like I was about to get sick all over the gas tank. I didn't stop right away, I kept visualizing the look of amazement on the bikers face when he was hit with the shock of the large caliber bullet and I watched in amazement as he fell away from me onto his back. I hadn't gotten the shakes afterward and I hadn't even gotten the little knee shakes that I had gotten in the past before a fight.

The realization was hitting me now that I had felt none of those reactions and that maybe it was why I didn't do so well in the fight before the shooting. The margin of losing out there had been so close that I should be dead now. Maybe the tightness in my throat and the taste of salt in my mouth and feeling like I was just about to get sick was just reaction.

While I was an active Police Officer, I trained myself to expect trouble and set my mind and attitude for it every day for 23 years. When I practiced, I set a mental picture of a shooting confrontation and possible scenarios of fatal and serious shootings that I had researched so that I would always be prepared.

Most of the guys I worked with hated qualifications, never practiced and most of the time never carried an off duty weapon. I wasn't considered by many to be an outstanding police officer and I was likely to fall asleep once in while if I parked too long, but I did all of my work, and only once took a short cut in a minor investigation, which I regretted all the rest of my career.

But that was a long time ago. I still carried a pistol because I couldn't reconcile myself with not having it and always felt vulnerable with what I knew was always a serious element of lawlessness everywhere. I would have still been shaken, even if there hadn't been any shooting. It would have been most unlikely that all of them or only a few of them had not been armed. Had I hesitated even a moment, they would have taken her or assaulted her on the spot; because for all they knew, she was alone.

It was never my way to watch and see someone hurt or see a crime or assault committed without getting involved even if I got into trouble because of it. I hadn't always gotten excited or broken any traffic codes as a cop to get to a Bar fight, which I considered to be stupidity by mutual agreement, but I always responded quickly to any assigned calls I received.

One particular incident that haunted me more than any other was when William Bundy killed a woman at Monarch Ski resort with a tire iron then dumped her in a ditch in the snow and abandoned her car. I had skied from the lodge over the embankment directly to the parking lot where my car was parked and I had been able to get most of the way to my car before I lost momentum.

I had been looking around at the other cars yet I had not seen her yellow Volkswagen that may have been in the lot when I was there. I was always armed, even on the ski slopes then, because I had a small Beretta automatic that I could conceal easily. To think that I had been there and I had actually skied out to the parking lot and hadn't seen anything left me with a feeling of doubt in myself for many years.

As I continued in the direction of Joseph City, I started having second thoughts about continuing on into the small town. I starting thinking that it would be safer off the road behind a hill or in the rocks and small dry trees that were becoming more in number, rather than get spotted out in the open. They may not know who had interrupted them yet and may not know that her rescuer was riding a motorcycle as well. I still had the dead Bikers pistol and I didn't intend to be found carrying it until I knew I could safely turn it over to the authorities. Better to hide it somewhere and come up with it only if I had to make a case for self defense.

I had no illusions about what kind of situation I could find myself in if it related to this woman having been kidnapped and the dead biker being turned up as a murder victim instead of a result of self defense. I knew that no matter how well meaning any investigation can be, there is always the problem of logistics and finances that can cut short or limit any meaningful investigation.

I could be taken as a biker now, not quite as raggedy and rank as the others, but to most anyone else, still a biker. I could be in serious trouble trying to prove self defense, even under the circumstances. Getting convicted was an entirely different matter; I could be in jail for a long time waiting for a serious investigation to be carried out.

I didn't know if these men were just outlaws or just weekend renegades who got mob fever and decided to assault a woman. I tried to reason they had run instead of standing their ground because they were caught off guard and ran away just to put distance between themselves and some real trouble when they saw me. They couldn't have known that I was alone and they hadn't taken a chance that there may have been others somewhere out there with me. Whatever the reason, they weren't likely to startle or cut and run again so easily. I could only guess that in their haste, they hadn't taken time to count heads and didn't know that they had left someone behind.

The Movie Detectives have all the time in the world to make a thorough investigation and they always seem to solve the most difficult cases. Suspects always confess when they are confronted with the truth, but the trial still goes on to try to prove or disprove their guilt. That would be great if it were true; unfortunately, most detectives have a caseload of ten to fifteen cases in hand all the time, and upwards of fifty in some larger cities.

More importantly, suspects always lie and will continue to lie right up to the time the needle is put in their arm. Cases are placed into categories of priorities according to solvability by the Captain of Detectives or a Sergeant, and then handed out to Detectives according to their record of solving certain crimes or their preference, if it is possible.

Sometimes there are just no leads to the solving of a crime. I was part of a special team ordered to find ways to reduce convenience store robberies. We were given a special assignment and ordered to search for leads in the murder of a woman who was killed and dismembered in 1974. Even though there were suspects developed by association, none could be substantiated.

I had developed some leads through some Country Western band members, but they were ignored because the Detective Sergeant didn't like me and because of the cost involved in tracking them down and traveling to another city. The murdered woman was nobody and no one was going to spend any real money or time finding out who killed her.

Chapter Six

There were a few side roads coming up; if I could get off the highway and get back in those hills far enough not to be seen, then maybe I could get this woman to start talking and find out what the heck besides her I had almost gotten myself killed for. It had to be a certainty that I hadn't seen the last of the bikers. I had to find out who she was and then I could make a definite plan that may get me out of this mess.

The guilt over killing a man hadn't really set in yet, so I tried not to get into that train of thought. I could think about it later when I had a little more information to go on or plenty of distance. Having a whole bunch of guilt and confusion over what had happened wasn't going to make my thinking easier or faster.

I had been on the highway about fifteen minutes and it was pretty light out now and starting to get warm. I slowed down and started looking for a road I could turn off into. The woman had leaned against my back and leaned her head over my shoulder against the side of my head. I welcomed the slight bit of warmth it gave me, then felt guilty about the other sensations I was feeling with her pressed against my back. The sweater I had put on the night before had helped, but it was still cold and the cold morning air felt like a chill wind off a snowy mountain.

There were a few roads leading off the highway and I wanted to make sure the one I took didn't have a ranch close enough to the main road that I could be seen when I went by. With all the traveling I had done through most of the routes from California to Colorado when I was still in the Navy, I didn't know a thing about this area, the ranches, towns or cities. I had stayed on the main highways and driven through all the small towns and rarely stopped in any of them except to get gas. I had come out here to get some research and the layout of the area, not because I knew it, but because I didn't remember any of it.

I saw a road off to the left of the highway ahead and started slowing down for the turn across the median. I made the turn easily then kicked up the speed a little to backtrack back to the dirt road. For the first time I was traveling a little faster than I would have liked to on a dirt road. I always kept my speed down because of the flying rocks and sand which tend to damage anything it strikes on the under carriage of the engine and fenders of the bike. I was starting to feel a little confident that I had chosen a good road as it wound between the low hills and seemed to be on an upward climb.

There was a scattering of low brush and scrub Pine as I got further away from the highway. There were double rutted old trails leading into the main road in several places and I took one of them that seemed to lead between some hills and rocks. There were dry washes in this area and some of them are small but they can all become live streams when it rains. I got off the old rutted road and went in the direction the dry stream seemed to be coming from and stopped in a spot protected by rocks and low hills.

She didn't move after I stopped, so I kicked out the stand onto a flat rock and swung my leg part way over the tank to get off. She still didn't move, but she didn't resist when I raised her left arm to put it over my shoulder and lifted her part way off the seat by holding her around the waist. I guided her over to a rock and got her settled on it and looked around for something to make a small fire. It didn't take me long to gather up some brush and sticks and get one going. I got out the makings and made some tea to warm her up then walked over to see if she was going to talk to me.

"What's your name?" I asked her as I handed her a small Styrofoam cup with some tea.

She looked at me like I should have been asking her questions all along and said something that sounded like "Annastal."

"What did you say?" I asked her again.

"Anne Stall, spelled S, t, a, h, l," she said with some impatience in her voice.

"What were you doing with those bikers?" I asked her.

"I wasn't with them" she said. "Who are you?"

"Miguel Maxwell." I said.

She looked at me strangely, probably because of the Mexican first name.

"My great grandfather was English, my great grandmother was a Navajo Chief's daughter and my grandmother was Spanish," I said.

"Miguale?" she asked, almost pronouncing my name correctly.

"You can call me Mike. Some of my friends call me Chico," I said.

"Are you with any of those men?" she asked.

"No, not likely, I just happened to be there when they stopped where they did and found you, besides that, I haven't missed that many showers yet."

She stopped talking and looked at me carefully for a minute then looked down and starting shaking. I didn't ask her any more questions for a couple of minutes until she stopped shaking and wiped tears from her eyes and cheeks.

"I feel so stupid," he said.

"Do you know any of them?" I asked her.

She just glared at me, or through me, I couldn't tell which.

"Well how did you get out here?" I asked.

"We were riding from my father's ranch and following the highway; the men who were following me were with a large group of others on motorcycles. They saw us riding near the fence by the highway and they stopped. My sister got off her horse and just rode off with them. Two of them came back and tried to get me to go with them. When I started to ride away, they shot at me and I fell off my horse. They came after me, but I ran into the hills and they didn't follow me. I was trying to stay close to highway so I could get help when they found me again, but I got away from them."

"Have you ever seen them before this? I asked.

"My sister talked to them in town and they tried to get me to talk to them, but I walked the other way and waited for her across the street. She finally came after me, and I asked her what she was doing talking to those men. I guess she thought it would be fun to talk to them, and then when they stopped on the road, she left with them," she said.

She looked around at the rocks and asked, "Where are we?"

"We're about ten miles from Joseph City, I would guess, but I'm not sure," I answered.

"Why did you stop here in the middle of nowhere?" she asked.

"I had to get off the highway until I can figure out where the men who were after you went," I said.

"Will you take me home?" she asked.

"I want to make sure we can make it there," I replied.

"What would keep us from getting there?" she asked.

"The men who were after you are still out there somewhere. They won't be happy that you got away from them and they'll want to get even with me for driving them off. I want to leave at a time that'll give me the best chance of not getting caught out in the open or on the highway," I answered.

"Wouldn't it be better to leave in daylight when they can be seen as well as they can see us?" she asked.

"Yeah, it would be best, I just wanted to get off the highway long enough to see if I see any of them. Where were you going when you left my camp this morning?" I asked her.

"What camp?" she asked.

"Where we just left. Where I parked my bike all night and you slept in my sleeping bag, that's where," I said.

She looked at me incredulously, like I was making up a story. "I don't remember anything about being in your camp. All I remember is that I was trying to get away from them and I was afraid to go near the highway."

"Do you remember anything about last night?" I asked.

"No. I just remember falling asleep in an arroyo. When I woke up I didn't know where I was or what direction I should go to get to the ranch and I was afraid to go to the highway to get help."

"What about your sister?" I asked.

"I think they may have hurt her, they were trying to catch me and I thought they were going to kill Me." she answered.

"Do you remember anything about last night when I found you and put you in my sleeping bag?" I asked.

"I don't remember anything before you put me on your motorcycle and started down the highway."

"Do you remember falling off the horse?" I asked.

"I went over the horse and almost landed on my head. I remember wondering why it didn't knock my breath out," she said.

It was pretty clear that she didn't remember anything about the fight and the shooting at my camp. She may have gotten a mild concussion when she fell off the horse and the shock was just wearing off and she didn't remember, or she had just shut it all out. I was hoping for the latter. I didn't need another witness to what may lead to me getting arrested for murder. If I could put it all behind me, I would, but with those bikers surely still out there, it wasn't anywhere near likely that this was over yet.

"Where is this ranch of your father's?" I asked.

"The ranch is north and west of here about four or five miles from the highway and is owned by Hal Holt now. He was a friend of my father's. My father died two years ago while I was in California and my mother and sister moved to Holbrook."

"So, what about your sister?" I asked.

"Her name is Rebecca and she's younger than I am. She just finished High school. We never got to town much when we lived on the ranch and I think she wanted some excitement," she said. "She just didn't know what she was in for."

Then she shivered before continuing. "I don't think they would have bothered me in town, but after my sister went with them out there on the highway; they came back after me."

She paused and looked at her jeans and her shirt sleeves. "I just feel dusty and sweaty and my clothes stink."

"You could have died out there in the prairie," I said. "Believe me I would like to get you back and be out of here. Nothing would be better than getting away from this so I can head on down the road."

Terror showed her eyes. Her eyes were large and gray blue and they were deeper blue with the whites of her eyes more enlarged. She may have just recalled more of the incident and realized that she had barely escaped being taken and she had barely survived the desert, only yards away from the highway.

"We were going to ride along the fence near the highway for a little way then head to the road back to the ranch," She went on. "My sister saw them coming on the highway and she got off her horse and walked out to the fence without a thought or a word. I was afraid of them so I didn't ride to the fence. The man she was talking to held the fence and she was already through and was getting on the motorcycle with him before I could even make a move to stop her. I started to ride away, then put my horse at a run when three of the men went through the fence and shouted at me to stop."

She seemed willing to continue to talk about her ordeal, so I let her go on. I looked around behind me and found a place to sit on another rock and sat down slowly so she would continue to talk.

"I was going to keep riding and head away from the fence so they couldn't follow me, but one of them had a gun in his hand. I kicked the horse and got him into a run, and then I heard the gunshot. The horse stumbled and I fell off after I was over the hill away from them. The horses ran off and I didn't want to take the chance they would catch up with me if I went looking for them."

"That doesn't necessarily mean anything has happened to her," I said. "The other possibility is that whatever they had in mind for you and her won't happen unless they have both of you. She could be safe as long as you're still free."

"So does that mean that I have to keep hiding out?" She asked.

"You're safe as long as they don't find you and it's her best chance at not being harmed. Stay put here, I'm going to check around here before we leave," I told her.

"What are you checking for? She asked.

"I have to prepare for the worst. We may have to hide out and this is as good a place as any. It isn't visible from the highway and the sides of the road are clear for a good distance, so they don't have much cover if they're anywhere nearby watching for us."

"They may not know where we are, and it isn't likely they would search every road in the area and risk getting any attention. For now, I want to look around and see if I could stand them off if they find us here."

"What do you mean stand them off?" she asked.

"They tried to take you by force twice, according to what you've told me," I said. "They shot at me and they may have planned to kill you, so there's no reason to believe that they wouldn't shoot if they find us."

"What do you think you can do against them if they start shooting?" she asked excitedly. Her gray blue eyes were large and I could see that she was frightened near the point of terror.

"I'm as afraid as you are, but I have no intention of getting shot or taken by them or anyone else," I said.

"What about me?" she asked. "What will happen if they start shooting at us, what can you do?"

"Our best defense is not to be found," I said. "We have to get to the authorities, but we have to get to town to do that. I can't outrun them if we're seen outside of town and if they trap us anywhere out here we won't be able to get away from them."

I realized by her questions that she may not even know that I was armed. A lot of people don't expect someone to be armed and they don't recognize concealed firearms or knives unless they're looking for them. A holster hanging below the line of a jacket or a large bulge on the hip or under the shoulder is suspect to a police officer, but not likely to be noticed by most anyone else.

Not everyone goes to action movies and the general public doesn't look for weapons when they look at someone. They're more likely to avoid looking too closely at scruffy looking persons, especially bikers, for fear of antagonizing one.

I had been standing several feet from her and now I walked to where she sat on the rock, went to my knees and sat back on my heels and looked directly in her eyes. "I have to tell you this. If they find us, there will certainly be some shooting."

She watched my face intently; her large eyes showing surprise at my statement that there would be shooting.

"I'll be right back," I told her.

Her expression didn't change and she made no move or indication that she had to see where I was going. I walked away from her and around to the side of my bike away from her. She didn't look my way, so I took the bikers pistol out of my pack and walked away from the camp into the rocks. I wanted to hide the biker's pistol for a couple of reasons.

First, I wanted to make sure I didn't get caught with it and not have a way to prove that I had shot in self defense. I still didn't think she was aware that one of the men that had been trying to catch her was dead, so I decided to keep it that way for now.

There was a chance that if I got her home or to the authorities without running into the group of bikers again, then I could go on my way before I could be tied to the dead man. I placed the pistol in some plastic wrap and buried it among the rocks in a place I could find it later. I looked in both directions and made mental picture of several objects that would serve as markers that I could find in any weather.

Chapter Seven

A kidnapper buried his ransom in the snow near a fence in the winter after shooting the father of the woman he and his partner had kidnapped in North Dakota in 1970. Thinking he could find it because he had marked the fence, he went back to recover it and all he saw was miles and miles of fence and highway and not a clue or mark where it may have been. The suitcase with several hundred thousand dollars was found in the spring of the following year by a motorist who noticed it leaning against the fence. I wanted to be sure there was more than a tape on a fence to help me find this location.

I looked in the direction of the sun then looked around, getting a mental picture in my mind. I remembered reading that while traveling, it is wise to stop occasionally and look back, so you can remember what it looks like from both directions. I looked around again and thought that I could remember the location. When I was sure, I started back to where I had left her. I picked up my sleeping bag and my gear and tied it on the motorcycle, then put out the fire and I buried the small amount of trash away from the camp and brushed away the tracks and scuffs.

She looked more than capable, taller than me and physically fit. I couldn't help but notice the firmness of her when I carried her out of the wash, and though slim, her shapely legs were smoothly muscled. She had survived a pretty serious trek in the desert prairie without water and not much cover.

She was a little burned but not injured or in the worst condition, considering she was dehydrated and could have died from exposure. She didn't seem affected by the ordeal except for the condition of shock she had been in and apparently wasn't able to remember anything up to the time I put her on the bike. She survived when anyone else would have gotten captured or would have simply given up and died of exposure.

"I was thinking that if we left while it was still daylight there would be less of a chance being seen," I told her.

"From what you said earlier, I thought you wanted to leave when it was dark" she said.

"In the movies, everyone uses the cover of darkness to make all their sneaky moves, which is fine, if you are on foot and you're wearing dark clothing. The headlight of a motorcycle is a giveaway in the dark and they certainly would be able to see me from miles away and I wouldn't be able to see them until they came after me with their headlights on," I told her.

She looked at me with a blank expression on her face, surely doubting what I had just said.

"We could leave later after it gets dark if there's a moon," I said. "I would be able to travel with the lights off as long as possible, but we'll stand a better chance if we leave right now."

She didn't reply so I walked over to her and said, "come on, we have to get moving."

She followed while I pushed the bike away from our camp to the road. I walked back and brushed away the tracks leading into the rocks to the site of the camp.

I got her on the bike behind me and was about to hit the starter when she asked, "Why are you taking the time to brush out the tracks?"

"You never know when you might have to return to a place and use it as a hideaway. It wouldn't be likely they would know we had used this place for a camp if there are no tracks. This is almost like any other place on the road for several miles in either direction. They can't check them all and it would be a good place to come back to if something happens and I have to hide out again," I said.

What I told her was only half true. If there weren't any tracks to give the location away, I could take a chance and come back for the pistol, not that they were likely to be looking for it. I rolled the bike slowly down the road and looked at both sides of the road and stopped once to look behind me, a practice that I was starting to appreciate.

Had it not been for the circumstances we were in, I would have greatly enjoyed the panorama before me as we went towards the highway. Dry or not, the hills and valley before us were as picturesque as anything you would want to see, with the widely rolling hills and the milky blue sky shading darker, into orange, red, then purple closer to the horizon.

We had to get into town and contact the authorities and get some help before we were caught out in the open. I wasn't even sure we wouldn't be attacked in any town we were found, though there was less chance of it happening in a public place. I doubted they would recognize me anywhere they saw me alone, but they would certainly know who I was after they saw us together. Right now, they had every advantage. I didn't know any of them by sight, which they may not know; but they had the force of numbers.

The bike bounced a little as I left the dirt road and entered the highway and I leaned into the left to make the turn. I appreciated every bit of horsepower of the 100 cube Revtech when I accelerated slowly into a low cruising speed. I didn't want to get a Harley engine when I built this bike and then have to alter all the wiring and try to match the custom components to the wiring and the frame.

The sound of the engine and any loud pipes of most motorcycles would be easily heard into the hills where they may be waiting me out, were they still in this area. Unfortunately when I had ordered the pipes and all the other accessories, I had no idea that they would be straight pipes with barely a baffle in them.

I appreciated the still cool late morning that made it easier on the engine. The day would warm up the closer it was to noon and heat up a lot more into the late afternoon. Then in the early evening it would be very cool and at night so cold it would frost the metal of the bike. While I admired the beauty of the almost dry hills and plains that stretched for miles I had to respect the harshness and unforgiving emptiness of it. It could be traveled during the day, but I had to be careful and be aware of the effect of the heat on the engine.

Anne leaned into my back and held on tight, leaning her head against the side of my head. It made me relax a little and for a moment it felt good that she was close and holding on, even though it was a feeling I shouldn't be thinking about. I had enough worry right now without taking on a false sense of closeness with a woman I had rescued and would have never been in contact with otherwise.

I should be thinking about getting her back to where she belonged without her getting into a panic and running away and getting herself caught again and possibly killed. I could only think of time and distance right now. I had to get away from this area and get somewhere I didn't feel so vulnerable and hopefully get the authorities involved. There was always the chance too that she and her sister had already been reported missing.

The bikers would be, to any law enforcement they may encounter, just another group of weekend riders going to a rally or traveling through. It wasn't a bad thing in itself, after all; I may have been traveling through here in better circumstances. I certainly wouldn't ever want to travel anywhere there were a lot of bad feelings toward riders in general. The bad dealings with biker types and the stigma of Hell's Angels of many years ago had somewhat diminished, at least in these areas.

I was hoping, for our sake, that the bikers didn't know that we hadn't made contact with the Police. They may know that one of their own may be dead and there was the possibility that they may have gone back to check on him to make sure. What I didn't need was being caught out in the open where they would have all the advantage.

I was heading east now and I had gradually increased my speed to eighty miles per hour. For this bike, it was an easy cruising speed, provided I didn't hit any stretches of road where the climb was steep. That would start the engine lugging down unless I shifted down and that would make even more exhaust noise.

Cruising at about seventy was the easiest and most economical on fuel when the engine was barely turning 2300 RPM. The five gallon tank would give me a range of about two hundred miles at sixty five to seventy, which would be over forty miles per gallon. I used to think that the old standard Harley dual tanks would have looked too big for this type of custom machine because of their width, but now I appreciated the extra gas.

I had just passed Exit 257 a few minutes ago and was getting closer to Exit 264. I was just at the right distance to see the outskirts of Holbrook and I didn't want to go into the middle of town right now. The new interstate seemed to go over the town because of the height of the road, but the old highway went right through the main business area.

What I wanted was to find a small motel on either end of town and hide out for a while and contact the authorities. There was too much of a possibility that the house was watched and I wanted to avoid going there at all until I knew where the bikers were. I was beginning to see the tops of some of the buildings on the edge of town when I saw a small motel.

I was hoping no one would recognize Anne at this end of town and it would help if there wouldn't be anyone who may start asking questions, at least for the time being. However, it was a certainty that she was well known even if she had been back from California for only a short time. I took the first off ramp and reduced speed until I saw a suitable motel and went alongside a multiple unit that had a *Manager* sign in front and pushed out the side kick stand. I told Anne to stay around the side of the building for the time being on the outside chance that they hadn't seen her yet.

"What do you want me to do?" She asked.

"Just try to stay out of sight for the time being," I told her. "Those men will know you on sight as will anyone else who lives around here. If they're anywhere in town they'll try to grab you again. They won't be as easily startled as they were when they left my camp earlier. I don't think they would recognize me, but they will certainly know who I am if they see you with me and they've already tried to kill me once."

I went inside and an Arab looking woman came up to the counter. I told her I wanted a room on the far side of the court away from the highway. There appeared to be a few cars in front of some of the units, so I thought, lights on in any of the other units later on wouldn't seem unusual. I paid for three days in advance for the unit and she placed the keys on the counter top after I signed the card. I took the keys to unit 29 on the East end of the court and headed the motorcycle around the back of the building.

"Walk straight out from here in that direction," I told Anne, "until you get to that last building there, then head behind it to the last unit on the East end of the lot."

"Why are you trying to keep me out of sight?" She asked.

"The longer it takes anyone to notice you, the better." I said.

I watched until she was out of sight, then I rode the bike straight across the lot to the side of the court where my room was. When I got there I opened the front door and pushed the motorcycle straight into the room.

The managers may not be too happy about me parking a motorcycle in the room, so I was hoping they wouldn't look to see where I had put the bike. I hoped that if they didn't see the bike outside the room they would only think I had left for the time being.

I put down a license number that I made up, but the clerk at the office didn't look at the card and just took the money.

There seemed to be plenty of room once inside, so I walked out of the room and half closed the door and called out to Anne.

"Come on in now, quickly so you can get out of sight."

Once I got her inside the door, I set about turning the bike around to face the door. I wanted to be able to haul ass if I had to move quickly. I would have to edge out the handle bars, but that would be a lot easier than backing out and lining up the bike to get moving.

"Why does it matter that I not be seen with you?" She asked.

"They aren't looking for me," I said. "They're looking for you. If they see you with me, then they'll know who they're looking for. I don't want to lessen the chance of your sister being found by giving away my involvement right now."

"Why would that complicate finding her?" She asked.

"We don't know where your sister is, or how she is," I answered. "The men who are looking for you attacked me when they saw me in the dark. I don't know what they would have done with you if I hadn't been there and I don't know why they ran off so easily."

"Wouldn't it be easier if you just took me to the house and I could call the Marshal?" she asked.

"If they find us again, now that you're with me, anything can happen and they may not be startled so easily again. I doubt that they left because they were afraid," I said.

"I'll call the house and see if she got back," she said.

I waited until she had hung up the phone. She turned to look at me with a worried look on her face.

"No answer?" I asked.

She shook her head and looked at me, more worried than before.

"Why can't you just take me to the house?" she asked again."

"It will be better for you and your sister if no one can connect you to any bikers, me included. We made it to the edge of town, but some of them may be watching the house, or hanging around in town waiting to see if you show up," I said.

She breathed out as if she was resigned to what I told her.

"I still don't understand," she said.

"If we can find your sister with the help of the Police it would be the best thing, but if they see police of any kind they may hurt her. They meant to take you by force, but as long as they don't have you, they may not hurt her," I said.

"How will we be able to find her?" she asked. "They may be anywhere."

"I don't know how the Police will go about finding her. They could set up a large scale search of all the possible locations of any bike gatherings," I said.

"This is a big country out here, how could they possibly find her?" she asked.

"It's true. They could be anywhere, but they can't be too far off. That bunch was with a large pack and if they were heading west when they took your sister, they could be somewhere between Winslow and Joseph City," I said.

"Her name is Rebecca," she said.

I nodded to acknowledge and said, "They've been in town for a few days and have probably been in this general area, so they must have found a place to have a large gathering."

"It may be impossible to find her," she said as she sat back on the bed looking exhausted and afraid.

"You need to rest. I'll try to contact the police and see if they can be of any help," I said.

Part of this was true, but if her sister had been harmed, I could be mistaken as being one of them and if Anne was seen with me it could be taken as being against her will. We were in a room with only one bed and despite my gray hair and my tired to almost exhausted look, she was giving me a worried look with her blue gray eyes looking larger than they were.

"You can quit worrying," I told her. "I have enough to think about just to do everything I can in contacting the authorities and helping you find your sister."

"What does that mean?" she asked.

"I'm a lot older than I look and that alone should leave out much chance of me being much of a threat to any woman," I replied.

She continued to watch me with a puzzled look on her face.

"I'm too old and tired to be much of a threat to you," I said. "Get some rest."

I didn't know what else to say to her and I wasn't sure what I was doing keeping her with me, when calling the local Police would be the sensible thing to do. However, I was in this deep enough now with a man dead and not knowing how I could get her somewhere safe without being seen by any of the bikers.

"My car is at the house," she said. "I can get it and look for Rebecca."

"What will you do if you find her?" I asked.

She gave me a worried look, probably not knowing how to take my question. So far I had only made statements that I was trying to protect her and stay out sight. She apparently hadn't given more thought to the character of the men who had come after her, but I wouldn't try to convince her otherwise if she insisted on leaving and contacting the police. If she did, I wouldn't have any reason to stop her and I would be free to be on my way.

"They might not know where you live or they could be watching the house," I said. "If they're watching the house and they see us going there, we'll never get out of their sight again."

My last statement got her to thinking again. She paled and started to look faint and bent forward until she held her head in her hands.

"It very well could be that your sister, uh, Rebecca is all right, but it may take some time to find her. In the meantime you have to stay out of sight," I told her.

"The police should be able to find her with less difficulty then you and I would have," she said.

"Are there enough officers here to be able to mount a search?" I asked.

"They will have to call in some help and the State Police will have to be called," she answered.

"She may just show up at home too," I said. "If she doesn't the best situation would be then, that the police get involved and find her and I could be on my way without any more problems."

She didn't look convinced, but she looked too exhausted to argue any further. I was ready to let her go wherever she wanted to go and be out of this mess as soon as possible if she had continued to insist on leaving and contacting the police on her own. She lay back on the bed and was asleep before I could talk about it any further. I covered her with the blanket by folding it over her.

Despite what I had said to her to make her feel at ease about being in a room alone with me, I felt the softness of her arm and shoulder when I covered her and it made me a little uneasy. The smell of her was warm and stimulating, even though she was still a little dusty and her hair was a mess. I wasn't in the best condition either so I took off the sweater and washed up a little in the bathroom. I really wanted a shower, but it might make me sleepy and I still needed to contact the police.

Chapter Eight

The Police station is listed in the phone book as being located on East Buffalo street, which is a fair distance into town. I thought for the time being that I didn't need to identify myself as someone on a motorcycle or as a retired Police Officer unless it was necessary. I probably couldn't accomplish much without Anne, but I wasn't ready to wake her and drag her through town and I didn't want to take her on the bike and make it known that she was with me.

I thought about her sister and that the longer she was missing, the more difficult it would be to find her safe. Time may be of the essence, but on the other hand, if she was dead, then it wouldn't make any difference and it would be sheer luck if she was found at all.

I stood on a chair and looked outside the window by looking over the top of the drapes. Moving the drapes aside to look outside is a dead giveaway and can be seen from a distance. I didn't see anything out of the ordinary, except the back walls of the other motel units and a partial glimpse of a car parked in front of one of them.

I left my jacket on the floor where she dropped it and I had removed my chaps. I had no clue as to how to proceed, except that I had to get something started with the authorities involved. It could mean restricting my movement or it could get me detained, but I doubted that anyone knew of Rebecca being missing at this time.

Letting myself be known right now and in the company of the sister of a possible missing girl in the company of bikers was not smart. I had to see if there was any way out of this without giving away my complete involvement. For now I had to think about keeping the shooting unknown, at least until I knew what the police would be willing to do. I was in this deeper than I could get out of legally and I realized that I was discouraging her from leaving and contacting the police because an investigation could lead to the dead man and I would never be out of this.

The man was dead. He was dead because he and his friends had tried to kill me, yet I could end up on the wrong side of the law, in jail and every one of the slimy bastards could escape or get off without any charges. I wasn't going to miss one dead outlaw biker who had taken a shot at me and I wasn't willing to make myself known until I knew what was going on. I was probably getting the false sense of security that the longer the incident remained undiscovered by any law enforcement agency the safer I would be. Yet, I could be out of this without any further complications if Rebecca turned up safe.

I looked around the room then took off my holster. I moved it around to the middle of my back so that the belt would go over it and press it against my back and make it less visible. I felt uneasy about carrying a pistol into town, but I didn't know what I would run into. I held the pistol behind my back and guided it into the holster. It was getting warmer outside, so I hoped I could get where I was going without sweating too much. I got a pullover knit shirt out of my bag and slipped it over my head. I didn't tuck it in so it would cover the pistol on my back.

The local Police building is two story brick among single level structures. It looked like many other buildings across the Southwest, built in the early 1900's out of red brick. The red clay is plentiful in this area and throughout New Mexico and Colorado, except that in Colorado a lot of the municipal and government buildings were built of natural sandstone or red sandstone during that time. Few buildings if any are built from brick or block any more because of the cost of production. Most are steel framed and covered with insulated corrugated steel or cast cement panels.

I walked up to the door and found that it was open. I wasn't surprised. Most small towns open up early in the morning. They are rarely or minimally patrolled, except for traffic at the edges of town and they are sometimes very unfriendly. I had learned early in my years of patrol and investigations, that small town officers and sheriffs are highly territorial and outwardly unfriendly to the point of being officious. They were in the chain link of gossip and local and regional information, if they chose to be. There wasn't much they didn't know and little they weren't interested in.

It was 1130A.M. when I walked into the lobby and found it empty. There was a counter inside the room near the inner wall, but there was no one there. There were no sounds from the narrow hallway leading to the back of the building or from the stairs on my left, which apparently lead upstairs to some of the offices.

I chose to walk up the stairs, recalling that most of these types of buildings had the police offices on the upper floors, and sometimes the City or Town administration offices on the lower floors. There was a large lobby facing the street and several glassed in offices in the back of the building. I still didn't see anyone in the upper area of the building.

I was about to walk back down the stairs when I heard footfalls in the rear of the building. I heard a door open and I stood in plain sight of the hallway leading to the back, so that anyone coming into the building would easily see me as they made entry. An almost middle aged man, short and tough looking and younger than me, in a neat tan uniform, had just entered from the back. He looked at me and he didn't seem concerned, he just looked sharply and steadily like he wanted to make me avert my eyes. He stood there and looked at me and didn't say anything for what seemed enough time for me to become nervous, but I didn't.

"I would like to talk to you about someone I'm trying to find," I said.

He still didn't say anything. So I walked toward him and repeated my self.

"I'm trying to find someone," I said. "She may have been hurt, or worse.

He walked toward me then, almost as though he was going to walk through me. He was right in front me and close enough, that if he continued to walk; he would bump into me. I waited a few seconds then looked to my right at an office door before I moved aside so he could pass if he wanted to. He didn't. He just continued to look at me without speaking.

"Am I in the right place? Or should I find the State Troopers office?" I asked.

I still didn't get a response. I looked at him for a moment more and I turned around and headed for the stairs. The sudden anxious feeling that I had made the wrong choice by walking into a small town police station washed over me and I wanted to get out of there. Ordinarily, I would give the greatest respect to any police officer, but I was tired, still scared and wondering how much more complicated this was going to get and how much deeper I was bound to be in it. I got to the first step when he spoke.

"What are you doing here," he asked in a deep low voice. It sounded more like, "Why are you where you shouldn't be?"

"I think I already answered that question," I said over my shoulder and started down the stairs.

I was almost to the bottom steps when he said more loudly, "Hey, I asked you a question!"

I thought the worst as I headed for the front door, thinking at any moment that I was about to be shot at or tackled before I made it to the street. He had either had a bad day, was expecting one or he was just not someone I was going to have a successful conversation with. I continued down the street and I walked between two buildings to get to the road which led to the motel.

I came out on the next street and started to walk back in the direction of the motel when I saw a clothing store. It took me only a couple of minutes to find a pair of canvas tennis shoes about the size that would fit Anne and a man's light blue denim shirt that should be about her size. If I hadn't, she would need to stop by her mother's house to get a change of clothes; I didn't want to do that yet.

I hadn't eaten anything since before noon yesterday. I doubted that Anne had anything but the water and tea we had since long before that. I walked out of the clothing store and into a convenience store a short distance in the same direction of the motel. I didn't waste any time looking around. I walked directly to the cooler, took out some bottles of cold tea and water and grabbed a couple of microwave soup cartons and headed for the counter. It was probably the best choice. She would still be dehydrated and anything but soup was bound to upset her stomach.

It took me a few minutes to walk the distance, but I didn't see anyone follow me into the street and it wasn't until I had entered the front door of my room that I heard a motor behind me. I looked out through the corner of the drape without moving it and I saw a tan Police car moving down the street in the direction I had walked. I started to think about how we could get out of there and get to a trooper station without any problems with the local authorities. The best time to leave was now, while it was still early in the day, but I wanted Anne to rest for a while.

I waited until later in the afternoon before I decided to wake her and make a phone call. I took a quick shower and changed clothes before I laid out the shirt, a pair of my jeans and a package of women's briefs I had picked up for her; then I woke her so she could clean up. She picked up the package of briefs, looked at the other clothes and looked at me with a faint smile, but didn't say anything. I got the phone number for the Arizona State Police in Winslow from the phonebook, and then I walked out to the phone booth in the lot next to the motel and called. I talked to a clerk or operator and told her what the call was about.

"Have you reported this to the local Police Agency?" She asked.

"No," I said. "It may have happened outside the area of Holbrook, out on the highway."

"Where are you now?" she asked.

"Outside Holbrook at a phone booth; can I meet an officer somewhere near here?" I asked her.

She told me that she would try to locate an officer that was on the highway closer to Holbrook.

"Give me about an hour. If he could meet at about five o'clock on the highway on the west end of Joseph City I can be there," I said.

"Will you be in a car or on foot?"

"There's a diner or gas station at the edge of town. I'll wave him down when I see him coming," I said.

I cut off the phone before she asked any more questions. I decided that the best thing to do was to head West on the highway and meet him coming out before he got to Joseph City. I felt nervous about not telling the operator about the involvement of the bikers, but there was also the nagging worry that the whole affair was about to get more complicated and dangerous.

There would be a better time to go into more detail after the State Police were notified and I knew what they would be willing to do. No one knew about the dead biker yet and Anne didn't seem to remember anything that happened before I got her on the bike and we had left the scene of the shooting.

Anne had put on the denim shirt and jeans before she came out of the bathroom. The jeans were loose in the waist and the shirt was at least a size large, but it was filled out by her breasts even though I was sure she didn't have a bra. Her hair was wet, so I handed her my brush so she could brush it out.

She didn't seem to talk much unless she was asked a direct question, and she didn't waste any time asking questions about the tennis shoes and the clothes. She just walked out of the bathroom and looked at me when she sensed that I was watching her and sat on the bed to put the tennis shoes on. She looked at me again as if finding something in my appearance that she hadn't seen before.

"You don't look like any Indian I have ever seen," she said as she tied her shoes. "I don't mean that to be belittling; I thought it may be some levity on your part to make me feel better."

"True story; my great grandfather was half Navajo, dark skinned and blue eyed. My paternal grandmother was fair and green eyed," I said.

"Do you go by Miguel or Mike?" she asked.

"Either one will do," I said as she looked at me wide eyed as if believing me for the first time.

She was strikingly beautiful, slightly tanned and also sunburned from her ordeal, and the jeans and shirt couldn't cover the fullness of her figure. I tried not to openly stare at her and create any tension or give her any discomfort to add to the ordeal she had already experienced. I wasn't calm and I hadn't forgotten that a man was dead and I had killed him. I could have been beat up, shot or killed.

The air between us was tight but not overwhelming. I knew she was a pretty woman when I found her, but now that I could see her in the light; I saw clearly that it was much more than that. She had finely shaped eyebrows; dark eyelashes that made her eyes look large, and finely shaped almost full lips. Even in the flat soled tennis shoes, she stood taller than me, with long firm legs. She was looking at me at eye level without making me feel shorter or smaller. Her body looked firm but not muscled like an athlete.

She stood across the room looking at me wide eyed and calm and didn't seem uncomfortable with me almost staring at her. She was well aware of her looks and was probably used to being looked at, stared and even gaped at. Had I seen her in another place and under any other circumstance, she would not have noticed me or made eye contact. She had the beauty of a model, not thin the way models are expected to be, but more like a professional dancer.

Professionally, I had met beautiful successful business women in the years I was a police officer. Most were polite when I had occasion to interview them and others only tolerated me as someone in their service as a police officer and would have had no reason to have any conversation with me otherwise. All my experiences with beautiful women were that they were aloof and without words, they clearly let me know they were way out of my class.

I didn't get that feeling with Anne Stahl even though she was more than out of my class. She had been terrified when I found her and may have been uncomfortable in my company after her thinking was clear, but she had not been impolite, nor had she given me the feeling that she was above any conversation with me.

She always spoke clearly and had the clear language of someone with a complete education, who was accustomed to speaking to others at the same level of education as her own. Yet, she didn't seem to notice that my language was common and influenced by my years of dealing with the best and worst of society. I broke eye contact first and looked in the direction of the phone.

"You should call your mother again and see if Rebecca has checked in or called," I said.

Anne said, "My mother isn't here. She left for Oklahoma about a week ago to visit with my aunt. I don't even know if she means to come back."

"Don't you talk to each other?" I asked.

"We don't get along. She has been drinking since father's death and it isn't getting any better. She still resents me for leaving to go to California when I did and worse now that my marriage didn't work out. I stay there to be with Rebecca, but we are always uncomfortable in each others company," She said.

She answered directly and politely and hadn't questioned the reason for any of my inquiries since I first started questioning her. Her fear and shock at almost having been kidnapped by the bikers was traumatic to say the least. Any fear she had displayed then was well founded, but she seemed in control now, although somewhat subdued, as if allowing her emotions and absolute terror show was something to be ashamed of.

"You have nothing to prove to me, and it's all right that you were afraid. I was afraid when I was facing those men out there. Believe me, your experience with the bikers was something that nothing in your life would have prepared you for. You survived the desert prairie and you're intelligent and tough enough to have kept on as long as you did. You had already gone beyond what anyone tougher and more prepared for the worst of conditions would have endured," I told her.

"I have lived here all my life," she said. "I have worked and ridden in the worst weather and I know about the desert, but being chased through it was more than I could manage."

I had a few moments when I was frightened enough that I could have lost control of my body functions before and during the shooting. She had nothing to be ashamed of and there was still a lot to be frightened of for both of us. She looked down for a moment, shivered slightly and looked at me again.

"I think I will be all right now," she said.

"What about the ranch? Is there anyone there who would be looking for you and Rebecca when you didn't return with the horses?" I asked.

"Mr. Holt would be there. I don't know if he would have called the Police or gone out to look for us," she said. "He may have been gone somewhere and the horses returned unnoticed."

"Where is the house?" I asked her as I handed her a fresh bandanna.

"It's on the east end of town on Third Street," she replied evenly while she tied the bandanna around her hair.

"Can we get there by skirting around the town a little?" I asked her.

"Yes, I've lived here long enough to know the few streets," she said.

"Are we going to the house now?" she asked.

"No, but I want to be able to find it in a hurry if I have to," I said.

Chapter Nine

I checked my bag for extra magazines for both pistols with my back turned to her and took two extra magazines for the Smith and Wesson and two for the Colt. I put the magazines in my pockets. They would be a little bulky, but it would be worth the trouble if I needed a reload. I didn't have any more ammunition than what was in the extra magazines.

I had been carrying Black Talons in one of my pistols and magazines and silver tip hollow points in the other. I had removed all of them and replaced them with 230 grain full metal jacket Ball ammunition before I left on the trip. The Talons and the silvertips were for sale only to Law Enforcement agencies when I bought them and I still had a lot of my own left over from my last years as a cop. A small nagging apprehension about having the ammunition while traveling convinced me to leave it behind.

I used the microwave in the room to heat the soup.

She took it reluctantly. "I don't know if I can eat anything."

I had thoughts that eating out of a Styrofoam microwave bowl was not something she had ever had to do.

"You haven't had anything as long as you've been with me and that's since last night," I said. "It isn't much, but you had better have something, or you'll be sick," I told her.

"I can handle a little fast food," she said. "I found it necessary while I was at the university and in a rush between classes."

While she took sips of soup, I opened my small pack and threw in a couple of cans of stew and a packet of plastic spoons and forks, and the plastic bottles of water. I didn't have any trouble getting the bike out of the room and rolled it around behind the building.

"Can we leave the back way and head to those warehouses?" I asked.

"Yes, there is a road that passes them on the other side," she answered.

"Is there any work going on there? I asked. "I don't want to run into workers or anyone else there. I want to check for any traces that the bikers may have used the building to get out of sight. If they haven't been there and there's no one there now, it would be a good place to hide out if needed."

"I don't think I've ever seen anyone in those buildings," she said.

"Whatever was there has been gone a long time," she answered. "There used to be trucking businesses here, but they lost a lot of their business and many of them closed years ago or started to build on the north side of the road when the Highway bypassed a lot of this area."

I motioned for her to get on behind me. As soon as she was settled, I started the motor and gritted my teeth because it made a loud exhaust noise before I settled it into an idle. I took off slowly, headed toward the warehouse and took the way around the left of the building when I came to it. I stopped in front of a large double sliding door, which was partly open, then moved ahead and pulled inside and killed the motor. I looked at one end of the building, then the other and noted that there were workrooms or tool rooms at each end of the large room.

There were large multi paned skylights at the top of the roof about 30 feet up and a lot of steel framing. The platforms in several locations on the ceiling girders looked like additional storage areas. They would make good hiding places if one could climb up there onto one of the platforms.

The bike could be hidden in any of the tool or storage rooms on the ground floor if we needed a quick place to get out of sight. I looked around, then I walked to the South end of the building to some of the rooms on that end. As I got closer to the rooms I noticed a large rectangle in the floor, like a scale or elevator.

I was hoping it was what it looked like, an underground storage, maybe an old repair pit, now covered up. So it was possible that I could find an old access to the main pit from one of the rooms, or close to the wall. If it was, I could hide the bike down there, and it was less likely to be found if we had to walk out around town anywhere.

However reluctant I was to leave the bike anywhere, it might become necessary. The other choice I had was to leave it inside my room. I could notify the office not to do anything in my room until I called them. It may still be likely that the management would find the bike in the room, if I had to leave it there, but all they could possibility do was complain, kick me out or scold me for it.

"How did you get out to where you and Rebecca were riding?" I asked.
"Mr. Holt picked us up. He had been in town and stopped by to check on us. He insisted that we ride out with him. He said he would be glad to bring us back whenever we wanted," she said.
"I don't think I'm ready to check on the house yet," I said. "If they are there or watching the house then they'll know who they're looking for. I don't think they know we're on a bike yet, unless they were watching and saw us come into town."

I got on the bike and motioned for her to get on behind me again. I rode the bike through the open doors and headed South to the end of the building and toward a road that seemed to go West out of town and to the main highway. I rode slowly to take my time for now. I could see the motel on my right as I headed out and I could already see the highway. Judging by the signs, I was on the old Route 66, and headed for the interstate. I was going to take the first right turn which led to the highway.
As it turned out, the turn in the road which went north was still Route 66. I took the turn and went another three miles, then reached the highway where the road went under the overpass to the on ramp access on the other side. If I continued directly ahead I would be in Joseph City. I took the first left and I got on the frontage road headed for the highway. I couldn't see anyone behind me and no other traffic on the highway.
I continued west past Joseph City and on further to the road which led to the rocks and hills where I had hidden the bikers pistol. It was as likely a place to wait for the Trooper as any. We would be able to see him coming from quite a distance from there, then go out to the highway and wave him down, or make contact with him if he went into Joseph City. I knew after about an hour that he wasn't coming or that we had somehow missed him. I thought about the cell phone I had somewhere in my pack and decided I could call again if I still had enough battery left.

It took me only a second thought to decide that it wasn't a good idea to use the cell phone unless it was an emergency. Any calls I made from the cell phone would be traced here by the phone logs. If this woman's sister returned safely and I left here without any further incidents, I didn't want anything linking me to this area.

I was beginning to have second thoughts about reporting the incident at all now. We were still not out of danger and I didn't think it likely that the bikers would report one of their own as missing and draw any attention to them if it could be avoided. I was beginning to think that it might become necessary to conceal everything that had happened and see if I could get out of this whole mess in one piece.

Everything depended on finding Rebecca if she was all right; if she wasn't, there was still plenty of time to make the report and start an investigation. What I had to do for now was to stay out of sight until we could see anything that would give me any clue they were anywhere near here.

I gathered some wood and made a small fire and then dug around in my pack for a small can of stew. I hadn't eaten since early morning yesterday and the little bit of soup helped by not making me sick after the shock I had been through. Now I was feeling empty. I was afraid to go anywhere in the night because I knew that my headlight could give me away. It was possible the bikers would hole up somewhere for the night later this evening, if they were still in the area. I was going to count on them being settled in for the night once they did and not move again until daylight.

She didn't seem willing to talk for the time being, so I heated up the can of stew in the can and gave her a small paper bowl and a plastic spoon. I had a little bit of water in my small canteen to drink and a couple of bottles of water and tea I picked up when I got the soup. I was lucky to be carrying even the smallest amount of items with me. She didn't complain, so I found a rock to sit on and ate the small amount of stew. I was starved, but I couldn't eat more if I had wanted to. I drank some water from my canteen and handed her one of the plastic bottles.

Thinking about all the possibilities over the years, had allowed me to prepare myself for fights and other confrontations. However, I was much older now and I was rapidly losing speed and flexibility and I even had trouble remembering small things sometimes. I already knew I couldn't stand up in a fight with any of them. The fight I had almost lost earlier had made it clear that any one of them had the clear advantage of youth on me.

I didn't feel any guilt for having shot a man and burying him to hide the incident. The bastard had tried to kill me and now that I had time to reflect on it, I was so pissed off that I turned over the fight in my mind and thought I should have shot him a few more times. I had never imagined that I would find myself in a situation that I would have to feel that I was wrong and that the actions I had carried out might be outside the law. I was retired now. I didn't have any justification to enforce the law. The only reason to use deadly force would be one of self defense; and even so it could be a matter of proving it, even if it had been to protect myself and what I believed to be an innocent person.

There was a dead man buried in the sand in the middle of nowhere and unknown to anyone except the bikers who had run off. They may just have gotten out of the area or they may be looking for both of us. I would be happy if they had left the area and I didn't have to worry about them again, except that Rebecca Stahl was still missing. I felt a responsibility to stay as long as I could and search until I knew where she was.

If I could in good conscience turn the whole matter over to the Police, I could leave the area and let someone else worry about the whole mess. I knew after trying to contact the authorities in Holbrook that nothing good could come from reporting it to them and getting me arrested. Walking out now and leaving it to Anne to report it to the police was likely to get Rebecca killed.

The more I thought about it, the more I knew that it was all wrong. I wasn't thinking clearly about what I could do to find Rebecca and I was only putting off reporting it to the Police because I didn't want to get arrested. Anne had suffered some heat exhaustion and a mild concussion and was in shock when the shooting took place. It didn't seem that she remembered anything of the shooting.

I looked around the camp at the rocks and low hills. The highway was visible from here, but far enough away that I felt relatively safe for the time being. Neither of us felt the need to talk and I lost myself in thoughts and apprehensions about the likelihood of another contact with the bikers. I knew that wherever I ran into them, everything would depend on the first move and where it was that the encounter occurred.

I could walk right by them in the street alone, as far as I knew and I wouldn't be known. If I was seen with her, they would know immediately who I was. I could do a lot more about finding Rebecca if I could find a safe place for Anne; maybe it was time to try to get Anne back to the Ranch.

There were a few small ranches around here and I was sure, several large ones. It wasn't likely that the bikers knew about the ranch, so it would be a good place to start, just in case she had gotten back safely. Whoever was there had to know that Anne and her sister were late in returning or had some problem, since they hadn't returned with the horses.

I had been standing several feet from her and now I walked to where she sat on the rock, went to my knees and sat back on my heels and looked directly in her eyes, "I have to tell you this. There will be shooting if they find us. They've already demonstrated their willingness to shoot at you, they most certainly will shoot at me."

Her eyes got large again, but I didn't see fear in them.

"What can you do?" she asked.

"What are you prepared to do?" I asked her. "Would you shoot back at them to keep them from taking you?"

"I don't know, I've used a rifle and I've shot a pistol, but I never considered shooting at anyone." She said calmly.

"What are you willing to do to get your sister home safely and keep them from taking you? Can you prepare yourself to shoot at someone that has a pistol and has already shown you that he would take you by force again?" I asked.

"Who are you?" she asked. "Have you been in a situation like this before?"

I looked down involuntarily, partly because I didn't want to qualify my ability to get into a shootout, and because I didn't easily talk about being a cop. It had taken me many years to change my attitudes and avoid looking at everyone with the same suspicious and scrutinizing looks of a cop.

"Right now I see no way out of this mess and I'm not willing to let them capture me or let them take you by force. They would certainly kill me to get you," I said.

Letting them have her without a fight wasn't something I would be willing to do. I had never allowed anyone to be bullied or hurt in my presence, even before I was a cop. A lot of people don't expect someone to be armed and they don't recognize concealed firearms or knives unless they are seen.

"I'm trying to prepare myself for the worst," I said, looking directly at her. "You have to too. You have to be willing to shoot and kill to stay out of their hands and stay alive. Do you think that you can do that if I give you a pistol and show you how to use it?"

"I've been around guns," she said, looking at me directly and emphasizing her words by leaning closer to my face.

I reached to my left side under my bulky sweater and pulled my pistol from the holster.

"Like this one?" I asked.

"No," she said. "My father had a Smith and Wesson; it had a cylinder. I have seen pistols like that, but I have never even thought of shooting one."

"This is a Smith and Wesson 45 automatic," I said. "Actually the common name isn't accurate, it's actually semi-automatic. The older automatics were single action. That is, you had to pull the hammer back in order to shoot it, but after the first shot the hammer stays back and the second shot just requires a small amount of pressure on the trigger to fire it."

"Is that one different?" she asked.

"This one is fired just by pulling the trigger, just like the pistols you have probably shot, but after the first shot it's more sensitive and requires much less pressure on the trigger to fire it," I explained.

"When someone not familiar with a double action automatic shoots it the first time without having had training, they sometimes fire the second and even a third shot involuntarily."

"Is that the only one you have?" she asked.

"No, I have the old style, single action automatic. It shoots better for me but it's harder to handle than this one. This one is heavier and bulkier, but the weight will counteract the recoil a little better. I'll show you how this one is fired. It'll be easier for you to handle because you don't have to worry about learning how to operate the safety," I said.

I let her digest what I had told her. She looked away to her left thoughtfully; her face becoming calm as she looked into the rocks behind me, then looked at me again.

"I'll try," she said.

I went back to my backpack and took out the Colt 45 to replace the Smith and Wesson 645 on my belt. I walked back to where she was, placed the Colt on a rock close to her and unbuckled my belt to remove the Smith and Wesson I had under my sweater. I had been carrying it on my belt in a nylon belt holster in a cross draw position with the butt forward. It was still fairly light out, so I took the time to show her how the Smith 645 worked. It was large for her hand and she held it in an ungainly manner.

"Am I going to be able to handle this thing?" she asked. "It feels like it weighs ten pounds."

"It's heavy but it'll be easier for you shoot than the other one. There isn't a whole lot to remember to make it work, and the weight will help you handle the recoil," I told her.

"It'll take a lot less time before you can be effective with it in the time we have. If it comes to a shooting, you're going to need every microsecond it takes for you to react and shoot."

The holster with the pistol in it looked ungainly and bulky on her left hip, so I moved it around slightly to the front of her right hip. I wasn't worried about concealing it out here and it could be removed if we got into town. I took the pistol from the holster, removed the magazine and pulled the slide back to remove the chambered round from the barrel. The magazine safety was still intact and wouldn't allow the hammer to operate without the magazine in place, so I put the magazine back in so that I could instruct her by allowing her to dry fire it. She was reluctant, but she caught on quickly and was dry firing it without jerking it.

"Remember, the first shot requires a long pull on the trigger, then when it fires release it slightly and the second shot only takes a slight pull to fire. Keep in mind that the gun will make a very loud report, jump in your hand and you have to consciously keep it on target because of the recoil," I told her. "If you have to shoot in the dark, it'll make a huge flash and almost blind you for the second shot."

I had her practice unsnapping the holster, drawing the pistol and bringing it up to eye level, holding it with both hands and squeezing quickly and smoothly so she could feel the resistance of the double action. After a little practice pulling the trigger in double action, I pulled the hammer back so she could see the difference firing with hammer back already. I showed her how to remove the magazine and replace it, so that she could reload if necessary. She did it easily, and then I had her remove the magazine and held it so she could pull the slide back and release it as if she had just inserted a full magazine.

"This is hard to pull back," she said. "I don't know if I can do it."

"Get a full grip on it with your left hand and jerk it back and pull it solidly back until it stops. If you pull the slide back with a full magazine in it, it won't lock back. It will slam the first round into the chamber. If you don't intend to shoot, then you have to lower the hammer by toggling the safety," I said. "If you fire until the magazine is empty, the slide will lock back and you have to use the slide release for the slide to move forward and load the next round."

She had more success on the second try and the slide locked in the open position.

"It will lock back when you fire the ninth round and stay locked back when you lock in the next magazine. You have to release the slide lock so it will load," I told her.

"If you remember to count your shots, all you have to do is load a new magazine and not have to pull the slide back. I always counted my shots, so that I would only shoot eight and reload while there was a round still in the chamber; that way I didn't have to pull the slide back to chamber a round to fire again. It's faster and you never really run out of ammunition, until you run out of magazines."

"That sounds like a war," she said.

"Like I said, we have to be prepared. If we get into any kind of situation, which I'm hoping doesn't happen, you'll have extra magazines," I explained.

"I don't think that I will remember to count. I've never done anything like this," she said worriedly.

"If it happens and all of a sudden you remember that you should have been counting, the slide is still forward and you don't remember how many times you fired, replace the magazine anyway. You may remove a magazine with rounds still in it, but you'll have a fresh magazine with more shots than you would have had," I said. "Will you be able to shoot?"

"I don't know," she said, looking at me with doubt in her eyes.

"Think about it now," I said. "These men shot at you. They found you again and tried to take you by force and shot at me. It's pretty clear that they'll try to take you again or shoot you or me if they find us."

"I didn't know they had shot at you," she said. "When did that happen?"

"You wandered out of my camp this morning," I said. "They found you and they shot at me when I surprised them."

"Were any of them shot?" she asked incredulously.

I was certain now that she didn't know about the dead biker at my camp and I wasn't willing to tell her and complicate matters any worse.

"You just have to consider what they're capable of," I said.

"What are you trying to convince me of?" she asked.

"You can't think about it later," I said. "You have to decide and set your mind now or sometime very soon, that you are going to shoot before we run into them again, if you hesitate or you don't shoot at all, you'll be dead."

"I don't know if I am more afraid of meeting them again or having to kill someone," she said.

"You're tougher than you give yourself credit for," I told her. "You got away from them and survived the desert. If we see them again, just remember what they tried to do and what they'll do if they take you again."

She looked at me carefully for a couple of minutes, then understanding seemed to reach her.

"You stopped them from taking me," she said. "I don't remember it, but I remember them coming after me yesterday."

"Who would be at the Ranch if we went there now?" I asked Anne.

She started out of whatever quiet thought she was having and said, "Mr. Holt should be there. They have a couple of boys but they don't live there any more. Mrs. Holt is not there. She has not returned from a trip to visit relatives and she may not. Mr. Holt is there a lot on his own. He has a couple of hands who work for him and some of the Indian locals work for him on occasion, but they don't stay on the ranch. They stay on the other ranch at Mr. Holt's old ranch house."

"The horses may have been found by now and he most certainly would have reported both of you missing by now," I told her.

"Are you going to take me to the ranch now?" she asked.

"It's a little early yet. We should wait until late afternoon, about an hour before dark," I said.

She gave me a questioning look. I was sure she was confused that I had said it was better to move around during the day and now I was telling her we should move just before dark. I took the time to check the bike for any loose bolts. I had lost the toe shift lever when I took it out for my first long ride. I had done a lot of the assembly, but I had ended up taking it to the shop where I had ordered most of the components so they could finish it. The owner had done some of the adjustments, but the mechanic who had done the remainder of the assembly, including the assembly of the clutch and primary case had left a lot of things loose.

I took the light weight blanket out of my small bag and took it over to her. "You can sit on this and then wrap up a little if it gets cool; I'm going to rest a while and maybe I'll even fall asleep."

I sat next to her and leaned back against the rock and felt myself falling asleep. I woke up later in the afternoon to find her leaning against my right shoulder with the blanket covering both of us. The fire had gone out, but there were still embers glowing in the circle of rocks. It wasn't dark yet, but it had cooled off quite a bit, leaving me almost chilled.

Chapter Ten

I checked my watch and saw that it was Friday, May 9, and it was late afternoon. Anne seemed calm and I hoped she was resigned to the possibility that she may not be able to go home until we knew where her sister was. I was still a little concerned about having left most of my gear at the motel but it was probably the best for the time being. If I had to leave without it, I could always try to get the owners to ship it to me. I got the bike maneuvered around so we could leave. I didn't have much gear to stow in the small bag I had brought. She was still wearing my leather jacket and I hoped it wouldn't get too cold before we made it to the ranch.

She said, "The Holt ranch is west of here."

"How far do you think?" I asked.

"I am not good at guessing distances." She answered. "It may be ten miles from here and another five or ten miles from the highway."

It didn't take long to get back on the Highway and we had been on the road for about fifteen minutes when she pulled on my shoulder and indicated that I make a turn to the right. The road we were taking now wound to the right, so it was probably a lot closer from the ranch to the highway directly across the prairie. She may have made it to the ranch when she was trying to get away last night, had she been able to sense her direction.

She tugged on my shoulder again.

"This is the turn," she said close to my ear. "It's about five miles from here."

It was dry, but there were scattered clumps of grass and green growth around the area of the ranch buildings. There were foothills close to this area and probably ground water, which may have accounted for the scattering of Scrub Pine over the low hills and Willow and Russian olive trees about the Ranch. The large frame house with wood and stucco siding, may have been 50 years old or more. It was all single level and it looked like many houses in the

Southwest and Midwest which had been built in the 50's and remodeled or enlarged until they were their present size.

There was a large light colored Suburban parked alongside the house and I could see a large "dually" pickup part way around the back. I headed directly into the yard, which was cut off from the road by another cattle guard and a pole and log fence extending out of sight over the small hills to my left and right.

Mr. Holt was a tall man, not strongly built, but lean and capable. He didn't look like a working rancher, but more like a rancher who hired hands and worked part of the time. He eyed me suspiciously, no doubt he knew the story from either Anne or Rebecca about the bikers who were trying to pick up Rebecca in Holbrook, but he nodded when Anne introduced me to him.

"This is Miguel. He was camped near the highway and agreed to help me get back," she said.

He looked at me with surprise, just as Anne had when I told her my name. It was still light out in the late afternoon and he could clearly see that my eyes were blue and though sun darkened, my skin was almost fair.

"That was yesterday," he said. "Why did it take you so long to get back and where is Rebecca?"

Anne said. "She rode off with someone on a motorcycle."

"She did what?" he asked.

"She talked to some men in town who were on motorcycles. They stopped when they saw us riding near the highway and she left with them," she said.

"What happened to the horses?" he asked. "They showed up here a couple of hours after you left on your ride."

"Two of the men startled them after Rebecca left with one of the others," she answered. "My horse stumbled and I fell off. Both horses ran off and I couldn't see where they went. I went out to the highway to see if I could get some help after the other men rode off in the direction of Holbrook."

"So is Rebecca alright?" he asked.

"As far as I know she is," Anne replied. "I just don't know where she is. Did you try looking for us when the horses came back without us?"

"I went out to the highway to try to find you, then I called the State Police. They told me to call back in twenty four hours. They won't even take a report until I call them back and tell them she hasn't returned," he said. "What happened after you lost the horses?"

"Two of the men came after me and I had to hide in the rocks," she answered.

"How did you get in the company of another biker?" he asked.

"He was camped near the highway halfway between here and Joseph City." she answered. She didn't volunteer any more than that and I knew that she would not be capable of lying without giving herself away. "I stumbled into his camp during the night and he offered to help me."

"Were you out there in that hot sun all afternoon?" he asked.

"Yes," she answered. "I was afraid to go near the highway. I don't know how I ended up where I did and how he found me."

He looked directly at me after that statement, probably thinking that I was just another biker and the unlikely possibility that I wasn't part of the other group.

"So what are you going to do now?" he asked.

"I would like to try to find her, but I have no idea where to look," she said. "I have to call the house. If Rebecca isn't back, I will notify the State Police that she hasn't returned and see if they will try to locate her."

"She could be in danger," he said. "Or she may just show up here any time."

"I should return to town. She may call there or just go home. Miguel can take me home so you will be here in case she calls or shows up," she said.

"You should wait here. I can return you town," he said firmly, clearly not liking the idea of her continuing on with me. "It should be reported to the police now."

"I'll call the house now and see if she returned," she answered.

I excused myself and said, "I'll wait out here if you don't mind Mr. Holt."

He looked at me, but he didn't reply as I turned to walk back to my bike. She came out while I was still adjusting the small pack behind the seat.

"Your expression tells me that you didn't reach her at the house," I said.

She handed me the Smith 645 still in the nylon web holster, so I put it back into my pack.

"There was no answer, but that could just mean she wasn't at the house right now," she said, and looked at me expectantly.

"It could mean that she hasn't returned. It would be easier to think that she may have gotten back all right, but they were still trying to catch up with you. They missed you twice and given that they tried to take you by force and shot at me in the process. They'll try again," I said.

"What should I do?" she asked.

"Stay here, until you hear from her. If you don't, then call the State Police in the morning," I said.

"What will you do now?" she asked.

"I'll head back to my room at the Motel," I said. "I'll look around and see if I can see anything unusual in the hills as I head back."

"Are you going to leave before I find Rebecca?" she asked.

I hadn't given it any thought before she asked, beyond looking for any possible camp sites on my way back to town. I hadn't expected to be asked to do any more than finding out where Rebecca might be, letting them call the police and then being on my way.

"There has to be something I can do to find her," she said. "You would know where to look."

"Meaning, I'm a biker and I should know some of their habits and where it's likely that they'll camp out?" I asked.

"They may hurt her if the Police go searching one of their camps or go after them." She said.

I knew she was proud and she didn't like to have to ask for my help beyond what I had already done to get her away from the bikers, but I knew she was afraid for Rebecca's safety. I felt a little ashamed and guilty that I hadn't thought for her safety, only that she had gone voluntarily and she may be returned before the bikers left the area.

"Give me the number here. If I see anything, I'll call and the Police will be able to go there and search for her. If you don't hear from her by morning, call the State Police so they can start a search," I said.

"They could be anywhere between Holbrook and Flagstaff," she said almost in frustration. "What if you don't see anything before you get back to town? Will you give up looking for her?"

"They could be closer too. They didn't just show up at my camp because they knew where you could be found," I said.

"How did they know where I would be? I don't even know how I got there!" she said.

"They must have been riding from their camp or returning there from Holbrook or Joseph City looking for you," I said. "They found you because they saw you near the road when you left my camp."

She stood there looking bewildered and frightened, but I knew there was nothing I could do, unless I had an idea where they may have taken her.

"Isn't there anything you can do?" she asked in a voice low and thick with emotion.

"I don't know what I can do, unless I see something that would tell me where they might be. I would guess that they aren't far away. They would have had to be close if they kept searching for you most of yesterday and this morning, then found you in my camp," I said.

"Take me with you. I know this area and I know where the ranches are. If they're out in the open somewhere and they have a fire, I will know if it's them or one of the ranches," she said.

I hesitated just long enough that she must have thought I had agreed with her. She turned and went into the house and returned in less than a minute, wearing a leather Bomber jacket and was tying a scarf around her head as she walked. There was no turning her away now, so I waited until she lifted her leg over the seat and settled behind me, and then I started the engine and headed out of the yard.

I couldn't help being fascinated with the ranch and what I could see of it and I would have liked to see the layout and the surrounding hills. It looked like a sound location and not as dry as the rest of the high desert that I had seen on the way out here. I could smell moisture in the air from the slight breeze that was blowing in from the direction of the edge of the foothills behind the house.

There must be a stream or a spring fed pond back there somewhere. It left my thoughts when she tugged on my shoulder for me to stop as I approached the intersection. I didn't make a move to shut off the engine or get off the bike. I just looked over my shoulder expecting her to say something.

"What happens now?" she asked.

"I don't know. We could go to your house and take a chance on being ambushed there, or we could stay out of sight a while longer and see if they show up again," I said.

"They could be anywhere between Holbrook and Flagstaff," she said almost in frustration.

"They could be closer too. They didn't just show up at my camp because they knew where you could be found," I said. "They must have been riding from their camp or coming back from Holbrook or Joseph City and found you only by chance."

She leaned her forehead on my shoulder and groaned, "oh no, I almost got you killed and I don't even remember any of it."

"You can't be to blame if you don't even remember walking away when you did," I said.

She leaned back and didn't say anything more, so I turned into the road and headed for the highway. I turned east when I reached the highway heading in the direction of Holbrook. I found myself somewhat relieved that everything seemed to be all right on the ranch. I wondered why I had conflicting thoughts about Rebecca returning on her own and yet feeling that the safety of anyone at the ranch could be at stake. If Rebecca was any where but at home, we may never find her or see her until she returned or they returned her, if they were inclined to.

I had no idea where the bikers may settle in if at all. They may have headed on to Flagstaff, or East past Holbrook by now, even if they had remained in the area last night. There wasn't much to see this late at night, except the road and the occasional fence line on the side of the highway so I tried to concentrate on the road and the sound of the bike. I saw some light off to the right of the highway. It wasn't bright, but it looked like either a large fire in the distance, or some type of Sodium outdoor lights.

Most of the night lights I had seen away from the highway since I had traveled east of Flagstaff were blue Mercury type lights, except in the cities, so there was a chance that it could be a gathering at a bonfire out behind the low hills. I couldn't see a road leading off to the right so far and the way roads meander over the low hills, the access road could be anywhere behind me. I slowed down at a rise of the highway going up a long hill and pulled off into a parking area on the right side of the highway. I kicked out the stand and leaned to my left to lift my leg over the seat and got off the bike.

"Why are you stopping here?" she asked.

"I saw some light out there. I'm going to get a better look," I said.

I found the small binoculars and took off my glasses so I could adjust the focus. Looking through the eight power binoculars, the glow looked like a fire in the distance, but I wasn't sure. I handed her the binoculars.

"Take a look and see what it looks like," I told her.

"It's not one of the ranches," she said. "It has to be one of their fires. Most of the ranches out here except for one or two of the larger ranches, use the blue lights; I don't know of any out in that direction."

"I'll take you back to the ranch, and then I'll go out there and check," I said.

"Wouldn't it be better to check now?" she asked. "I'll be able to find her if she's there."

"Yeah, I know, but we won't be able to get her out if we do find her. We can't ride with more than two on the bike. We won't fit on the seat and we could be in real trouble if they see us and come after us," I said.

She said nothing more as I got on the bike and she settled behind me again. It didn't take as long to get back as it did on the way out. I stopped in the yard and she got off, then hesitated and reached to take my hand off the throttle and embraced me, with her face against mine.

"Be careful," she said. "If you see her and can't get her attention to get her out, come back right away and we can go back out with the Police."

"If they're near enough to the highway for me to see anything of their camp or a fire, I'll take a look, but I have no idea what she looks like," I said.

"If you see her, you'll know it's her," she said. "She's wearing a light denim shirt and tan jeans and boots."

With that, I took it to mean that she looked like her, except younger. I started the engine and headed out of the yard through the gate. It troubled me greatly that there really wasn't anything I could do, but I could still see the helpless haunted look in her eyes as I headed down the road to the intersection that led to the highway.

I really had no idea of Bikers and their activities. I had been out of the system a long time, and even then, any information I would have had on the activities of bikers would have been because they had done something to bring Police attention to them. I also knew that I would have to try. I had no idea where the bikers were, but seeing lights where there shouldn't be any, was a good start. They may have headed on to Flagstaff, or East past Holbrook by now, even if they had remained in the area last night.

There wasn't much to see this late at night, except the road and the occasional fence line on the side of the highway so I tried to concentrate on the road and the sound of the bike. Thinking in that train of thought, I supposed it was foolish to be looking for them on a bike; they would be curious and decide to check me out if they did see me.

Chapter Eleven

It wouldn't take long to get back to the pull out at the side of the road. I had to start from that location and start checking any roads that lead off in the general direction, hoping one of them was the one I needed to check. Looking again in the direction I had seen the light before, I could see it flicker as a light would with dust moving or a light wind blowing the flames.

I couldn't see a road leading off to the right so far and the way roads meander over the low hills, the access road could be anywhere behind me. I slowed down at a rise of the highway going up a long hill and pulled off into a parking area on the right side of the highway. I kicked out the stand and leaned to my left to lift my leg over the seat and got off the bike.

I found the small binoculars and took off my glasses so I could adjust the focus. After stowing the Binoculars back in my pack, I started the bike to head a little further east down the highway. I didn't think there would be any chance of checking on the location until I saw a road that seemed to go in the right direction.

There weren't many roads leading to the south of the highway and none at all from beyond Joseph City all the way to Holbrook because of the railway. I had nothing to lose by taking it and checking in that direction, so I made the turn and headed south. I tried to keep the engine at low RPM on and take a chance that it wouldn't be heard if this was the biker camp I was looking for.

The road started to bear off even more to the right and seemed to be headed almost west. I continued to follow the road until I saw the light off in the distance and I could see that I was getting closer. I looked for a place to pull off the road and hide the bike. There were shadows on the left side of the road which appeared to be hills or rocks just past a ninety degree right turn. I stopped and turned the headlights in that direction until I could see that there were rocks a short distance away and the ground was fairly level. I had a thought to call Anne at the ranch, then thought better of it, thinking it was no use getting her in danger again before I knew if Rebecca would even be there.

The bike bounced slightly when I went over the shallow drop at the side of the road. I headed the bike for the rocks and found a flat area of ground that lead around behind them and settled the bike on its stand on some flat rocks. I walked back to the road and looked back to see if I could see the bike from several different angles.

Satisfied that it couldn't be easily seen, I picked up a willow scrub branch as I walked, so I could brush out some of the tracks closer to the road. I hoped that if I wasn't able to get back to the bike before daylight and had to hide out, there would be nothing visible on the ground to give the location away. I should be able to find the rocks when I returned in the dark, because I would be looking for them with my flashlight.

I reached what seemed to be the summit of the gradual incline I had been on for most of the way up the road. I could see the crowd of people, motorcycles and trucks with campers, once I reached the highest point in the road. There were rocks and scrub brush on the sides of a large flat area about the size of a football field. Most of the people were fairly close to the fire or sitting on rocks or motorcycles that were parked around the circle, twenty feet or so from the fire. I continued to the right to an area that I could see had a lot of larger rocks and boulders with more scrub brush and small dry trees.

I found my way around the large boulders, hoping that no one was out of the light behind or among the rocks. I lost sight of the crowd when I went behind the rocks and started working my way in the direction of the fire carefully. It felt like loose sand and some small rocks and dry weeds on the open ground between the larger rocks. I found a large terraced shaped boulder and started to climb up on the side away from the fire.

I was a lot closer to the fire than I had thought. I took my glasses off to avoid the chance of anyone seeing the reflection of the fire on the lenses and put them inside the neck of my sweater, hanging by one of the crown earpieces. I bellied down and looked carefully behind me to make certain no one had been watching me while I climbed.

This was a large crowd, mostly men, dressed in denim jackets, some cut off at the sleeves and others wearing a variety of denim vests over their leather jackets. Some were wearing ball caps and others had bandannas tied on their heads. The few women mixed in with the crowd were wearing blue jeans, some of them cut off and many in a variety of shorts. They were in small groups and almost everyone I could see had a bottle or can of beer.

A woman with a light denim shirt and tan trousers and what looked to be light western boots was sitting on the rocks just below me. I knew by the difference in her clothing and her hair that it had to be Rebecca. It was getting colder now and it must have been close to nine o'clock and nearly pitch dark, except here in the glow of the fire.

Just about the time I was going to move off my vantage point to get closer, one of the men from the crowd walked to where she was sitting. I could hear him talking to her, but there was too much noise from the crowd to discern any of the words. She shook her head, and then he shrugged his shoulders and walked back toward the fire.

There didn't seem to be a way to reach her or get her attention without being noticed, but I started down off my perch to my right anyway. I reached the ground and started moving toward her carefully, keeping out of sight behind the rocks as I moved forward. Just when I thought it was going to be impossible to get her attention and find some way to get her to come to me, a loud bunch of whoops and screaming started and most of the crowd started moving closer to the fire. Some kind of group activity was about to start and it looked like everyone wanted to move closer to the action.

I didn't waste any time. I made a quick move to get behind her and reached the rock she was leaning against. I put my left hand over her mouth and nose and felt her stiffen as if to fight or scream. "It's all right Rebecca; Anne sent me, keep quiet and come with me."

She was shaking but she didn't make a sound when I pushed her in front of me to the back of the large rock I had just climbed. She turned to look at me in the dim light of the fire reflecting from the rocks as if trying to identify me and I put my finger in front of my mouth for her to be quiet.

"Move quickly and quietly," I said close to her ear. "If they look around for you, we'll be in trouble."

I took her arm and guided her to the road where I had walked in. My heart was beating wildly and almost loudly and my chest was starting to burn as I held on to her arm and pushed her ahead of me. I hadn't even run yet, so I thought to slow down so I wouldn't pass out or start having some serious chest pains. I walked a little slower so my breath and heartbeat would slow down in case we had to run for it.

After a couple of minutes of walking a little slower, my heart slowed down and I felt myself breathing a little easier. The return trip to where I had left the bike seemed to take a lot longer than the trip in, but we managed to get there without having to run for it.

The rocks weren't visible in the near pitch dark, so I checked with the flashlight and I found a slight depression of the tracks, beyond where I had brushed them out. I guided Rebecca in the direction of the rocks and we walked around behind them to where the bike was. I was trying to listen in the direction we had just come from to see if the same level of noise was still going on. Nothing seemed any different. The loud voices, screaming and hollering and some engines revving up and down continued as before.

"You have a motorcycle too. Are you one of them?" she asked, sounding a little frightened.

"Just coincidence," I said.

"How do you know Anne? And, where is she?" she asked.

"She wandered into my camp after she got away from some of your friends last night," I said.

I didn't think this would be a good time to question Rebecca and find out if she had told anyone anything that may lead to Anne or the ranch. I was more occupied with listening for sounds from the direction of the gathering and looking carefully for movement of any kind coming down the road.

"Come on. I don't have time to explain now. I have to get you out of here before they figure out where you went and come looking for us,"

"Help me push the bike to the road," I told her after I got the bike balanced and got the kickstand up.

She put both hands on the sissy bar and I started pushing the bike. The sand was soft, but the way was downhill and though difficult, I was making headway toward the road with her pushing with one hand on the seat and one on the sissy bar. I got the bike on the road, set it up on the stand and went back and brushed out the tracks with a piece of brush. I wrapped my bandanna around the tail light and hoped it would cover the light when I turned on the switch to start the bike. I got on and leaned forward partway onto the tank to make room for her behind me and put my glasses back on.

I leaned forward and pushed with both feet to get the bike rolling. If I got it rolling fast enough downhill I could try starting it without using the starter, but even if it didn't start, we would be going downhill and could roll for quite a distance before I had to use the starter. There was nothing I could do about the headlights. All the lights would be on as soon as I turned the key to start the engine, so I had to let it roll as long as possible.

We started rolling slowly at first and I thought the added weight was going to keep us from speeding up, and then we gradually gained some momentum. Once we had gained some momentum and the bike seemed to be slowing a little, I had the presence of mind to reach down and turn the petcock before I squeezed the clutch to shift into gear; then turned the key and squeezed the clutch and kicked the lever upward into gear.

I toed the lever up one more time, so it would be either in third or fourth gear and the heavy 100 cube engine would turn over and start. When I let the clutch go and turned the throttle slightly, the heavy engine grabbed and the bike almost felt like it was going to stop from the compression. It coughed once and the engine started without backfiring.

Quickly, I grabbed the clutch and squeezed it and shifted down and luckily it seemed to be in second gear. I accelerated slowly and got up to about forty miles per hour. It took about twenty minutes to reach the highway and I was hoping that we might be able to reach the ranch before anyone noticed Rebecca was missing.

I looked over my left shoulder and saw dancing bright lights that had to be on the road moving in this direction. It had to be bikes coming this way. I wished mightily now that I had altered the lighting system back to the way I had it the first time, so that the first click of the ignition would allow the bike to start, but the lights would be off until the switch was turned to the second position.

There was no choice now, I may not be able to outrun them or stay out of their sight if they had discovered Rebecca was gone. They would be able to overtake me once they got to the highway or at the very least, they would know where I was going. The best I could do was to head west and try to find the road where I had hidden the pistol. I didn't think it mattered how much noise my pipes made now, they probably couldn't hear them over the sound of their own engines. I thought I might be able to get far enough down the highway that they wouldn't see my lights if I got moving in that direction quickly.

"Hang on tight," I yelled over my shoulder. "I have to kick it into high speed."

I felt her arms tighten and she leaned forward against me with her face at the back of my head. I was still moving pretty fast when I reached the intersection with the highway, so let up on the throttle gradually to keep the exhaust noise down as much as possible until I reached the pavement and I could make the turn. I had to head east and find a place to cross the median. I accelerated rapidly and shifted gears until I reached ninety miles per hour.

I couldn't risk much more speed than that with her behind me, especially if there were any serious bumps in the pavement. I didn't know what kind of rider she was. She was probably scared shitless already and I didn't want to take a chance that she would lose her grip on my jacket and fall back against the sissy bar and bend it or break it off.

I was about to take a chance and cross the median through the soft sand and grass when I saw a crossing just ahead. I slowed quickly and made the turn and headed west, hoping that they wouldn't see my lights before I got far enough down the road. I had seen the lights dancing off the rocks on the sides of the road, but I hadn't seen any headlights when I reached the blacktop. I still couldn't see any lights directly behind me as I went up an incline in the highway and headed down the other side.

I kept looking for the road to my last camp or any likely road that could offer us some cover. With any luck I could find it in the darkness and get off the highway and cut off my lights before I was seen. I was about to give up on finding it, when I caught sight of the depressed ruts of old tracks on the road and slowed quickly to make the turn without using the brakes. After I made the turn I quickly found the place where I had gotten off the road to get to the cover of the rocks.

"Get off quickly and help me push the bike into the rocks," I said, as I quickly turned off the engine and the lights.

It seemed to be taking too long to push the bike across the sand, then through the rocks, where I thought we would be out of sight. Rebecca stumbled and lost her grip on the seat and fell. I continued on until I was sure the bike would be out of sight and set out the kickstand. I moved quickly to reach Rebecca where she had stumbled and helped her to her feet and guided her to the cover of the rocks.

"Get behind the rocks quickly," I said.

Chapter Twelve

We stood in the darkness until I could hear the sound of engines and I saw the lights of the bikes as they went by in the distance. It was only a short distance to the highway and I couldn't be sure, but it looked like at least three bikes as they went by. If they went all the way to Winslow, we would be safe here until they decided they weren't going to find us and maybe they would head back to their bonfire. If they didn't know they were trying to catch up with another bike, they would be looking for tail lights of a car or any other vehicle.

Only a few minutes had passed when I heard the sound of engines again. I looked back toward the road and I saw the bikes heading back in the direction of the bonfire. It was cold now, but I couldn't make a fire here; it would be seen reflecting off the rocks on this side of the hill. We had to stay out of sight until I was sure they wouldn't go by again and we would be seen. I decided that the best way was to find a way to the other side of this hill, find some more rocks and make a fire that would reflect into the desert and not toward the highway.

"Come on, we're moving," I said. "Start back to the road. I'll get the bike to the road and then we can head farther away from the highway."

I got back to the road and positioned the bike for her to get back on.

"Why can't we just go home?" Rebecca asked.

"I can't take the chance that they'll see my lights in the dark and I can't outrun them," I said. "We need to stay out of sight a while longer and leave just before first light in the morning. It's a good bet that they may party hard and sleep in and we can get back to the ranch before they get moving again."

"I'm freezing to death," Rebecca said.

I felt guilty about not offering her my jacket before we hit the road, but in the excitement, all I could think at the time was to get out of there as quickly as possible and not be seen. I slipped out of my jacket and put it around her shoulders.

"Don't bother to zip it up," I told her. "We won't be too long finding another location, I hope."

She got on behind me and I headed up the gradual incline, taking us further away from the highway. I continued on until I could see that it topped off on a hill and started in a decline on the other side. There was a moon rising over the low hills now a little to the right of the direction we were headed, so we must be heading almost east now. I could see more rocks to my left on this side of the hill. It would be a good location to camp and make a fire behind some cover. I looked for a low place on the side of the road and turned left to go through the packed sand and rocks. I stopped when the wheels started to bog down.

"Get off and follow me into the rocks," I told her.

I found a way through the rocks and it looked like an ideal place that couldn't be seen easily and stopped and propped up the bike. I located some thick dry brush and grass and some cactus boughs that would start a fire just as she reached me. I got a fire going and opened a can of stew and put it near the fire to get hot. I handed her a couple of paper bowls and some plastic ware from my small bag then took the can out of the fire with the pliers of my Leatherman. I put the can on a rock beside her and went back for my canteen. I drank some water then handed her the canteen and went back to the fire.

"Get close to the fire on this side and warm up," I said. "Then you can tell me why it was so easy to get you away from the party."

While she was settling down closer to the fire, I rolled a rock closer to the fire so I wouldn't have to sit on the ground. I didn't think my tired and cramped legs would let me sit on the ground and once down I didn't know if I could stand up again. I looked at Rebecca then and saw a younger version of Anne. Her hair was the same color and possibly a shade darker, but longer and her eyes were large and light colored in the light of the fire. She didn't look afraid, but it was not a trusting look either.

"Who are you and where is Anne now?" she asked.

"She's at the ranch with Mr. Holt," I answered.

"You're a biker too; how do you know Anne?" she asked.

"I'm a rider, there's a difference, and the name's Miguel," I told her. "Anne wandered into my camp Thursday night after she got away from the two men who took a shot at her."

"They took a shot at her?" she asked incredulously.

"Yes, and the horse stumbled and she had to get away on foot," I said.

"What happened to the horses?" she asked.

"They were startled and ran off back to the ranch. After she fell off and wandered around most of the afternoon, she happened into my camp," I answered. "Several of them found her in my camp this morning and took a shot at me, but we were able to get away from them."

"Oh my God!" she said. "What have I done?"

I waited a while before talking to her again, letting her brood in her thoughts until she looked up at me.

"So, what happened?" I asked Rebecca. "Something must have changed that you wanted to leave the party."

Her face took on a look of resentment, and then she let her shoulders drop and her face softened.

"I thought it would be fun to ride with them. Brooks, the one I went with, seemed nice. He said I could ride with him while they were here and if I wanted, I could go with him to a rally in Texas to a place called Goldwin or Goldwain or something," she said.

She paused and I said, "You were with them almost two days."

"I know, I thought we were just going to ride to Winslow and be back before it got dark and cold. I thought it would be cool to ride up to where there are trees and it's green. Flagstaff is a beautiful view of the mountains," she said.

She went on to say that instead of heading farther west, they had stopped at the camp where I found her.

Then she went on. "There were a lot of bikes, trucks with trailers and even some campers and tents. It looked like a bike rally which was turning into a party and it looked like fun until it started getting dark. Then the party really got going and got louder and rougher. Fights broke out and almost everyone seemed to have a knife, even the women."

"The women spoke dirtier than the men," she said. "They didn't like me. One of them pushed me and took a knife out of her pocket. She said she was going to cut my pretty face, and then Brooks wouldn't like me so well. Brooks got between us and led me away with some of his friends to one of the tents."

She looked down and I could see that she was embarrassed to go any further, and then she shrugged her shoulders and said, "He wanted me to take my clothes off. I still thought he was nice and I would have, but I saw his friends just outside the tent watching. I knew they all wanted me, so I said no, I didn't want to do it. He talked nice and kept trying to convince me, but when I kept saying no, he forced me to take off my clothes. I screamed and tried to keep him away, but he held me down. His friends came in the tent, but I started to scream again and he told them to get out, they could have me tomorrow."

She paused again and sobbed then continued. "Later, I fell asleep in the tent after he went back with his friends. He was still asleep when I woke this morning. Most of them just sat around and talked all morning and later one of the women brought me something to eat. I tried, but I couldn't eat anything. They didn't bother me all day, but I was really scared when it started to get dark and the party started again. I sat as far away from everything as I could. I was scared to death when you grabbed me from behind, but when you said Anne sent you, I just hoped you were telling the truth."

"Was that Brooks that talked to you just before I found you?" I asked.

"Yes," she replied.

"How did you know I wasn't one of them?" I asked.

"I didn't, but you don't sound like them. They knew it was my sister when they went looking for her. They wanted her too, but I never told them her name. They didn't ask her name or seem to care," she said. "I saw Brooks' friends leaving last night and I asked where they were going. He told me they were just going to town, but I knew his friend Jinx wanted to find Anne."

"Was Jinx at the party?" I asked.

"He didn't come back with his friends last night," she said. "I saw Brooks talking to the men who left with him and they almost starting fighting."

She paused then looked at me worriedly and asked, "Why did you ask?"

"I just wondered who it might be that was with that bunch that shot at me last night," I said

"Is Anne all right?" she asked.

"She suffered a little exposure, but she's all right," I answered.

"We'll wait until it starts getting light, then I'll take you to the ranch. I left her there with Mr. Holt."

"She is surely so upset with me for going with those men," she said.

"Do they know where you live?" I asked.

"Yes. I talked about where we lived in town. Then they asked me where Anne may have gone when they came back the first time," she said. "I told them she may have gone back to town."

"Did they ask about the horses?" I asked.

"I told them we rented them at a small place not far off the highway. I told them she had probably taken the horses back before she went back to town," she said.

"Did they know about the Holt Ranch?" I asked.

"No, I didn't say anything about the ranch," Rebecca said. "If I had been out there any longer, they may have asked, or they may have taken me to look for Anne."

"Both of you are going to have to leave town for a while," I said.

"Why do we have to leave?" she asked.

"Because, I don't think they're going to stop looking until they find you and Anne, but I can't see that they'll hang around town looking for you for very long if they don't see you right away. The longer they hang around, the more they'll be seen. I don't think they want any more attention than they already have. They'll head down to their rally or wherever else they were going and forget about you," I explained. "If they do come back this way, which is not likely, they can't find you if you're not here."

What I didn't tell her was that they would continue looking for her and Anne and whoever had helped them and shot their missing friend. I knew they would want some blood now that they figured out their friend "Jinx" was probably dead. The only thing in my favor right now, was that they didn't know who they were looking for, besides Anne and Rebecca and they may not know where to look.

"It wouldn't bother me if we left here forever," she said.

Brooks turned around to look into the rocks where he had left Rebecca. She was still frightened and didn't want to get near the fire where most of the rest of the crowd was. The party was winding up higher and the drinking was getting more serious as the night went on. He was thinking about taking her to his tent again before he got too drunk. Zero and Baker had been pressing him to let them have her while the party was still going strong.

"Hey Brooks, come on let's take that sweet thing over to the tent and have a little fun," said the one called Zero. "You said Baker and me could have her."

"No, Goddamn it!" said Brooks. "You'll have plenty of time with her later."

"Hey, ok," Zero said. "No offense man, we just want to party too."

He didn't like the look in Brook's eyes. He was usually calm and joked around with him and Baker, now he stared a lot and was stalking around and drinking a lot more since morning when Jinx hadn't returned. He grabbed Zero by his open jacket and drew him close, breathing into his face.

"You guys lost Jinx," said Brooks. "He was worth four of you and Baker. We been riding for a long time him and me. He was my partner."

"Hey, we had her. We didn't see the guy in the dark until Knuckles started shooting," Zero pleaded.

"So why didn't you shoot? Motherfucker! There was eight of you out there, what the fuck, are you a bunch of chicken shits or what?" shouted Brooks.

"So, where was Jinx?" he asked Zero.

"Doan Know man, I thought we was all together headed for our rides. There was more shots when we got on the highway," said Zero.

"So why didn't you go back and help Jinx?" he almost shouted at zero and looked at Baker.

"It was dark man. It could've been a bunch of them shooting at us out of the dark," said Zero. "I thought we was all together when we pulled out. I thought they was shooting at us."

"So, who the fuck are they?" shouted Brooks. "Did you see any of them?" "What are they? Some local shit kickers partying out in the desert or what?"

Evan, president and one of the charter members of the Silent Wing approached them.

"What's going on?" he asked in the general direction of the three of them.

"These two motherfuckers lost Jinx," said Brooks.

"So, what's going on?" he asked. "Where's Jinx?"

"We don't know Chief," answered Baker. "Jinx wanted the other bitch, was with this Rebecca. So we went with him to find her."

He was reluctant to add that there were others who went with them. Evan didn't know about any of his riders leaving to look for a woman and wouldn't have approved had he known. Members who went looking for trouble instead of staying within the clubs activities while on a Run were not tolerated for long. Members and visiting club members didn't involve outsiders or do anything that would bring the attention of the law.

"What the fuck. I told you Brooks, we didn't need the grief. There's plenty of women traveling with us or comin' out, what the fuck did you have to go messing with the locals," said Evan. "Now you got the bitch over there and someone knows you got her. Next thing you know there'll be Mounties and farmers all over the place looking for her!"

Brooks took a half step back. He didn't want to brace Evan. Evan didn't cuss unless he was agitated and he rarely talked much except with a few select members who hung around him; other ranking members of the Silent Wing club.

"Doin' something on your own could get you before the board, but taking others in on it could bring real trouble," he told them.

He knew Evan would act suddenly and without warning, not right away, but when least expected he might find you alone and walk up and just shoot, then walk away like nothing happened. He had the support of most of the visiting groups too, and a few trusted members of his club were always watching Evan from a distance. You might be able to get the drop on him only to find yourself looking at the wrong end of a couple of shotguns.

"Fix it Brooks. Take the little bitch back where you got her and find Jinx; any Mounties come around here looking for her, make sure you a'int here. You two," he said looking at Zero and Baker, "get her out of here and find out what's happened to Jinx. If you don't find Jinx, you'll be up in council."

"If you find Jinx, make sure those two bitches get back to town. As long as they get back, it don't matter what they say, nobody will come lookin' for us. Nothing happened to them that'll get the Mounties after us and we're still in the clear as long as the law a'int looking for those two women," he said. "Do you understand?"

"But what about Jinx?" asked Brooks.

"Jinx went outside without orders while on a Run," Evan said as he leaned his face closer. "So did you. If you find him, he's up on council and so are you. If you don't find him he don't exist and if the law comes looking for either of those women, you don't either."

With that, Evan walked away to the fire. They watched as he went back to the chair where he had been sitting with some of his closer associates, charter members of the club. Brooks didn't need it explained any further. Going out without orders while on a Run could get you expelled at the least, worse if it brought trouble on the club.

The mixed group of clubs was headed south to settle a conflict of territory and distribution with some of the Bandits. The clubs were on a run without colors until after that meet to avoid any interest by any law enforcement. Anything that happened to get them noticed would complicate any negotiations they were to have with the other associated groups.

They all knew about the recent skirmishes the Hells Angels had with some of the groups in Canada which put all the clubs in that area under scrutiny. It was not a time for any of them to get noticed. Conflicts over territory and distribution were part of the cost of dealing and being organized, but many of the clubs throughout the country had been cooperating to some extent to avoid conflicts over territory.

Most of the hard corps clubs had virtually gone underground except when on Rally Runs. Getting in any scrapes with the locals during a Run to a closed conference would certainly get the attention of all the law enforcement organizations along the way, but if there was no major law being broken, it would amount to no more than getting a ticket or two.

"Come on," said Brooks. "She'll tell us where to find the bitch."

He turned in the direction he had last seen Rebecca. She wasn't there.

"She a'int there!" said Baker.

"Goddamn it, I can see," said Brooks. "Let's go, get your mules and get ready to go before Evan knows she a'int there. I'll go look around. Meet me over by the road."

He walked to the large boulders where he had left her. Not finding her, he circled the rocks then made his way to the tent to see if she had sneaked off to get away from some of the women who were with the group. None of the women were riding on this run. They were running support only, driving trucks and campers as support for the combined clubs on the road. The two men headed for their bikes where they were parked on the side of the fire nearest the road. They ran into another of the men who had been with Baker looking for the second woman after she had lost her horse.

"Well, let's go. Brooks is looking for the little bitch and said meet him on the road," added Baker.

Brooks reached the tent only to find Darla there, standing to the side of the tent flap with her right hand on her hip.

"Well, where's your little bitch?" she asked insolently. "I want to have a little talk with her."

He reached out and grabbing a handful of her long dark hair, pulled her close and said, "Get lost you fuckin' cunt. I won't tell you again."

"So what, you too good for me?" she asked.

She grunted in pain when he twisted her hair in his hand and made her lose balance to the right as he put the pressure on. He pushed her away and she lost balance as he released her hair and she fell in front of the tent. He started after her as if to kick, but not before she scrambled to her feet and walked quickly away to the fire. It was hard going in the dirt and sand walking his bike away from the tent, but he didn't want to attract any attention his way, especially if he was leaving without Rebecca.

"Goddamn it," he said under his breath. "I'll find you and that bitch too, and get rid of both of you."

The three of them were on their bikes waiting on the road when Brooks approached them rolling slowly in first gear. He looked back in the direction of the fire to see that Evan was still sitting and talking with several others. He didn't see Knuckles until he caught movement in the shadows over to the left. Knuckles pushed his bike onto the road before starting it and pulled up behind. Brooks said nothing more as he passed the other three on the left side and headed down the road away from the Rally. The Group of five men on motorcycles had reached the main highway west of Joseph City. Baker was riding next to Brooks when he stopped.

"Which way?" he yelled.

Brooks was looking to the left, trying to decide whether to go toward Winslow or go east. He thought he had seen something in that direction, but he couldn't be sure. He knew Rebecca hadn't been gone long. He hadn't seen her on the road between the area of the bonfire and the highway, so someone from the rally must have gotten her out of there, or she was on foot somewhere behind them.

"You two and Tank head that way," he said pointing to the left towards Winslow. "I thought I saw lights just now. Check it out, and then be back here. I'm gonna check the road back again."

He watched while Baker, Zero and Tank got onto the pavement and were headed toward Winslow, and then he entered the highway and made a turn on the wide pavement. Knuckles followed him as he headed back in the direction of the bonfire. Finding someone in the dark is virtually impossible; all the person hiding has to do is find cover and be still. The only way someone on foot could be found would be if they were moving in the open and in this case, on the road. Baker, Zero and Tank had gone at least fifteen miles when Baker decided that they weren't going to see anything that would tell them if anyone else was riding in the area.

There were a few roads leading off the highway, most of them just ruts, but he had looked in the direction of one that looked like it was a farm or ranch road and was a little better maintained. Something had caught his eye for a moment, but it could have been a shadow changing shape in the moonlight by the effects of his forward movement while going down the highway. Fifteen miles east, Brooks was becoming more impatient by the minute. She had to be close to the Rally, she couldn't go very far on foot and she wouldn't want to be very far from the road. Zero and Baker had told him of catching up with the other woman; she had been walking close to the highway.

"She was tryin' to walk in the direction of Holbrook so she must have been headed for one of the ranches in the direction of town," he spoke to himself as he rode scanning the road and as much to the sides of the road as he could in the glare of their headlights.

He slowed down after the last turn of the road about two thirds of the way back to the location of the Rally. He didn't want to go any further and be observed by someone at the bonfire. If he was discovered, it was sure to get back to Evan and he would be in deep trouble. He slowed down and stopped on an upgrade of the road so that he could back the bike down easily while turning, then it wouldn't be hard to make the turn to go back in the other direction. His companion did the same and they headed back to the highway.

"What now boss?" Knuckles asked him after they had stopped at the intersection with highway.

"Nothin' yet," he replied. "We'll wait and see if Baker saw somethin."

The other three riders were in sight coming toward the intersection with the highway shortly after Brooks and his companion had reached it. The three slowed and made the turn and stopped alongside them.

"You see anything?" Brooks asked while looking in the direction of the three riders where they had remained on their bikes after they shut down their engines.

Baker looked his way and spread his arms as if to say, "I don't know."

"I'm gonna head to town and wait there and see who comes this way. Maybe somebody picked her up. We can light them up with our lights when they get close enough and check them out," Brooks said in the direction of Knuckles to his right.

"Head back that way again and stop somewhere and watch the road," he said to Baker. "She's got to come out somewhere."

Baker thought he'd seen something a few miles back down the road. It could have been some rancher on a side road but he had to check which way Brooks was going first. He wanted her without Brooks around. He watched as Brooks and his companion made the turn onto the pavement before he pulled off the highway to the right to make an easier turn to head back in the direction he had just been.

He hadn't said anything to Tank and Zero so it wouldn't be mentioned to Brooks, in case they thought it was something they should tell him. He slowed down after about twenty minutes so the engine and the pipes made less sound as he was getting closer to the side road he had seen. There was a slight breeze blowing in their faces when they headed off the highway toward a wide hill with large boulders sloping up for some distance. He saw the twin ruts in the road leading off to the left.

"Damn, what a good place to hide," he said to himself as he headed into the large boulders to a space between them.

Brooks had only gone a few miles when he decided to go in the direction Baker had gone. He stopped at the edge of the highway and waited for Knuckles to come up beside him.

"Baker must'a seen something," he said to Knuckles. "He left too easy. C'mon, were goin' where they went."

Baker heard the sounds of the two bikes coming up the highway. He looked over at Zero and Tank.

"Someone's comin' this way," he said.

They looked in the direction of the highway and saw the two men on motorcycles go by.

"Must be Brooks goin' to check farther down the road," he said.

He was certain it was Brooks, but it didn't matter, there didn't seem to be anything here but the ashes of a fire. It could be days old and he had no idea who had been here. Had the slight breeze been blowing in the other direction, he may have smelled the smoke in the wind from the other side of the hill in the direction away from the highway.

Chapter Thirteen

I had just gone in search of more sticks to put in the fire when I thought I heard motors rumbling in the distance, but I couldn't make out the direction. The hills and rocks tend to deflect sounds and the breeze will sometimes carry the sound, so it's hard to tell which direction it is actually coming from. I walked out a little further from the camp closer to the road where we came over the hill to the new camp site. I kept looking back to my right toward the highway and the campsite in the rocks where I had hidden the pistol.

It was one of those sensations of hearing something and you're not really sure it's the sound you think you hear. The desert is so quiet that the silence is audible and loud to the ear. There is no white noise when you are listening for sounds in the desert when the wind is still or quiet. I heard only the slight breeze which sometimes rustled the dry sage and mesquite.

There might have been the sound of little rustling critters had I been sitting quiet, but there was no other noise. I listened more intently and I heard it again; it sounded like the low rumble of an engine. I had to be sure. We couldn't get caught out here in the middle of the desert, far from people and from help of any kind. If they were here, they meant to kill me; they had tried before and they would be more intent now that one of their own was missing. I turned around quickly and went back to the rocks where I had left Rebecca.

"Wait here and stay down," I said. "I need to check back down the road."

I took the Smith 645 out of the holster in my pack and handed it to her.

"What can I do with that?" she asked.

"If anyone besides me comes back, point it at his stomach and start pulling the trigger," I told her.

"I can't shoot anyone!" she said in a strained voice.

"These men tried to kill Anne, and they tried to kill me Goddamn it! If they're here, they mean to kill me and take you back or kill you too," I told her.

With that, I put the pistol in her right hand, guided her finger into the trigger guard and guided her left hand to grip her right hand over the grips.

"Point it down for now. I'll call out when I come back, so don't shoot me," I said.

I had no idea what to tell her to do if I didn't make it back. I didn't go all the way back to the road. I walked alongside it to the point where it started to rise, then back in the direction of the highway toward the location of our first camp. They may have seen me turn off the highway and weren't sure where I had gone and could be searching the rocks where we would have been.

I walked along the edge of the hill and got closer to the large rocks and boulders until I could see the shadows of the rocks where I had parked the bike before we moved up the road to the other side. The Moon wasn't full, but it was bright enough that I could see the rocks and shadows and the road leading back to the highway off to my left. Just as I saw the furrows of tracks which could only have been made by motorcycles, I saw a glint of light off to my right.

I looked that way but it was dark and quiet now. Just when I was about to move in that direction skirting the edge of the boulders, I heard a rustle of sound behind me. I was scared enough and I had been running the thought through my mind of meeting face to face with bikers with guns in their hands.

I was carrying on my left hip again and pulled the Colt 45 clear, pulling the hammer back as I made a complete turn to my left, then dodged slightly left and dropped to my right knee. Now I was facing in the direction I had heard the sound. For the first time I realized that my sights were visible as I lined them up with the shadow in front of me just as I completed my turn. I had the flashlight in my left hand, holding it away from me to my left, but I hadn't turned it on.

Just as my right knee touched the ground, I saw the large flash and heard the echoing crack of his pistol and the loud clap of a bullet going past me at supersonic speed. I didn't expect the flash of a gunshot before I was able to shoot, but the instant I saw it I reacted and squeezed the trigger twice. Turning and making a movement to my left onto my knee had kept me from being shot.

The moon had been at my back before I turned; now it was a little to my right. I fell backward onto my back to make myself a smaller target and dropped my flashlight. I realized that I was consciously thinking and I hadn't been shot. Looking between my knees, I could see the dark figure on the ground about twenty or twenty five feet away.

I bent my right knee to roll to my right and rose smoothly by straightening my leg to stand up without having to put my hand down. I picked up my flashlight and walked to the figure on the ground. I turned the flashlight on just long enough to see that he was shot in the chest and the stomach. I could see the large spots of blood clearly on his light colored T-shirt under his open Levi jacket.

His eyes were open and his right foot was twitching. I reached down and grabbed his right arm and pulled it across his body to turn him over to check his back. I levered the safety up on my Colt and pushed it into my holster then picked up his pistol, which I recognized as a large black Smith and Wesson revolver.

The bullets had both gone through. I walked past him, looking in the direction that would have been behind him. I could barely see his tracks leading in the direction behind the rocks in the moonlight. I dragged him into the rocks with his right arm and left the pistol by his side and started out into the open again.

I heard the small shuffle of sand being moved and I dropped down to my knees close enough to the rocks that one of them was at my left shoulder. I drew my colt out of the holster as quietly as I could and waited and listened until I heard it again. I wasn't stalking these men, but I was past the point of realizing that they would kill me if they saw me first.

Just when I was thinking that I would have to be the one to get off the first shot this time, a shadow appeared in the direction I had heard the sound. I remembered that wild animals sometimes don't seem to see you if you stand still, even if they're looking right in your direction, and so it is with the human eye. He might not see me this close to the rocks unless I moved.

Watching as he turned, I waited to see if he would come in my direction. Just as he started coming toward me, I realized that my pistol was pointing downward all this time so I brought it up and toggled the safety lever down as he was closing the distance.

The moon was at my back now and directly in his face. I could almost see his features change when he looked directly at me and he started to bring up his right arm. The decision had been made before I saw him, but even so, something was in his hand and his eyes seemed to widen even though I couldn't see his eyes in moonlight.

My pistol bucked in my hand three times, making a blinding flash with each carefully aimed shot. His upper body bent away from me with the first shot, but I had fired twice more carefully and rapidly, aiming lower each time. Just as I saw that he was on his back and not moving, I pressed my back against the rock and looked in both directions then snapped the safety up with my right thumb.

I waited only a minute or two then stood up and walked to where he had fallen. He was hit in the neck and on the lower right torso. I turned him over and I could see that the bullet that had struck his neck had severed the Carotid artery and the other had passed through his torso. I had missed with my third shot.

I lowered the hammer on my pistol, holstered it, then dragged him into the rocks and went back and picked up his pistol. It was a large automatic. I placed it on the ground near his right hand and started walking in the direction I had come. I used my flashlight to follow my tracks back to the rock and looked to my left for my casings.

I saw them easily with the flashlight and picked them up. I continued back to where I had dragged the first body into the rocks and then to where I could see the scuffs made by my boots. I looked in the direction my ejected casings would have to go and I found them too. I turned to my right and headed toward the place in the rocks where I had heard the engine noise, keeping the road to my left. I heard only the sound of my feet shuffling softly in the sand and walked as directly as I could to the opening in the rocks.

I saw the glint of the moon on chrome and the shapes of motorcycles and stopped to look in all directions. There were three motorcycles parked closely together. I walked past them past more rocks until the ground under my feet was on an incline. There was at least one more of them out there. I ran back past the bikes and angled to my left toward the road.

My chest started to burn as I tried to move quickly, then my arms started feeling heavy and I started feeling burning sensations at my wrists. As soon as I topped the hill where the road went over the crest, I slowed to a fast walk, and headed to the left toward the rocks where I had left Rebecca. The moon was to my right and slightly behind me as I continued at an angle on the down slope of the hill.

Just as I saw the dim light of the remains of the fire in the distance, the sound of pebbles being kicked sounded somewhere off to my left. I stopped and went to my right knee and brought my pistol up to point in that direction. Just about the time I was going to go flat on my belly he came into view over the crest of the hill.

He was clear in my sights and about fifty yards away and it was too late to move or go flat. It is not a shot that any one with any sense would make even though I thought I could hit him. The distance is out of the effective range of most 45's and in the moonlight, even though clear, it would be an almost impossible shot. My brother shot as a Marine pistol team member on course ranges which were from twenty five feet up to fifty yards. I remembered him telling me about shooting the fifty yard course with a reconditioned and balanced military Colt 45 Semi-auto.

One of the guys with us of course snorted and said, "You can't hit anything that far."

My brother John had replied, "Well, get out there and start running, you'll see if I can hit you or not."

I had shot a few competition courses years later, even though I didn't like to compete on a regular basis. I only went to the meets to accompany my friend Tom, who competed regularly and was a top competitor and instructor. The pistol I had in my hand was not a military Colt 45. It had a tighter slide and I had found it to be very accurate in practice over the years.

He didn't seem to have seen me yet but I didn't want to chance a shot at this distance and miss. Carefully, I set my flashlight down on the ground beside me and reached to hold the pistol in both hands. I put my left elbow on my knee and placed the butt of my pistol in my open left hand and clasped my fingers together. I continued to wait because I could see that he was still walking toward me, but looking over his left shoulder in the direction of the fire.

He was less than fifty feet away when he leaned to his left and almost turned to go in the direction of the glowing embers. He must have clearly heard the almost soundless click of the hammer being pulled back with my thumb or seen me silhouetted in the moonlight and stopped in mid stride as if to drop or turn.

It was too late; the first shot hit him and turned him to his right. I must have hit him in the side because it turned him to his right facing me as I shot again. He fell backward on his butt and his upper body fell backward away from me. I shot once more, trying to hit him in the legs or groin and I knew I couldn't shoot again because the slide had locked back.

I had fired exactly eight times. I dropped the magazine into my palm; something I would have never done in practice or in a shooting in any other situation. Taking the time to catch your magazine from an automatic pistol or catching ejected casings from a revolver is a deadly mistake, but I could see that he wasn't moving. I placed the empty magazine under my belt and pushed another up from my pocket and snapped it into the butt, locked it into place and released the slide lock.

I got up and walked slowly in his direction. He didn't move. I turned on the flashlight to look at him closely and could see that his pistol had dropped away from him to his right. He had been hit high on the right shoulder and on the inside of his right leg; the third shot had missed altogether.

He was shot through the muscle on his right shoulder and through the Femoral artery of the right leg. He had already stopped breathing when he turned his head to try to look at me where I knelt beside him. I lowered the hammer on my pistol, pulled it slightly back again into a half cock and slipped it into my holster.

The Ball ammunition had not been stopped by tissue or bone yet. All the shots had gone through each time. That meant that the bullets were not likely to be found, especially since I had moved each of the fallen bodies. I went back to look for my casings but I couldn't find any of them this time.

His pistol was another nondescript automatic, a large caliber Argentine Llama, probably ten millimeter or 45 caliber Colt clone. I picked it up carefully, let down the hammer and pushed it down into my right front pocket. I took him by the arm and dragged him in the direction away from the road a short distance to a small wash and rolled him into it. I dropped his pistol next to his right hand and walked the remaining fifty yards to where I had left Rebecca. I walked past the rocks and called out to her.

"Rebecca! It's me Miguel!" I said loudly.

She didn't reply, but I walked in carefully and found her lying low about fifteen feet from the fire that had rekindled in the breeze. She sat up when I approached and stared at me wide eyed with shock on her face. She was holding the Pistol with both hands, pointed downward, but in my direction.

"It's all right, don't shoot," I said.

I walked closer to her and reached out carefully and gently pushed the barrel away with my left hand, then gripped it to take it out her hands.

"Come on, we have to leave fast," I said.

"Where are they? Were they shooting at you?" she asked

"They may have seen me in the distance and shot in my direction, but I wasn't close enough," I said. "Come on, we have to move."

"They're going to follow us until they catch us," she said.

It was clear that she knew something had happened.

"They won't be following us," I told her quietly as I put the Smith 645 into my pack.

I got the bike to the road then walked back and picked up a mesquite bough and brushed at the tracks quickly from about twenty feet out and back to the road. I got back on the bike and motioned for her to get on behind me. I went quickly up the rise and down the other side toward the highway and kept looking to my right to see if I could see any more movement in the moonlight. I tried not to look directly at the lighted road ahead of me. Whatever vision I was to have in the moonlight off the road was going to depend on my eyes not being affected by the bright light from my headlight on the road.

The old ruts at the side of the road were visible when I stopped next to them.

"I have to stop here for a minute," I said.

I looked in the direction of the rocks and turned the headlight to see if any tracks were visible. The rutted tracks didn't show any new tracks or ruts from the motorcycles. I started moving forward again toward the highway and turned easily onto the pavement. I accelerated quickly to about eighty miles per hour hoping that she wouldn't have any trouble hanging on behind me.

It took about fifteen minutes to reach the turnoff to the Holt Ranch and then I saw the lights of the house in the distance. I pulled into the yard just as several bright lights lighted up the front and sides of the house. I had just set out the kickstand when Anne opened the front door and stepped out onto the large step. Rebecca met her halfway as she stepped off the large step onto the driveway.

They embraced and Anne said, "You're all right! I could only think the worst."

"I'm all right, I'm all right. What are we going to do?" she asked Anne.

"What do you mean? We're going home," she answered.

"They know where you live," I said as I stepped off the bike. "You have to consider leaving town for a while, at least until they've left this area. It's likely they'll want to head down the road to whatever rally they had planned on going to before they picked up Rebecca."

Mr. Holt walked up just as I made the statement. "They'll be safe here," he said.

"With all due respect, they won't be safe and if either of them is seen on the road or in town; they'll come here and you'll be in danger as well," I said.

"Why would they come here?" he asked.

"They shot at me when they found Anne at my camp and they followed me when I took Rebecca out of their camp," I answered.

"Does that mean they'll come here?" he asked in a tight voice, with his voice rising at the end of the question.

"I lost them in the hills as far as I know. I didn't see anyone following me on the highway, but I think they may continue to look for them," I answered.

"I don't think they should have to leave," he said.

"I think we should go," Anne said. "If you can take us home I'll get my car and we can leave right away."

She turned to me then and asked, "What will you do now?"

"I can follow you into town; they know where you live and may go there. I'll know if any of them are around. As soon as you leave, I'll head to Colorado," I said.

"All right," she answered. "Hal will take us to town."

I watched the three of them walk back into the house and got on my bike and turned the ignition on as I got ready to start it. They walked out of the house and Anne walked out to me carrying my jacket in her hand and wearing a Bomber type leather jacket.

"Hal will drive Rebecca to the house. I'm going with you," she said.

I looked at her face that was shadowed in the light from the house behind her, wondering if I should just distance myself now and didn't answer right away. She didn't wait for an answer, she stepped up to the bike, raised her left leg over and settled down behind me and began tying a bandana over her hair.

It seemed only about ten minutes later and it was near midnight when I saw the lights of the town ahead. This would be Joseph City. Holbrook was about ten or fifteen minutes farther. I remembered that their apartment was on the east side of town and I hoped I could reach it by taking the McLaws Road turnoff and bypassing the main part of town.

There was no traffic and little or no lights on the sides of the town away from the main streets and buildings. McLaws road became S. Whiting, then W. Romero, then Navajo St. I crossed the tracks and turned right, then made the turn on 7th Street. Anne tugged at my arm and I stopped in front of some small apartment sized houses. A blue Honda sedan was parked in front of the one Anne pointed at. I turned off the ignition switch and the lights and she got off and went to the door.

After checking to both sides and behind me, I pushed the bike into the driveway and turned in to the right in front of the blue Honda and turned to look out to the street to watch for Hal Holt's dually. He turned into the driveway and parked next the Honda and Rebecca exited the passenger side just as he turned the lights off. I heard them in one of the rooms to the right of the main room as I entered the front door then closed it. I stopped just inside the door and watched while Anne threw clothes into a large suitcase.

"Come on Rebecca, get your clothes. You don't need anything else right now. We need to go now!" Anne said in excitement.

Rebecca walked into another room and Anne turned to look at me.

"I'm afraid they will still be looking for us. What can we do?" she asked.

"The first thing to do is get you out of here fast," I said. "You may not be able to come back for a while if at all. Will anyone miss you being here or seeing you around town?"

"No, I don't think so. Mother hasn't been here and Rebecca and I both left with Mr. Holt. I doubt if anyone would take notice if we didn't come back," Anne said.

"What are you going to do now?" she asked.

"I'll follow you for a while until I can see that no one is following us. Then I'll head north and go to Colorado," I replied.

She stood in front of me and placed her left hand on my shoulder and said, "I don't know anything about you, where you're from and how you happened to be there to get me away from them. All I could think about was me and Rebecca and how in the world we were going to get away from those men."

Tears welled up in her eyes and she went on, "I didn't think about you or what may happen to you. I just wanted to find Rebecca."

"We need to go." I told her. I reached up with my right hand and patted hers on my shoulder. "We can talk later if we can stop after we get out of this area."

Rebecca came into the room with her suitcase. I already had Anne's in my right hand, so I grabbed hers with my left and headed out the door. She had found a handbag somewhere and pushed Rebecca ahead of her and went for the door. She opened the door and waited until I had gone through, turned off the lights and closed it securely. It didn't take long to throw the bags in the car, one in the trunk and one in the back seat.

"Let's go," I said. "Back out and head out of town toward Albuquerque. You can gas up at the first stop outside of town. I'm going back to the motel to get my gear; you head out and gas up.

Don't wait more than ten minutes for me. If I catch up with you and I recognize your car, I'll shift my lights to bright twice and no more."

"I'll wait for you," she said. "That's the least I can do."

"No, don't wait," I said. "I can catch up before Albuquerque. They still may not know who they're looking for, except you and Rebecca. They may pass me by anywhere on the road, but not you."

"Will Hal be all right?" she asked.

"He will be if he leaves now and goes back home. Talk to him and make sure he doesn't follow you out of town," I said.

Chapter Fourteen

I followed N.W. Central Ave. back along the tracks and continued back to the freeway and my room at the motel. It didn't take me more than two or three minutes to get my gear and tie it on the seat. I still had a couple of days left on my room and I had signed in using a false name and I hadn't listed a license plate. I had paid in cash so it was not likely I could be traced unless they had gotten a close look at the bike. I didn't go back through town, but went directly to the highway, got on the onramp and headed east.

Nothing seemed to stir as I went through. I saw car headlights to the west of me, but nothing headed my way. My license plate is not visible except from directly behind, since it is on the right side of my rear wheel. I had thought of covering it up with a piece of cardboard and tape to get through town then decided against it and it was just as well; I might forget to take it off and get arrested.

Twenty minutes later I stopped at a small station which, surprisingly, was still open. It was close to 2 A.M. when I checked the clock on the inside wall of the store and gas station. The realization came to me that I had been running on fumes for most of the night. We must have covered more than a hundred miles since we first left Holbrook and headed west out to the Holt Ranch. I patted the tank of my bike then and I was grateful that the bike was good for almost two hundred miles on the five gallon double tank. Even carrying two, it was good for almost forty miles per gallon if I stayed under 70.

I traveled over a hundred twenty miles without finding another place to get fuel. The Honda was good probably all the way to Albuquerque. Anne must be keeping a pretty steady seventy miles per hour, because she was staying ahead of me. The big Revtek was barely turning almost three thousand RPM at almost eighty miles per hour in sixth gear and I had a lot of room for much more as long as there was no traffic.

This was as fast as I wanted to go for the time being. I doubted it, but it would not be impossible for a State Police cruiser to be out, even if it was past four in the morning. It felt good to ride and feel the cold air going by, even with the events of no more than just hours ago still looming darkly behind me. The cold air didn't cut through my jacket or my chaps and I had taken the time to put on my leather kamikaze cap. It was getting close to the light of morning and I almost lost the tension of the last two days as I put more distance behind me.

I kept trying to think of things that could be traced to me everywhere we had been. I hadn't left much but the three casings of the last shooting. Those, I knew, could be found and matched to my pistol if it was ever checked. I knew then that I would have to come back and I would be taking a chance that more of them were still in the area looking for Anne and Rebecca.

The bikers may or may not go in search of the other riders, unless they were well known to them. There is a lot of desert out there and a lot of hills, rocks and plateaus, with ruts, arroyos and dry creeks everywhere. They would have to have an airplane to check all the possible camp sites we may have had or any likely hideouts their friends may have found while they were looking for us.

I had buried the first biker in a place I hoped would'nt likely be checked. There were tracks to my first camp, but they ended there. A little breeze would soon erase any other tracks and all other signs of any camp out there in the open. It could be years before the natural elements, rain or wind or a curious Indian would find the first biker and his bike.

The others that I left at the other camp among the rocks would be found, but who knows how soon and there were the casings that I hadn't found that could be matched to my Colt 45. I knew that I may have to get rid of it as soon as possible. If I had to lose it before I got back home it would have to be where it could never be found. The trouble was that I had bought it through a licensed dealer because I was honest and so, it was registered to me. If I got home with it or was able to get to Colorado I could melt it down at a friends place.

If a rancher found the three dead bikers that I hadn't the time to bury or hide, he would call the State Police, maybe. Ranchers didn't like outlaws of any kind. They might just as likely bury them and not have anyone poking around looking for trouble. If one of the local Indians found them, they might strip their bikes and whatever else they found on them and bury them; the bikers might do the same. They had no idea who may have dusted their brother bikers and if they found them, they would just as likely hide the bodies and take their bikes and forget about them.

These were not just ordinary riders out riding their bikes on a weekend or holiday. This kind of lawlessness, shooting at other people without provocation, was the behavior of outlaws, not Joe citizens out for a couple weeks of riding and a rally. I seldom read the paper, but I would have seen an article for an open bike rally if one had been publicized. These men were outlaw mean and may in fact have been headed for a confrontation with the Banditos down in Texas.

I was just about ready to switch to reserve and find a place off the road to camp, but I found another place to get fuel as I was nearing Albuquerque, and it was just about time. I went on after fueling and upped my speed to about eighty for a while.

It was full daylight now and the bike was running cool in this cold air and I was feeling good. I would go on for a while before I went any faster to make better time. I was thinking I would never catch up with them and it may be just as well as long as they kept up their speed. They could gas up and head on through to Oklahoma.

I reached Albuquerque in the early morning. It had changed a great deal in the last 45 years that I had been through there on an occasional trip. The old city is right on route 66, which comes in from the higher side of the vast prairie from the west. The new city and part of the old is in the lowest area of a large river valley and extends much farther north.

The new Interstate 25 cuts across the southern part of it almost from north to south. The city I knew was still there, but all the businesses had moved across the river to the "Heights," new developments on the south side of Sandia Mountain and west into and past the area of "Corrales" along the river. The area northwest of the old town is vast and extends well over what were just foothills. The north side of the Sandia Mountain slope is a ski resort. I could pretty well transit the old city on Route 66 and never see a Police car.

The last time I entered Albuquerque from this direction, there was a diner on the down slope of the prairie about five or ten miles from the city on the old route 66. Like a lot of businesses on the old route, it may have disappeared many years ago. I was about to give it up as thing of the past when I saw it ahead; it was on the right side of the highway and there was only one vehicle in front and two parked on the side of the building. I recognized the blue Honda as I got closer and recognized Anne walking around to the side of the car.

I slowed down and started into the lot, but I didn't go all the way to the building. I went only close enough so that Anne would be able to recognize me. She looked right at me when I passed within forty feet of her car and I continued on past and then back to the highway. I went on for a couple of miles and stopped at a wide part of the road which looked like an old rest stop.

When I saw the headlights coming up behind me, I got off the bike and saw that she was going to turn into the parking area. She parked the car and got out and walked toward me. I couldn't see Rebecca in the car, but she could be sleeping in the back seat or lying down in the front seat. Anne walked right up to me and hugged me over the shoulders and put her head against mine. I put my arms around her waist and we stayed that way for what seemed a few minutes.

"Are you going to go on?" I asked her.

"Yes, if I can. I am still scared to death. I won't feel better until we are in Oklahoma."

"All right," I replied. "If you don't mind, gas up at the next stop and see if you can buy a five gallon gas can. Don't fill it up completely, just put four gallons in it and screw the caps tight so the fumes don't get out. I'll wait for you up ahead at the first place where I can get off the street. You can follow me out of the city."

"I am not sure I know the way out from here," she said.

"You wouldn't happen to have a road map would you?" I asked.

"Yes, I got one when I bought gas outside of Holbrook."

I looked at the map she handed me and looked for Interstate 40 on the other side of the city. I found it and handed back the map and described her route to get on Highway 54 to Amarillo.

"I got gas a few miles back so I'm ok for another two hundred miles," I said. "I'll need more gas later, so if I travel ahead of you, you can see when I stop. You or I traveling separately can make it through the city without anyone paying a lot of attention at this hour of the morning. Its full daylight already and it's going to get warmer, so I'd like to be out of Albuquerque and find a place to stop and rest."

"How far is it to Amarillo?" she asked.

"It's over three hundred miles. I have to gas up at least once before we get there. I can gas up once from the can if we have a long stretch of highway," I answered. "I'll stay with you as far as Amarillo, then I have to head north on Highway 385, but right now I'm exhausted. I've been tired since before we left Holbrook. I'll figure out a way to hide the bike and your car so we can rest part of the day."

"I saw an intersection with Route 68 on the map, which looks like about ten or fifteen miles on the way to Santa Fe," she said.

"Take it even if you don't see me," I told her. "There should be a place to stop and it would be off the main highway and out of sight."

I left the parking area and headed into Albuquerque ahead of her and went past the large abandoned buildings of the old city. It looked like a ghost town, with all the buildings nailed shut or fenced off with chain link fencing. I passed a gas station before I could see that she had stopped there so I pulled off the street into a large parking lot and waited for her. I pulled out of the lot and onto the street when I saw her leave the station. It took about thirty minutes to get out of Albuquerque and on the highway heading toward Amarillo.

I found the turnoff to Route 68. It looked like a well kept two lane highway into the mountains. Luckily, there was a small motel about two miles north of the turnoff and it looked like a good place to stop. She pulled into the lot and drove past me and I caught up and stopped beside her.

"Go ahead and get a room," I said. "I'll get a room, hide the bike and come over and talk to you."

I waited at the entrance to the parking lot while she went to the motel office. She walked out and went back to her car and headed to the far end of the row of rooms. I went inside and rented a room and asked if I could park the bike in the rear of the building.

It had taken all night to reach Albuquerque. It was still early morning now and it would be the ideal time to travel. It was still warm out and it wouldn't be too hot now that I was off the desert plain of Arizona, but I was exhausted.

It was a virtual miracle that I had made it this far and just as amazing that Anne had driven for the past six hours to reach here. I took the bike around back and walked the short distance around the side of the row of motel rooms to get to the front door of my room. Anne had taken one of the rooms between the row of rooms where I was located and the highway. I continued to walk around to the front of that row of rooms and knocked on the door of the room in front of her car. Anne came to door right away and looked at me expectantly.

"Let me have your keys and I'll park your car around the back," I told her. "This place is out of the way enough so that they couldn't possibly find us, but it's just as well not to take any chances until you're in Oklahoma."

"It's all right," she said. "I will do it right now."

With that, I raised my right hand and walked to my left to go around the building to my room. I heard the car's engine just as I walked around the back to get my bag from the bike. I looked the bike over carefully for any loose bolts or leaks. It shouldn't be leaking anywhere, but it would be a good indication of anything being loose.

After a few minutes of checking I slipped the thin cover out of my large bag and covered the bike carefully and tied it down to the lower frame. I went back inside my room, dropped my bag on the floor near the bathroom and took a quick shower. My mouth tasted like five days of bad food, even though I had eaten only once yesterday. It felt good to brush out all the bad taste and drink some more water.

I had just walked out of the bathroom when I heard the knock at the door. I slipped on a pair of clean trousers quickly and slipped on a shirt, buttoning it as I walked to the door. I went to the door and opened it slightly. Anne was standing at the door wearing a light colored shirt hanging out over her jeans. Her hair was still wet and her eyes were large and darkened by her dilated pupils in the shadow of the building behind her. I stepped back and she walked past me into the room. She was standing about two feet from me looking at me, with a look of apprehension or fear in her eyes.

"You need to rest for a while. We can talk after we both get some sleep," I said.

She moved close to me and put her head on my left shoulder and held on to me lightly with her hands almost on my hips. Years ago I would have responded differently to a woman standing this close to me, but now it just made me nervous and a little apprehensive. She was leaning against me and I could feel her breasts through her shirt pressing against my chest. She smelled like fresh wet skin and her hair felt cool and wet but I could feel the warmth of her head coming though her wet hair where it touched my face.

"I'm still terrified," she said, her voice low and thick.

I put my arms around her shoulders and tried to hold her lightly, trying not to show the emotion that was going through me. She held on tighter and I could feel the heat of her body through my shirt. I was so tired that I had the anxious feeling of exhaustion and the reaction to her closeness at the same time.

"I have to sit down, before I fall," I said quietly when I started to feel faint.

I didn't push her away but I brushed past her to sit on the bed.

"Rebecca is my daughter," she said as she sat on the bed beside me.

I turned to look at her and she glanced downward.

"She doesn't know it," she said and looked at me directly. "I was still in school when I became pregnant. I finished school and went to California to go to college. I came back just before she was born. I had her in the hospital in Flagstaff and mother raised her as my sister."

I let her continue without asking any questions.

"I went back to California to continue with school and mother took care of her," she said. "I got my degree and started on graduate courses when her father moved to Los Angeles and came to see me at college. We got married but I left him after less than three months. I didn't know that it was he that had raped me at a party that I had gone to."

"How did you find out?" I asked.

"He drank a lot and he would get violent and I couldn't be around him," she answered. "He threw it in my face because he was angry that I wanted to continue to go to school. He accused me of being with other men while I was away at college."

"Does he know about Rebecca?" I asked.

"He wasn't certain, or at least didn't let on that he did," she said. "He may have suspected because other people here seemed to suspect it. Some of the men here treated me like I was trash."

"Where is he now?" I asked.

"He was killed in an auto accident in California. I came back here when they returned him for the funeral," she said. "Rebecca didn't know anything about him. She was only five years old when he died."

"Did your parents know about him?" I asked.

"They didn't know he was Rebecca's father. They suspected he may have been when I married him, but I never told them," she said. "I stayed here after he died and only returned to California three years ago to try to finish my master's degree. I returned when father died."

"Why are you telling me?" I asked. "I would never have questioned you about matters private to you."

"You took a great risk to help me and Rebecca. I wanted you to know that I'm not the so perfect innocent woman you think I am," she said.

"Why are you concerned whether I think you're perfect or not?" I asked her quietly.

"You didn't hesitate to put yourself in danger and you made me stay with you because you were concerned for my safety and now we are leaving and I will never know anything about you," she said.

"I reacted to events in the last couple of days out of survival. I don't know any other way to react to violence. I took on the responsibility for your safety the moment I found you and kept them from taking you," I said.

"Yet you keep me at a distance as if you're afraid I'll run or scream if you stand too close to me," she said quietly.

"You would have every right to if you did. Keeping you safe doesn't give me the right to expect anything from you," I said.

She stepped up on the bed with her right knee and moved around behind me and held me around the shoulders tightly, leaning her head against mine. I leaned to my left to lie down and raised my feet onto the bed. I was trying to remain facing away from her about to fall asleep, but she pulled on my right shoulder and pulled herself over me to lie down directly in front of me. I felt the softness of her as she slid over me, leaving her left leg part way over my thigh. She pressed herself against me, her head on my left shoulder and her mouth open on my neck.

I tried to lean my right shoulder back and move away from her to lie back and just hold her, just as she started unbuttoning her shirt. She shrugged her left arm out of it and pressed her bare breast against my chest, reached down and unbuttoned her jeans and pushed them down her legs with both hands. My right hand was over her left arm when she reached for it and pushed it down over her thigh.

She kicked her jeans off the bed and unsnapped my jeans and pressed them open with her left hand. She had either not put on undergarments, or they had come off with her jeans. She pressed her left hand down my hip, pushing down on my jeans, so that I would remove them. I had only taken the time to pull on my jeans with nothing on underneath when I had heard her knock on the door. I turned slightly on my back and started to push them down when she put both hands on my hips and pulled my jeans down over my thighs.

She pulled on my shoulder to draw me over her before I could kick the jeans down off my legs. Her large soft breasts were pressed against my chest as she tilted her head back, closed her eyes and moved her legs apart. She pulled on my hips and arched up against me. She moved against me and moaned softly while I was trying to catch my breath. She shuddered, then relaxed and circled her arms around my neck and pressed her face against mine. Her body shook again, and then she began sobbing softly.

I remained as I was for a moment or two, then relaxed and dropped to my left shoulder to move slightly away from her. She rolled against me and kept her hips pressed against me, with her left leg over my thigh and her arms around my neck. She continued to cry softly for several minutes, then became quiet and seemed to be falling asleep.

I reached behind her and pulled the edge of the blanket over her. I felt guilty and weak for becoming physically involved with her, even though I had not initiated it or encouraged it. I looked back at her and watched her sleep for several minutes. Her features had softened until she looked much younger than the thirty or so years I had thought her to be. After a few minutes I relaxed and quickly fell asleep.

Chapter Fifteen

I woke in the late afternoon slightly disoriented and wondering where I was until I realized I was looking at the ceiling in the motel room. It felt like something I had dreamed as the result of the long two days and the long night of fright and the tension I had been under. I was as tired as I had ever been in my life. Anything was possible under the stress and exhaustion I had experienced.

I hadn't asked her if she remembered what had happened that morning after she wandered out of my camp. It was just as well. The less she remembered and wasn't sure of, she wouldn't have to account for later. I would have been content to have taken a shower and lay down on the bed and fallen asleep and dreamed of having held her and letting the tensions flow away while she slept in her own room, but it was no dream. I could still feel the closeness of her as I listened to the softness of her breathing as she slept. She woke when I started to move away from her to get out of bed.

She pressed against me tightly and said, "Don't go yet."

She started to relax her arms and I thought she wanted to move away from me. Instead she kissed me then pressed her face against mine and pulled me over her again. She sighed as she moved against me, then she tightened her arms and shuddered, gasped and then moaned loudly as if in pain and then lay still. I stayed that way for a few moments, and then I rolled aside to move my weight onto my left side. She pulled me back and held on and moved her hips against me for several minutes and breathed loudly in long breaths.

After what seemed several minutes she stopped moving and relaxed. She kissed me until my breathing became difficult and held me tightly a little longer, and then pushed against my chest gently until I settled onto my left shoulder. She held herself against me a little longer, then moved away and swung her feet out to stand up beside the bed. She turned without haste to stand there for a moment with no apparent reluctance and showing no effort to move out of my view of her.

She picked up her clothes and making no effort to cover herself with them, turned away to go into the bathroom. I found myself watching her walking away, her hips swaying only slightly, admiring her statuesque and graceful movement. I was unable to avert my eyes, thinking that at any moment she might turn to see me staring and I would be embarrassed that she would see me watching her.

She stopped at the bathroom door to turn slightly just before I was able to look away. Her face softened to a faint smile before she walked in, as if to say that it was all right and pushed the door part way closed. I heard the shower running for a few minutes then she came out into the room fully dressed in her shirt and jeans. She sat on the bed and looked at me with a slight smile and softness in her eyes and reached to touch my hand.

She held my gaze until she stood up and walked around the bed toward the door and asked, "Can you come to my room in a few minutes?"

"Yes, I'll be there soon," I said.

I got up after the door closed and got into the shower. I allowed the hot water to run over my face and head for several minutes. It was time I went to their room and found out how they felt and see if they were ready to continue on. I went by the Motel office first and purchased a long distance calling card good for three hundred minutes. I wanted her to be able to call me and let me know how they were doing.

The calling card would identify me as the caller, calling my cell phone. It wouldn't identify her as the caller. I didn't know that she would call if I asked her to, but this was the best way to let her know that she could. She opened the door almost before I had moved my hand away after knocking on it.

"Come in please." she said. "I took the time to find some fast food a little way up the road. It will save some time not having to stop somewhere along the way."

Rebecca met me part way into the room and hugged me and put her head on my shoulder.

She stepped away then and looked at me and said, "I'm so glad you're all right."

I was looking at her with some surprise realizing that she was as tall as Anne and was looking at me at the same eye level.

"I have no idea what you had to do to find me and get us both out of trouble," she said, then stepped away. "I'm so glad you're all right. I feel so badly that we aren't going to get a chance to know you better. Anne said you have to leave us and go on north after we reach Amarillo."

"I'm afraid it's sooner than that," I replied. "I need to finish my trip north, make a couple of stops in Colorado before I head back to Seattle, then head back home. The trip is going to be a little longer than I had originally planned, so I may as well get on my way."

I looked at Anne while I was talking. She looked downward and didn't lift her gaze until I had looked away. I couldn't tell if it meant that she was sorry that I was going my own way sooner, or that she regretted going to my room. I realized with the thought that the feeling was only my own selfish thought of inferiority and that it shouldn't matter.

Whatever happened between us was over before it could ever start. They were leaving and I was headed back to my cabin and they could both put the nightmare behind them. Rebecca hugged me tightly after I loaded the suitcases, then looked away and got into the car.

Anne watched me for a moment then said, "I'm never going to see you again am I?"

My chest got tight and I couldn't answer her question right away.

"You'll be safe when you get where you're going and then you can work on putting this all in the past," I said.

She stepped closer to me and put her arms over my shoulders and pressed herself against me then relaxed and held my shoulders at arms length.

"Will I be able to find you or call you?" she asked.

I handed her the phone card from my pocket and said, "Call me anytime of day or night, but don't feel that you are obligated to call."

"I don't need a card to call you," she said with a hurt sound to her voice.

"You do. I don't want you to be connected to me by phone calls or mail until this is well in the past," I said. "Any calls you make will be on this card as if I am calling my own phone. I wrote my landline and my mobile phone number on the back of the card."

"Where are you going now?" she asked.

"I need to make some stops and see friends that know I'm on the road and will be wondering where I am," I said. "Then I'll head back to my cabin and take care of some things there. What about you and Rebecca?"

"I'll go back to school and finish my degree and try to get my life together," she said. "I'm never going back to Holbrook. Even if mother was there I would not stay. I don't think I can live with her either so I'll find a place as soon as I'm working. Rebecca will stay with me and go to school too. Father left us some money that I will use for school."

She pulled me close and held on to me tightly for a couple of minutes and shuddered slightly and I felt tears on my neck when she pressed her face against mine.

She let go, looked at me directly with her face inches away from mine and said, "I don't know what to say to you and if I did I don't know if I would say anything. I'll just hope that somewhere, sometime, I may see you again."

"Just stay away from here," I said. "I'll be thankful with knowing that you're all right. That's the best we can do for now."

She turned away and started walking to the car. I didn't say anything more as I watched her walk away from me, already feeling like yet another part of my life was closing behind me. I still hadn't seen her smile more than just slightly and she seemed to be fighting back tears as she opened the door and got into the driver's side of the car.

I stood in front of their room watching until the car was out of sight going south to the highway. It took me only minutes to pack my bag and walk around behind the room to tie it on the bike. I left the parking lot slowly and headed towards the main highway. When I reached it I turned right onto the highway to head back to Holbrook.

It didn't take too long for me to get back. I traveled the three hundred miles in about five hours of road time; I reached Holbrook about midmorning on Sunday. That was the average, traveling much more than the speed limit at times, but I had made a couple of stops. The road time included a stop at a small motel about halfway back, to get some rest before midnight. I didn't think I could find the turnoff from the highway to the Holt ranch at night and in any case, it would'nt have been a good idea to arrive there in the dark. The best time to arrive was in the morning when Mr. Holt was more likely to be there and could see clearly who it was that was coming into the yard.

I knew as I continued past Holbrook, that by staying on the main highway, I was taking a chance being seen by the bikers that may still be somewhere in the area where they had held their rally. Mr. Holt had been placed in danger by the events of the week and the least I could was to check on him in case there was any chance that the bikers would somehow trace Anne and Rebecca to his ranch.

They didn't seem to have a lot of trouble finding us and it didn't take very long for them to arrive after I took Rebecca from their camp. There was the possibility it could have been just chance that they happened on the camp, just because it was a likely place for me to stop and try to stay out of sight.

I saw what I hoped was the right road ahead and I made the turn easily and increased my speed to make better time. It didn't take long to get to the ranch. I was running over in my mind a way to find out if Mr. Holt had any knowledge of the events of the last couple of days, beyond what I had already made known to him. He walked out the front door just as I was turning into the yard. He watched as I balanced the bike onto the kickstand and got off to walk to the house.

"Good morning," I said as I walked closer.

He replied, not impolitely, but he didn't offer his hand when I got close.

"I wanted to assure you personally that Anne and Rebecca are safe," I said. "They should have arrived safely at their aunt's home in Oklahoma by now. I followed them as far as Albuquerque and I saw that they left before I started on my way back."

"Let's go in the house," he said.

I followed him inside to the living room. The house had the look of having been remodeled. It had modern hardwood cabinets and newer appliances in the kitchen area and a beautiful old hardwood table and chairs in the dining area.

"Would you like anything to drink?" he asked.

"A glass of water would be fine," I said, even though I was dying for a beer.

I looked around the wall near the entrance to the kitchen when he walked away. There were some family pictures on the mantle above the fireplace and two others above the mantle on the wall of an older Navy Destroyer. The numbers on the side weren't very clear. It looked a lot like the ship I had been on from 1964 to 1968, but a little older, clearly a Stoddard class. Next to it were pictures of a man in Dress Blues and a White Hat.

"I was in the Tonkin Gulf in 65," he said. "I got out of the Navy in 66 after one tour. You have the look of an ex-cop or a boxer. Ever do any service?"

"Tonkin Gulf, three tours," I said. "Served on a can and went through the Taiwan Straits in the worst weather I ever thought existed. I got out in 1968 and was a cop for twenty three years."

"You have the look," he said. "I could tell by the way you looked at me, polite, but sizing me up."

"Yeah, I know," I said. "I thought I had lost most of my attitude after retiring fifteen years ago."

"I bought the ranch from my friend Bill Stahl," he said. "I think he struggled with it for years. It was originally five sections and leased land as well. He sold some of it off to make ends meet over the years. I bought the last two sections from him when he got sick."

"So, you're from this area yourself then?" I asked.

"Yes, I ranched here on the family's place for years then I retired a few years ago. My place is five sections, plus leased BLM land. I leased it out and released the BLM leases when we left. My wife wanted to live back east where she was from originally. We didn't spend much time together anymore, so I bought Bill's place just to get back here. Mine is still leased. I still have friends here and my ranch went a long ways back through my family," he said.

"So why are you back?" he asked.

"I wanted to see that you were all right," I said.

"Why would I be otherwise?" he asked.

The look he gave me was one that seemed to tell me that he already knew, but he was waiting for me to tell him more if I was inclined to. If he knew more than I was willing to tell him, he gave no indication.

"We had a bit of a scuffle out there where I found Anne and later when I found Rebecca. We were followed, so I had to get off the highway and into the rocks to hide out. They found us anyway," I said.

I hoped the answer was going to be enough.

"I saw some light out there and I heard some gunfire. They must have been getting a little wild," he said. "I went over past Jack Rabbit Road yesterday then out to the hills the other side of Joseph City to check it out and see what kind of a mess they made with their camp."

"What did you find?" I asked apprehensively, knowing that he would have easily found the three bodies and the motorcycles there.

"A lot of motorcycle tracks at one location and the signs of a fresh camp farther in on the other side of the hill," he said.

"I was a little curious myself," I said. "I had an idea to check there on the way through."

"Where are you headed to?" he asked.

"Back toward Seattle," I said. "I left my rig and trailer there before I came this way."

Although in truth, I had planned to go to Colorado first. I wanted to go back to the camp now, especially since he may have been there already. My curiosity was growing since he wasn't volunteering any information that he had found anything of interest there.

"Are you going there now?" he asked.

"Yes," I replied. "I'm curious about what I might find there. Rebecca told me that she found out that the purpose of the gathering there was sort of a rally to get more support for a confrontation in Texas, if there wasn't any agreement. I suspect that there is some kind of rally going on down there by some of the local clubs. That's Bandido country down there. They're a Mexican outlaw gang that's into drugs, general crime and maybe even slave traffic. They may have been heading there in force to show a united front or it may be a planned confrontation."

"Any idea where these bikers are from?" he asked

"Rebecca didn't know where any of them were from. She saw license plates from several states, but no one said anything around her about where they came from. It would seem likely that there were several clubs represented from several states," I answered.

I knew the biker's bodies would be easily found if anyone had found the bikes. It would be difficult to conceal a large number of bikes and other vehicles on the highway if they were already there and in the process of moving the bikes. Anyone else going by on the highway would have seen them. He had been polite but not friendly thus far. It was time to make my exit and leave it at that. He didn't say anything more so I turned and walked out the door. I didn't look back when I left the driveway and headed out to the main road leading to the highway.

It took about twenty minutes to reach the highway and another ten minutes to reach the road leading to my camp. I made the turn and found the double rutted road leading to the rocks. There were other tracks there now. The faint marks on the hard packed ruts had surely been made by motorcycles and there were tracks made by other vehicles as well all around the rocks and to the sides of the road. I had just parked and was heading to the hideout where I had left the pistol when I heard the sound of a vehicle from the direction of the road.

I continued to the location and found it easily. It didn't seem disturbed, but I moved the rocks out of the way until I could see the plastic wrap where the gun was hidden. I covered it back up and walked back to the clearing. I saw Holt turn onto the ruts of the old road just as I reached my bike.

"I saw all the tracks here when I checked," he said. "Then I went over the hill and checked over there too. I didn't find anything of interest."

I didn't know how to take his statement, but since there didn't seem to be anything here to see I thought I may as well check around the rocks and see if anything was there that would indicate a shooting had taken place.

"I'm going over there in a minute," I said. "I wanted to take a walk around these rocks and see if I could find anything here."

He followed me at a distance as I went around the rocks to my right on the side leading back to the road. I looked for any scuff marks I may have left when I kneeled and fired at the first biker. I walked around farther to the right then back to the rocks to see where I had leaned against the rocks to shoot the second time. I found tracks leading into the rocks, but nothing else to show that someone had been dragged there. I saw what looked like dried caked blood in a couple of places, but no large pools of it anywhere.

I was certain I had found all my casings that would have been here that night, but I had a nagging thought that I should be sure there was no more to be found and no other sign of the fight. I walked back to the bike and Holt was already at the side of his truck.

"Leave your motorcycle here," he said. "I'll show you where the other location is. It's just over that hill."

He pulled off the road and headed to the rocks where I had taken Rebecca. He stopped the truck about fifty feet from the rocks and got out to walk around the truck. I walked around the back of the truck and headed at an angle up the hill where I thought I had been when I saw the third biker and shot him. I saw something shining in the sun as I walked upward along the ridge. It was one of my casings. I looked around and I found the other two then I walked over to the small wash where I had left the third body.

Holt was walking up behind me when I reached it. I had a moment of apprehension that the third body would still be there and then a second thought that he would have found it if it had still been there when he was here before. I found a small indication that could have been a mark made by dragging a body out of the ditch but not much else. I started to turn when I saw something shiny to the right of where the body would have been. I looked back to see where Holt was, but he was close enough to see what I had.

There wasn't any purpose in trying to hide it, so I walked over to it and reached down to pick it up. It was a survival type knife, new with a large blade and cut out serrations on the top of the blade close to the haft and a stag handle. I picked it up carefully by the edges of the haft, which were the smallest surfaces and the least likely to show fingerprints, my own or the owners. He saw it when I held it up to look at it more closely.

"I guess I missed that," he said, looking at me intently. By his manner and the way he said it, I guessed that he may have found other small items when he walked over this area.

"You don't mind do you?" he asked, holding his hand out.

"No, I wouldn't have any reason for keeping something like this," I said.

I handed him the knife carefully and he took it by the handle and wiped it completely with his bandanna.

"I guess there's nothing more here to see," I said as I started past him back to the truck.

He took me back to my bike and walked with me back to where I had left it.

"You can come back out to the ranch if you like," he said.

"Thanks, but I need to make up some time. I need to be in Seattle in the next day or so," I said.

It was a friendly gesture, but I was feeling a nagging thought back in my mind that it was time to head down the road.

"There isn't anything more to find here," he said.

"No, I guess I didn't really expect to find anything," I said. "I just wanted to be sure. I camped off the road a little way from here in the direction of Holbrook when I first got here. That's where I found Anne near the road."

"I checked there too," he said. "I had intended to check most of these roads to see what kind of mess any of their camps had made. There were tracks leading from the highway for a short way. I checked over the hill in some of the larger washes there too. If there was something there to find, it isn't there now."

"I'll never know whether or not the bikers knew they had been looking for someone on a bike when they were looking for Anne and Rebecca," I said.

"Is that important?" he asked.

"There must have been a lot of motorcycles around here. Why would that make a difference?" he asked.

"They all know each other and would recognize an outsider wherever they saw him. If they had seen me once, all of them would know who they were looking for. I didn't want to take that chance," I said.

Again he had given me the suggestion that he had either found the bodies or he had checked thoroughly and not found anything. If Holt had found any of the bodies here or at my first camp, he wasn't going to make it any clearer for me. If he had been able to find my camp and checked farther away as well and found the first body, then he would have been able to find the bike I buried in the arroyo too. I was getting more apprehensive the longer I was here. I had the last of my casings and I hadn't lost anything out of my pockets that would be identified as belonging to me.

As far as I knew, no one other than Holt had seen me with Anne and Rebecca. We had arrived at Mrs. Stahl's house in town well after dark and left right away. There wouldn't have been enough light to identify me or my bike even if it had been seen, except by any of the bikers. The Sheriff's officer in town had seen me but he didn't know anything about me and the woman at the clothing shop would only remember me as a tourist who bought some items of clothing. He held out his right hand and grasped mine firmly and smiled faintly.

"Thanks for looking out for Anne and Rebecca," he said.

"I'm sorry I can't take you up on your offer. It looks like there's nothing here for the authorities to get interested in, other than a herd of bikers heading south, so it's time for me to go," I said.

I watched his truck until I could see that he was heading east toward his road to the ranch. After a few minutes I checked my bags and headed to the highway. I was pushing my luck, but I had to be certain. He was a friend of the family and there wouldn't be any reason he would want Anne and Rebecca connected in any way to four bodies, but it wouldn't feel like it would have a chance to be put to rest until I knew.

I found the site of my first camp easily, but I took my time making the turn completely off the highway. I stopped short of the cattle guard for a few minutes and looked toward the large mound where I had camped before I continued on up the road. I went past the large mound and continued up the hill following the large wash and stopped on the other side and settled the bike on the kickstand.

After looking in both directions, I walked to the arroyo where I had entered the stream bed. I walked to the farther wall to check where I had collapsed it and buried the first motorcycle. There were tracks on the arroyo floor and most of the wall that had collapsed was still there. It didn't look like it had been disturbed but it wasn't deep enough to cover the bike that had been there. I went back to the ditch where I had covered up the first biker.

The tracks were faint leading to the ditch where I hadn't brushed all of them out. I could clearly see the scuffs in the side of the ditch, but the sand was down level with the bottom of the ditch. Someone had removed the body and done a thorough job of moving the sand around and brushing the bottom of the ditch. I would have felt better if there had been a body there.

Now I would never know who had moved it. The bikers would have moved it and buried it somewhere else or taken it with them and then put as much distance between themselves and here as soon as possible. They would have taken all of the bikes too. Many of the motorcycles that outlaws ride are made up from stolen parts or so called after market motors and transmissions. Most of them always have the money to buy the best and they do most of the time, but later they add stolen motors and accessories as theirs get older and wear out. Most of the parts from the four bikes would very likely be spread out as far as possible and the motors would be replaced.

I gave up on the original plan to go to Denver. I still had both my pistols. I could ship both of them out from Seattle by any one of the shipping companies and be through Canada in about four or five days. I could be in Winslow in less than a half hour if I kicked it into gear, gassed up and be past Flagstaff in a little over an hour.

Heading west would put me at the intersection of Route 66 and U.S. 93 which would put me in Reno in about 4 hours. I intended to continue to travel north through Eugene, Oregon, Portland and Bellingham. The guns would have to be shipped from Tacoma or Seattle.

Chapter Sixteen

It continues to be pretty cold most nights even in late May in Alaska but working in the woods during this time of the year is not too bad. I found myself thinking about the warmer days coming up and being able to get the bike on the road again. I had missed riding all the way out to Colorado and the research I had planned on doing while I was in California, Nevada and Arizona.

Unfortunately, research has to come from traveling, seeing and photographing the area, the monuments, parks and all the little towns. Pictures would have been useful to recall what I had seen as well as to give me an order of writing down the information.

I was already planning a return trip, but I was going to wait until the roads were clear. The roads from Anchorage to Tok and from Beaver Creek in Canada all the way to Haines Junction are on and off icy. There would have been no way to travel by motorcycle through most of northern Canada at the time of the year that I had headed out on the last trip earlier this month. The bike could be taken by trailer all the way to Montana.

The large cabin where I live is on a forty acre subsection of the original homestead of 160 acres. So anyone driving to my place has to transit sixty acres and about a mile and a half of gravel road. Not even the clerks at the post office know where I live. My thoughts as I was cutting some downed spruce into stove length logs were of my trip earlier in the month.

I hadn't thought about it much in the last week for good reason. It took a lot out of me just to get out of Arizona without getting shot or arrested. I knew I was still not in the clear. For anything that happens and more than any one person knows about it, there will be at least several more that will get the information. With that, it doesn't take long before more have heard it and are passing the information around freely.

Anne Stahl seemed to have been in shock and was'nt aware of what had happened before I found her near my camp, except that she had fallen off her horse and had to hide to escape the men following her. She must have realized that it had been a real possibility that she could be killed and her killers never found or prosecuted.

More than that, the fear leading up to her near capture by the bikers had to be much more than she ever imagined could happen to her. Everyone watches movies and all the elaborate escapes, wild chases and near death experiences, but the truth of life is; it never happens that way. Most movies have to end with heroes and bad guys; otherwise no one would go to movies.

I'm sure she had seen violence of some degree while in California, but nothing like her own real experience. I knew it was'nt over, but at my age with so little ahead except riding and keeping my place in the woods going by cutting wood every late fall and early spring, worrying about it for the short remainder of my years wasn't going to change anything.

It's not easy to move through the woods anywhere and harder to move within less than two hundred feet of earshot without being heard by someone. Moose can be heard moving through the woods sometimes more than a quarter mile away and more than a half mile away at night. I have always felt relatively safe out here because any vehicle coming out has to use my road to get there and can be heard almost a half mile away. I can hear the vehicles on the highway more than a mile away, especially trucks and I can hear when motorcycles go down the highway.

Safety is relative to the way you live your life. You can trust to luck or you can take precautions in everything you do. Today, I hadn't heard moose moving and I had heard few birds moving in the trees, but that could be because of the time of the month. I am always startled by new sound because of where I live and what I have become accustomed to hearing.

As an active Police Officer, I had sometimes worried about having to take extra precautions to guard against someone stalking me out of retaliation. I probably should have been more aware all of the time but I never had anyone stalk me. My whole view of safety changed since the incident at Holbrook. I had taken to carrying a pistol all of the time while outdoors and especially in the woods and all sound and movement around me had become suspect.

I didn't know how many of them were involved in stalking Anne in the desert. Two left with Rebecca and three went after Anne. There were at least eight of them at my camp when they tried to take her by force from me, but only three that I knew of when they found us at the last camp near Joseph City.

If they had seen my bike and the license plate, they could trace it to me and find me by the description of the residence location on my registration application. Unfortunately, all that information is available to the public. They would have great difficulty finding Anne and Rebecca outside of Holbrook, unless they talked to someone in Holbrook who knew of their aunt in Oklahoma and would be willing to tell them.

That too, was a serious possibility. Any number of ruses could be used to contact someone in Holbrook and get that information. However, I hoped that no one knew of the Aunt. Since Anne's mother had become a heavy drinker, she may have

gradually lost contact with friends and associates in Holbrook otherwise she may have had friends that would have helped her with her illness and given her a reason to stay.

The guilt and fear of discovery had been with me since I returned. I didn't expect to be found here by friends of the four men I had left in the desert, but it was always in my thoughts, like a nagging daydream about another encounter with any of them. I found them in my dreams as well, but they weren't always bikers. I would see their faces as I remembered them when I saw them lying on the ground and they were alive again and stalking me or confronting me with guns in their hands.

There was still a lot of work I had to finish in the woods in the next few days. I didn't remember much of the evening before and I wasn't sure I had done much in the cabin before returning to the stack of cut logs in front of me the next morning. I heard a twig snap behind me, making me quickly alert and I turned my head to look suddenly. I had reacted too late.

There were three men standing there with guns in their hands. I had been carrying my 44 Magnum Smith/Wesson into the woods as a matter practice but I hadn't drawn it yet. I turned, expecting to see a moose in the distance somewhere behind me, not three guns at close range.

I had nothing to lose at this point. I dodged to my left, bending my right knee to balance my move and started to draw the large six inch barreled pistol from the holster under my left shoulder. I have always had difficulty drawing it quickly because of the size of the pistol and the tightness of the holster.

My body had gone into high speed as it had done at times in the past when faced with a physical confrontation and now I had the pistol in my hand but I can't understand why they haven't shot at me. In panic I pulled on the trigger and I watched the hammer draw back and drop at the end of the trigger pull.

I felt it snap down and heard it click as it dropped to strike the primer, but it didn't fire. I pulled again and again and I could see the cylinder turning but the bullets weren't firing. I panicked and the gun still didn't fire. They extended their arms and pointed the pistols at me and I couldn't breath because I knew they were about to shoot.

I heard a phone ringing behind me and I was afraid to look because I was about to get shot. Suddenly I became aware that I was looking at the ceiling in my bedroom. I have learned that there is a delay of time between the beginning of a sound and the time it takes the mind to register it during sleep. Then there is another delay before there is conscious thought and recognition of the sound for what it is.

My cell phone was ringing upstairs. It will usually ring three to four times before it will switch to my voice mail. I couldn't tell how many times it had rung

already but I swung my feet out of bed and grabbed my robe to head upstairs. A feeling came to me that I knew who it was even before I picked up the phone to try to answer the call before it switched to voice mail.

"Hello, this is Anne."

Her voice on the phone was calm and it sounded like it was coming to me from a long distance with the echo of a stone cave even though her voice was as clear as a bell. I realized that I was fully awake when I recognized the voice.

"Hello?" she said again.

"Yes, this is Miguel," I answered. "Is everything all right?"

"Yes, I'm all right, so is Rebecca.

"Where are you calling from?" I asked.

"I'm in Holbrook at the ranch," she said calmly.

I had a feeling by the tone of her voice and the hesitation that she wouldn't have told me unless I had asked, but I remembered that I didn't believe she was capable of lying.

"You are there only because you have a compelling reason," I said, more as a question than a statement.

"Mr. Holt called me. He seemed a little concerned about us. He would not tell me at first until I pressed him. He said a small group of men on motorcycles was seen in Holbrook," she said.

"That in itself shouldn't be unusual. The sight of men on motorcycles is becoming more common," I added, but even as I said it, I had a growing apprehension about it.

"He did not believe that they were just passing through," she said.

"Did he think they were camping in the area?" I asked.

"He did not say he was certain," she answered. "He learned from conversations with some of his friends that they had come in from the direction of Albuquerque and may have gone in the direction of Winslow. I was afraid for Mr. Holt's safety and terrified to have to be back, but I would recognize the men who were with the others who were after me."

I didn't think that questioning her wisdom in returning and placing herself in danger again would serve any purpose. Placing blame in addition to admonishing her for returning wasn't going to make anything better either. She was afraid for Holt's safety, and I didn't voice my confidence that he and his friends were probably more than capable of taking care of themselves because it would sound like I was trying to distance myself.

It didn't take me more than a few minutes to load the motorcycle on the truck and decide when to leave after I talked to her. I remembered the difference in her voice from the time we had been running and hiding in the hills, trying to stay out of sight, and the way she spoke now.

She was concerned about Mr. Holt. I didn't know what she thought she could do by going back and getting back in the middle of danger, but I knew that I would never live long enough to forgive myself if anything happened to her or Holt. I had no idea what I could do except continue to be involved in events that I had no control over. But it wasn't a matter of having it happen close enough for me to see and making a choice whether or not to get involved. I had become involved as soon as I dragged Anne Stahl out of the arroyo and now the problem was mine as well.

It may have been more enjoyable at another time under better circumstances, but the drive through Canada was uneventful. I crossed the border into Montana without any difficulties and drove on to Billings and found a parking facility to leave the truck. I hadn't been willing to take a chance and have my pistols confiscated at the point of entry into Canada, so I shipped them to a friend who lived south of Colorado Springs.

I unloaded the bike after a few hours of sleep in the truck and headed out for Denver. With any luck I could be there before morning, depending on how many miles I could cover before stopping for rest and some sleep when I needed to. By pushing hard past Denver before stopping at Castle Rock on I25 going south I could make it to Holbrook early Tuesday morning. I could ride four to five hours in a stretch with some rest in between and an overnight before reaching Holbrook.

The five gallon tank would allow me a range of almost two hundred miles, but I wouldn't push farther than 160 miles to allow some margin to find a gas station. My timing would put me outside Holbrook before sunrise and hopefully, some things, like the sidewalks rolling up at night, are still common in small towns. There wasn't any traffic when I headed through town and reached the west end where the small motel where I had stayed before was located.

The same sleepy eyed Arab woman came to the counter to check me in. She didn't give me any indication that she had ever seen me before and I had just a passing thought of worry that she had seen more than one biker come through and some may have even stayed there recently. I pushed the thought aside and filled out the registration card, paid cash for five days and neglected to list a license number. I used a false name as before to avoid any problems later if someone started looking for a name they could trace.

I left my larger bag in the room and took the smaller one with my Smith 645 and three extra fully loaded magazines. I chose to put the Colt on my belt and pocketed the two extra magazines I had for it. If the worst happened, I could get rid of the Colt if I got into trouble again, or ship it out before I left, provided I recovered all my brass.

I had never been able to find replacement barrels for the Smith, but I had already replaced the barrel and the ejector on the Colt while I was at home, which took care of it being matched to any bullets if they were found. I hadn't expected to use it ever again.

All the loads were Ball, full metal jacket 230 grain standard loads that I had for over 20 years. I qualified with the supplied ammo reloads from the Police department but I kept a good stock of Ball ammo and the department approved silvertips and Black Talons while I was still active. I had carried extra magazines fully loaded with the approved ammo over the years, but I had never fired more than a few rounds of it.

I would have preferred to use the Talons if I got into any kind of trouble because of their obvious stopping power, but I felt more confident using more common 230 grain jacketed rounds that I knew from experience would be more likely to pass through. I was less concerned about the so called lesser stopping power of the Ball ammo over the lighter hollow point Silvertip and Talon, than having ammo that may be found and traced.

I had read first hand reports by officers who investigated shootings where attackers had been shot several times with small caliber bullets that didn't stop them. One particular incident involved a man who had shot his attacker with 9 MM hollow points. The attacker had his weapon out first and made threats with it, but he didn't shoot until he had been shot six times by his would be victim with the 9MM hollow points. He finally returned fire with two shots of 230 grain 45 Caliber Ball ammo from an old Colt 45. He missed with one shot. The other struck his victim in the stomach, went completely through and struck a bystander who was behind him, killing them both.

I continued to carry a pistol on and off over the years after I retired, not because I intended to shoot anyone, but because I had never reconciled myself to not carrying a pistol. It's still legal to carry one in most of the United States and legal in Alaska, except in bars and public buildings, but illegal in Canada. In states that have laws allowing concealed weapons, the catch is, the person has to be a resident of that state. Some states have reciprocal carry laws, allowing persons from concealed carry states, to carry them in that state as well.

For those of us traveling back into our country through Canada from Alaska it's always been a problem carrying firearms. It has never been allowed, but it has been done anyway with some risk of having them confiscated. U.S. efforts to fight terrorism and illegal weapons entering from Mexico have only been successful when they are transported in vehicles. I wasn't searched the few times I crossed the border into or out of Mexico and I didn't see any of the card holding aliens being searched either but it was not anything I would ever have tried.

Twenty minutes past Holbrook, I started looking for the turnoff to the Holt ranch. I slowed down gradually to keep the exhaust noise at a lower level and shifted down until I was in second gear. I made the turn easily then accelerated gradually and kept the speed under fifty. I reached over with my left hand and turned the ignition switch to the left and the headlights went off. One of my priorities when I left here was to fix the ignition so that the lights were off on the first position of the switch and the bike would continue to run.

It was still early morning and it would be sunrise in another twenty minutes, but I could see pretty well in the dusky light. I was counting on habitual behavior being difficult to change and that any bikers that were in the area hadn't set up any observation on a continuous basis, but I wasn't taking any chances. Coming in with the lights out would give me time to get close to the ranch house without being seen.

Chapter Seventeen

It caught me completely by surprise. Three motorcycles were in the yard, still moving forward toward the house when I topped the rise in the road just past the fence posts that were on both sides of the cattle guard. They must have been traveling side by side slowly after they made the turn from the main road to the road leading through the old gate to the main yard of the ranch.

The sound of their pipes hadn't allowed them to hear me coming up behind them. That had to be why I didn't hear them either and I knew why I hadn't seen their lights. They were traveling with their lights off just as I had. They had slowed down, but hadn't used their brakes to stop yet.

I had closed the distance to them quickly after I had made the turn and found myself almost a hundred feet behind them. Their surprise was more complete than mine. Instead of turning in different directions to spread out, they froze and tried to look around behind them.

They had counted on arriving and catching anyone at the ranch by complete surprise. They hadn't expected someone to approach them from behind and had not heard my engine over the noise of their own engines. I reacted immediately in the only way I could. I hit the brakes to slow down to what I hoped would be about thirty miles per hour, then released the front brake, locked the rear brake and turned slightly to the left to go into a controlled slide on my left side.

I had done it on a 1961 Triumph on the beach in Formosa when I was stationed there and later, on the Torrey Pines beach in California when I was deployed back to the U.S. many years ago. I had done it on my 1976, 900cc Kawasaki when I caught a patch of sand on pavement at forty miles per hour on my way home from work in Colorado. That time I had almost torn off my left boot, half my pant leg and I had scuffed my duty belt. I had never done it on a big bike.

I felt the left foot peg dig into the soft packed dirt at the edge of the ruts in the driveway as I lifted my left leg to get it clear so it wouldn't be trapped under the tank as I went down. I had no choice; it was either this or roll the bike right up to them, which would have put me too close, or worse, be stupid and slow down and try to make a turn to go the other way.

The bike was still sliding when I put my right foot on the seat and pushed off. I slid on my left hip and left leg, keeping my left arm up so I wouldn't injure my elbow. I felt myself stop sliding with my feet pointed toward them and my bike, which was down on its left side. I was almost on my back and had stopped with my back touching the ground when I reached across to my left to pull my Colt out of the holster. It cleared the holster easily and I pulled the hammer back with my thumb as I raised my shoulders slightly and moved my bended knees apart to aim between them.

Not more than a few seconds had passed and they hadn't moved other then to put their feet on the ground with the engines running. They were no more than thirty five or forty feet in front of me, slightly to the right of the line of fire between me and the house. It looked like they hadn't been able to decide whether to make a turn in different directions, stop to see who was behind them, or just drop their bikes and scramble for cover.

The man on the right fell over, motorcycle and all, with his right leg trapped under the bike just as I shifted my aim in his direction. He had just positioned himself on his belly, trying to prop himself on his left elbow. The one on the left had his left foot on the ground and decided to raise his right leg over the tank, turning so his left foot pivoted and he started to make a full turn to the left. He had both feet on the ground and pivoted so that his left shoulder turned and his upper body was facing me as he was reaching to his right hip.

I shifted my aim to the left and fired three times, rapidly but not in quick taps. He was clearly hit and seemed to jerk twice when he was struck, knocking him almost backwards away from me just as the bike hit him in the legs. I shifted quickly to the right to fire at the middle one who had gotten off his bike and let it fall and was now facing me and in my sights. The engine was still running as the bike fell to the right, grazing his right leg when the rear tire momentarily grabbed, jerking the motorcycle forward slightly before the engine stopped.

He jerked back when I fired twice and I was about to fire again just as I saw a big flash from the direction of the house and heard the loud clap of a large caliber rifle. He bent forward suddenly from the waist as if to bow. The rider on the right was still trapped with his right leg under his motorcycle. He appeared to have a pistol in his right hand and was trying to get me in his sights.

I saw a bright flash in front of him just as I fired two close shots and he was jerked backwards hard enough that he jerked forward against the pressure of his leg trapped under the motorcycle. I realized that I had been breathing in gasps in what had seemed like minutes during the time I had been shooting. Only seconds had gone by and I felt myself breathe a couple of times like I was out of breath.

I hadn't remembered to count my shots but I knew it was time to reload. I was conscious that the slide was still forward on my Colt, so I hadn't fired more than seven times. I felt the bulge of the extra magazine in my left front pocket and reached down to push it up far enough to grab it by the bottom plate just as my thumb pressed the ejection button and the spent magazine dropped out.

"Who's out there?" a man's voice yelled.

"It's me Miguel!" I yelled back, just as I jammed the magazine into the butt and slammed it upward.

A spotlight and lights from the front of the house lighted up the yard out to where I was and I realized that it was not yet morning light. It was light enough that I had seen the three bikers clearly, but dark enough so the lights from the house made everything starkly visible and cast shadows from the bikes between me and the house.

I heard the man's voice yell out again, "Wait, don't go out there!!"

I saw someone come out the front door almost at a dead run. I pointed the Colt straight up and levered the safety up when I saw a shadowed face and a woman's hair billowing above it and to the sides. I recognized her as Anne when she haltingly slowed to a fast walk about ten feet from me. I propped myself up on my elbows. She came up to me on my left and went to her knees. She bent forward and reached out with her hands to touch my chest and shoulder.

"Have you been shot?" Anne asked in a hoarse almost forced whisper.

"No, I'm ok, but I think I lost some skin off my leg and back sliding into third base," I said.

She almost smothered me when she pulled me forward by my shoulders, pulling my face into her left breast and the left side of her face. I couldn't struggle even if I had thought to and just relaxed until I felt my right hand touch the ground to my right. I released my grip on the Colt, let my shoulders sag and relaxed my head against her shoulder and got the shakes.

My shoulders shivered as if from cold and I felt a cold sweat on my forehead and face. She held me tightly until I stopped shaking, then I realized that I could smell her hair, her soft skin and the freshness of her clothes. She loosened her grip slightly and kissed me on both sides of my mouth and held me against her again.

"I thought you said you would never see me again," I said, in a strained, low voice.

She released me just enough to look in my face and let out a short laugh and smiled.

The smile faded and her beautiful face stiffened as if from the cold and her eyes were large when she asked, "When is this going to be over?"

She relaxed her arms and pushed away slightly to stand up and I felt another hand on my upper arm pulling me forward so that I could stand up. My thoughts shifted to the present.

"I'd better check and see what we have here," I said.

I recognized Hal Holt as I was being helped to stand upright. My legs were a little shaky and I felt weak and almost faint. I steadied myself and felt Anne place my left arm over her shoulders and her arm behind me holding me up and steady on my feet. Holt bent down and picked up my pistol from the ground. She didn't let go and I forced myself to walk to the bikes on the ground in front of me. I walked around to my right and pulled back on Anne's shoulder, forcing her to slow down and follow behind me.

I went first to the man on the right, who had fallen back on his face and was still trapped by the right leg. I saw that he wasn't moving and I looked quickly across the other bike to see if there was movement from the one who had been riding on the left.

Both his legs had been trapped under the bike. I didn't see any movement there, so I stooped down to check for a pulse. He was wearing a leather jacket, jeans and red bandanna around his neck. I went down to my left knee near his head and felt the right side of his neck through his shoulder length greasy hair for a pulse. There was none.

The rider in the middle had been slightly ahead of the other two. He fell face down almost in front of his bike. It had fallen on its right side with the rear wheel over the front wheel of the bike on the left. I knelt down by his right arm and turned my hand enough so that I could feel down the right side of his neck.

I could see a patch of blood in the middle of his back, staining the back of his denim jacket with cut off sleeves that had been fitted over a leather jacket. It looked at first glance like an exit wound that had puckered a hole outward. He would have had a clear shot, had I not fired first and he would have been dead even without the shot from the house. I couldn't see anything else even in the light from the yard lights.

It was getting lighter now that the sun was barely starting to light the sky but hadn't risen yet in the distant hills in the direction of the house. The first man I had shot had been trapped by his motorcycle and had fallen in an odd position with the back of his legs trapped under the tank of his bike and his upper body turned so that his right shoulder was on the ground and his left shoulder almost in contact with the ground as well.

I looked back in the direction of the first one I had checked. Anne was standing there, facing in my direction with her arms hanging loosely, her hands on her thighs and her head slightly bowed forward. She looked as if someone had struck her on the back of the head and she was trying not to fall forward. I walked over to her, reached over her right shoulder and turned to my left to walk to the house. She walked quietly and didn't utter a sound until we reached the front steps leading to the front door. She moaned twice as she stepped up the two steps to the wide landing in front of the door.

I glanced over my left shoulder, sensing that Hal Holt was walking behind us. I noticed for the first time that he was carrying an M-1 Garand military issue 30.06 in his left hand. That was the bright flash I had seen and the loud high powered blast that had hit the middle biker. I walked Anne to the dining room table and pulled out a chair for her to sit. As soon as she was seated I turned around to talk to Mr. Holt. He held out my Colt in his right hand until I took it and pushed it back into my holster.

"What happened to make you get concerned about the bikers?" I asked Holt.

"I saw them in town a couple of times, which I didn't worry about until I had seen them again and they seemed to be looking around like they were trying to find somebody" he said. "They had been here about a week. When they would leave town they would go in the direction of Joseph City."

He looked at me as if apologizing and said, "I didn't mean for Anne to come back here. She asked me if any more bikers had been through town and I mentioned that three large groups of them had been seen on the south side of town on McLaws road headed for the south route that goes through Show Low. I didn't worry about them so much as those three out there that came back a couple of days ago."

"It has to be near impossible that they were able to find this place and connect it to Anne and Rebecca, unless they saw Anne in town and followed her out here," I said.

"I didn't go to town," Anne said. "I took a flight to Flagstaff and called Hal from there."

"How did he pick you up?" I asked.

"He was driving the truck," she answered.

"Then it had to be by process of elimination," I said. I looked at Anne and asked, "do you recognize either of those three out there? Have you seen any of them before?"

"I don't know. I couldn't look at them," she said.

"We'll have to now. It's the only way any sense can be made of any of this," I said.

Her face was cold and her hands were shaking. I held out my hand so that she would stand up and follow me outside. She held out her left hand reluctantly and I took it in my right hand, then moved my hand up her arm and held it lightly and walked towards the door. I walked over to the one who had been riding between the other two, who was still lying on his face. She looked at him when I turned him over on his back.

"He is the one who talked to Rebecca in town," she said. "He is the one she said was Brooks."

"Is he the one she rode off with when you were out on the horses?" I asked.

"Yes, he's the same one," she said.

I remembered him too. He was the one who had talked to Rebecca at their rally just before I took her out of their camp. Next, I checked the one who had been riding on the left. He had both legs trapped under the motorcycle up to the back of his knees. I reached and pulled him free just as Holt lifted the bike, then I turned him over.

"I don't remember seeing him," she said.

I walked over to the last one and she looked at him carefully now that it was light in the yard.

"That is not one of the men who were trying to catch me," she said.

I reached down to pick up something shiny that was on the ground next to his right arm. Holt came over to look at what I picked up.

"It's a pair of brass knuckles," I said. Interestingly enough, I thought to myself, that they would be called a "pair," when it was actually just one. Anne started to shake, so I walked to her and turned her to head back to the house.

"It has to be a process of elimination," I said. "He went looking for Rebecca when we left their camp. He must have gone back to the only other place besides town he had seen you or Rebecca."

She turned to look at me directly with her eyes large.

"Where they first saw you on the horses," I told Anne. "All they had to do was find a place to watch the road near where they saw you that day and see who came out or went in. They might have found the ranch earlier if they had watched the road any time after I took you to town or before we hid out. They had no way of knowing anything about the ranch, but they must have guessed that you hadn't rented the horses," I added.

"They had to have believed you lived out here not too far from where you were riding. They may have been about to give up and saw you in Mr. Holt's truck when he brought you in from Flagstaff. They waited just long enough for you to settle in, made their plan and headed out here hoping to catch you unaware."

"There are other ranches on this road," she said. "How did they find this one?"

"They may have seen Mr. Holt drive out of here and return. It had to be just chance that no one else drove out of here and returned in the time they watched the road. They saw you in the truck on your way back and followed you down the road until they were sure where you were going. They would have planned to hit late night or early morning when you would be the most vulnerable," I said.

"Do you think it's over now?" asked Holt.

"I don't think it will be over as long as Anne is anywhere in the area," I answered. "If these were the only ones still here from the rally, none of the others may know about the ranch. They were only able to find the ranch because they saw Anne; otherwise they may have given up and left."

"The longer they were in the area, the more attention they would have gotten. I'm surprised that they didn't get the attention of the Marshall in town or any number of State troopers. There may still be some out there who know Anne by sight or would know her by her resemblance to Rebecca."

"How long are you going to stay?" I asked Anne.

"I don't know what to do right now," She said.

"I need to go outside and see what condition my bike is in," I said and headed to the door.

Holt followed me outside and walked away from the house with me to where I had dropped my bike. He helped me stand it up and held it up until I kicked out the kick stand. I checked the left side carefully and felt the fuel lines to see if anything had been loosed in the fall. Everything was in place and there didn't seem to be any damage other than the clutch handle being a little out of alignment that I could see. At the very least, the left foot peg and gear shift should have been bent or damaged, but they weren't.

"What do you think we should do about them?" he asked.

"I'm not sure what can be done about them. It's your call. You live here and any heat that comes from this will certainly come down on you," I said. "I didn't ask you before, but I suspected that you may have moved something you found out there where I ran into them when I found Anne."

He looked at me soberly and said, "I didn't find anything."

I looked at him disbelieving and said, "There were at least eight of them that came into my camp for Anne and I got the drop on them. One of them shot at me and they all ran and left on their bikes. The one I shot had tripped over Anne, then got up and shot at me and missed. I dragged him into a ditch and covered him up with sand and buried his bike in an arroyo."

"I think I know where that was. I went there but I didn't find anything but a lot of tracks," he said.

"What about the other location where I found the knife?" I asked.

"I went there, but I didn't see anything," he said.

I had thought wrong. He didn't say anything to me because he didn't know. He was letting me know that he was willing to cover for me, because he suspected something had been there, but he wasn't going to ask.

"There were three men there and their bikes. I didn't try to bury them. I dragged two of them into the rocks and the third one into the small arroyo where I found the knife," I told him.

He looked at me soberly, not showing any indication that he had known.

"The other bikers must have found them," I said. "They wouldn't want any of it known. It would just draw attention to them and they would want to avoid any involvement with the law, no matter the reason."

"What about you?" he asked. "They can still come after you; if not now, then sometime later."

"I don't think they ever saw me. They had no idea who took Anne from them, other than someone who surprised them in the dark. It was too dark for me to see any of them and remember what they looked like, so it's reasonable that they didn't get a good look at me," I explained. "My bike was parked out of their sight when they found Anne at my camp. If they had seen it and me before I saw them, they would have ambushed me. I didn't see any more of them when we left there."

"What about the way you were dressed, your jacket and all?" he asked.

"I wasn't wearing my jacket that night. I took it off when I wrapped up in my blanket and put Anne in my sleeping bag. I was wearing only my sweater when I found her missing from my sleeping bag and came up on them," I said.

"If they did see you, they know your license plate," he said. "They can find you through public records."

"How well I know that," I said. "I'll have to take that chance, but I don't think Anne should. She needs to get to the airport and out of here as soon as possible."

Anne had walked to where we were standing beside the bike.

"I don't want to go to the airport. I want you to take me back," she said.

"That's a long ride," I told her.

"They have caught up with me several times and you were there each time. I don't want to be alone if they find me again," she said.

"My rig is in Montana. We can ride there and get it and I'll drive you back," I said.

I looked at Holt as if asking what we were to do about the bodies and whether or not report this to the Police.

He looked at Anne and said, "Go ahead and get ready to go. There's a leather coat in one of the closets. Don't worry about taking any more with you than you can tie down."

"I can't leave before we report this to the police," she said with a strain in her voice.

Holt looked at me and all I could do was look back without a word. She walked away and looked back at us over her shoulder and she continued on to the house. He waited until she had gone through the door.

"What do you want to do?" he asked.

"I don't know what to do about them. They were shot in self defense but in these times where everything is big news, there's liable to be a coast to coast story about them getting shot out here. Everyone in the country will know where they were killed and who did it," I told Holt.

"If you just leave, I'll take care of all of this. If I'm the only one who knows about them there's much less chance of anyone finding out what happened here," he said.

"I can't just leave you to take care of this," I said.

"I'll take care of anything you leave here and get it to you," he said.

"I enforced and obeyed the law all of my life. Hiding this is the hardest thing I will ever have to do and I would almost rather face charges just to stay on the right side," I answered.

"But then it's like you said; you'll have to hide from every outlaw biker in the world," he said.

"I know. I can't go on looking behind my back for the rest of my life," I said.

"There's an old hand dug well that never had water a ways from here back that a way," he said as he pointed in the direction of the house and the barns. "I've been putting off filling it in for a long time."

"What if someone ever gets wind of this and comes around looking, not that they're likely to trace any of them here," I said.

"It's a big lonely country out here," he said. "No one will ever be excavating around here while I own this ranch. After I'm dead and gone, I won't care much what anybody finds here."

"It seems the worst of things to do, to just dispose of them like trash," I said.

"Either that or look behind you for the rest of your life," he said. "These boys came here to kill me and I don't think any one of them was going to grieve over my dead body."

"What do you want me to do?" I asked.

"I'll lead off. You take those cycles back there and I'll take care of the rest," he said. He walked around the house to his dually.

Anne was standing in the doorway when we walked past the landing so I walked over to her.

"What are you going to do?" she asked.

"We have to do something about them," I said.

"Are you going to bury them?" she asked.

"That's the only thing we can do. This many men being killed out here, bikers or not will be the sensation of the country. The only way we can put this behind us is to keep it from being known," I said.

"It seems evil to just bury them without notifying the authorities," she said.

"I would have the understanding and the advantage of being known as a retired Police officer in my home town and that my actions and explanations would be believed first until proven wrong," I said. "I wouldn't have any problem turning myself in to the Police and surrendering my weapon so that an investigation could begin if this had happened where I had worked and retired."

"These men are dead because of me and Rebecca," she said. "I can't help feeling guilt even if they were trying to hurt us."

"I find it a little hard to feel anything but relief that they are dead and can't come after you any more," I said.

She was still standing there when Holt brought the dually around and we loaded the bodies into the truck bed. He waited long enough to see if I could start the first bike, then he drove around the house headed for the barn. I followed him around the barn and then onto an old road with cattle tracks all over it. He went about a mile farther to the foot of some low hills covered with brush and dry grass.

I could see the marks of an old foundation off to the right. He had stopped next to some pallets stacked high over long boards about forty or fifty yards from the old ruins. I rolled the bike next to his truck and helped him pull the bodies out of the truck, dropping them on the ground and then we went back for the other two bikes.

"The old well is under there," he said. "The hole is about six foot wide and over fifty feet deep."

I took the bikes one at a time and rolled them to the well and dropped them in. They seemed to fall for a long time before they hit the bottom.

"I don't think I want to see their faces in that well for the rest of my life," I told him.

"I understand what you're saying," he said. "Let's get back to the house so you can get ready to get on the road."

"What about them?" I asked, looking over at the bodies and the bikes."

"I'll bring over the tractor with the bucket and take care of it," he said.

Holt looked at me and I said, "I have to stop in Holbrook to pick up my bag at the motel."

"Give me your key" he said. "I'll pick it up and ship it out to you from Flagstaff."

"No," I said. "Just get rid of the bag and everything in it. There isn't anything in it that I'll miss and nothing in it that ties it to me."

"You should bypass Holbrook before you head north," he said.

"I guess I can go to Flagstaff first and take 160 into Four Corners," I said. "I can do it as long as I get good weather into Durango."

"I got some maps at the house," he said.

I looked over at the bodies on the ground behind his truck.

"I'll take care of this," he said. "You took all the risks. Now you let me do what I can."

He left me at the house and walked around to the barn. A minute or two later I heard the sound of the tractor when he started in the direction of the well. Anne walked to where I was checking the bike. She handed me a small back pack, which I tied on the back of the sissy bar after I had retied my small bag. I handed her the Smith 645 in the holster and drank some water from my canteen while she put it on her belt. She tied a large scarf on her head and waited until I started the bike and balanced it to get ready to leave.

I made the turn onto the road leading to the highway as soon as I reached the intersection. I looked over to the left in the direction of the ranch and I could see smoke rising from the area of the old ruins. Anne gripped the sides of my jacket tighter and leaned her head against my right side of my face. I stopped to get a better look to confirm to myself that the stack of lumber and pallets was burning. The small billows of white and grey smoke would be seen up to ten miles away but it shouldn't give the appearance of a possible grass fire. I knew that she had a momentary fear that the ranch buildings were burning.

She was looking in the direction of the ranch when I looked over my left shoulder and said, "It's just a pile of pallets burning."

"Will anyone find any of those men?" she asked.

Even with the frightening events of the past weeks and maybe even relief that they were dead and unable to pursue her any longer; she still had the capacity not to dehumanize them. I had referred to them as bodies and bikers and felt some remorse for having shot them, but I didn't regret that they were dead.

"There shouldn't be any interest in someone burning some old pallets out here and there's no reason anyone would come looking out here," I told her. "In any case there won't be anything for anyone to find."

The highway was clear at this time of the morning while we rode to Flagstaff at a pretty good clip. Most of the earlier traffic going from one town to another or to work was gone. I stopped at a phone booth on the edge of Flagstaff. Anne got off the bike and stood beside me as I leafed through the phone book.

"What are you looking for?" she asked.

"Motorcycle sales," I answered.

I continued into Flagstaff until we reached the Hwy 89 turnoff that would take us north to U.S. 160 and Four Corners. I found a Harley dealership that looked like it would have some leather and pulled into the parking lot around the side of the building. I could see that Anne was a little uneasy about me buying leather for her to wear.

"I would surmise that your plan is for me to look more like a biker," she said when I picked out a jacket and chaps for her.

"That would be very difficult," I said. "Find yourself some boots, just plain, even if they cost more than the ones with buckles and designs. Make sure they're a good size large and almost loose. Don't wear them. Leave the box and just bring the boots."

I paid for the goods with cash and started for the door. She followed me out the door carrying the boots. She didn't say anything as we walked out and I headed around the side of the building where I had left the bike. I stopped at the end of the pavement near the dirt lot next to the building out of view of the street and the Harley shop.

"Aahhhh," she moaned as if in pain when I tossed the jacket and chaps onto the dusty pavement, and watched almost in horror when I stomped on the new leather and ground it into the pavement with my boots.

She sighed when I picked them up and dragged them back and forth like I was washing the side of a car.

"Now the boots," I said.

She handed them to me painfully and I did the same with them, scuffing them before I stepped on the toes and crushed the square tips down. Then I took a pair of gloves and did the same with them, taking care not to tear them or break the stitches. I looked at them, satisfied at the result and walked over to the building to a water faucet. I wet my bandanna, wrung it out and wiped the dust from the jacket and chaps. She watched me closely when I drew my knife and cut off the legs of the chaps, so they wouldn't be too long.

"Ok, lose your boots and put these on," I said.

She leaned her back against the building and I pulled off her almost new western boots. I helped her on with the chaps, feeling the closeness and the contact with her when I zipped the chaps and helped her buckle them. I was standing close to her with my hands on her waist after I buckled the belt of her chaps. She put her arms over my shoulders and put her head on my shoulder. I didn't move for a moment, then she let me go and I handed her the jacket.

"It's a little warm, so don't zip it all the way up," I said. "Just zip it a little and buckle the belt before we get started again."

I took her jacket, boots and the scraps of leather and put them into the dumpster and walked back to the bike so we could leave.

Durango is about 260 miles from Flagstaff, Arizona. I made it to within about 25 miles of four corners on the Arizona side in about six hours with a couple of rest stops along the way on highway 160. I had not been able to shake the bad feelings I had leaving Hal Holt to clean up the mess in his yard.

I chose a small clearing away from the road and out of sight of the rest stop where I could set up the small thin walled tent to stay overnight. The events leading to her being in my company had been forced upon her and had put me on edge and in a constant state of apprehension at possibly having another confrontation with more of the bikers. The real possibility of running into them and losing was still a real threat and I hadn't felt safe at any time since the beginning.

Chapter Eighteen

It was cool but not cold yet, so I hadn't thought about making a fire, which was just as well. Smoke could be seen and smelled from the highway or from the rest stop. Anne removed her chaps then she sat on her bag with her back against a large rock and watched me set up the tent.

She hadn't talked much on the way here from Holbrook when we stopped twice for a break at coffee stops along the way. I removed my chaps and walked over to where she sat and set my jacket down on the rock next to her so I could sit. She looked at me uneasily as if it was the first time she had ever seen me and was worried about what I was going to say.

"How do you feel?" I asked, while really wanting to ask, are you comfortable in my company?

"I'm a little tired from the ride, but I feel alright," she answered. "Is that what you meant to ask?"

"Yes and no. You've been through a lot in the last couple of weeks. You should be under a lot more stress than you seem to be. Sometime soon, you're going to have to get some counseling," I said.

She looked at me questioningly but didn't reply.

"You've had more happen to you than happens to soldiers in the field in the middle of a combat zone. They need counseling after each stressful and deadly encounter to defuse them and get them to come to terms with death and their part in it," I told her.

"I never imagined anything like this happening to me," she said. "I have watched news reports at one time or another and I have been shocked at some of the things people do to each other, but nothing I have ever experienced could have made me more terrified than what I have been through."

"Do you mean the shooting at the ranch?" I asked.

"Yes. I was shocked at what happened. I couldn't have fired a pistol at them even after you instructed me how to do it," she said.

"What were you doing when the shooting started?" I asked.

"I was awake early because Hal wanted to go out to the range and check on the livestock," she said. "I had just finished dressing and I was getting ready to go out and get the horses ready."

"I didn't see any lights when I came into the yard. If there had been lights they may not have come to the house when they did," I said.

"We never turn on the lights in the morning if we are going out into the yard," she said. "There is always enough light to get dressed at that time of the morning unless it is in the winter."

"So you probably didn't have the chance to see if you could do anything because it was over before you could prepare yourself for it," I said.

"I had not thought about it that way. It was just so shocking when I realized what was happening. It seemed that I was still half asleep when I saw Hal at the door in the darkness holding a rifle and firing it," she said. "The most frightening was when I was trying to get away from them out there in the prairie. I was angry and scared and I couldn't believe that they had so little regard for me that they were going to take me without any feelings about what was right or wrong."

"That's the way it is sometimes," I said. "But your anger and determination is what kept you alive."

"How can that be? Who are these men that have no regard for the law and anyone they run into?" she asked.

"There are the rest of us that obey the law out of our moral regard for it and the rest of them that have no morals and have the highest disregard for the law and the rights of others," I said. "It isn't isolated to any particular group of people any more than it is to these men."

"How do you feel about having to take me with you?" she asked. "Did you feel trapped into helping me just because you had to get me out of trouble?"

"That wasn't your choice and it wasn't mine. There isn't anything you did to cause it to happen and it certainly wasn't anything I did," I said. "For their own selfish lawless reasons, they were going to take you any way they could. I just happened to be there and all I could do was try to stay alive."

"You didn't really answer what I asked," she said. "How do you feel about having to bring me along? Wasn't it enough that you had to get shot at because of me then insisted that you take me back?"

"You're asking me exactly what I asked you," I said. "How do you feel about avoiding being taken by them and then me not allowing you to go home or report it to the police?"

"You put yourself in danger to help me. I'm not certain what happened before you put me on your motorcycle, but I know that everything you did after that was done to keep me and Rebecca safe," she answered.

"I did everything I could so that they wouldn't take you, but I kept you from going back to Holbrook and reporting it to the Police because I would have been arrested," I answered.

"Would you have been arrested if it was known that you were a Police officer?" she asked.

"It wouldn't matter who I was if I was charged. I'm not going to tell you that I did something selfless and brave. I found myself in the middle of it when they came up on my camp and tried to take you. I didn't have to try to reason whether or not I would do what I did," I said. "I had to keep you from being found, but I also had to keep them from finding me."

She waited a moment before she spoke again.

"My life feels like a big wreck. I got divorced from a selfish and abusive man who tried to make me feel inferior and accused me of being unfaithful and vain. I didn't want to believe that he was mean until he became physical," she said. "I left him because I was afraid of him, not because I thought our marriage had failed."

"I have never been on a motorcycle or even thought of it," she said. "When I saw those men in town, even before Rebecca talked to them I was disgusted by their appearance and arrogance. They were just people in another life that I would never have considered being associated with."

"Have you been here all of your life?" I asked.

"I grew up on my father's ranch. I don't remember much before that. We raised cattle and horses and went to auctions and fairs and worked on the ranch. If I had not gone to California to go to school, I would have been there on the ranch before he died."

"I don't know anything about the kind of men who ride motorcycles and fight in bars except what I have rarely seen in a movie or in the news. I feel as if my whole life has been rolled up side down." She went on. "I feel guilty having left and even more so that my father died and he lost the ranch. I felt so helpless that there was nothing that I could do to help him keep it even if I had known."

She stopped talking and the silence became long. She wiped tears from her eyes and looked at me as if to question me about how I felt.

"It's horrible that this has happened and those men are dead," she said. "I know that this kind of fighting and killing goes on, but I never imagined that it could happen to me."

"You did nothing to cause any of it," I said.

"I will never be able to escape the guilt I feel for not having reported their deaths and what happened," she said.

"It became something way beyond the law after the second attack," I said. "You and Rebecca could have been assaulted and killed. Any publicity from any of this would make it necessary for you to hide out for the rest of your life."

"I took my life for granted," she said. "I didn't realize what a sheltered and relatively safe life ranching is, even with the harsh winters and the occasional serious incidents."

"I'm from another life altogether," I said. "I came out here to research a book and do something I never gave myself time for before I retired. I felt uneasy about setting up camp and staying overnight in a tent with a woman who would never have chosen to be in a place like this."

"I didn't know what to think about you," she said. "You seemed thoughtful and calm, almost cold."

"You seemed uncomfortable being in my company, most likely because being with me had not been of your choosing. I'm sure you felt that you had escaped being taken by those men only to find yourself captive by someone else. I shot and killed someone who attacked me in circumstances that will put me in further danger if it's ever known," I said.

"I don't understand what you are trying to say," she said. "I'm not afraid of you and I don't feel uncomfortable with you. I felt a cold panic when I thought you were going to leave and I would still be in Holbrook worrying about running into more of those men."

"If I had ever seen you anywhere in any other circumstances, I would have never have dreamed of being in a conversation with you," I said.

"Why would that matter to me?" she asked.

"You're a beautiful woman from a distant and totally different life than mine. I would have never met someone like you or otherwise come into contact with you even when I was young, if not for the events of the past weeks," I said. "I feel like just being with you is taking advantage of some obligation you must feel because I got you out of danger."

She had listened to me all the while watching me intently, her eyes wide and her lips parted slightly. An almost impatient look came over her face and she looked away for a moment then she reached for my right hand and gently pulled me toward her. I didn't know if she was going to stand or continue sitting on her bag as she guided me to stand in front of her.

She drew me to her until I bent my knees to kneel in front of her and sat back on my heels then she pressed herself against me until she was sitting on my thighs with her knees bent. She tightened her arms around my neck and pressed my face against her neck and breast. After a moment she drew away to look at my face.

"Those lines represent years, not character," I said.

"Did you bring me with you because you felt you had to?" she asked.

"It doesn't matter," I said. "I'm just happy that you're safe."

"I'm not as young as you must think I must be." She said. "Rebecca is just out of high school but I finished school a long time ago. I was afraid for my life and for Rebecca. It didn't make me less aware of whom you seem to be and the different worlds we have lived in. I crossed over into another life because I became aware how easily a safe orderly existence can be shattered without warning. My husband gave me the first lesson. Those men gave me the second."

"I was searching for some kind of reasoning that would reduce my feeling of guilt for being intimate with you," I said.

"Do you regret it?" she asked.

"I regret not knowing you when I was younger," I said.

"Do you think you would have felt guilty then?" she asked.

"Maybe, but more than likely, it would have never happened," I said.

"None of these things would have happened if not for me and Rebecca," she replied.

"There is nothing you've done that gives you any reason to take responsibility for any of what has happened," I said. "You didn't do anything wrong and you can't help who you are. You're beautiful and because of that they wanted you."

"It wouldn't have happened had she not offered herself to them," she said.

"She was being what she is; a young woman wanting to live her life. She can't be blamed for trusting that she should be safe in any company she chooses. Those men could just as easily have been decent human beings who drew the attention of a trusting young girl," I said.

"You have the right to expect more of me than just allowing you to fade away after you had to break the law and place yourself in danger," she said.

"Just as long as you know you can go on with your life with no expectations from me," I said. "Your safety would have been more thanks than I would ask."

"Well, thanks" she said and held me close again.

I couldn't tell if she smiled or would have laughed, because I couldn't see her face.

"At least I've been on a bike before and I'm worn out," I said. "You have to be as tired as I am."

She said no more but I held her until she relaxed her hold and stood away from me. She walked to the tent, sat with her back in front of the tent flap, smiled at me and leaned back and to her side and slid herself into the tent.

She was in my sleeping bag with her back to the inside fold of it when I entered the tent. I raised the unzipped side of it and tried not to crowd her into physical contact when I got in. I put my head on the rolled blanket for a pillow and settled back to try to sleep. She pressed against me and put her leg over mine and her arm across my chest and seemed to fall asleep.

"Did you know that I would call you?" she asked.

"I knew it was you as soon as I heard the phone ring," I said.

She pressed herself tightly against my hip and rose up on her elbow and kissed me. Her closeness and the softness of her body aroused me quickly, but she relaxed and I knew she was falling asleep. I awoke with her hair against my face and the smell of her warm skin. I let her continue to sleep and left the tent trying not to disturb her.

I started a small fire with some dry sticks to minimize the smoke and heated water for tea. It was still cool when she emerged from the tent with her jacket half open. She looked as fresh as when we left Holbrook except for her tousled hair and slightly wrinkled shirt.

"That confirms that you're from a totally different life. You're unbelievably beautiful even after spending the night in the dirt in a sleeping bag," I said.

"I probably look as bad as my mouth tastes," she said puckering her lips slightly.

"Try this. It'll burn a little, but it'll make you feel better," I told her, handing her a small bottle of mouthwash.

"We're about three hours out of Durango. We can make a stop in about two hours and get cleaned up. If you can hold out until then, we can have some food and stay there and get some rest. I'm still tired, so you must still be exhausted," I said.

"I have a lot left yet," she replied. "You don't have to adjust to how I feel."

"We may be out of range of any of that group of bikers, but we can't let our guard down," I said. "We should be safe if we run into any of them from that same bunch in any of the towns on our way, but we won't have anywhere to go if they decide to follow us."

Chapter Nineteen

Outside Flagstaff a large group of motorcycles was turning from the highway onto a mountain road. They had been traveling since early morning after leaving a campsite south of Showlow, Arizona. They turned into a clearing large enough to accommodate most of the riders and some of the trucks with campers that would be following.

"Tong, you and Buzz go back and bring the trucks back here," Evan told the two who usually rode close to him on the Runs.

"Find Juice," he spoke to another rider who had pulled alongside when he stopped in the clearing. "Tell him small fires only, no partying, no noise."

More of the riders were gathering around him now that most of them had found parking around the outside edges of the clearing.

"How did you find this spot, boss?" another of the riders asked him.

"I used to camp around here sometime back," he said. "It's close to Flagstaff and they don't have to know we're here until we go through and pick up 89 to head up to Silverton or Durango."

"Why not just go up through Santa Fe and Albuquerq'?" the rider asked.

"Too much traffic. We just need to get back to Denver and get this Run over. It went sour with Baker an' Brooks an' his bunch almost bringin' the Mounties down on us over those women," Evan replied.

Only a select few of his trustee's were made aware of the death of Jinx, Baker, Tank and Zero. Brooks and two others who went against his order to leave the women alone were still missing. He nodded his head at three riders who had just parked their bikes near some large trees and a small clearing.

"Hey boss," one of them said as he approached, lighting a freshly rolled reefer.

"Go easy on that," he said. "We got business."

"What's up boss?" the one called Cody asked.

"Never found out where Brooks and knuckles and Cass went off to or who else went with them," said Evan.

"He prob'ly figured to go off on his own again. We didn't check all the places he could'a been if they got themself shot too," said Cody. "Who you think they're tangling with? You think it's some other riders?"

"Doan know. We couldn't check every place out there," Evan said.

"Too much nosy farmers out there. Sooner or later the law was goin' to start lookin' for us and ask questions. We found Baker and the two was with him, but no sign of Brooks an' the other two."

"We could'a looked aroun' Holbrook," said Cody. "See if we could find that bitch was with Brooks or the other one they were after."

"No, too much trouble. We been here too long already," replied Evan.

"He might'a caught up with the little bitch and headed south already," Cody said.

"We head back in the mornin'," he said. "We can make Denver some time tomorrow if we light out first thing in the morning. We three, four hours out of four corners and then another five, six out of Denver."

"What about four corners?" asked Cody?

"Some of us stop at Durango, some at Silverton and the rest at Farmington. The trucks and women go on and start setting up at our camp past Durango," he said. "We got another Run come up in June. We get the law on us and we have to go in small Runs for a while, or we got trouble."

"Why we got to cut our numbers?" asked one of the others.

"Too much happened at the big rally in Holbrook. These lawmen, they talk to each other. We stayed too long because of Baker and Jinx goin' off and tryin' to pick up that other bitch like they did." He replied.

"We got four dead and Brooks and Knuckles and Cass are out there somewhere."

"We gonna look for them?" asked Cody.

"No, we gotta move on," said Evan. "They may show at Durango or Silverton. They know the plan we had of stopping there on the way back from the Run down south."

I wasn't in any hurry to leave in the cool morning. Farmington is much higher in elevation than Holbrook. Four corners is the site of the connection of four states; Colorado, Arizona, New Mexico and Utah. It's colder at night and much cooler during the day than it is in Flagstaff and Holbrook and it's still frosty at this time of the morning at this altitude.

We were well off the highway, out of sight of the traffic and far enough from the rest stop that we shouldn't have been seen by anyone stopping there. The smoke from our fire was drifting north away from the highway and the little of it there was, was mixing into the trees. I heard the rumble in the distance and I knew it for what it was; a large group of motorcycles was heading our way toward four corners and Durango.

"Wait here," I told Anne. "I'm going out to the road and watch from there for a little while."

I started in the direction of the highway and stopped short of the small clearing between our camp and the rest stop. I looked carefully in the direction of the small parking area, checking for any movement from anyone who may have stopped in the lot. I heard movement behind me just as I was about to start across the small clearing.

"I heard something in the trees back there," Anne said.

"I'll go have a look," I told her as I walked to her and took her arm for her to walk with me.

I skirted the small clearing of our camp, trying to keep from stepping on fallen boughs or rocks and avoid making noise. I motioned for her to drop down behind some rocks and I continued around our camp, all the while checking to my left into the trees. Not seeing anything or any movement, I turned around to head back to where I had left Anne. I felt the slam against the outside of my right thigh before I heard the loud report of an automatic pistol, followed by a two more loud dull reports which sounded different.

The second two shots were from a slightly different angle behind me, but I was already falling from the force of the first shot or I would have been hit again. There is a little difference in the sound of gunshots. I could recognize the sound of a revolver, especially if it is a large heavy caliber like a Smith and Wesson Magnum. The revolver makes more than one sound because of the escape of compression from the clearance between the cylinder and the barrel, followed by another sound as the compression escapes between the bullet and the muzzle when it clears the barrel.

The sound gives the impression of a loud cracking explosion. An automatic has a single loud clap of sound when the compression escapes behind the bullet when it leaves the barrel. I heard the loud clear explosion and knew it for the sound of an automatic, smaller than a 45 caliber.

I felt my self twisted slightly forward on my right side and I let myself fall on my right shoulder. I fell into the foot high grass and rolled twice, just enough to get under the brush at the side of the clearing.

"If you fall and you aren't dead, don't lie still, move and get to cover; then lie still. They don't expect you to move when you get hit, so when you find cover, lie still and listen," my brother had told me, when he told me about one of the times he had been wounded in Vietnam.

I crawled quickly to where I had left Anne behind the rocks and went into the small hollow inside the brush just as she looked like she was about to yell. I motioned for her to lie down close to the ground and I tried to move quickly around to my right to circle back to where the shots seemed to come from.

I looked down quickly and put my hand over my thigh where the blood was welling from my jeans then wiped my hand on the upper part of my thigh and drew out my Colt, cocking it as it cleared the holster. My thigh went numb when I was hit, but now it was starting to come back and it felt like I was getting a stab from a knife each time my foot dragged on the ground. Blood was all over my upper pant leg so I took my bandana from my neck and tied it around my thigh over the wound.

I stayed in a crouch and kept moving through the brush while keeping away from the boughs to avoid the sound of my clothes brushing against it. I heard movement to my right, which would have been from the clearing between where I was when I had been hit, and the trees. I got down low so I could see a little better under some of the brush, which thinned out closer to the ground. I saw the color of denim and ducked my head lower to see one man walking toward where I had fallen. I moved to my left to a break in the brush so I could have a better look.

"Over there, that's where he fell," a man's voice said.

I was about to move forward when another man came into my vision slightly to my left. He would have seen me if I had moved.

"First rule of searching or hiding; look and listen and don't move if it's quiet," my brother had said. "Second rule; move small distances at a time, stop and listen again before moving and change directions slightly each time."

I could see their backs clearly from the knees up. This was the first time I had seen their colors, two gold wings behind a gray and black screaming skull. They were sweeping their vision left and right to check both sides of the clearing to see where I should have fallen. Only seconds had passed when I lined up my Colt, center body mass on the back of the man on the right, who was slightly ahead of the other one about sixty feet away.

There was no word of warning or thought of hesitation. Only cops in the movies give warning before they shoot at men with guns in their hands, whether they are pointed at them or not.

There is no rule of law that says you have to give warning when the danger to yourself or others is imminent or when you have someone in your sights who has already demonstrated his intentions. Means, opportunity and intent means he has a weapon, there is someone in front of him or in his sights and he has made a motion or movement that shows he will shoot or he has shot at someone already. That is, if the rules in a court of law haven't changed since I retired. However, this is the woods in the middle of nowhere and they would have to be alive to testify.

These thoughts raced through my mind as I fired two closely spaced shots and watched him jerked forward onto his face in the grass. I would have shot at either one, but I shot the one on the right, because he was slightly ahead. The other one would see him fall from the shot and he may not move if I didn't shoot again. He didn't. He dropped something from his right hand and raised his arms.

"Don't shoot!" he yelled. "I dropped it!"

He started to turn to his right trying to look over his right shoulder as he turned.

"Don't move!" I yelled. "Or you may just see me when the next shot hits you. On your knees, now!"

He didn't hesitate. He dropped forward to his knees. Had I been active and making an arrest in the so distant past, I would have had him clasp his hands behind his head into the standard handcuffing position. This wasn't that day. I just wanted him to hold still until I could get close to him. I reached down and picked up his pistol, a standard four inch barreled Smith and Wesson.

Out of habit I picked it up with my thumb and forefinger by the trigger guard. If I didn't handle it any more than I had to just to dispose of it, I could wipe it easily. I looked to my right where his companion had fallen. I sidestepped to my right, trying to keep the first one in my vision. I pushed his pistol into my waist band between my shirt and my trousers then looked down and saw the first man's pistol. It was an older Browning Hi-power replica, 9MM, Luger.

Chapter Twenty

I was shot in 1965 in the outer thigh with a 7.62 by 39 from a Russian type Ak47. The bullet had entered just outside my large quadriceps at an angle toward my knee; either because my leg had been going up to step forward or the shot had come from above and behind me. It stopped just short of taking my knee off at the joint. It left a large hollow in the outer part of my thigh and a long wide scar in both directions up and down my leg.

I never knew where it came from. I had been walking towards the MAAG compound in Saigon. It may have just been a stray bullet, because I never heard a gunshot and I didn't hear anything until the next day in the hospital. Had this been the first time I had been shot or injured, I might have gone into shock, or not moved fast enough after I was hit and they would have found me lying just where they'd been looking for me.

Blood from my leg had just reached my ankle. It wasn't bleeding fast, but it was fast enough that if I didn't do something soon, I was going to pass out from the loss of blood. It had really started to hurt now, as if the shock from the blow had worn off and the place in my leg, just behind the old scar, had just been seared with a hot iron. I heard Anne behind me, even before I turned to look at her. I backed up so she could hear me if I talked in a low voice.

"Give me your scarf," I told her.

She handed it to me and I untied my bandanna from my thigh with my left hand.

"Here fold this and hand it to me and then tie the scarf around my leg," I said.

I reached down and felt the tear in my pant leg just over the wound. I stuffed the folded bandana into the tear over the gash the bullet had made and she tied the scarf over the bulge of the wound.

"Go back to the rocks where I told you to wait the first time. Don't go back to camp," I said. "I'll be right there."

"Is he dead?" she asked dully, without emotion.

"I don't know. I haven't had time to check on him yet," I answered.

"What about him?" She looked in the direction of his companion.

"I'll make sure he doesn't follow us for a while," I said, all the while thinking, *You can't follow me if your dead, you Bastard,* but not thinking I could cold bloodedly kill him now that he didn't have a weapon. I waited until she was out of sight headed back around the rocks before I walked back to stand behind him.

I placed the muzzle of my Colt on the back of his neck and asked, "How many more of you mother fuckers are still looking for us?"

He was tough. He had no fear in his voice when he answered. "At least a hundred of us."

He didn't react when I stepped back slightly, then I shot off his right ear. The muzzle blast turned his head and knocked him forward on his face. I reached forward and grabbed him by the back of the collar of his leather jacket and pulled him back to his knees. He appeared too stunned by the concussion to yell in pain.

"Ok, talk to me!" I said in his left ear. "The next one takes off your elbow. It's a 230 grain Colt. It may take off your whole arm."

"Just me and him," he said grunting in pain as he talked.

"Who's him?" I asked.

"That's Tong. Me and him was supposed to check for the trucks that was followin' us," he answered.

"What's your name?" I asked.

"Buzz," he answered.

"How far back?" I asked.

"Bout Flagstaff," he said.

"How many are in the group you were with?" I asked him.

"Bout forty left by now. The rest is gone home. We was splittin' up into small bunches to head back," he said.

"Why only you two are after us?" I asked. "And why are you doing it?"

He didn't speak, so I put the muzzle at the left side of his head.

"You can still be dead. Why are you after us?" I asked again.

"You got Jinx and some of us. They was our partners," he said.

"Why were you after us in the first place?" I asked.

"We was after the bitch," he said. "Brooks got the younger one and Jinx wanted the other one. We caught up with her once and you come out of nowhere and shoot Jinx. Jinx was Brooks' partner. We was supposed to pull out and leave her be and get the young one back to town so the law wouldn't come after us, but she got away and Brooks wanted to get even for Jinx."

"It was Baker still wanted the older one. We found Jinx where we caught up with her that morning. We knew whoever was with the older one shot Jinx and buried him and we found Baker and Tank and Zero, but Brooks and Knuckles and Cass di'nt come back. Maybe they was gone off because of Evan."

"Who is Evan?" I asked.

"He's the president. He told Brooks and Baker to take the little bitch back and find Jinx, but to leave them be," he said.

"So, why are you still after us?" I asked him.

"I wasn't. We was riding scout and seen you leavin' Flagstaff," he said.

"How did you know who to look for?" I asked.

"We di'nt know you was a rider," he said. "I saw the bitch. I knew it was the little bitch got away from Brooks. We followed you here and went back to meet Evan in Flagstaff before they left. We stayed with the Run until here, then we dropped back and started lookin' fer your camp."

"Where are they going to camp tonight?" I asked him.

"A few miles past Durango, pointed rock or somethin'," he said.

I walked up to him and pulled on his bandanna until the knot was at the back of his neck where I could untie it.

"What you doin'?" he asked.

"I got a wound here one of you put in my leg," I said.

"Was Tong shot you," he said. "We just wanted the bitch. We wasn't gonna shoot."

"Well, you did," I said, and untied the bandanna.

He shook as if to brace himself for the coming shot, and then relaxed when I didn't shoot. I took my finger out of the trigger guard and pushed the pistol into my holster. I took out the set of brass knuckles and put them on my left hand, wrapped the scarf around them and swung my arm in a wide hooking punch and struck him on the neck slightly behind the ear.

He went out like he was struck with a bat, falling over to his right and slightly on his back. His eyes rolled back and I couldn't tell if he was still breathing or not. I had meant to drag him into the bushes and leave him, but thought better of it and started dragging him to the small rise across the clearing. He was still breathing. I felt a wave of nausea, thinking I may have killed him too.

I could hear the wind past the small rise, giving me the thought that there might be a large gully or stream bed there. I left him just past the trees and walked a little farther until I could see that there was a gorge that went deeper with some rocks and trees down the side of it. I dragged him to the edge and confirmed that he was still breathing.

It didn't matter. I wasn't going to leave him in a position to hunt me some more. I rolled him over the bank above the small gorge and eased him over edge and released him. I watched him slide down the sandy bank and stop on a sandy ledge about twenty feet down. I wiped his pistol with his bandanna and tossed it over the ledge. I went back and dragged his dead companion to the ledge and rolled him over too. I wiped his pistol clean as well and tossed it over the edge.

Had there been more of them besides the two, I would have been dead. If I hadn't shot when I did they would have found me and they would have found Anne. They were going to pursue Anne until they caught up with her and they were prepared to kill whoever helped her. It was sheer, dumb luck for me that they were alone, or seemed to be so far.

From what he had told me, they had been ordered to back off and let Anne go and they hadn't known who was helping her until they saw us leaving Flagstaff. I quickened my pace to get back to where Anne should be. If there had been others, they would already have found her if I had told her to go back to the camp and there wasn't anything I could have done about it. I had to do something or she was not going to get through this. I reached out with my left hand and took her right arm.

When she didn't respond I said, "Anne!" loudly and shook her lightly.

She looked directly in my eyes, blinked and said, "I'm all right. I'm just frightened."

"Let's get back to camp," I said. "We have to get out of this area."

"What are we going to do? They seem to be ahead and behind us too," she said.

"It has to be only a few of them that are still determined to find you, but there is no way to know how many more there are," I said. "One of them told me that the main body of riders is camped east of Durango. There are probably still a few stragglers coming in from Flagstaff."

"What can we do to get out of here without being seen again?" she asked.

"We can't stay here and we can't go on in the direction we were going," I answered.

"So what can we do?" she asked.

"We're going to have to take a long shot and head south. It seems that too many of them think they know who you are," I said.

"They think that it's Rebecca. Everyone who was at the bonfire must have seen her," she said.

"I don't think the rest of them know about me," I said. "I'm sure that they know someone has been with you and helped get Rebecca out of their camp, but they may not know who it is or how many. These two were part of the first group of bikers who were after you from the beginning."

"We're heading south," I told her.

"That would be Ship Rock," she said. "They may go that way too."

"They could, but I'm hoping that they are trying to keep a direct route out of here on their way to Denver. That is, if the biker gave me the correct information. I really don't want to travel right now and I don't want to get caught out in the open, but there's no choice," I told her. "We have to get out of this area right away."

What I didn't tell her was that I had no intention of leaving until I could do something that would end this search. The search for us, that is.

"How do you know that he didn't lie to you?" she asked.

"He was probably certain that he should tell me what I wanted to know," I said. I thought to myself. *He hadn't been sure whether I would kill him or not.*

I left Anne with the bike just short of reaching the rest stop parking lot and went to look for the two bikes. Their bikes were parked about sixty feet past the parking area hidden in the brush. After checking for traffic on the highway I went back through the brush and put a bullet through the engine casing of each of the bikes. I would have shot the engine cylinder, but I wasn't certain that the 45 caliber slug would penetrate the iron piston sleeve.

We were just over two hours from the little town of Shiprock. I continued on and found a small motel just short of the main area of the town. The bleeding had stopped or slowed down in my leg, but it was swollen tight inside the jeans. She checked us in, got a room then I pulled around behind the unit, so the bike would be out of view for the time being. I could get the bike inside later in the after noon or as soon as it got dark; something that happens early in the mountains. Anne removed her chaps and the motorcycle jacket and placed them on the bed as soon as we got into the room.

"Do you think you can find some supplies?" I asked her.

"Yes, of course. I know all these little towns. What do you think we will need?" she asked.

"Peroxide and some kind of disinfectant; Neosporin or one of those, if not, get some kind of Iodine if nothing else and some first aid pads and tape," I said.

"Is that going to be enough?" she asked, worriedly.

"It'll have to do. Get a small sewing kit that has some white thread," I told her. "It doesn't seem to be a deep wound. It just cut a gash in my leg."

"What if they don't have any disinfectant?" she asked. "This is a small town."

"Just anything you can find, even if it's animal strength Iodine," I said.

"This is cattle and sheep country, especially sheep. If there isn't anything else, there will be livestock Iodine, I can thin it out," she said.

She started to leave when I stopped her.

"Wait," I said, and pulled her shirt up out of her jeans. She looked down at my hands, but she didn't try to stop me or pull away.

"Tie it like you did when you worked around the ranch," I said. "Walk normal, not in a hurry. Hopefully you won't get too much attention on the way there. See if you can find some Bromelain or some pineapple juice."

I followed her out the door and watched her walk up the street. There was no traffic and I didn't see anyone on the street between the motel and the store. I knew she would stand out like a large flower in a basket of dandelions if anyone saw her walking around in the little town. I waited until she seemed to reach the store before I went outside to the phone booth to make a collect call.

Using my phone card or the one Anne had with her would immediately record our location. Not that anyone was looking for either of us; that is other than the outlaw bikers.

The motel was out of sight of the main road coming into town, but the store was right next to highway. Our room was in a unit out of sight of the motel office, but I could see the small convenience store clearly from here. I waited outside the door until I saw her come out of the front of the store.

"Did you run into anyone you know?" I asked.

"I don't think so. It has been a long time since I have been here," she replied.

"I have one change of clothes," I told Anne. "I'll wash these out in the sink if I have to and hang them on the furniture to dry. We'll be here long enough."

"I have a change of clothes," she said. "I tried not to bring more than I had to."

"If you don't mind, I'll clean up first so I can get all this blood off me. I've been seeping blood through the bandanna, but I think the swelling has helped slow it down," I said.

I got into the bathroom and was able to start the pant leg off my swollen thigh. I thought I was going to have to cut it off, but fortunately, my leg, like everyone else's, is smaller below the quadriceps. The trousers started slipping off just as she opened the door and saw me sitting on the closed lid of the stool with pain showing on my face.

"Let me help," she said, slightly impatient as she dropped to her knees in front of me.

"I'm sorry," I said. "I wasn't giving you credit for being capable."

"I grew up on the ranch. We had to do everything. I can handle heavy equipment and drive a Semi or a Bulldozer. Rebecca was too young while I was still here. She didn't get an opportunity to do much of the heavy work," she said, as she helped me take the trousers off and I slipped out of my shirt and socks.

I took everything out of the pockets and threw the jeans on the shower floor and poured Peroxide over the blood on them. I stepped into the shower and pored more of the Peroxide over my leg and watched it foam the blood away and made it start bleeding again. I showered while trying to keep the water from hitting the wound directly so it wouldn't be any more painful than it was already.

She handed me the bottle of Ibuprofen, so I took three of them. The three inch gash caused by the near miss was welling out and made me nauseous watching the blood run down my leg. I dried off while trying not to rub the towel on my leg and make it any worse.

I filled the wound with the slightly watered down iodine that burned like crazy. I started to black out, but I managed to hold the small wash towel against the wound to slow the blood until I could start some quick stitches. I stepped out of the shower without trying to cover myself and I felt like I was going to pass out. She met me at the shower door and helped me to a sitting position back on the stool lid.

"I have done this before," she said. "Our horses were always running into fences. We lost some of them when they were cut badly."

"Thanks, that really makes me feel a lot better," I said.

She took the needle and thread and managed to sew the gash deftly in about ten stitches and the bleeding stopped.

"I should have known you would be able to handle wounds of this kind," I said. "But as you can see, I can't think and feel nauseous at the same time."

"It's still seeping blood through the stitches," she said.

"Put some more Iodine on it and let dry. Once dry, I'll put a light amount of the Neosporin on it and a bandage pad over it," I said.

She showered next and changed into a fresh shirt and jeans. They looked a little too new, but it didn't matter for the time being. I opened the small can of pineapple juice she had found and drank some of it for the swelling in my leg.

"See if you can change your appearance some by rolling up your hair and covering it with your scarf," I said.

She twisted her hair and let it settle behind her head like a braid. It covered pretty well with the bandanna tied with the knot behind her neck.

"I don't know if I can, but I'm going to try to put on my other set of jeans. They're not as tight fitting as the ones I was wearing," I said.

"We don't have to go anywhere," she said. "I can go get something for both of us."

"You aren't going to get out my sight, until we're out of this, if we ever are," I said. "My leg may swell up more, but it may start it healing a little faster if I walk on it."

"Is there anything you can say that will make me feel a little less helpless?" she asked quietly.

I started to answer, but I didn't know what to say right away. She took a step closer and pressed against me with her head on my shoulder.

"Nothing I have done since this started has been the right thing. There are dead men out there that I killed. Something I may have had to do when I was an active police officer, but never like this," I said.

It was painful and I hobbled until we reached the small Café, then I managed to hide my painful walk to look as normal as possible. It had been early afternoon when we returned to the room and I fell asleep without trying to undress. I remembered lying down and seeing her standing beside the bed looking concerned at my discomfort but I wasn't aware that I had fallen asleep.

Then I realized that I was awake and I saw her when she walked out of the bathroom. Her hair was tied back and she was wearing one of my white t-shirts that didn't quite cover her hips and didn't cover the swelling of her breasts. I became completely aware of her sensuality and painfully aware of the throbbing pain in my right leg.

She raised the blanket on my left and I moved over slightly to make room. She slipped into the bed and pressed her breasts against my shoulder and put her arm across my chest. I could feel the heat of her body against my leg and my left hip but she lay quiet without moving. I felt myself dropping off to sleep wondering how close it was to sunrise.

Morning came more swiftly than I had imagined, it seemed like only moments ago that she had lay down beside me and now it was almost light outside. I heard the knock on the door before Anne did. I raised the blanket and slipped off the side of the bed quickly. My leg still throbbed, but it wasn't as sore as the night before. I grabbed my jacket and stepped out the door before putting it on.

"I'm glad you came as quickly as you did," I told Holt.
"Where's Anne?" he asked.
"Hopefully, still asleep," I said.
"Will she go with me?" he asked.
"She doesn't have any choice; I have some things to do in Durango. If it works out well, I'll see you at the ranch this evening or tomorrow. If I don't show up, tell Anne that I've gone on to Colorado Springs and then back to my cabin," I said.
"So, what's going to happen after this?" he asked. "How do I deal with these people if they keep after Anne?"
"I don't think that'll be a problem after today," I said. "From what one of the bikers told me yesterday, only a few of them were after Anne. It was a small group of them that included one of the men who showed up at the ranch. Now the main group is heading back to the area of Denver or wherever else they're from."
"It sounds like Anne is moving around," I told Holt when I heard movement coming from the room. I reached out and touched his arm and said, "Give me a couple of minutes to get some of my things, then I'll be on my way."
I went back into the room and saw that Anne was in the bathroom. I picked up my small pack and checked it to see if my Smith 645 was in it. It wasn't. Anne had kept it to put it back on her

belt as soon as she was dressed. I took a quick look around to see if I had left anything else in the room. Holt was waiting beside the door of his dually when I came out of the room. I walked up to him and he held out his hand. I took it and squeezed it slightly and let go.

"How close are you to Anne?" I asked.

"What do you mean?" he asked, a little embarrassed.

"You know that we were thrown together by circumstance only, but she has real respect and affection for you," I said.

"That's because her father and I were friends," he said. "She could be my daughter. I'm at least twenty years older than she is."

"And you're at least ten years younger than me," I said.

"Don't sell yourself short Holt. You have everything going for you. She loves the ranch, which you saved by buying it from her father and I'm sure you bought it to keep it for her. If your sons cared about it, they would be there or on your old ranch."

He looked at me sharply when I said it.

"I don't resent you because she's with you," he said.

"You wouldn't. But I knew there was more to your reserve when I first talked to you," I said. "I know you won't hold it against her because she found herself in my company."

He looked down at his boots, then looked up at me and shrugged his shoulders.

"No, I wouldn't," he said. "What about you? Why would you give her up when she wants to be with you?"

"I have nothing to give up," I said. "She came with me because she was still afraid and she didn't want to continue to put you in danger. She belongs here. We are from completely different worlds. She belongs on a ranch here or somewhere else, it'll just take time to put this behind her."

I didn't take any more time to talk; I had wanted to be down the road just as soon as I could get my pack from the room. I started the bike and let it idle a couple of minutes and started out of the parking lot with the choke still on. I reached the end of the lot and started onto the pavement before I reached down and pushed the choke button back in. I was less than an hour from Farmington, less if the road was clear at this time of the morning. I made Farmington in less than the hour I had estimated, found a phone booth to make a call then continued east for another thirty minutes.

I picked a road at random that went for about a half mile before narrowing into a two rut jeep path. I turned around and headed back in the direction of the highway and stopped at a wide part of the road to set up camp. The road looked fairly unused since at least the last hunting season, so I set up my tent and made a small fire. I waited until early evening before picking up the camp so I could head to Durango, less than fifty miles north on U.S.550. I had no idea what I was looking for, but I had a feeling that I would know when I saw something.

I reached the intersection of U.S.550 and Highway 160. I made the turn heading east, which would take me into the Alamosa plain in southwest Colorado if I continued east. I was less than ten miles east of Durango in a likely area for the bikers to set up camp if they were still in this area.

I had a feeling that they were. It would have taken a day or two for the whole caravan of trucks and campers to catch up with the riders if they were going to meet here somewhere. I found a road off to the south of the highway and looked at the ruts carefully to make sure there were no motorcycle tracks on it.

Chapter Twenty One

It would have been a lot easier to look at the traffic heading east on the highway in an earlier part of the day, but I had to be sure I could hide out in the darkness. Any traffic I saw moving in the daylight would also be able to see me. I was there about two hours when I heard traffic coming from the west. It was what I was waiting for. I watched several trucks and campers go by in the distance about forty or fifty feet from my vantage point off the highway. I waited only a few minutes after I heard what I hoped was the last of the caravan.

I started my bike and rolled close to the intersection and couldn't see any lights in either direction when I stopped at the pavement. I pulled out, still worried that I may have pulled out too soon and another one of their caravan might come up behind me. I was committed now. If any of them came into view now, I wouldn't have any choice but to go on east after I saw where they were going.

I accelerated and kept a steady seventy five miles per hour, until I saw tail lights about a quarter of a mile in front of me. Excitement hit me when I saw the tail lights brighten in the distance. They were slowing down to make a turn. I switched off my lights then turned the ignition switch one more stop and shut off the engine so I could coast to a stop without having to gear down and make a lot of exhaust noise. I took a chance that I could at least see the road, or stop before I went into the ditch at the edge of the pavement. I looked into my rear view mirrors and I saw that there was no traffic behind me. I stopped and breathed a sigh of relief that I was still on the pavement and on an uphill level of the highway.

I could see that some of the vehicles ahead were turning off the highway to the left side of the road and some of them were continuing east on the highway. I waited until all of them were out of sight and looked around until I could see in the darkness. I let the bike roll backwards and turned the handle bars to the left.

When the rear wheel reached the edge of the pavement, I turned to the right and started rolling in the direction of Durango. I turned on the ignition and kicked the toe shift a couple of times until I got it in third gear. I released the clutch and the bike started with a jerk. I accelerated gradually and found the road which lead to the site of my camp. I had to get back to their camp and scout it out.

There wasn't any traffic all the way out to where I had set up camp. I knew it was at least a quarter of a mile to where I had seen the trucks and campers turning off the highway. It was very dark and there was no traffic, so I walked on the pavement and found the road. I continued walking on the road until I heard sounds coming from the woods off to the right.

Moving slowly, I was able to get close enough to where the clearing and camp site should be, that I could see light from their fires. The approach could be guarded, so I headed into the woods and crouched low while I moved until I could see the light from their fires again. I crawled slowly until I got in position to see into the clearing.

I had been watching the well lighted clearing for about an hour. It wasn't hard to figure out who it was that seemed to be the center of attention at the fire. Two men who were sitting close to him, left at different times and returned and others stopped to converse briefly, but he remained. When he put a beer bottle down another was brought to him. He had to be the one called "Evan." It was going to be a long wait. It confirmed that this was the right camp when I saw one of the men wearing their colors. It was definitely two gold wings with a skull.

The gathering was in motion, but quieter than the rally in Holbrook had been. It was almost ten o'clock, but it didn't matter. I had to wait until I found out where he slept. I had slept for a long time last night; that and the painful throb in my leg should keep me awake. For the first time since I had been watching for the past hour or so, he got up from his place at the fire and started walking away. He made his way to a camper at the edge of the clearing

I had stopped frequently to look around me as much as I could, while I had been getting close to the clearing and I hadn't seen or heard anyone moving in the woods. That didn't mean they weren't out there. I scanned the edges of the clearing again and located two of them that had positioned themselves to watch the road coming into the clearing. I would have to find another way out to the road and check carefully for any other sentries watching the woods.

It was after midnight when the last of them finally went to their campers or tents or just lay on the ground to sleep near the fire. I waited for another hour until I was certain it would remain quiet. I backed up deeper into the brush I was using for cover and started to make my way out. It would be a lot different in the daylight, so I had to be sure I could get back early enough to give myself enough time to position myself long before daylight.

I didn't know what effect it would have on the camp when his two scouts didn't return with the support group in the campers and trucks. It might cause them to take a little more caution and set up more sentries, but chances were they were confident that no one would consider coming in uninvited. I kept moving in the direction of the highway, taking care not to make any noise. I was just about to move again when I heard talking off to my left. I went to the ground and started crawling in the direction of the noise.

As I moved to higher ground, I realized that there was a large formation of rocks at the top of the upward slope. There was a defined path leading from the camp clearing to the formation of rocks. I waited to see if the conversation was going to continue then I heard someone walking my way from the path above me and to the right. I watched while the shadow moved past me and headed down the path to the camp. I would have missed this one and been in real trouble if I had moved farther to my right where Evan's camper was parked.

I went quietly off to my right and about fifteen minutes later I was on the highway. It took me another fifteen minutes to get to where I had left the bike. I pushed the bike out to the highway and onto the pavement. I pushed it to get it moving on the downhill grade then swung my leg over and allowed it to roll until I was far enough down the road that the engine wouldn't be heard when I started it.

Twenty minutes or so later I was entering Durango. The motel I was looking for was on the west end of the city near the airport road. I checked in and went to my room so I could check the bandage on my leg. It was red and the swelling was down more, but it was still painful when I put a fresh dressing on it. The liquid hair colors darkened my hair and beard enough to change my appearance. By washing out the dye later and shaving off my beard, I could change my appearance again. I put on a ball cap and my gray sweater before I made a phone call to another room.

"Are you ready?" I asked.

I watched the path leading from the main clearing to the sentry's vantage at the top of the rocks. It was still very early morning and I could see the path clearly in the diffused light from the moon that was to my left. There was a lot of time left before sunrise. I wanted the new relief to get up on the rocks then I would try to get close to him undetected. He may be more alert on his way up than after he got there and he was focused on watching the clearing. The man who had been on watch came down after a couple of minutes and I watched his shadow going down the path towards the clearing.

It took me what seemed to be about a half hour of very slow quiet climbing before I could see the top of the rocks where his perch must be, then I had to wait for him to move or shuffle his feet before I could locate him. I counted on him to be looking into the camp so he would be facing away from the approach to his vantage point. I took no chances that there would be a struggle. I punched him just slightly to the side of his spine at the back of his head with the brass knuckles on my right fist.

His knees buckled and his chest hit the large rock in front of him, then he slid to the ground. He didn't have a bandanna, so I wouldn't be able to use one to gag him. I had come prepared to restrain any of the sentries I would be able to take out. I used two electrical ties on his wrists, two on his ankles, and then I tied his wrists to his ankles with another. Then a light came on in my head and I thought then to strip his trousers with my knife. I removed one of his boots and stuck one of his socks in his mouth and tied the strip of denim around his mouth to hold it in.

A half hour later I was in position to locate another of the sentries at the edge of the camp's clearing. He had just gotten relieved and gave me an opportunity when he decided to move off to his right a short way into the trees. I watched him for a moment to see what he was doing before I started moving. I crawled to a point where he would either have to walk by or stop, otherwise he would be out of sight of the clearing in the darkness. He stopped and looked back over his shoulder then unbuttoned his pants to relieve himself. He must have been pissing on a rock for the loud noise that it made and perfect to cover the rest of my approach.

I tried not to hit bone when I hit him just under the left ear before he got his head turned back. The heavy brass knuckles had the same definite effect as they had on the sentry up on the rock. He was out cold. I listened for almost a minute for him to breath. I rolled him over quickly and gagged him with one of his socks and his bandana. I half expected to pull the boots off only to find that he had no socks on. I tied his bandanna tightly in his mouth and behind his head. He might choke, but I wasn't too concerned because I was running out of time. It would be light soon so I had to make my move now.

It took me a couple of minutes to locate the third sentry and another ten to crawl to his location. I reached him and waited for another opportunity to move. It was almost a disaster when I got within range. I had watched until he turned to look into the clearing then I started to get up to make my move to get behind him. I couldn't talk to him like they do in the movies, saying, "Don't move I have you covered," or put a pistol to his head and tell him to be quiet. He had to be incapacitated quickly and efficiently. He looked off to his left to the left side of the clearing and jerked like he was startled.

I moved quickly when I saw that he was going to walk back to the clearing. He was moving forward with his right foot about to touch the ground when I reached him. I stepped hard on the back of his left leg, grabbed his left arm just above the elbow and hit him hard at the base of his neck trying to miss the spine. He fell forward and his head struck the tree right in front of him. All that remained now was to position myself for the next step.

I waited at the side of the camper that I had seen Evan enter last night. It would just be my luck that he had not stayed there all night. It was getting lighter now and there was movement in different areas of the camp. I thought I was going to have to use the cover of the noise of activity around the camp to get into the camper if he didn't come out soon; but I heard movement inside.

I didn't have to wait long. I positioned myself at the right side of the camper to keep out of view of the rest of the camp. The door opened toward me and I waited until I saw his foot reach the lower steps of the camper. I pulled the door open wider and stuck my Colt 45 in his ribs on his left side behind his arm then gripped his left arm.

"It's a 45 caliber 230 grain load. With the muzzle pressed tight against you they won't hear more than a pop and you'll be dead before they know where the noise came from," I said just loud enough for him to hear.

I took a quick look inside the camper in case anyone else had been in there. There was no one else.

"What you want man?" he asked.

"I'm here to end this," I said.

"If you shoot, you'll be dead too," he said.

"If I was here to kill you, you'd already be dead and I would be heading back through the woods and my friends would drop about a dozen of your friends before they could figure out where it was coming from," I told him quietly.

"What friends?" he asked.

"There's a scoped Bushmaster out there looking right at you. He's never missed," I added.

"Your play man," he said.

"Why did your boys keep coming after us?" I asked.

"Who are you? And who is it that we're after?" he asked.

"Does the name Jinx mean anything to you?" I asked.

He didn't answer right away, but didn't hesitate or try to evade the question again when he did answer.

"They weren't supposed to," he said. "That's not what we do."

"So what do you do?" I asked.

"We were goin' to a meet in Texas, business you know. Was it you got four of our boys?" He asked.

"There were more than that came after us," I said.

He didn't answer but started to turn his head to the left to get a look at me.

"Don't look at me," I said. "Or this cannon could go off."

Even if he could see me I looked like any other citizen in any place he had ever been. No one could see me where I was standing and if they could, the light was too poor to get a good look.

"There was no more," he said.

"Are you missing Tong and Buzz?" I asked.

"That's six. Those were tough boys," he said. "If they were after you, they would've got you."

"They almost did. One of them is dead. The other one may still be alive with maybe a broken arm or leg, but I didn't shoot him," I said.

"You owe us," he said.

"I don't owe you. It was your boys come after us," I said.

"What you want?" he asked.

"It ends here or you're dead now and my friends drop about a dozen more of you," I said.

"How do I know it ends from you?" he asked.

"You came after me and you're still alive, that's how. It was your boys that were ambushing me. What I did was out of self defense; I just want it to stop," I said.

"So what do I get then? Whatever deal you want a'int enough," he said.

"You and about more than a dozen of your boys get your lives," I said. "Is that enough?"

"Where's Tong and Buzz? We want 'em, we take care of our own," he said.

"I'll give you Tong and Buzz, but you have to wait until tonight to go get them," I said.

"So you think you got all the cards, why you still wantin' to deal?" he asked. "We could still get you."

"It's the law of odds," I told him. "You keep coming after us and I keep making the deck smaller. Sooner or later my luck will run out and your boys may get me or one of the women, but you'll be the first to fall. That's a promise."

"So how I know you won't do it anyway?" he asked.

"I think you're smarter than that sounded. I already told you, had I come here only to kill you, I would have already done it and been halfway home by now. They shot and missed," I told him. "I don't miss."

"Where's Tong and Buzz then?" He asked.

"First rest stop in Arizona going out on 160. Walk directly north until you reach the canyon. It won't be easy, but you'll manage. Their bikes are about sixty feet west of the parking lot in the brush," I said.

"So how you know I keep my end?" he asked.

"I'll be watching the road. If I see any of you headed in that direction before six o'clock this evening, I'll scout you out again. You'll never make Denver," I said.

"Deal," he said.

"Turn around and face into the camper. Stay that way for five minutes. If I see you trying to look, my friends take you out first," I said.

Chapter Twenty Two

I looked behind me and to my left and started backing out of the clearing into the woods as soon as I had removed my pistol from his side. It took me only five minutes to reach the rocks where I had taken out the first of their sentries. I stopped and listened before I continued to walk past the rock. I went directly through the woods until I reached the road. I knew I was being watched from across the highway as I crossed to the other side. I entered the woods and started making my way to my camp about a quarter mile in the direction of Durango.

"How did it go?" he asked as he stepped out of the brush to walk with me.

"They're heading out of the area for Colorado and beyond. I won't know unless I see them again," I said

We walked close to the edge of the woods, keeping out of sight, where I could look back to see the road a couple of times before heading directly to my camp.

"They won't move until six tonight if he believed me. Even if they move now we still have a head start and can get back to the motel and be down the road," I said.

Walking through the woods takes a little longer than just walking a straight mile, which would take about fifteen minutes at a good pace. I was avoiding walking into any brush and Tom was being careful not brush his gun case at all. The noise would be heard a greater distance than stepping on brush, which we were both avoiding. There was still no traffic on the road. It was almost six in the morning now and we had been walking for almost fifteen minutes.

"We're well out of sight of their camp, but I'm still not willing to walk on the highway," he said.

"We're only about ten minutes from your truck," I said.

"Great. I wasn't up to walking all the way to Durango through the woods," he said chuckling.

"Me either. It's not likely they would follow us through the woods, but you never know, some of them may even be good woodsmen," I said.

We reached Tom's SUV just a few minutes later. He headed it to the highway and stopped short of the pavement. I watched carefully to the right for any traffic coming from the direction of the biker's camp. A small truck went by going in the direction of the camp, but I waited a while longer. I saw a compact car and full size sedan coming in our direction going towards Durango. I waited until the small car passed.

"Now, go ahead and pull out," I said.

He timed it perfectly and we were traveling in front of a blue Buick.

"Are you going to head back to Alaska right away?" he asked.

"No, I'll follow you to Farmington. We can pick up U.S. 44 there and head east to Albuquerque and stay there overnight," I said. "If we head north then it's unlikely that we'll see any of them and even if we do, they won't know me."

"It seems like a round about way to get back to Colorado Springs," he said.

"It was my understanding that they're headed for Denver. They'll want to stay out of traffic, so it's likely that they'll stay on 160 until they reach Monte Vista, then head north on 285 to Denver," I told him.

"What about Anne?' Do you think you'll see her again?" he asked.

"Anything's possible, but I hope she stays put this time," I said.

"Where is she?" he asked. "Was she going to stay in Holbrook, or head back to Tulsa?"

"She may stay in Holbrook for now but the safest and surest thing would have been if she had gone back to Oklahoma right away," I said.

"Do you think they'll still try for her again?" he asked.

"I had hoped that this would end but that's probably not possible. Sooner or later one of them may get a wild hair and show up down there looking for her," I said. "That's why I thought she should stay away from here."

"Well, you put away six of their boys," Tom said. "They have a lot to do to break even."

"Nine. Eight, if the one I didn't shoot is still alive. There were the three who went out to the ranch. She and Holt could have been dead had they showed up at any time since I left here and before I got back. It was just sheer luck that they didn't figure out how to find her before that," I said.

"Well if she had stayed in Tulsa, they wouldn't have found her," he said.

"No, but they could have gone out to the ranch looking innocent and killed Holt in the process. They would have never known if they had the right place, but it was the closest to where they first saw Anne and Rebecca. So now there are eight of them dead and I'll never know for sure if it's over," I said.

"So what do you want to do?" he asked.

"I'll call Holt from Albuquerque," I said.

"This is Holt," the voice on the phone said.

"This is Miguel," I said and paused.

"Anne went back to Tulsa," he said. "You can call her there."

"She didn't want to stay?" I asked.

"I made her an offer to stay a while," he said. "She said it was too close to where it all happened. She said she would keep in touch."

"It's probably the best for now," I said. "It'll give her time to get over some of it, though I doubt anything will ever be the same. Only time will tell. Don't give up on her though. As long as you stay in touch she may decide to come back once it starts to fade out a little."

"Are you headed back to your place?" he asked.

"Yes. I've done all I can do for now," I said.

"It's out of your way, but I have something Anne left for you," he said.

Tom was back in Colorado Springs by the time I called Anne from the Holt ranch. It sounded like Anne, until she spoke again. "This is Rebecca."

"I just wanted to check on Anne," I said.

"She went into town a while ago. I know she will want to talk to you," she said.

"Ok, tell her I called. I'll be on my cell phone after sunset. I'm headed north in a while," I said.

"Are you going to travel at night?" she asked.

"Yes. I'd like to travel for a while before I stop somewhere in Wyoming. I have to pick up my truck in Billings," I answered.

Tom was home and Anne was safe in Tulsa for the time being, all that was left was for me to get back to Alaska. It had been a tiring two trips and I hadn't had time to enjoy the camping yet…but I still had a lot of time after all. I hadn't counted on returning to the Holt ranch but Anne had left my Smith 645 there. I would have returned if Holt had asked me to anyway. I still didn't feel safe anywhere on this route, but I couldn't go on avoiding it or letting it change the rest of my life. There wasn't enough of that left to let even the disastrous events of the last month change everything I was going to do for the rest of it.

Evan didn't seem to be aware of how I had gotten Anne and Rebecca out of their reach and he didn't seem to know how much help I had. He knew I had everything to do with the disappearance of at least six of his brother riders, who must have been close associates in his club or known associates from other clubs.

I was able to pull off a direct threat to him and anyone else that may come after me. Now it was just a matter of whether or not he had control of his club members and other associates to end their pursuit. It sounded like it had been only a group of them that had acted outside the knowledge of the club, according to the one named Tong, and Evan himself.

I was almost sorry that I had almost killed the man named Tong. I had meant only to knock him unconscious, not kill him. The only choice I had was to dispose of him along with the one I had shot, and they were certainly trying to kill me. I hadn't taken the time then to search for my casings. I may have gone back to see if I could find them, but informing Evan of the location of his two boys had taken care of the problem of having to. No one would ever search that area without evidence of anything having happened there and I doubted that Evan would report it.

It was late afternoon when I pulled into the yard at the Holt ranch. I would be on my way as soon as I could, once I had picked up my pistol. Holt was walking around the side of the house when I got my bike stopped and kicked out the kick stand.

"It doesn't look like you're able to stay away from here," he said when he approached me. "You're welcome. Don't get me wrong."

"Thanks. I appreciate that," I said. "I would have welcomed being here under better circumstances."

"Come inside," he said. "I'll get your pistol. You don't have to leave in a hurry this time. Stay as long as you want. I can even show you around the ranch."

"Thanks. I'd like that," I said. "I admired it the first time I saw it. I would have always wondered how the rest of it looked."

I had brought in my small pack so I took off the holster with the Colt 45 in it and placed it in the bag. He handed me my Smith 645, so I placed it in the bag too for the time being.

"Your large bag is in the bedroom there," he said.

"Can I put this one in there too for the time being?" I asked.

"Of course, then we can walk around back on the hill behind the barn," he said. "Most of the layout can be seen from there in all directions."

He continued to talk as we walked out of the house and continued up the slope of the hill behind the barn. There was still a lot of the afternoon left to see the rolling hills and the extent of the nearly two thousand acres of the original three sections of the Stahl ranch.

"My old place is over there," he said, pointing to the east. "You can't see it from here but it's pretty much like this one."

"It looks pretty dry," I said thinking out loud.

"It's early in the year," he said. "It'll green up with some of the spring rains. I have cows east of here and horses on the old ranch. I keep only a few here to ride close in. Most of the range is checked with four wheelers or the truck."

We walked around the side of the house just as a full size gray Buick was pulling into the yard behind my bike. I stayed back when Holt approached the car. A dark haired very attractive woman got out of the car and approached my bike. She looked at it carefully as if trying to memorize the license plate and the paint. She looked at me appraisingly before she walked to where I was standing.

Her dark skin and clear and even features would have made her beautiful; except for the intense and officious attitude she was trying to demonstrate. Her straight dark hair pulled into a braid and her severe business suit added to the coldness I supposed she wanted to display.

"Can we talk?" she asked.

She seemed to be trying to make me nervous, as if letting me know that she knew I had something to hide.

"Well talk," I said.

Holt walked away and went into the house, leaving us to whatever conversation we were about to have.

"Do you know anything about the group of motorcycle riders who went through about two weeks ago?" she asked.

"Who is asking?" I asked her.

She produced an identification card marked "Federal Bureau of Investigation, Special Agent." I started to look down at the name and the picture when she said, "Kathleen Stephenson."

"What is so significant about a bunch of bikers?" I asked.

"They were a large group, probably from several clubs from California, Wyoming and Colorado. If you've been on the highway anywhere between here Winslow you would have seen some of them," she said.

"There are a lot of bikes on the road this time of year," I said.

"Were you riding in the Four Corners area in the last couple of days?" she asked confidently.

"This is as far north as I've been," I said.

"Are you riding alone?" she asked.

"Why don't you just get to the point?" I asked. "Why don't you just ask me what you really want to know? I'll see if I can help."

"I have information that a woman may have been kidnapped by men in one of the groups that rode through here," she said.

"What would I possibly know about that?" I asked.

"You were in their camp near Durango," she said.

"Is there a woman missing?" I asked. "If so, what have I got to do with it?"

"Let me see your identification," she said officially.

I handed her my driver's license. She took it and seemed undecided what to do with it.

"I can take you in," she said. "Sooner or later you're going to tell me what you know about it."

"I can't tell you what I don't know and all that will do is delay my trip," I said. "That is if you have charges of some kind to make."

She didn't have anything she could hold me for. Whatever information she was looking for wasn't about a missing woman. No report had been made to the police or the troopers, except the phone call I made to the State Police in Winslow and the call Holt had made that they didn't follow up. No one showed up to investigate and no other report was made of anyone missing, unless someone else was missing other than Anne or Rebecca.

She was working alone, so there was more to this inquiry than checking on rumors. She looked at me as if trying to decide whether or not to detain me and question me further at a location that would put me at her advantage. She walked back to her car and got into the passenger side of it. She opened an attaché case and took out something that looked like a computer. I waited where I was for about five minutes before she opened the door and walked back to face me.

"Why didn't you tell me you were in the system?" she asked.

"That depends on what system you're talking about" I said.

"You're a retired cop from Colorado," she said. "Let's quit playing games, you could have told me who you are."

"You didn't ask. Anyway I'm retired; it means I'm not active and I'm not required to be anywhere and I can go where I want without missing work," I said.

I thought that should have done it. She would tell me I was going to be detained before she got any more frustrated or she would let it go as a dead end. She had me worried as soon as she identified herself, but her questions left a doubt about what she could do with what she thought she knew up to now.

"Can we sit somewhere and talk about this?" she asked.

"I don't live here, he does," I said and I pointed at the house. Holt had walked to the door and she looked at him.

"Why don't you come inside?" he said. "I have some things to do outside before it gets dark."

She walked into the house and I followed. Holt walked out the door from the kitchen and out of the house. She sat at a chair at the table and I pulled out a chair and sat facing her.

"I'll trust that as police officer you can keep confidential information," she said. "What I'm going to tell you could get me killed or at the very least, destroy months of undercover work."

I just looked at her and held my right hand out, giving her the go ahead sign by turning my palm upward and gesturing towards her.

"I penetrated the biker's club that is at Durango now," she said. "I was in their camp when you showed up."

"There's more to it than someone who looks like me showing up at a biker camp," I said.

"So you're saying it wasn't you?" she asked,

"I can't be in more than one place at once. You can talk to Mr. Holt about where I've been for the last couple of days," I said.

"I was trying to get the confidence of one of the men close to the leader. He has since disappeared. I wasn't forthcoming about the kidnapping, I was aware that he brought a young woman into the camp near Holbrook and she is missing," she went on.

"Maybe she just went home," I said. "If she didn't, maybe she went somewhere else. You're fishing for information that I don't have."

"If you know anything, you can tell me," she said. "I would just like to know what happened to her. It may have something to do with the biker leaving before I could get his confidence."

"Yeah, right," I said. "You don't know anything more than that I may have seen bikers on the highway. That isn't a crime. Have you ever been to Sturgis? I've been there too and run into thousands of them."

"You don't believe me do you?" he asked. "You think I'm trying to trap you into saying something."

"Now you're trying to act as dumb as you think I am," I said.

She didn't reply and I knew she wasn't sure it was me she had seen.

"Why are you here? What lead you to this ranch?" I asked.

"I heard a small bit of the conversation between the two men who picked up the young woman and the president of the club. They said they had found her riding near the highway close to where the rally near Holbrook was held. The president wasn't happy about it but I didn't hear any more of the conversation," she said. "I tried to talk to her once but the man who picked her up got between us."

"So how did that lead you here?" I asked.

"It didn't," she answered. "I was going to look around the area and check all the ranches. I was in Holbrook when you went by, so I just followed you on a hunch."

"Did you talk to anyone in town to see if the girl is actually missing?" I asked.

"Yes, I talked to the marshal. No one has been reported missing. He didn't remember anyone by that description in town, or else he wasn't completely forthcoming with me," she said.

"So if she was at the rally, where did she go?" I asked.

"I don't know. She was in a tent where he had left her. I went to check on her and she was gone. I thought that she must have left the camp just before I went looking for her. He came to the tent looking for her too then left with some others after that, so I know they went looking for her. I haven't seen any of them since," she said.

"And no one in the camp knew any more about where they went," I stated as a question.

"The women aren't allowed to know what's going on, not even the woman who drives the president's truck and camper," she said. "Only a select few members have access to the president."

"So what happens now?" I asked.

"I may not have access to their camp anymore," she said. "One of the men who didn't return was my contact."

"So are you out of the loop now?" I asked.

"No. I still have another contact. I was running supplies and driving one of the campers for another of them. I may still be able to get back in," she said.

"Aren't they going to be missing you by this time?" I asked.

"No, they pulled up camp. Some of the campers started leaving in the late afternoon. I pulled out shortly after that and came here after I picked up a car in Durango," she said.

"So what was the great significance of the visit to the camp by this person you thought was me?" I asked.

"It worried the president," she answered. "According to rumor and what little I was able to overhear, he called in his closest members and prepared to leave the area right away."

"I'm sorry I couldn't have helped," I said.

"You're saying that it wasn't you at the camp?" she asked.

"Coincidence that you even found me here; I happened to be riding and camping near here and trespassed on part of this ranch. Mr. Holt here was hospitable and allowed me to stay and tour his ranch before I leave," I said.

Chapter Twenty Three

I was almost sorry that I couldn't help in some way; anything I would have told her would only start an investigation that could expand into a search for the missing bikers. The bodies would have burned to ashes and the only thing that would be found even if the well was found would be burned metal resembling a motorcycle frame.

The two motorcycles near Durango would have been disposed of by the club as well as the other four in this area, if true to form; Evan would have enlisted only trusted members to dispose of the bodies and the motorcycles. Any investigation or outside knowledge of the missing bikers could only complicate and interfere with club activities.

"My time outside the camp is limited," she said. "I have to get back and continue support for the Run or lose all the time already given to penetrating the club. It would take years to get information on the missing bikers, if ever. Most of these men have no home or address of any kind."

"Believe me, I would help if I could, but there isn't anything I know that could be of any help. I've been retired for almost fifteen years and definitely out of the loop," I told her.

"There has to be something you have seen or know that could help me," she said.

"I can appreciate your frustration. I tried to investigate members of some of the clubs in Colorado Springs only to find that there was no way to get information on their members," I said in support. "They live for the club and hardly, if ever, leave the group. The clubs own their member's bikes. They register them like a company fleet and if they had family, it's in the distant past."

She told me what I needed to know, I thought; that they had pulled out and headed back to Denver or wherever else they called home.

"This isn't over," she said. "Where are you going to be for the next few days?"

"Hard to say. I have some research to do and some friends to see in Colorado, then I'm headed back to Alaska," I said.

"You know I can keep you here," she said.

"You can find me easily enough. I'm not hiding," I said.

Holt stood at the door and watched her drive out of the yard and head for the main road. She would be able to track me down through Department of Motor Vehicle records, through the physical address, if she was astute enough to figure out the Alaska address, which wasn't accurate or clear. The maps kept by the Boroughs are never clear or accurate and the roads named in them may or may not be current and the maps are never up to date. If she tried to find me, she could, but it would take a while.

"Did she know anything?" he asked.

"She knew a lot more than she was willing to tell me," I said. "The main group of bikers was camped near Durango until last night. I went into their camp a couple of days ago and made a deal with the leader."

"What was the deal?" he asked.

"He didn't get killed and half his camp didn't get shot up by one of my friends," I said.

"What was his part of the deal?" he asked.

"He called it off and said they would pull out of the area if I would give him his missing men," I said.

"How many more were missing?" he asked.

"Two more came after me and Anne where we stopped near Four Corners," I answered. "I dropped them into a canyon and hoped it wasn't a traveled area and they wouldn't be found easily. Part of the deal was that I would tell him where they were."

"So what's to keep them from calling in the police with the evidence of two bodies with your bullets in them?" he asked.

"It would have been a problem. One of them was shot and I'm sure he was dead. It looked like both shots went through him but I'm not sure," I replied. "These are outlaw bikers and most of the outer fringe clubs don't report anything to the police. It screws up their unlawful operations."

"What about the rest of them?" he asked.

"So far, my shots have all gone completely through. I chose to use full jacket ammo because I didn't want to get found with police issue or police approved ammo in case I ever got stopped. The hollow points I would have been using almost certainly would not have gone through," I said. "I didn't plan to shoot anyone when I started on this trip, but had I not been reluctant to carry the other ammo it would have added another factor to the problem."

"I had words with the Marshall in town about Anne and Rebecca," he said. "He was curious about not seeing them in town and no one had been at the house."

"What did you tell him?" I asked.

"I told him they were out of town and wouldn't be back for a while and would not be staying in town when they came back" he said.

"That's why the agent didn't have much to go on," I said. "She talked to the Marshall and he had no reports of anyone missing as far as he knew."

"What if they come after you or Anne anyway?" he asked.

"They may. Sooner or later one of them who was in it from the beginning will come by here and try for some payback, if they know where to look," I said. "It can be a long time before Anne and Rebecca can be safe here.

"What about me?" he asked.

"They don't know anything about you. I think it was just coincidence that those three checked this particular road and spotted Anne in your truck," I said.

What I didn't say was that they could come back as tourists to search the area for them at a later date. But it wouldn't be of any use worrying about things that may never happen.

"It's a hell of a way to live, worrying about some bikers looking for
Anne," he said.

"They may just give it up. As far as I know they had no idea who helped Anne or who got Rebecca out of their camp. And they would have no reason to believe that I wouldn't carry out my threat," I said.

"Would you?" he asked.

"They're outlaws and they have a lot more experience fighting than I would ever have and they're not stupid. I doubt they would take a chance any time soon against odds they have no way of knowing," I said.

"What do you mean?" he asked.

"I don't think they know who helped Anne, otherwise the agent who just left would have known more than she did," I said.

"She was pretty observant and thinks she recognized me from their camp at Durango, but I wasn't on the bike there or anywhere she would have seen me. It was just coincidence and good investigation that she put it together when she saw me coming here today."

I stayed overnight at the ranch with Holt to rest before heading back to pick up my rig and get on my way back to Alaska. He had made a life for himself as a Rancher and retired, then returned and had given up his family for the loneliness of the life he loved. I would have liked to stay longer, but there was some strain between us because of Anne and there was only so much of the ranch I was going to see.

Thoughts of Anne were always with me. Had I been younger, any woman attracted to me would have given me second thoughts about spending all my time alone in the Alaska woods. It wasn't a matter of choosing to be alone, but more a matter that after years of being retired and having little contact with anyone socially, it was a way of life. There are people living alone everywhere, most of them by their own choice and beautiful or not, I was still afraid of the consequences of such an involvement.

There are more retired people per capita living in Alaska than anywhere else. Most of them live alone and have few or no close friends. Had I stayed in Colorado after taking early retirement I would certainly have spent time with one or two close friends I had developed while I was an active police officer.

My friend Tom continued to live in a house he had bought shortly after his last divorce and he seemed to have little or no contact with active and retired former associates from work. I didn't contact him at all for the first five years after I retired and that was after he had been retired about a year. I rarely saw any retired officers come to the Police Station to visit in the years before I decided to retire. Most of them retired and faded into obscure lives they had chosen some years before deciding to pull the plug.

We had a picnic and gathering every year that was always attended by most of the active and some of the retired officers and many were seen with a number of friends, but I believe that few of them kept in close contact. I visited with only two of my friends during my off hours and then later only one of them. The other became estranged as a friend because of his petty attempts at discrediting the rest of us after he was promoted to Captain.

Every personality and range of character exists on the job as in every other occupation. There are thieves, sociopaths, liars and altruists in every range of profession including any police department. Mistakes are made in every job and profession which can cause serious problems, but most of those that are minor to mildly serious anywhere else can cause very serious consequences for a police department. So even though the camaraderie exists there is still a limit to their trust. Police officers deal with criminals, sociopaths and murderers all of the time so they become distrusting of everyone, including each other.

The job irritations and conflicts with co-workers in any work place influences the friendships police officers develop and keep. There is no greater range of job irritations and conflicts between co-workers in any other line of work. The flaws in character and personal problems are kept from surfacing for the most part by the demands on their time and they rarely maintain friendships with other police officers even though there is a common bond due to the demands and danger of the work.

Most of them will respond and support fellow officers when they are called upon, regardless of their personal feelings towards them. They know that they need each other when important situations arise and their petty differences or dislikes will be forgotten for the moment.

Fourteen officers were investigated early in my career as a police officer. Some of them had committed crimes in my beat that I had investigated and I never knew until the later that they were the ones involved. Many others had given police information to a local wannabe crime boss who had a relative in the City Manager's office who controlled the promotions. Places on the promotion list could be bought through him and his niece, for at least the higher positions. He had a big dream of controlling the promotions of the higher ranks of officers and according to his plans, would later owe him and be loyal to him.

Not all of the officers involved in the misconduct and corruption were ever convicted of all the charges, although other violations of department policy were discovered in the process that lead to further dismissals and forced further resignations. Some of those investigated that were guilty of other violations weathered the inquiries to remain on the job. For others the charges that had been brought against them were either not proven or were unfounded.

There were always cases of dismissals and resignations from the job over the years for other issues related to misconduct. There were even firings and forced resignations because of minor charges against a few and that successfully caused their departures when other methods and charges had failed. The real cause of trying to force them out of the job hadn't been successful because of lack of evidence or the fact that some of those seeking their dismissal had been guilty of the same violations sometime in their past.

There were supervisors and command officers who would have loved to have fired me over minor issues because of job irritations and personal conflicts on the job. One of those supervisors was my captain, who was a close associate and former friend and another was the commander of a task unit I was assigned to and there was more than one sergeant with whom I had differences.

I wasn't completely innocent. I fell asleep on the job more than once, was borderline insubordinate on more than one occasion and had used excessive force a few times when I felt it was warranted. In my own defense, none of those were innocent or helpless citizens and in more than one case they were hardened criminals who had assaulted police officers as well. One of those sergeants who hoped to find evidence against me for excessive force had been guilty of more than one case of brutality, not just excessive force.

These were some of the reasons that most of us didn't have a lot of close friendships. There were a lot of job irritations, conflicts and jealousies that created hard feelings between us and created a lot of mistrust. They exist in every job in the world, but in deadly dangerous occupations like policing or front line military combat, those conflicts can cause serious consequences. As a police officer you always had to watch your back and that wasn't only from the criminals.

The lack of constant danger on the scale of front line combat makes the conflicts and friendships between soldiers and between police officers a lot different and more uncertain. The incidence of other officers withholding support to another officer in the line of duty is real, yet the exception. So it is, that once they retire they become separated and remain distant from their former associates and friends.

We had fewer friends than most people in other occupations because of our differences, those differences being out of proportion because of the nature and demands of the job. Another reason for lack of contact for me and for many of those that retire and leave some friends behind is that we are mostly loners out of choice. That was the most important reason I had been in the desert that night when Anne stumbled into an arroyo and I found her. I was alone on a lonely ride in the desert because I didn't have any close friends that would accompany me on a long run to the middle of nowhere.

I had gotten involved with Anne Stahl in a relationship which would have otherwise never been possible had I not found her in the desert and saved her life. Not more than a day passed that I didn't think about her with the hope that she would find her life again and be happy. There was nothing I could offer her in the short remainder of my life that could be more than just a selfish thought to end my own loneliness.

I sought companionship and relationships in the times between failed marriages only to have them fail because I hadn't taken the time to make them work or I had gotten into them too easily and for the wrong reasons. This was a relationship I had not sought or had any hope of being successful. That had been part of the reason I had called Holt and asked him to meet me in Ship Rock to pick up Anne. The other reason had been to keep her safe while I did something drastic to put an end to the confrontations with the bikers.

During the past year I had thought of calling and checking to see that she was still safe and had gone on with her life but I was reluctant to push myself into her life again. There was no relationship to try to maintain, only the memory of the warm closeness of a beautiful woman who wouldn't have given me a glance in any other circumstance. Any further contact with her would only make her life difficult and hard for me to return to the solitary life I had resigned myself to.

Chapter Twenty Four

"This is Miguel," I answered the phone. Knowing that it was she, sent a cold shock through me that something had happened to Rebecca.

"Hal Holt passed away," she said, without identifying herself to minimize the shock that it wasn't anyone else or that anything had happened to her.

I couldn't answer right away, just letting out my breath in a sigh that she must have heard at the other end of the line. It had been almost a year since I left the Holt ranch to return to my cabin in Alaska. It was with surprise and shock that I got the call from Anne on a day and time when I had been thinking of her. Anne hadn't returned my call when I called her from the Holt ranch before leaving Arizona. Knowing that I thought she may have felt obligated to me for taking the risk in helping her and Rebecca may have kept her from calling me.

It took most of that year for the events to fade enough that I was almost sleeping most of the night again. I still took the motorcycle out a lot, but I hadn't been out of the state since. Most of my Runs had been short rides and an occasional trip north to Fairbanks or to Valdez. I had since changed the barrel on my Colt 45 and had honed the cartridge receiver on the slide and replaced the extractor.

The receiver and extractor on any automatic pistol can leave identifying marks on a fired casing so that had been changed first. I could just have melted it down but there was no need to, since it was a different pistol now.

"He had been ill for a few months," she said. "I sensed that something was wrong even though he didn't tell me when he called. I came to the ranch in February to see if everything was all right. He died suddenly two days ago."

"What about his family?" I asked.

"His wife died in November. Rebecca came with me for her services, but she was too broken up to come this time," she said. "His sons called because they knew I would be here and informed me that they were not attending. I think they were angry because Hal and their mother were separated when she died."

"I'm really sorry. I know he was a friend and he had great regard for you," I said. "I thought of him as a friend and I regret I didn't know him better."

"He thought a great deal of you" she said.

"I can be there on the earliest flight if I make arrangements right now," I said.

"I want you to come but there is no hurry. He arranged to be cremated and there were no services," she said. "I'm sorry that I called after it is all over, but it was sudden and he had made his own arrangements."

"Then it'll be in about a week," I told her. "It'll take me about that long to haul my bike to Montana and ride the rest of the way."

"What route will you take to reach here?" she asked.

"It will be south on 285 from Denver then 550 until I reach 89 to Flagstaff, more or less the route we took to Four Corners," I said. "I have a feeling that I should avoid Holbrook for the time being."

"Why would that be necessary after all this time?" she asked.

"I don't know. Maybe it's just a hunch on my part. I get those feelings every now and then and when I don't ignore them I seem to avoid problems," I said.

"Do you think any of those same men may be here?" she asked with a worried tone to her voice.

"I don't know why they would, but I want to bring the bike and I would be a lot less noticeable either just driving the truck or riding the bike down there," I said. "I can always go back to Montana for the truck."

The uneventful trip through Canada took five days because I didn't make any long overnight stops. I traveled during the day or night and stopped to sleep when I got too tired to continue. It would have taken less time but I stopped for a little extra time at Liard River to rest and enjoy the hot springs. It brought up old memories of when I left Colorado to retire in Alaska. It had been one of those periods between marriages that had been difficult and had taken me a couple of years to get over, even though I knew I was better off.

It had been a year since I had been in the area of the Four Corners, but I still traveled with a tightness and wariness through there because of the incident which ended with another man dead and the other a possible. Knowing that no one from the group knew me enough to recognize me didn't help.

I had never felt completely safe from retaliation even after fifteen years from those I had arrested over the twenty plus years on the job. These more recent events had been different than the arrests during those years. Men had died. The memory would never fade and I would never feel safe anywhere in the Southwest or Midwest while I was on the road on my bike.

I was returning to Holbrook along the same route into the desert near where I had camped almost a year ago. It would be midmorning before I reached the ranch. It had been almost a pleasant trip even with the dark cloud over me because of the news of Hal Holt's death. I had chosen to ride part of the way so that my trip here would remain flexible and I could leave at any time. I didn't know how long I would stay, but I was already feeling out of place even before I got there.

It must have been a wet spring this year. I could see small tufts of green in the dry grass near the road leading to the ranch. Grass in the prairie clumps up and holds moisture in the roots while the dirt and sand around the clump is worn away by the wind. The spaces in between the clumps will fill in with grass during the rains then dry out during the dry season leaving the clumps that look like tied corn shocks in an autumn cornfield.

It was surprisingly warmer the closer I had gotten to the turnoff to the ranch. It had been cool when I left Flagstaff and I had expected it to be cooler at this time of the morning. I stopped about twenty feet in front of the house and turned off the ignition. It looked deserted or abandoned and I couldn't hear any sounds or movement from the direction of the barn. Just as I was becoming a little worried that something was wrong I heard the distinct sound of horse hooves trotting on packed earth from behind the house.

Just the same, I looked in the direction of both sides of the house and got off the bike to look behind and to both sides at the surrounding low hills. I could see part of the barn as I started around to the right, back in the direction of the house. The dark colored dually was parked almost behind the house where I had seen it when I was here before. There was no sign of the SUV.

Walking carefully and looking right and left as I walked, I approached the back of the house. The blue Honda which I recognized as Anne's car was parked in one of the stalls of the equipment shed next to one of the tractors. Still not trusting what I had seen so far I continued walking towards the barn. The corral where some of the horses were kept was visible where it attached to the back of the barn.

I walked past the equipment stalls attached to the barn and continued past it in the direction of the old road to the building ruins. I heard the sound of leather against wood just as I got past the corner of the barn. I looked to my left through the large open barn through the large arched entry on the other end where it led to the corral. I went between the fence rails of the fence where it attached to the back of the structure.

Inside, the barn was shadowed but everything was clearly lighted by the late morning sun shining through the open part of the barn. There were bridles and hackamores hanging on the short walls in front of stalls to one side and saddles on stands on the other. I waited there to allow my eyes to adjust to the lower light and shadows inside the barn and still didn't see anyone. I decided that the sounds I had heard must have been horses moving around the small corral attached to the barn outside.

There were no visible marks in the yard or toward the barn that I could see other than the car or truck tracks I had seen when I walked in this direction. Looking to both sides and up into the loft, I continued to walk towards the front of the barn to return to the house. I stopped to look to my right, once outside and I could see horses in the corral attached to that side of the building. It was possible that Anne left in the SUV and had not returned. I decided to enter the house through the back door and walk through to check it inside. The air in the house was fresh and had not been closed up except for a short amount of time.

There didn't seem to be anything amiss, so I walked out to my bike and started it. I thought it would be a good idea to park it inside one of the equipment stalls and cover it up to keep it out of sight as well as out of the weather.

I had just parked it and walked out of the stall when a gray SUV came into view heading through the cattle crossing at the end of the yard. When I was sure that I could see the driver and could see that it was Anne, I started walking to the house. I walked around the dually into the front yard just as she was opening the door to exit the vehicle.

She was wearing a light blue western shirt tucked into blue jeans. Her hair was tied back and it was longer and a lighter colored gold brown than I remembered. She was looking down and closing a small brightly colored handbag and wasn't looking in my direction when I stopped near the front door. I didn't want to startle her, so I waited until she looked up and saw where I was standing about forty feet away. She dropped the bag and her eyes were wide and startled at seeing me, as if I had appeared suddenly or dropped out of the sky.

I walked out to meet her and stopped in front of her close enough to reach out to touch her. Her face seemed to melt from a startled look to a look of sadness and then she closed her eyes and reached out to embrace me. She pressed herself against me and I held her tighter when she started to sob as if in pain.

Her knees gave out and she started to slip to the ground in front of me and I held on to her until we were both kneeling. After several minutes she became still but she didn't speak or pull away to look at me. She let go and it felt as if she was going to move away; instead she put her arms over my shoulders and held on tightly kissing my neck and the side of my face.

When she leaned away, she looked at me directly and said, "It was another tough day."

I didn't reply because I thought that she would talk to me when she was ready. We had not had any long conversations during all the time we were running and hiding, even when we had been at the motel outside Albuquerque. The longest she had talked was when she talked about school and the failed marriage and the death of her ex-husband. We stood up from the ground at the same time, but she didn't move away from me right away.

She turned away as if to head into the house and took my left arm in her hands and pulled herself closer as she turned away. She held my left hand with her right and held onto my upper arm with her left hand and guided me to the door. She waited quietly while I removed my jacket and chaps. A shower and a change of clothes would have been the first thing I needed, but I knew there were some things she wanted to say first, or she wouldn't have taken a seat at the table when we came in.

"Would you like a drink or something else?" she asked.

"Just tell me where the glasses are. I can get a glass of water," I said.

She looked at the cupboard just before I started to walk to the sink. I sat across from her after I had gotten a glass of water. I was thirsty enough to stand at the sink to drink it, but I thought it more polite to sit and drink slowly for now.

"He left me the ranch," she said quietly.

"What else has happened?" I asked, avoiding making a comment about the ranch.

"He talked about giving the other ranch to his sons before I knew he was ill. He talked to them on the phone at different times and was very depressed after the last call. He told me later that they didn't want to come out and arrange to transfer the papers. They just wanted him to transfer ownership through an attorney. He changed his mind about it then. He knew they would just sell the ranch without even coming out to see him," she answered.

"What will happen to the ranch then?" I asked.

"He left it to me." she said. "That's the problem. His sons may try to take it to court and contest the will. I don't want his ranch and I don't want this one."

"It was his to give as he saw fit. I don't know much about these things, but it would seem that they have no legal claim to it," I said.

"I don't care if they get it. It belongs to his family. So does this ranch," she said.

"That makes the solution easy. Give it to them and you're out of it, whether or not you care what they think," I said.

"I can do that without any second thoughts," she said. "The real problem is this one. He didn't take ownership of it and the papers were never transferred to him. Father transferred ownership of the ranch to me and Hal continued to make the payments on the mortgage."

"So what is the problem then?" I asked.

"If they contest ownership of the other ranch I will let it go. I don't want it and I don't want this one but Rebecca is entitled to it if she wants it," she answered.

"Then you're making obstacles before they happen," I said. "If it bothers you, give up the Holt ranch and don't worry about this one. They can make noise the rest of their lives, but there is nothing they can do about it. The ranch is in your name. It doesn't matter who made the payments on it."

"If they take it to court it will create a lot of publicity. There is a lot of resentment already from some of the other ranchers who wanted to buy it. Father sold off parts of the ranch to an outside corporation because they offered more for it," she said. "The local ranchers are angry because they didn't have the cash or collateral to buy it and Father didn't want to carry the mortgages for any of them."

"Let them scream until they're blue. They would resent you regardless of what you do because they couldn't make the deal with your father in the first place," I said. "If you give in now and let any of them have it, they'll resent you just the same because someone else got it. No one'll ever be happy."

"It didn't end there," she said. "The corporation that bought sections of the land offered it for sale after Father died."

"I can see why they're frosted over the whole thing then," I said. "You had nothing to do with any of that. Let them be pissed off with your father the rest of their lives if they choose."

She got up then and walked around to stand behind me.

"I have to apologize. Why don't you freshen up and rest for a while," she said and placed her hand on my shoulder. I reached across with my right hand and held her hand on my shoulder then stood up and turned around to face her.

"You smell like a biker," she said with a slight smile. "The shower is over there."

"Where did you smell the rest of them?" I asked with a straight face.

"You seem to have forgotten that they were always upwind," she said.

Her face sobered then and she said, "That is all I can remember of them when they found me. They all smelled of sweat and urine and stale beer. And their awful breath; I think that was what frightened me the most. It smelled like what I would have imagined the doorway to hell to be," she went on.

I didn't want to press her to talk about it further. She would talk about it again now that she had the courage to recall more of it. With that, I walked out the back door to the equipment stalls to get my bags. I didn't see her when I walked in the back door and passed by the kitchen. I walked part way through the living room until I saw her opening the rear hatch of the SUV. I laid out a knit shirt and jeans to change into and took them into the bathroom with me. I changed before I left the bathroom and started into the front room to see if she was still outside.

Chapter Twenty Five

A tall man wearing western clothes and a large hat was standing with his back in my direction talking to Anne and gesturing with his hands. A new dark blue four wheel drive pickup with oversize tires and a lift kit was parked to his left. I was going to stay in the house and not interfere with any of their conversation until I saw him make a move toward her. She tried to push away from him to get distance but her back was too close to the parked SUV.

I started out the door almost at a run and he might not have heard me because she was protesting angrily. She slapped him twice, once with a right and then a left, sending his head back a little, but it didn't stop him. He had just grabbed her right arm in his big hand and was about to slap her when I reached him. I didn't announce myself or give him any warning.

My punch to his right kidney buckled his knees when I hit him. I stepped behind him and took a tight grip on his shirt collar. He went completely to his knees when I stomped behind his left knee with my right foot and put my arm over his shoulder and put his throat in the crook of my arm.

Before he could recover from the kidney strike, I pulled him against me and put my head tight against the side of his and clasped my hands together with my left elbow levering downward behind his left shoulder. As soon as I had him gripped securely with my head tucked tightly behind his, I slipped my grip so that my right thumb and wrist were in the cleft between his throat and the left side of his jaw.

The instant I had the position of my hands secure, I cranked the pressure upward into the Hypoglossal nerve under the jawbone and cut off the circulation of the artery as well. It was the dreaded "Choke Hold" that I had taught in the academy years ago, which was prohibited from use because of improper application by officers. With improper application or deliberate misuse it had caused more than one death in California, when it had been used to put pressure in the front of the throat.

This one wouldn't kill him, unless I kept constant pressure on the Carotid past the point of him blacking out due to the lack of circulation to the brain. I waited only until he slumped into unconsciousness, which past this point he could start losing brain cells every second that the blood was even partially cut off from circulating to his brain. The other danger of collapsing the Hyoid was avoided because I knew well enough not to center the pressure in the front of his throat.

His ten gallon hat had come off and was crushed into the ground into the packed earth and sand when I shifted my weight. While keeping his neck secure in my right arm, I reached down and pulled up his left wrist. As soon as I had his arm secure behind his back, I removed my right arm from his throat and pulled his left arm up so I could grip his wrist in my right hand.

This was the most dangerous point in the fight for me. He was a big man and strong enough to shrug me off his shoulders even before he was fully conscious. With his left wrist securely gripped in my right hand, I slipped my left arm under it until my palm was against his left shoulder blade and his arm and wrist were secure in the cleft of my left bicep and my forearm.

I quickly put my right arm over his shoulder again until his throat was in the cleft of my right arm before he could regain consciousness. I felt him start to move as he was regaining some of his senses and probably about to go into a panic. He would not be aware of what had happened to him past the point of being struck in the kidney hard enough to make him wet his pants and I was surprised that he hadn't lost control of other body functions as well after he lost consciousness.

With my left arm securely under his wrist and the palm of my left hand near his shoulder, I cranked his arm hard upwards while I kept his throat in the crook of my right arm. He was almost conscious enough that he would feel the pain in his arm and shoulder and not buck up like a Brahma bull.

"Aughhh...!" he yelled when I put the pressure on.

I hadn't looked up to see where Anne was when this was going on. All of my attention had been on choking him until I had him under control. I kept him in control in a sitting position in front of me with my right knee on the ground until I was sure he was almost fully conscious.

Only seconds had gone by from the time I had punched him in the kidney through the seven seconds it had taken to put him out. Only a few seconds more had passed until he was regaining consciousness. I spoke directly into his left ear now that I had his full attention.

"I don't know what this is about you big stupid motherfucker, but if you try to move, I'll put you out again," I said.

"You're breakin' my arm," he moaned painfully.

"There is only one reason I am not going to break your arm right now," I went on. "That is, if you don't give me any shit. I'm going to let you go now and I expect you to leave peacefully. If you give me any trouble I will have to permanently scar your big ass. Do you understand?" I asked him.

"I got it," he said. "Just let go of my arm."

He slumped back onto his back on the ground when I released him and stood up and stepped away.

"This a'int over," he said. "I'll be back and you won't jump me from behind."

"It had better be over. There will be a police report made to the Arizona State Police. If you're seen anywhere near here again you will be arrested for trespassing and assault," I said.

I walked quickly to his truck and took two rifles from the Redneck rack. I opened the bolt on the high powered rifle and released the bolt lock, pulling it completely from the slide. I threw the bolt across the yard out of sight and threw the rifle into the bed of his truck. I walked to the front of his truck and jacked the cartridge out of the chamber of the lever action rifle. I swung the rifle against the bumper of his truck, breaking off the stock past the trigger guard and threw it into the truck bed also.

I looked over at Anne where she was leaning with her back against the SUV. She looked at me with a startled look which was almost a look of fear. I couldn't tell at the time if it was fear of me or shock at what had just happened. She started to walk toward me and I waited until she had reached me before I turned to walk to the house.

"Let him get up on his own," I said. "I don't want to have to fight him if he changes his mind now that I don't have control of him anymore."

"Is he all right?" she asked.

"He shouldn't have any permanent damage except maybe to his pride and a wet pair of pants," I said. "He'll have a bit of a headache and a lot of hate for me and you as soon as he figures out what hit him."

We reached the house and turned around to watch him leave. He backed the truck with the wheels spinning and pulled out of the yard in a cloud of dust.

"He can cause a lot of trouble for me," she said.

"Who is he?" I asked.

"Mark Raymond," she answered. "I knew him in school. He was always a bully." "He started coming after me even before I was out of school. It seemed that everywhere I went he was there. He wasn't the only one, only the most obnoxious. I returned before Rebecca was born and went back to school as soon as she was big enough for Mother to take care of her. I came home every break, including part of summer break. It wasn't over even after I came back after so many years. They still remember."

I looked at her as if to ask.

"They suspected that I was pregnant before I finished high school. He threw it in my face that I was an easy mark. That is why I left when I did to go to college in California," she said.

"How is it that Rebecca didn't know?" I asked.

"If she does, she has never mentioned it," she answered. "I guess people stopped talking about it before she started school. Father put her in school in Winslow and she grew up without anyone there knowing about it."

She was quiet for a while and I didn't press her for any more conversation about it.

"You must be tired and hungry," she said. "You have been on the road for almost a week."

"Are you going to call the State Police about Raymond?" I asked.

"That would just make more trouble," she said. "It's his word against mine and it will cause trouble for you."

"Do you think he'll go to the police?" I asked.

"He would if this had happened in town and there was a way for him to take advantage of it," she answered.

"Well, then we'll just have to weather it I suppose," I said.

"Do you want lunch?" she asked again.

"Sure," I answered. "I would like to see the layout of this place too, if it's possible."

"We can do both now if you don't mind taking a little drive," she said.

"Sure." I said, not knowing what she had in mind.

"It looks like you need to clean up again," she said. "I can put something together while you wash up again."

I washed up in the bathroom and took out another shirt before I went back to the kitchen. She had a cooler on the floor with the makings for sandwiches on the table.

"Is beer alright?" she asked. "I have some juice and water too."

"A little of both would be nice," I answered.

I walked back to my bag in the hallway between the bedrooms and took out my Smith 645. I put it on my belt and put an extra magazine in my pocket before walking back to the kitchen. I picked up the closed cooler and headed out the front door to put it in the SUV. She came out the front door with a folded blanket under her arm and a lever action rifle in her right hand.

"That's something I didn't expect," I said.

"Coyotes," she said. "I have never had to shoot one but Rod said they were bothering the cows. I may have to shoot at one if there are any around the calves on that range. Rod White Hawk is one of Hal's hands. He lives in the house at the other ranch. He and his brother take care of the cows and bring in other hands to help when needed."

She drove the SUV around the barn toward the old road which went by the ruins of the old house. The road didn't go near the old well where Holt had burned the stack of pallets. She didn't glance in that direction, she followed the road around the low hills going east. The sun was at just past high noon during this part of the day. The land leveled out but I could see that there were more hills and large pastures with bunches of new grass appearing in the distance.

"It is a lot greener than I had expected it to be. It looks like just a lot of dry prairie from the highway and even from the house," I said.

"The ranch is nearer the foothills than it looks from the ranch house," she said. "There are large green pastures all along the range this side of the mountains. There are running creeks that cross the ranch and small reservoirs that have water in them most of the year."

"Nearly a thousand acres isn't it?" I asked.

"More than twenty five hundred in addition to five sections of BLM land, but it isn't a lot for some of the dryer ranches around here" she said. "It takes a lot of prairie grass to keep cows or sheep here. This ranch has water in a couple of places and large areas of green pasture."

I could see larger hills with green brush and bushes and a lot of green grass in the hollows. She continued to follow the line of the hills to our left until we reached an area with a lot of cedar scrub and tall dried grass and shrubs. The road continued towards large car size boulders and rocks.

There was larger scattered pine and the trees coming into view in the distance and thickening brush and tall dry grass until we reached a large pond that could almost be considered a lake. She turned almost into the rocks when we neared the pond. The trees were Pine and Spruce around the rocks and there was a blanket of short green grass starting to cover the ground. There was a small stream coming from behind the scattering of rocks in the direction she headed.

She stopped the vehicle and said, "We can walk up the hill from here."

I got out and opened the back door and picked up the cooler. She took the blanket and the rifle. I followed her up the sloped hill to a grove of aspens near the rocks. A new cover of green grass was all around the area of the rocks and beyond the rocks, a hot springs.

"Father and Hal cleared a pool here. The water is hot and it runs into the pond all year round," she said.

"All I've seen so far makes this a valuable property. I can see why they wanted it," I said.

"There are a lot of things that make it a great ranch," she said. "It's harsh here in the winter too and there were always losses of the small herd every year, but Father managed to make it successful every year until he became ill and couldn't manage it any more."

We sat on the blanket and made sandwiches and I chose to drink water. It was very warm in the shade even with the small breeze coming up from the east through the meadow. She looked down first then leaned her head back as if her neck was stiff then shrugged her shoulders before she spoke.

"I worked on the ranch off and on during summer break and then for a couple of years before I decided to go back to attend graduate school," she went on, "father turned the ranch over to Hal and moved into town a year before he died. I have lived in town with Rebecca and mother for almost two years."

"Can you manage the ranch?" I asked. "Or, a better question; do you want to?"

"I can but I'm not sure I want to. Too much has happened here now," she said. "I don't want to think about it any more for a while. I have to meet with the attorney in Flagstaff tomorrow to finalize my ownership of the ranch and sign the papers for Hal's ranch."

We returned to the house in the early afternoon. All the equipment, tractors, four wheelers and tools were in working condition. Holt had purchased new tractors or equipment as needed to work the ranch while he had been there.

"Rod White Hawk and his brother are knowledgeable about all the workings of the ranch. They spend most of their time on the old Holt ranch, traveling here only when they are needed," she said. "Most of their time is spent checking on the cattle and horses and mending and checking fences around both ranches. Hal worked Dad's ranch mostly on his own with the help of two other part time hands who checked in with him in the middle of each week."

"Where is the other ranch located?" I asked Anne when we had reached the house.

"The main road goes north past the hills and turns east after a few miles. It goes past the road that goes into the Holt Ranch," she said. "The cattle guard is about seven miles from the intersection of this road and the main road heading north. It's the only one that turns off to the right. I can show you the other ranch this afternoon."

"I'm about worn out for one day. I thought I could sleep last night but I was a little restless," I said.

"You can rest while I do some things outside," she said.

"I will if you don't mind. I could wash some more of the sweat off and lie down for a while," I said.

"I'll be tending to the horses for a while," she said. "If you don't see me later you can find me out near the corrals."

The house had three bedrooms, which included a large master bedroom and two smaller ones set up with double beds. I had taken another shower and slipped on a pair of clean jeans and a t-shirt and lay down on the bed on top the covers. I had never slept so deeply in any time that I could remember. Most of the time over the years my sleep was fitful and I would wake several times and get up during the night, then nap during the day. I thought I would wake up after a couple of hours of rest but I didn't. I woke up in the darkness of the middle of the night in the smaller room I had chosen, disoriented and wondering where I was.

There was a light blanket over me and I was still on top of the blankets. It was a little cool in the room and I hadn't moved or looked around the room yet. I had awakened looking at the ceiling in the almost totally dark room. I looked around now and felt someone beside me under the blankets.

The smell of her hair was unmistakable and I could hear her even quiet breathing as she slept. Not wanting to disturb her sleep, I slipped out of the bed quietly and walked out of the room after slipping some socks on my feet. The moonlight outside lighted the kitchen so I was able to find the sink and a glass of water.

I walked back to the hallway next to the bedroom and took my jacket off one of the wall pegs. I carried it as I walked through the kitchen to the front door. I opened the door quietly and stood on the landing to put my jacket on and sat on the step to look around the yard in the moonlight. I heard the soft movement behind me and Anne opened the door and stepped out on the landing behind me.

"It's beautiful out here at night," I said. "The air is clear all the way out to the horizon in the moonlight."

She knelt behind me and put her arms over my shoulders and pressed against me with her head on the right side of mine. I could feel the softness of her through the robe she was wearing.

"I'm sorry I made you come out here," I said. "It's cold out here even under this leather jacket."

"I have been coming out here just like this as long as I can remember," she said. "I would stay out here until I got cold then I would go back inside and sleep a little better."

"I suppose you'll stay out here and get cold unless I go inside," I said.

I stood up to go inside and followed her through the door. Her hair and her wispy robe flowed like a beautiful apparition when she walked to the bedroom. I took off my jacket and went to the bathroom to rinse out my mouth and drink some more water. She was in bed under the blankets when I walked into the room.

"You don't have to sleep with your clothes on," she said.

I removed my t-shirt and my jeans and socks. I lifted the blankets on my side of the bed and sat on the edge and leaned back to lie down. She moved across the bed when I settled down on my back. She reached across my chest and pulled herself over my left arm until she was lying partly over me with her breasts pressed against my chest.

She circled her arms around my neck with her elbows over my shoulders and straddled me with her legs. I moved my hands down her smooth back, over her hips and thighs and she pressed more tightly against me when my hands reached the back of her legs. She held on to my neck and shoulders and she rolled onto her back, drawing me over her.

I felt her loose hair on my face and the smoothness of her firm neck and shoulders as she moved against me. She moaned softly and pressed upward against me until I shuddered and then pressed against me tighter until I relaxed. She moved softly against me with her mouth open against the side of my neck and face, and then lay still until I thought she was falling asleep.

I woke up lying over her in the dim light never knowing when I had fallen asleep. I heard her sigh when she woke up and she started moving against me again. Her movement became more urgent and I felt my body shudder and she pressed her mouth against my neck before she relaxed and lay still.

Anne was on the way to Flagstaff before I had taken a shower. I left at about midmorning after taking the time to look around the ranch again. There wasn't any reason to expect some kind of retaliation from the Silent Wing or any remaining friends of the eight men I had shot, after a year. Just the same, I wanted to look the ranch over carefully to see if there were any dead spots that could make it vulnerable to attack.

I had never expected to be shot at in the desert and I had never imagined that I would have to help someone escape from a biker camp. My quiet, sometimes boring and almost solitary existence had been changed by my choice of camp sites. I could have just as easily chosen a campsite, miles away in either direction.

Rebecca had gone with them of her own choice and would have been raped repeatedly and then abandoned at the very least. Had Anne been discovered anywhere but at my camp she certainly would have been raped and possibly killed and her killers would have never been known. That was the kind of reasoning I would have had to present in court defending myself for the deaths of any of them. Rebecca's innocent choice to be with them could well complicate my defense and I could well be convicted of Manslaughter at the very least.

I didn't know what kind of retaliation I could expect from Mark Raymond. The outcome of our scuffle would have been a lot different had I met him face to face instead of with his back turned. He had expected Anne to be alone. Apparently he had not approached her before this because Holt was a respected rancher in the area and it was unusual that he would take a chance of being censured by the other ranchers for molesting the daughter of a rancher. But like all occupations and lines of work, all kinds can be found within any segment of population.

"So who is this Mark Raymond?" I had asked her in our conversation last evening.

"I knew him in school and through the association of Mr. Raymond and my father as ranchers," she had answered. "I had little contact with him during the years after that. I saw him once in a while and he seemed polite and reserved with me, as if he wasn't sure I would be sociable."

"Hadn't he ever approached you before this?" I asked.

"No, but he kept coming after me while I was still in school. He just stared at me at times, but he wasn't the only one who stared at me or talked about me," she said. "There were others who approached me and made overtures, some polite others not so and some outright insulting."

Chapter Twenty Six

The hills rose in height in the direction of the foot hills to the north of the ranch, sloping down into the inner valleys closer to the mountains. The contour of the land to the east behind the barn sloped lower in altitude south in the direction of the highway. There were not many blind spots where someone could approach hidden from the house unless it was done under cover of night.

A sniper could set up on the hills north of the ranch in some of the rocks or to the south in the direction of the highway. Someone intent on taking some kind of armed retaliation could carry it out in any number of ways from at least three directions away from the house. Even the barn itself offered concealment in any part of it where someone could hide out and wait for an opportunity to find anyone here unaware.

With this in mind I took Holt's lever action .30 caliber rifle and put it on the seat of the dually and left the ranch shortly before noon to contact Rod White Hawk and his brother. I found the right road on the second try. The first one had taken me into hills covered with dry grass clumps, pinion scrub and scattered bushes. Scouting the ranch and the surrounding hills had given me an idea and a means of turning any possible attack or pursuit. I didn't intend traveling anywhere in the area without a firearm.

I approached the former Holt ranch house where the brothers lived. The house was old like the Stahl ranch house, but it had not been remodeled. It was not run down but it was at least a hundred years old, built in the old gingerbread style with lathe and filigree on the porch and the gables of the roof. It was a pleasant and quaint old house that needed some care and paint to make it look attractive again. The house and most of the buildings had been built in a grove of cottonwood and aspen except for the barn which faced the morning sun.

There was no one at the house. The surrounding buildings were laid out much the same as the Stahl ranch, with tool sheds and equipment stalls and corrals to keep horses and some of the cattle. I could see the front of an old Chevrolet flatbed truck sticking out of one of the equipment stalls parked next to a faded yellow tractor with a front loading bucket on it. The corrals were much larger on this ranch, probably to keep the cattle penned and fed during the winter months.

The layout of the other ranch suggested that a lot of improvements on the Stahl ranch were made by Holt after he took it over. Whatever respect I had developed for him during the short time I knew him grew even more. It wasn't hard to understand why these ranchers were tough and capable. They made a living and were successful in a harsh dry country in the summer and through the harsh cold winters. The terrain was difficult and the land hostile even where there was adequate water available as on the Stahl ranch.

My sense of direction was off when I first drove the big dually pickup into the yard. Not until I exited the cab did I notice that the sun was to the right side of the house, which faced south instead of west like the other house. The barn and corrals were off to the left and the grounds level with the hills rising off to the right, with lower plains beyond and behind me. The contour of the land behind the barn and corrals to the north dropped lower for miles then rose into the foothills of the mountains.

I walked between the house and a large cabin that may have been a bunkhouse years ago. I walked through the large open sliding door of the barn and through the sunlit interior to the open double doors in back. Some of the stalls on the left of the barn were open and I could smell the mixture of manure and straw coming from them. The barn floor was hard packed dirt littered with bits of straw.

The sound of voices seemed to be coming from the area behind the barn surrounded by a corral fence. The corrals were all empty as far as I could see. Two young boys were walking into the open gate of the corral from a large mound of manure mixed with straw. One of them was pushing a wheel barrow and the other carried a wide long tined pitchfork resembling one I had used many years ago to load sugar beets into a truck.

As they came closer I could see that the dark haired boys were in their late teens and tall, one wearing a light colored plaid shirt and the other a light colored one of plain cotton. They didn't seem surprised at seeing me standing in the middle of the corral and stopped ten feet away looking at me with dark curious eyes.

"I'm looking for Rod or Stephen," I stated.

"They're out on the East Range checking the water holes," the older boy in the plaid shirt said.

"When do they usually come in?" I asked.

He shrugged his shoulders.

"I came over from the other ranch," I said. "How do I get to where they are?"

The boys looked at each other and the other one shrugged his shoulders.

"I'll show you where," he said.

I took the cooler off the seat of the dually and levered the driver's seat forward so I could place it behind it.

"This is Holt's truck," the younger boy said. "Where is miz Holt?" he asked.

"You mean Miss Stahl," I said, looking at the younger boy who had climbed into the truck and sat in the middle of the seat. "She had some business to take care of today."

The other boy had climbed into the seat next to him and they looked at each other then looked forward when I started the truck to leave the yard.

"Go that way to the road," the younger boy said pointing to south where I had come in off the main road.

I followed his directions until I reached a road that went off to the east and wound through low hills and followed an arroyo to the open prairie beyond. The grass was beginning to grow in the open areas between the clumps of dry grass. The road followed the edge of a long low mesa gradually turning to the north into a long valley covered with yellow brown grass and sparse brush and scrub pine. I had seen at least two of the old wind driven mills that I knew were used to draw water from the shallow water table.

I couldn't see whether they were active wells and there was no wind to show that they would turn to draw any water. It was too early in the spring to see if the area around the water tanks was green to indicate that there was water in them or had spilled over onto the ground around them. I could see two old pickup trucks close to a stand of sparse aspens and brush ahead of us. When I drove closer, I could see ruts and paths in the sides of the road, which had been made by the livestock moving back and forth in the direction of the tanks behind me.

I stopped behind the trucks and got out to walk in the direction of the small grove of aspens. Beyond the trees was a dry reservoir with caked dirt and dry mud in it. A small part of it had been a natural depression at the base of the rocks where a dry stream bed wound through the hills from a higher location beyond.

The two men were walking among the rocks in the direction of the dry lake bed where I was standing waiting for them. Both of them were lean and muscled where I could see their arms below their rolled up shirt sleeves and both were taller than me.

Both men had light tanned complexions and dark eyes and dark hair. They were not Caucasian, but it was not obvious that they were Indian. The older one stopped about twenty feet away from where I was standing and turned in my direction with a look that seemed curious yet suspicious.

The younger one clearly resembled the older, but with softer more handsome features. Both of them wore light colored plaid shirts; the older light blue checkered, the younger a light rose colored shirt with lines of multi-colored squares. They both looked in the direction of Holt's dually then back at me and their expressions turned from one of suspicion to interest.

"I'm Miguel," I said when I approached them to stand about five feet away.

"Rod White Hawk," he said and pointed at the other young man.

"This is Stephen. We worked for Holt."

"I'll be at the other house for a little while," I said.

"Are you taking over the ranch?" he asked.

"No. I'm not here for that and I don't speak for Miss Stahl either. I'm her friend," I answered.

Stephen looked in the direction of the dually as if to confirm that the boys sitting in the truck were out of earshot of the conversation.

"You the biker got Anne Stahl out of trouble with that outlaw bunch?" he asked.

I smiled at his direct and to the point question.

"Well, all I can say is that I wasn't one of that bunch. How did you get that information?" I asked.

"I heard them talking about it before she left a year ago," he said.

"Does anyone else know about it and why she left?" I asked

Rod White Hawk answered. "They didn't even tell me, I only heard part of their conversation and we don't talk about anything outside the ranch. People too nosy."

"That was you had words with Raymond too was it?" he asked.

"How did you find out about that?" I asked.

"He talks big. He was telling his father yesterday in town. I heard him," Rod answered. "He says he roughed you up some because you were having words with Miss Stahl."

"Well, you can see that I don't appear to be roughed up. He could have, had he wanted to, though. He's pretty big," I said.

They both smiled slightly and he said, "He had a fat lip and the side of his face looked like he skidded in the sand."

"He'll probably be trouble again," I told him. "What do you know about the father?"

"Frederick Raymond," he answered. "Hard ol' man, don't bother us; but he never hired us either."

"The pond looks like it's been dry for some time," I said. "What are you trying to do?"

"We'll bring a backhoe and see if we can free the stream from under the rocks and sand here," he said. "You can see all the moisture over in the rocks where it's seeping out but most of it is sinking into the ground before it reaches the pond. There's more water around the ranch but this one was the best when it was runnin' into the pond." I looked across the pond into the rolling prairie to the south.

"How much water was there when the spring was running?" I asked.

"It was always small but it was steady," he said.

"It's probably from a stream that comes off the mountain then goes underground," I said. "It looks like it came out of the ground here for a long time. Maybe the upper stream is dry or changed course."

"I went up quite a ways and couldn't find water in the original stream, but it's wet around here, like a spring trying to break out," said Rod.

"It could be that it found a new channel when it slowed down in the winter. It will either resurface here again or it will come out of the ground farther down the slope over there," I said and pointed to the south.

He looked around first toward the mountain then south in the direction the contour of the ranch sloped into lower elevation.

"If you dig deep enough for it to run out again it may resurface or it may take the direction of least resistance and the new channel under here will fill up with mud and clay," I said.

They looked at each other and nodded their heads in agreement.

I had seen a dark colored pickup coming up the road in the distance before I turned toward the ranch house off the main road. I knew I could have trouble when I saw the white dually parked in the yard. The pickup was coming at a pretty good clip and wasn't far behind me when I started into the main yard.

I slowed down to pass the truck in the yard on the left and turned right to stop between it and the house. I grabbed the 30.30 lever action when I opened the door to get out so the dually was between me and the white truck. I had just cleared the cab so I was looking in that direction over the bed of the dually. It was Mark Raymond's pickup that had followed me into the yard and stopped next to the white dually.

The driver of the dually, an older man, had exited the dually and had started to walk to meet me. I walked around the dually and approached the older man where he had stopped dead in his tracks and was watching me carefully. It looked like all the color had drained from his face and he was about to back step to his truck.

"Who are you?" he asked.

"Who are you?" I asked him.

"Fred Raymond," he answered in an almost strained voice.

"I let him go the last time he was here even though Anne should have had him arrested," I said.

He looked like he wasn't sure he should answer.

"You haven't told me who you are," he said gruffly.

"And I'm not going to," I said.

"He said you jumped him from behind when he came here to talk to Anne," he said.

"Well, it seems you already know who I am," I said. "It wasn't a friendly conversation and I did jump him from behind, but I was good to him, as you can see. He was about to hit her when I got to him."

"That's a lie!" Mark almost shouted.

"Well, she'll be along any time now. She'll tell you herself and then call the state police and have him arrested for trespassing and assault," I said.

Chapter Twenty Seven

We didn't have long to wait. Anne returned shortly after five o'clock. She drove past both their trucks and stopped the SUV next to the house. I still held the lowered the rifle in my right hand when she approached where we were standing.

"Why are you here Mr. Raymond?" she asked.

I looked in the direction of Mark Raymond just as she asked and watched him drop his gaze to his boots and his face flushed red at the cheeks.

"Mark said this man jumped him when he was here to talk to you about the ranch," he said.

"That is a lie," she said. "We had no conversation about the ranch. He insulted me and was about to strike me when this man intervened."

"I don't believe that," he said.

"I don't care what you believe," she said.

"I didn't come here to hurt anyone," he said. "Mark's pushy at times. I should have known he was stretching the truth; it's my fault for not making it clear I wanted to talk to you myself."

"It's a little late for apologies after he lied and you believed him," she said.

"Nothing happened and no one got hurt," he said. "I come to talk business with you."

"We have no business to talk about," she said.

"I was friends with your father," he said. "I offered to buy part of his ranch but he sold it off to strangers."

"You wanted to take advantage of him because he was ill; you were no friend of his," she said. "He had better offers from the corporations."

"You won't be able to manage all this," he said. "Maybe we can work out a lease for part of it."

"Whether or not I can manage it is not your concern," she said. "Good day Mr. Raymond."

I turned and walked away with her before he could answer her. I watched to see if they were going to leave before I reached the house. They both got in their trucks and drove away while she watched them leave. I was seated at the kitchen table when she entered the front door. Her presence would be felt in any room or crowd she walked into. She wasted no movement in her walk nor did she exaggerate any hip sway or shoulder movement as some do to attract attention.

Yet, she would certainly be seen and be given more than a glance. She walked easily and though the movement of her hips was slight it emphasized her gracefulness and her shapely long legs. Her look was sober and without emotion as she walked. She looked at me thoughtfully, not seeming offended at my attention to her movement and open appreciation of her. She was seated across from me and folded her hands on the table before she spoke.

"The attorney doesn't think the ownership of the ranch can be contested. It was clearly recorded in my name. Hal had made an agreement to lease the land and the buildings. I have the lease agreement," she said. "The only requirement Father made was that he pay all costs of upkeep and improvements. He would place a percentage of the proceeds of any sales of cattle or stock in a trust in my name."

"So was the lease for the purpose of operating the ranch or just a way to keep it in your name?" I asked.

"It was done to keep the ranch in my name so that no one could contest the ownership in the future," she answered.

"What about the Holt ranch?" I asked.

"He contacted Joe and Rainey's attorney about their intent to pursue a challenge to the will," she said. "They weren't interested in seeking ownership except to dispose of it. They both received a substantial cash settlement from Hal's estate that was worth much more than the ranch could be sold for. Getting the money was contingent on them releasing their interest in the ranch. So they dropped their claims to it."

"How big is the ranch?" I asked.

"The largest portion of the ranch was leased Bureau of Land Management property and totaled ten sections. The actual ranch is only five sections," she said. "He told me that recently. I never knew about the BLM leases and I never wondered about the size of his ranch."

"What will you do with it then?" I asked.

"I haven't had time to give it much thought," she said.

"I was certain that Raymond would try something to get even for getting his pride damaged," I said.

"I don't know him well enough to know what he would do," she said. "He has roughed up some of the boys who work for his father but no one has ever complained that I am aware of."

"What about the boys who worked for Hal?" I asked. "Has he ever given them any problems?"

"There was nothing ever substantiated," she answered. "They won't complain, even if it is serious."

"Are you considering Raymond's offer to lease or buy the ranch?" I asked.

"No. He offered to buy it from Father for a lot less than it was worth and he wanted him to carry the mortgage," she answered. "I have no objections against him personally or otherwise.

"What about the boys? How well do you know them?" I asked.

"Stephen is a little older than Rebecca. Rod is closer to my age and I have known him all my life. They seem capable enough. They've more or less been managing Hal's ranch and it seems they were taking care of this place too," she said. "Hal had a lot of confidence in Rod, but he was managing his ranch under his supervision. I don't know how it would be if they were completely on their own without Hal's influence. There isn't any doubt that they are capable, but managing on their own would place them in competition with Fred Raymond and the other ranchers."

"What about the thug Mark?" I asked.

"Mark got the worst of a fight with Rod a long time ago, then he and a couple of others jumped him one night. It could have gotten worse, but Father found out about it and talked to Mr. Raymond about it," she said.

"What kind of trouble would he give them now?" I asked.

"Mark will not try anything against Rod by himself," she said. "But they haven't had to compete with anyone yet. Hal made the sales and managed all the finances."

"What about the attorney in Flagstaff?" I asked.

"He could act as a financial advisor," she said. "They could operate the ranch through a power of attorney instead of directly as managers or leasers."

"That would help them get their feet wet and give them time to operate on their own." She went on. "They could find out during that time how much opposition they're going to have going head to head with the other ranchers. On the other hand, it may place the ranchers in a position to have to deal with them instead of opposing them."

My attention was shifted outside the house to the road when I heard the sound of approaching vehicles. I could see two pickup trucks approaching the house when I reached the window.

"It's the boys," I said. "I'll be outside until you're done talking business."

She got up to meet them at the door without any comment. She didn't need an audience while she made whatever arrangements she wanted with them. Holt had confidence in them to take care of his old ranch. Whatever doubts she had about her desire to manage the ranch or dispose of one or both of them would have to be settled. Rod and Stephen White Hawk were still seated at the table when I returned to the house about a half hour later. Both of them stood up from their chairs when I entered the kitchen through the back door.

"No need for that," I said. "You probably have more to talk about."

They both looked at Anne where she was seated across the table then back at me, but they didn't sit down again.

"Is there anything we should know about the bikers that were here a year ago?" Rod asked me.

"There isn't much to tell," I answered. "They were in the area for a few weeks and left, according to what Mr. Holt told me. Is there anything particular that you want to know about?"

"There was a lot of shooting one night west of here and no one seems to know much about it," Rod said. "Mr. Holt told us to report to him anything suspicious, like them hangin' around or checking the ranch roads."

"If there was anything at the time, I'm sure it's over," I said. "I talked to Mr. Holt before I left. There wasn't anything to worry about then."

"If you see anything suspicious you should call me or call the State Police," Anne said.

With that, they excused themselves to Anne, looked in my direction, and then headed for the door. Anne stood up and saw them to the door and watched them drive out of the yard.

"I may have made some hasty decisions, but I have decided to lease out Hal's ranch to them," she said. "I am not certain if I am ready to manage this ranch so I left it open whether or not I will need them to manage this ranch or if I will.

"What will you do then?" I asked, not wanting to ask whether she would stay on and oversee the operation of this ranch or go back to Tulsa.

I didn't ask because I didn't want to give the idea that I wanted to offer advice or get involved in her business.

"What will you do?" she asked me when she turned from the door.

"I haven't thought about it at all," I answered. "I hadn't thought beyond paying my respects to Hal when I came. My rig is parked in Billings. I have to pick it up sometime no matter what I do otherwise."

"When do you have to pick it up?" she asked looking at me calmly almost without emotion.

"Any time," I answered.

My thought that she wouldn't want to get into her life of ranching may have been wrong. She had turned over the Holt ranch on a lease to the White Hawk brothers but she had not talked about what she wanted to do with her father's ranch. She avoided, as I did, direct questions about how long I should stay or what I would do when she became occupied with running the ranch.

I had no right or inclination to advise her on how to carry on with her life, although I thought it was best for her to get on with her life on the ranch. That she had the desire to assume ownership and take up ranching as her way of life wasn't clear. She had been away from the ranch most of her adult life, but it was a life she understood.

"I had thought to leave tomorrow morning," I said. "It doesn't have to be early."

"Why do I feel like I am about to cross a line back into my life and you won't be on the other side?" She asked.

"I wouldn't ask you to give up whatever responsibilities you have just to keep company with me," I answered. "Ranching is a life you grew up with. I don't know how I would fit into this without being in the way."

"I didn't know where I belonged, but now that I have a reason to stay here, I don't want what I do to allow you to feel that you have to go," she said.

"It's selfish of me to consider anything else but what you choose to do with your life," I said. "I fell into your life because of an incredibly stupid act of lawlessness by someone intent on taking you, but I can't assume to have any right to be taking up your time."

"Would you ever deny me any choice I would make?" she asked.

"No one has that right, especially me." I answered.

She walked closer until she was standing less than a step away. She reached out and put her arms over my shoulders and drew against me. I encircled my arms around her back and waist and she pressed her hair into my face and kissed my neck then my cheek then my mouth. She drew away to look at me before she spoke.

"Nothing in my life ever prepared me for the horror I felt and the real possibility of being raped and assaulted. I was terrified of the possibility that you would leave and no one would know what to do to protect us. You took me away from them and stole Rebecca out of their camp then risked yourself when they came after us," she said. "You came back because I called but I don't know how you feel about being here with me."

"I just don't know what to make of your attention," I said. "I did what I had to do without any expectations of you. You could have any man you chose to give half a chance to, so you can understand that I'm more than just a little overwhelmed by you."

"I wanted you to hold me when you took me to your room the first time," she said. "I felt a little embarrassed because you said you were no threat to me. I was still afraid but I was too exhausted to say anything and I fell asleep. Those men made me feel violated even before they were close enough to touch me. Afterward, when I felt safe again I was so relieved that I hadn't been assaulted that I felt clean again. I was drawn to you because I trusted you with my life."

"It's not a sign of weakness to be afraid," I said. "Any one can be overwhelmed by the strength of numbers and circumstance no matter how strong we are or how we are used to dealing with dangerous situations."

"They were relentless and kept after us," she said. "I was shocked when you stalked them even though there were so many of them. I was almost afraid that you were ruthless like them. Were you not afraid?"

"Yes I was afraid, but I knew they meant to kill me if I hesitated," I said.

"I never imagined that I would have to be dependent on someone else for my very life," she went on.

"You should not have had to," I said. "Anyone should be able to live their life without ever knowing the threat of lawlessness."

"Was it wrong of me to offer myself to you?" she asked.

"You did nothing wrong, but it felt wrong for me to become involved with you beyond just getting you out of danger," I said.

"Would you change what has happened between us?" she asked.

"Thinking how life would have been if I had made other choices is not something that's easy to think about," I said.

"I'm not going to get a straight answer, am I? Would you miss me?" she asked with a slight smile and humor dancing in her eyes.

"I always miss you," I said.

"Does that mean that you want to stay?" she asked.

"I want to be with you as long as it doesn't interfere with your life and the responsibilities you want to take on here," I said.

"What is the real reason you called Hal and told him to take me with him?" she asked.

"I wanted you to be safe," I answered. "More than that, I was concerned about dragging you around the country on a bike just because I wanted your company. You have a right to a real life. The only way you will ever have that is if I step aside and allow your life to go back to normal."

"I don't want you to step aside," she said. "I feel safe with you and it feels good to be wanted without any demands on my life. I didn't know if I would see you again if you left without knowing that I want you to be here."

I had slept lightly during the night, waking every time she moved against me. She slept with her arms around my neck and the full length of her body against my side until late into the night when she turned away and pressed her back against me until I held her tightly with my left arm under her neck. She held my right arm firmly under her breasts and breathed softly in her sleep. I had taken my time getting ready to leave to give Anne any opportunity to talk.

I was feeling a little guilty for the first time about trying to convince her to get back on track and take up her responsibilities with the ranch; but more than that, I knew that it was time for me to let go so she could. I knew that I had to find a way to fade out of her life however great it felt to be with her even, with the impossible differences of our lives and the difference in our ages.

She watched me while I packed my bag and got ready to leave.

"What are you going to do?" she asked, her eyes wide in the dim light of the morning. "You're going to do more than just get back to your truck."

"I don't know what I'll be doing, but I want to make sure there aren't any more bikers in the area on the way through," I said.

I told her I would be back soon, even though I had a feeling that she thought I may just continue on north and not be back for a while if at all. She would become absorbed in her responsibilities soon enough and I would soon know if I could just cut myself off and make my way north and back to my cabin.

Highway 160 connects Flagstaff with the four corners area. It continues on east from Durango and through Alamosa, Colorado. It becomes busier closer to the intersection with U.S. 191 because of the traffic converging from all directions towards Farmington, Silverton and Durango. I expected a lot of traffic during the late morning and early afternoon in both directions traveling from Flagstaff north until I picked up 191 to head to Green River, Utah. It was still cold at night and almost until late morning north of Flagstaff this time of year.

The intersection with the road going north into Utah is about sixty miles from Four Corners. After that I would pick up Highway 191 for a short distance before the intersection with Highway 373, which would take me northeast to Interstate 25 on the way to Billings. It was turning out to be a pleasant, although cold ride through mountains and high prairie.

There was a lot less traffic than I expected there to be this time of year in this area of southern Utah. I had not traveled through Green River since I had driven to Seattle many years ago. Instead of going on to the northwest, I would bear slightly east after passing Green River. My fuel consumption was holding at about forty to forty two miles per gallon, slightly down from the trip south just recently. This was probably due to the gradual climb into the higher parts of the Rockies.

The high altitude of some of the passes took me through the cold, then warmer levels of open high mountain prairie. Green River is somewhat larger than when I had passed this way the last time, some thirty years ago, but it would be all right for a fuel and rest stop.

It had taken most of the day to travel the two hundred or so miles from Flagstaff. I would continue on in the morning if there was a good out of the way place to stop for the night. I didn't remember that highway 50 coming in from the east, bypassed the town by almost a mile.

I turned off the highway to Airport Road and turned left onto Green River Road, hoping to find a small café first and then I would backtrack and try to find a small motel to stay for the night. Amazingly enough, I found the Green River Motel shortly after turning onto Green River Road just before dark, which is not long after seven o'clock in this area of mountain country. I checked in and didn't bother to worry about writing down the license number. This was a long way and a year since the incidents in Holbrook, so it was a safe bet that I didn't have to hide myself from anyone looking at the check in cards.

I asked the location of the room before letting the clerk know if it would be suitable. The room happened to be directly behind the motel office with the back of the row of rooms hidden from view from the street. It was easy enough to check behind the room to see if I could conceal the bike in the back, then I took it around the front of the room and checked to see if my front door was visible from the motel office.

It was concealed enough from view and the door was low enough that I was able to roll the bike in. I was able to turn the bike around easily after I pushed the bed against the wall and didn't bother to move it back, once I had the kickstand settled on the phonebook.

I walked about two blocks to the small café and went in to find only a few people inside. I had taken the time to take off my chaps and leather jacket and put on a pullover sweater over my flannel shirt. It was still cool outside and it made my glasses fog over slightly when I entered the door. I sat in the farthest part of the room away from the front door so I could watch the street. I was still careful after many years since retiring and my wariness was returning even more so, after the incidents the year before. I should have been feeling that all of that was well behind me and the bikers had all left the area of northern Arizona, but there was still apprehension and a nagging doubt that it had really ended.

The traffic outside was light, with only an occasional vehicle going by. I was the last to leave the café and I was a little nervous when it came time for me to step outside. It was about eight o'clock and it was dark outside, with only the blue light of the mercury lights on the sidewalks. I walked through the parking lot instead of going directly to my room and circled around so I could see behind the units before I went to the door.

I felt it before I saw what it was that alerted me. I looked to my left at a line of office buildings and there was a shadow of movement. I shouldn't have felt any apprehension at seeing someone near the buildings, since it wasn't that late at night, but I felt the hair on the back of my neck stand up with a chill. I was about to walk towards the end of the row of units when I saw that the shadow was someone walking in my direction. I lost sight of the person walking as I moved in the direction I had started, then waited to see if the walker continued in my direction.

The faint sound of footsteps seemed to be moving closer to the other end of the lot. I saw that it was a woman walking in my direction. It could have been just another guest returning to her room, but I decided to wait until I could see her more clearly. The small amount of blue light from the mercury pole lamps on the street illuminated her. I could see that she had long dark hair and was wearing jeans and a dark sports jacket. I continued to watch with interest to see where she was going.

She stopped in front of number 7, which was my room. She stood away from the door then turned her head to look behind her, then scanned the parking lot and the buildings behind me. The suspicion I had been feeling was confirmed when I finally recognized her as the agent that had followed me to the Holt ranch a year ago.

I felt an ominous ripple creep up the back of my legs as I always had when I suspected a trap and serious consequences were about to happen. I made a nervous gesture of checking the middle of my back to confirm that my pistol was still in place, even though I still felt the bulky shape of it against my skin. I had been trying to remember her name so I could call out to her and not shock her into an aggressive defensive action. I was about to give up and just call out her last name when I remembered.

Chapter Twenty Eight

"**K**athleen Stephenson," I said just loud enough for her to hear me. She visibly flinched then looked in my direction and started to shift her weight to walk in my direction.

"Stay there. I'll come to you," I said, and walked to where she was standing in front of the door of my unit.

I walked right up to her, close enough to see that her eyes were almost round with apprehension. She was tall, but not tall enough to meet my gaze at eye level. I stepped to her left and unlocked the door and pushed it open and stepped in. She stepped in behind me and I closed the door. It was too dark in the room to see so I waited for my eyes to adjust enough to see where she was standing, just inside the door.

"I guess you know that I'm not going to put on any lights," I said.

I could hear her breathing and spoke to her again.

"Whatever you're here for, I'm amazed that you could have seen me coming here and I didn't see you," I said.

"I had been watching the road close to where you turned into town off the highway," she said.

"Well, you couldn't have been watching for me. That would have been the longest long shot anyone ever took after a year. So what were you watching for?" I asked. "And what would you be looking for here? It's been a year since the bikers were in Arizona. Surely they've long since gone back to wherever they came from."

"Well, are you going to tell me anything? Now I'm really curious as to what is going on. Or is it a secret operation?" I asked.

"Yes, they all went back to Denver," she said. "There's been some movement back in this direction by them and another group of bikers."

"The Bandidos," I said. "What have you got to do with them?"

"It isn't the Banditos," she said, pronouncing it with a "t" instead of "d," as I had. "But it's one of the groups that were here last year."

She hesitated as if surprised that I had mentioned something of the movement of the Banditos. I hadn't known anything about their location or their area operations until I had read about one of their members being arrested and held by the FBI in Montana.

"My partner was working inside a club that has been associated with them. I was in contact with him off and on, but he hasn't called me for over a week. I think he may have been found out and something has happened to him," she said.

"So what is it you think I could possibly do?" I asked. "I'm not a cop. I'm retired and I have no authority."

"There were rumors that someone stole a young girl out of a biker's camp," she said. "I don't know what credibility can be placed on any talk of that sort, but I know there was a girl in camp near Holbrook. I saw her and I knew who she was with. She disappeared out of their camp and was never seen again. She was local and no missing persons report was ever made to the local or state authorities."

"She may have just decided that the life was not for her and simply went home," I said.

"There was also a rumor about eight bikers who were in that camp and haven't been seen since, including the man who had her with him," she said. "Try as I might, I couldn't find out anything of their whereabouts or where they were from, other than the clubs they belonged to."

Now I was becoming a little nervous about what she actually knew. It would be a long shot, but there is always a possibility of finding out information if one is tenacious. Holt, however, was dead now, but Anne was on the ranch and she knew of the deaths of at least four of them, including Brooks, who had picked up Rebecca.

The possibility of discovering the deaths of at least the three on the Holt ranch was remote, but still possible. I was certain that the disappearance of the bikers hadn't been reported. Most outlaw bikers come and go and disappear all the time without anyone but a few within the clubs knowing about it. Those few were not likely to report it unless it was caused with some publicity or by a rival biker club.

"You're telling me that with all your resources, you can't track them down by name and license numbers," I said.

"Some of them must have been on record somewhere, but many of them have never been arrested or stopped for an identification check. Now with the newly expanded rules of Homeland security and the Patriot Act, a lot of the information on radical groups should eventually become available, but it hasn't yet," she said.

"I still don't know what you could possibly expect me to do," I said. "I was aware of the practice of most outlaw clubs taking ownership of their prospects bikes when they apply for membership. It would be a sure way to ensure their sincerity in wanting to be a member."

"You're my way back in," she said. "They think I'm just an outsider anyway; a groupie. It wouldn't be suspicious if I show up with another outsider at an open rally where some of the outlaws happen to be. I may be able to talk to some of them and find out more about what happened to my partner."

"You've got to be crazy to be working inside a biker group, but I'm not. I don't intend putting myself in the middle of the murder of an agent or an investigation where I have no authority. I can't even think of any possible reason, however remote, to be in any of this," I said seriously.

"I don't care about the missing bikers," she said. "I have a strong suspicion that you know more than I could possibly prove or that I even care to pursue about the girl in that camp."

"Right, like you're going to be talking through the same side of your mouth if it even looks like I may know anything about a missing girl that isn't even missing," I said sarcastically.

"All you have to do is get me into the rally. It's mixed riders and Free Riders. There'll be a lot of outsiders there, even old farts and fat women," she said.

"Thanks for the vote of confidence, but you could just as easily find a young rider you can influence," I answered.

"Once I'm in, you can leave and go wherever your wandering spirit takes you," she said. "I don't care."

"I'm not convinced that I'll see the last of you no matter what I do," I said. "You know who I am, where I'm going back to and probably have some plans where you would like to send me if you could find even a remote connection with me and what you're talking about."

"I don't know any other way to convince you," she pleaded. "I can't trust any other biker. If I asked anyone else it could turn out to be someone who can cause me trouble or connect me to my partner."

"Any investigation you make could do that for you," I said. "But I guess I don't have to tell you that. I'll take you there. Then I'm outta there and I'm going to tell you now; you get me shot at or in some kind of fight with bikers over this and there could be some serious consequences."

"I'm not sure what you mean," she said.

"You could get me killed," I said. "Once I go into that camp with you everyone there will know who I am. I have no defense against them if they choose to follow me; I won't even know who they are until they're shooting at me."

We'd been standing apart all the time we had been talking while standing in the dark. She moved closer to me and I felt her right hand on my arm. Instinctively, I moved my arm out of her reach and stepped back. She had clearly made a move to entice me with her wiles and I could see that in different clothing and a faint scent, she was quite attractive, but I didn't trust her. Everything about her made me uneasy, like a knowing hunch that kept coming back, making the hair on my neck stand up.

"I'm sorry. I didn't mean to startle you and I didn't mean anything by that," she said.

"You didn't startle me and you don't have to convince me any further," I said. "I can see that you're going to persist until you get what you want, so you need to help me change my appearance."

"I don't understand," she said.

"Since you know your way around you can go out and find me some hair dye and some sunglasses," I said. "I'll shave while you're gone and be ready to go. Make it dark brown dye, some of that shampoo kind, from one of the convenience stores and see if you can find me one of those novelty license plates with a nickname or first name on it."

While she was gone, I removed the windshield and front fender of the bike and removed the bolt-in upper part of the sissy bar. I knew it could still be recognized by the engine and design of the remainder of the bike, but they would have to be seeing it close up to do that. I didn't intend to be standing still any longer than I had to after this.

I heard her knock on the door about a half hour later. She didn't look cautious or worried, so I suspected that she had no trouble finding what I asked for. She watched while I removed my license plate frame and bolted the novelty plate on. It had the name "RON" on it. I put my own plate and the backing frame in my backpack and went to the bathroom with the supplies she brought.

I shampooed the dye into my hair and moustache. I had shaved off my beard and washed my moustache thoroughly while she was gone in hopes that the dye would stick to it. It didn't, so I took the brown shoe dye and colored my mustache with it. I left my chaps and jacket on the floor by the bed then tied a dark bandanna on my head so my newly dyed hair would show without exposing the top front of my head where my hair was thin. I would wear the dark glasses up on my forehead until I entered the area of the rally and pull them down no matter how dark it was.

"Ok, I think I'm ready to go," I said.

She was watching me with a startled and puzzled look as if recognizing me or seeing me for the first time. She may just have caught a glimpse of me if she had been there when I went into Evan's camp near Durango a year ago. I had darkened my hair and shaved clean except for the moustache before I went in.

"If you have any ideas, now is the time to hear them," I said. "Otherwise, I can't help you."

"I haven't changed my mind." She said. "But now I know why I recognized you."

"If your wheels just started to turn, forget it," I said. "All you can possibly know about me is that I look like someone that was in a biker camp. That isn't a crime as far as I know even if I *had* been there."

However, I knew that probable cause for holding me and questioning me could depend on making a case for a possible association with a known and identified outlaw club. She was probably weighing the value of going any further with trying to associate me with them just to hold me and question me further later, against finding her partner, if in fact she was telling me the truth about a missing partner.

I didn't have any choice in any case. She was going to get her way or I was going to be held and questioned until who knows when. My best move was to follow through and then get away from here and take another route to get to billings. She didn't know about my rig in Billings, yet. So, I could probably still get out of this; after that, time was on my side.

The longer it took for them to find me after that, the more remote the possibility of linking me to any missing bikers. I opened the door and stepped outside and waited for her to follow. She didn't seem inclined to want to change what she was wearing, so I didn't mention anything about it.

After I looked around I stepped back inside to roll the bike through the door. I cranked it and motioned for her to get on behind me and we headed out of the parking lot. I turned right onto the access road which would lead back to the highway. I stopped at the intersection. After waiting for her to give me directions, I asked her where we were going.

"We have to take Highway 50 in the direction of Las Vegas," she said. "You'll see Buckhorn Draw Rd. It's about five or ten miles past that. It should be a large rally with a lot of concessions out of Las Vegas and some towns up north. It won't be hard to find."

I hoped it would be as easy to get out of, I thought as I took a right turn onto the highway and headed west. About ten minutes out of Green River, I saw the turnoff for Buckhorn Draw and started looking for the turnoff she had described. The road ran almost parallel to the highway then took a turn north. I headed toward the light, which must have been from the lights illuminating the area of the rally.

She pulled on my shoulder and pointed to the right where I was approaching a road branching off the main road. I took the turn and saw tents and concession trucks set up all along the road leading to a large area. It must have been the site of a rodeo or a cattle loading site sometime in the recent past.

I continued through the large camp until I started seeing motorcycles parked side by side along the road. There were large bonfires scattered through the camp, but I continued until I saw men and women in biker garb near one of them before I slowed down to a slow roll. She tugged at my shoulder again and I rolled to a stop. She got off the bike, taking her time and I saw that she had already been noticed by some of the group around the fire. She stood to my right with her left hand on my arm and looked at me expectantly.

"Good luck," I said and I looked around to see if I could turn to the left and head back down the road.

"Don't leave yet!" she said.

"Sorry, you knew I wasn't going to stay when I agreed to bring you," I told her.

"Wait!" she said excitedly when I started to roll forward.

"See you," I said and pulled ahead and started into a left turn.

"Shit!" she said, as I pulled away.

Tough, I thought as I started back to the main road. My suspicions were correct. She had no intention of allowing me leave, but she was on her own now. She knew what she was getting into when she pressed me into bringing her and I had no intention of taking any more risk. There were no lights behind me when I turned left onto Buckhorn Draw Road, so there was no one following me yet. I picked up speed until I was nearing sixty when I reached the highway.

There was no traffic, so I continued at the same angle of entry to the highway and sped up to seventy five. It didn't seem long at all before I saw the small amount of lights from the town. I headed directly for the motel and pulled into the parking lot to head for my unit. I opened the door and quickly got the bike inside. The bed was still against the wall so it made it easy to start jockeying the bike around to face it in the direction of the door.

I had a nagging suspicion that I may be followed, so I didn't turn on any lights; even though it was almost black dark in the room. After watching for a while through the small opening in the drape, I decided I wasn't going to see anything. The shower didn't take out the color in my hair, but most of the dark dye in my mustache washed out.

I woke sometime after midnight to the sound of someone or something scratching on the door. I picked up my Colt 45 and tried to look past the drape without moving it. I stepped up on a chair and looked over the drapes, but I still couldn't see anything. I stood to the right of the door so that it would open away from me so that I could see who was there as it opened. I reached to open the door, keeping myself at arms length from the area of the door frame.

Someone pushed the door open and I saw the shadow falling across the threshold. Looking a little closer, I could see that it was Agent Stephenson. She had either fallen into the doorway or dropped down to see where I was without making herself a target. I made no sound until I heard a moan from her on the floor. I stepped to the right and around her form on the floor until I could look out the door into the parking lot. After I saw that it was clear, I reached down and took hold of the jacket and dragged her away from the door so I could close it.

She had some cuts on her face, a bloody nose and one of her eyes would be swollen almost closed. I left her on the floor and got a small towel in the bathroom and wet it and rung it out partially, leaving it sopping wet with cold water. There were no other bruises on her face, so she may not have had any broken bones in her face.

She didn't respond to the wet towel except to moan a little. I dragged her to the bed and picked her up by the armpits to see if I could drag her up on the bed without having to pick her up bodily. She wasn't as tall as Anne but she seemed as heavy. I guessed she must be about five foot seven and weighed about a hundred and thirty five. Anne was tall, at least eleven inches over five feet and weighed close to a hundred forty and firm. Agent Stephenson had well-muscled arms and shoulders and I guessed her legs were well muscled as well.

I had lifted Anne on my shoulders into a fireman carry to get her out of the arroyo, and carry her to my camp. It had just about made me pass out with the effort of having to crawl out of the arroyo with her on my back. This was just as difficult because I had to lift her bodily to get her on the bed. After I got her up on the bed I unzipped her jacket and removed it. Something fell out of the pocket of her jacket to the floor with a "thunk."

I looked down and picked it up to see that it was a cell phone. I put it in the pocket of my jeans for the time being. She was wearing a dark blue shirt with long sleeves. I unbuttoned the shirt down to her waist so I could check to see if she might have injuries that could be internal.

She had some reddening across her stomach and the middle of her chest and above her large breasts, but none of the bruises seemed to be serious. She had seemed a little flat in the chest and muscled like an athlete, but part of it was because she was wearing a sports bra under her shirt. I pulled her shirt closed and checked her head. She had a good sized lump with a gash in it on the top of her head that could be pretty serious.

Her eyes responded when I checked them with the flashlight, and not knowing any more of medical conditions, I wet the towel with cold water again and applied it to her face. She responded by moaning and turning her face from side to side, but she didn't open her eyes. I opened her shirt again and put the cold cloth on her stomach and up her chest. She responded by gasping and saying, "Ohhh." I mopped her face again and she took a sharp intake of breath and opened her eyes.

"Do you know where you are?" I asked her.

She stiffened as if startled and started to sit up.

"Just stay down for now," I told her. "Talk to me and tell me if you're hurting anywhere."

She didn't respond immediately.

"Come on," I said. "Talk to me."

"My head hurts," she answered as she started to reach up to touch the top of her head.

"Don't put your hand up there," I said. "You've got a pretty good gash there. It's probably why your head hurts. I cleaned it with some water, but you'll probably need a stitch or two at the hospital or you may get an infection."

"No, I can't do that," she said painfully. "I'll get something to put on it."

"Stay put," I told her. "I'm going to walk down the street and see if that convenience store is open. I should be able to get something to disinfect it and put on a bandage of some sort."

I found an all night store after a couple blocks of walking and bought a box of Band Aids, a small bottle of peroxide, bandages, a small sewing kit and a small bottle of Iodine. I took a bag of ice and a small package of sandwich bags as well. She was in the bath room with the door open washing her face and upper body with a small towel. She grabbed a towel and covered her breasts with it when she heard me at the bathroom door. She must not have heard the front door open and close when I entered the room.

"Sit on the toilet and I'll check the top of your head," I said.

"Come on, sit down," I told her when she balked at having me in the bathroom with her while she was half undressed.

I handed her a plastic bag with ice in it and guided it in her hand to the top of her head and she let the towel drop from her breasts. I could see that some of the bruising was over the whole upper part of her left breast.

"Ow!!" she said as the bag touched the cut on her head and she weaved forward as if she was about to pass out.

"You'll have a pretty good bump and you'll have a hell of a headache in the morning, but I have to get the swelling down so I can clean it and stitch it," I told her.

I cut away the hair from the three inch cut on her head so I could try to close it up. After clearing away a small patch of hair with the disposable razor, I cleaned it with peroxide and put the bag of ice back on while I cut a couple pieces of tape.

"You need stitches," I said.

"No, I can't go to a hospital," she said.

"What are you afraid of?" I asked.

"They might be looking for me," she said. "That's the first place they'll check."

"Just call the Police," I said. "You're official; get the Police involved and make an arrest."

"I can't do that," she said. "It's not serious and if I call anyone now it will flush away a lot of time I already have in this."

She looked directly at me for the first time and said, "Goddamn you for leaving me there!"

"Hey, fuck you," I replied. "You knew I wasn't going to stay when I took you out there. You knew damn well what you were getting into."

"Well, Damn it, you didn't have to leave me there alone," she said.

"I'm not in on this," I said. "This is your job, not mine. I don't know what the fuck you expect of me. I retired a long time ago and I'm not in any shape to be fighting with bikers who are all half my age, besides the fact that you can get more agents than there are bikers out here to help you if you make a phone call. I'm going to patch you up and then I'm leaving and you can take your job and your demands and shove them where the sun don't shine."

"I should take you in and sweat you for a while," she said.

"You know, I would like that," I said. "Then we can find out what is really going on and why you won't call for help."

I found a small needle and white thread in the small kit and stitched the cut on her head as best I could. She moaned with pain the whole time, but she didn't move until I had the last stitch in. I covered the cut with some diluted Iodine and put on a light bandage to keep out any dust. I handed her the ice bag again and gave her three Bromelain tablets for the swelling.

"What are these going to do?" She asked.

"I doubt that you've had anything to eat, so they should take down the swelling in about an hour, unless you develop an infection," I said. "If you do, you'll be in the hospital unconscious without knowing how you got there."

I had put the bike back together when I returned, so it was ready to go. I tied my bag on the back and pushed it closer to the door so I could roll it out. I hadn't noticed that she had dressed while I was tying on my bag and getting ready to leave until I turned to see if I could turn off the light before opening the door. She was standing in the bathroom door when I reached around her to switch off the lights.

She followed me to the bike and said, "You can't just leave me here!"

"I can and I am going to do just that," I said. "What is this? Don't you have other agents you can call for help?"

I opened the door and straddled the bike and rolled it through the door. I didn't bother to see if she was going to close it. I was just about to hit the starter when I heard the door close behind me. I glanced around to see her step through the door and walk to the side of the bike. She put her hand on my shoulder and put her leg over the seat behind me and grabbed me around the waist.

"You're not leaving me here," she said.

"Motherfucker," I said. "You just can't press me into service. I could go to prison just for being with you."

"I won't arrest you," she said. "I know where he is."

"So, make a phone call and get some help," I said. "All you're going to accomplish is get me killed."

"They have a place on the other side of Farmington, on the Colorado side. My partner and I were trying to locate a distribution point for guns in this area. The last time I talked to him he had a possible location and he gave me the general location. He was going there to make sure, but that was almost a month ago," she said excitedly.

"Does this partner of yours have a name?" I asked.

She hesitated before I got an answer, and then said, "James."

"Is that it?" I asked.

"James Kerrington." she answered.

I doubted that was his name, but I had a name I could call him by if we found him.

"He was going to give me the location as soon as he located it so we could start tracking the distribution" she said.

"You weren't going to stop it?" I asked.

"No. The object is to locate the guns and then track them to possible terrorist activities. We can't stop them from getting guns and it's almost impossible anymore to locate the dealers because there are so many, but once we are able to track them and tie them in to possible terrorist activities they may lead to more dangerous weapons" she said.

"This is way over my head," I said. "I retired before any serious terrorist activities started here, at least any visible ones. No one I knew had even any remote suspicions of that type of activity and they wouldn't have believed it if they happened to be watching it from ten feet away."

"This is serious," she said. "There have been some direct connections identified that should have lead to some suspected terrorist cells, but they turned out to be dead ends. The names we had on our watch lists don't seem to be active, or else they are using other organizations to move dangerous materials."

"Including some outlaw biker clubs," I stated as a question.

"Yes, that's why I penetrated some of the clubs through the Silent Wings," she said.

"How did you find out where your partner is?" I asked.

"I made another contact at the rally. He knew where James was going, but they made me as an outsider and tried to kill me. I was out cold in one of the tents for a while. I heard some of them talking about the location and I think I know where it is now," she said.

"How do you know your partner is there?" I asked.

"He was going to try to get into one of the groups that were taking a new supply of weapons to the storage location," she said.

"Why do you have to talk in such general terms and descriptions?
You describe them as groups and where they may be as locations. If I'm going on this trip, I have to know where and who," I said.

"It's too complicated," she said. "We have to get there as soon as possible."

"So what good is going there going to do? Won't it give him away?" I asked.

"He may be dead but I have to find out, and I have to verify the location before they move it. If I call in a large scale raid on the place, someone in one of these towns may be able to tip them off," she said.

"It doesn't look like I'm going to be able to get rid of you until I get myself shot," I said. "I suppose you know you can lose your job over this. You can't just press me into service; I'm a civilian now, retired cop or not."

"I won't tell anyone if you don't," she said.

"Yeah, right; who would believe me if I had anyone to tell?" I answered.

With that, I hit the starter button and the bike started with a pop from the exhaust. I went out across the parking lot at almost an idle trying to keep it quiet even though I knew I could be heard blocks away then realized it didn't matter now. We had to get moving. I reached the main highway and turned left to head south and stopped short of the pavement before I turned my head to talk to her.

"How far south do we go before we reach this place?" I asked.

"We go south to the Devil's highway," she said. "Then we go east from Durango. It's on a little used mountain road that intersects 160."

"You're going to have to hang on," I said. "That's a long way and we'll be lucky to make it before daylight and even then it's taking a chance that we'll be seen coming in. I'm guessing, but it's about a hundred and fifty miles to Farmington and about three to four hours away."

Chapter Twenty Nine

I kept the speed at about seventy five until I reached the intersection of U.S. 160 and Route 666, the Devil's Highway at Cortez and guessed it to be about another fifty miles to Durango. It was about three in the morning with about two hours until daylight at best. If it had been anywhere but in the middle of the steep Colorado Rockies, it would have been daylight about now. We continued on until I could see the lights of Durango about five miles away. I slowed down and stopped on the side of the road, which was fortunately clear of traffic.

"How much farther is this place from Durango?" I asked her.

She didn't respond right way, so I turned around as much as I could to look at her face. She was leaning forward with her head on my shoulder so I leaned back to shift her weight against the sissy bar. I pushed out the kickstand and stepped off the bike to the left and slapped her lightly on the cheek. She opened her eyes then her head dropped forward and she moaned.

"God, my head hurts," she said.

I could see that she was dizzy with pain and probably had a mild concussion.

"You belong in a hospital," I told her. "I'm going to find one in Durango and that's as far as you go until you get some of your FBI buddies here to help you. I've helped you as far as I can."

She reached forward and grabbed my jacket on both my arms and said, "No, I'll be alright. If we don't find him he'll be dead!"

"Oh yes, and in your condition you'll be dead and if I run into anyone on the way or when we get there, I'll be dead," I said.

"It's only another twenty of thirty minutes there from here," she said and looked up at me with tears in her eyes.

I couldn't tell if the tears were for her partner or from the pain on her head.

"Well, you better hope it's not more than that," I said. "It'll be daylight in minutes after that."

I put my leg over the bike and started it to continue into Durango. The streets were still deserted, so I continued to the intersection with highway 160 to head east. I accelerated to seventy five as soon as I cleared the edge of town. A half hour later she tugged on my left shoulder and pointed to the road off to left of the highway which was almost covered with high brush and trees. I stopped as soon as I turned into the road.

"How much farther from here?" I asked.

"I'm not sure. I was told that it's about five miles from the main road," she said.

"Well, I hate to tell you this, but we're going to have to hide the bike soon and walk the rest of the way in," I told her.

"How close can we get?" she asked.

"We're probably taking a chance not parking right here and walking the rest of the way in right now," I said. "I'm going to take a chance and ride a little farther in, but if there's anyone at this place they could hear us coming at anything less than a mile, that is if we can figure out how close we are."

"Well, I was told it was about five miles from the highway, and that it's wooded all the way in except near the complex," she said.

I knew I was taking a chance not hiding the bike before we went any further, but I was reluctant to leave it farther out than it would do us any good in case we needed to get out fast. I checked the mileage by the odometer and pushed it a little by going farther in than the four miles indicated on the meter. I stopped and glanced around at her behind me.

She caught my glance and understood that it meant that she should get off so I could get the bike into the brush. I found an opening in the brush and trees and moved the bike through at almost an idle until I found a suitable place to leave it. It was covered with brush on all sides so the bike could not be easily seen except from a foot or two away.

I looked in both directions trying to orient myself with the surrounding trees. I would have trouble locating the bike here myself, unless I devised a sure way to mark the trail without alerting anyone else as to the location. I walked back to the road a short distance until I couldn't see the bike parked behind the brush. I tied some of the red orange growth in the shrubs with some of the stems of the other brush. I walked out a little further to see if it was noticeable enough for me to see it. I broke some of the stalks as I walked out to further mark the trail.

I was certain I would notice it and I was counting that no one else would be looking for them as markers for something hidden here. When I got back to the road, I looked in the ditch alongside the road for some rocks. There were a lot of rocks, so it wouldn't make my next marker obvious except to me. I crossed the road and marked the opposite side with three rocks close together. Anyone seeing the rocks and recognizing that they might be a marker, might look on that side and finding nothing close enough to the road, they might not look any further.

"Ok, let's go," I told Agent Stephenson. "It'll be full daylight soon. We have to find this place and look it over before its light enough for us to be seen."

"You know, you don't act much like a civilian," she said.

"As in what?" I asked her.

"You marked that location in a way I wouldn't have thought of, and so far, you've been giving the orders," she said.

"You haven't questioned it so far," I replied. "So to me, that means you understand that it's a condition of me being here."

"You mean you'll pull out if I don't agree?" she asked.

"Exactly. I'm here against my own choice," I said. "I'm here because I can't seem to get rid of you, but I don't intend getting myself killed over it."

We had been walking along talking, but I had also been looking at both sides of the road and ahead for any changes in the road that might mean we were close.

"Let's get off the road," I said. "I think I see the clearing ahead. Whatever this complex is, we should be able to walk to the edge of the woods and look it over."

We reached the edge of the woods and I ducked down, hoping she would do the same before we got to the edge of the brush. The several buildings reminded me of a university work camp I had seen when I had been hunting near Creede. All the buildings were the same color and shape and were all arranged so they faced the same direction, not unlike a military installation. The place looked deserted or at least inactive. If there was anyone here, they weren't moving around yet. I could see no vehicles from this angle so I started circling around to my left so I could get a better angle of view.

"If he's here, we're going to have to search the buildings to find him," I told her over my shoulder. "Were you told anything that would give you any idea where he might be?"

I looked behind me and saw that she didn't have a clue as to where to search. She had a blank look, nearing panic or dismay, and probably not knowing what to do. There were three rows of buildings, two of them closer together than the third row. The complex was twelve buildings total; four to a row and what appeared to be two smaller buildings that could be storage sheds between the last row of buildings and the woods.

Each building had at least six windows and two doors in the middle. The second building in the row facing us had both doors open. I couldn't see the front of the other buildings in the other rows to see if all the doors were the same. There were power lines coming in from the woods to the building closest the woods away from us.

"It isn't going to matter anymore. It's almost full daylight now so we may as well start checking the buildings," I told her.

"Where do we start?" she asked.

"We go directly in," I said. "Stay with me until we check the first one. That way we'll know how to get into each one."

We got to the first building in the line to our right as we started towards the complex. We walked around the first building to find that there were two doors in the back of the buildings as well. All the doors in the other rows of buildings were closed and padlocked. I walked back around the first building to check the windows which were just about eye level.

The batteries in my flashlight still had a lot of life in them, so we should be able to see inside the buildings. The inside of the first row of buildings appeared to be arranged like a barracks, with nothing inside them. The second row seemed to be the same until we reached the second building in that row. It was packed almost to the ceiling with boxes of all sizes with debris and packing and broken boards littering the floors between the boxes and the wall. The third building was the same.

"I think we're wasting our time checking the buildings," I said.

"What do you mean?" she asked. "He has to be here somewhere."

"I don't disagree. We should have checked the obvious first," I said then started towards the sheds behind the last row of buildings.

I reached the shed, which had a padlocked door like the larger buildings. I kicked the door as hard as I could. There were tools of all types inside; shovels, rakes hammers and shelves with boxes and cans stacked on them; many of them strewn on the floor. I walked out quickly and kicked in the door of the second shed. It had tools in it as well, with a couple of lawnmowers and sacks stacked against the walls.

I continued to walk to the back of the shed and was startled when I recognized what appeared to be a body in the corner. I checked closer with the flashlight and found that he was alive and was obviously in bad shape. I saw that his hands were tied behind him and his ankles were tied together with strands of wire and I could see the swelling in his feet. He should be dead.

"Is he still alive?" she asked almost in a strained whisper.

"I don't know," I said.

I put my hand in front of his nose to see if I could feel any respiration. He shuddered just as I put my hand close to him, as if he felt the closeness of it. I reached for my knife which was clipped inside my left pocket. I snapped it open quickly and cut the electrical cords from his wrists and reached to his ankles and started cutting the wires on his ankles with the serrated part of the blade. He was a mess. He must have been here several days or longer without food or water.

"That first building in the row closest to us has to have a kitchen or facilities or something," I said. "Let's get him over there."

We dragged him to the first building and I wasted no time after I dropped his arms to kick the door solidly, hoping it would break on the first attempt. It did. I looked in and was rewarded with the sight of long tables and a walled off area that had to be some kind of kitchen. I kicked in the door and walked to a row of sinks and wash basins. The taps were dry, but I found bottled water stacked in the cabinets under a large counter. I walked out the door to where I had left him with Agent Stephenson.

"Let's get him inside," I said, and helped her drag him towards the kitchen.

I splashed water on his face and wiped away the caked blood from several cuts and abrasions. His lips were smashed to pulp and his nose was out of shape. His eyes seemed to be swollen shut and he had clots of dried blood in his hair. I had no doubt that he was bruised over most of his body and probably had broken ribs and internal injuries.

"He needs to be in a hospital," I told her.

"We can't get the local police involved," she said.

"He may be dead soon, even if we get him to a hospital immediately," I said.

"We have no way to get him out of here, and someone could show up anytime, then we'll be dead too. Now make the call!"

I handed her the phone she had been carrying when she fell into my room at the motel, just as she started to pat her pockets looking for it. I didn't wait to see if she was going to make the call. I went outside in full daylight and looked towards the road, then walked around the building and looked in all directions towards the woods. I sensed that there were vehicles coming in this direction even before I heard the motors, quiet though they were. It was the sound of cars or pickup trucks and no motorcycles so far.

"Come on," I said as I went in the door. "We have to move to one of the other buildings now!"

"Why?" she asked.

"We don't have a clear line of fire from here and if we stay here they'll be too close for us to hope they'll miss. Now, damn it, move!!" I yelled at her.

"We can't leave him here!" she said.

"He'll be better off here than we will!" I yelled.

Chapter Thirty

We went out the door and between the first and second buildings in the next row and into the back door of the second building in the row facing the entrance road. I had just enough time to turn over a heavy table almost in front of the open door and pointed to the other one so that she would do the same.

I just hoped that the doors had been left open and wouldn't cause suspicion that would tip them off that we were in the building. If she had any kind of firearm when she found me at Green River, it was long gone. She had nothing with her when she fell into my room and as far as I knew had no access to anything before we left. I had three extra magazines for my Smith 645, so I handed her the Colt 45 with two extra magazines.

"It's got one in the chamber, so don't jack the slide or you'll kick out the first round," I told her when she was about to check the chamber.

"It shoots true to about 25 yards before it starts to drop," I said.

"We can't shoot at them if we don't know who they are!" she yelled back.

"You can wait and find out if you want to; it'll be too late to do anything then!" I yelled back.

There were vehicles coming into the clearing and headed almost directly to the front of the building we were in when I positioned myself to get a good view of them without giving myself away. From my position low on the floor I could see the first one, a dark blue Suburban, which stopped about 50 feet away after turning slightly to the right.

The Suburban was followed by an older pickup and a medium size grey moving van of the type we used to call a Bobtail, which is a truck cab with a large cargo box attached. They were here either to unload and store something or pick up something that we hadn't found in our quick search of the buildings. We had given up a complete inspection of the buildings when I realized that we were searching for her partner Kerrington in the wrong buildings.

They had to be after what was in the large boxes if they weren't here to unload. The pickup stopped to the left of the Suburban and two dark haired men who could have been any nationality stepped out. The passenger stepped out of the pickup with an AK-47 in the port arms position, and turned to face the Suburban.

The driver started to walk around the front of the pickup to approach the Suburban and patted his right hip under his loose shirt as if checking to see if a pistol was still there. I waited until the driver was between the two vehicles next to the passenger. The van was still rolling and started to make a left turn to head around the west side of the buildings.

Not wanting to wait any longer, I had just started to line up the pickup driver and the passenger in my sights when the driver of the suburban opened his door and stepped out. I still hadn't seen any other passengers in the Suburban and I couldn't wait for the van to pull around the side of the buildings or we would certainly be flanked and trapped from at least two sides. I still didn't know if there was anyone else in the van besides the driver and the passenger that I could see. I didn't know who they were and wouldn't have known whether they were cops or not, but the Ak-47 certainly wasn't police issue.

I looked to my left at Stephenson just as she glanced in my direction. I pointed at her, and then I pointed towards our newly arrived company and slightly to their left to try to indicate to her to take the ones to the left. I pointed to myself and then pointed to the right and hoped she would understand. I wasted no more time and took careful aim on the pickup driver and his passenger. I hoped to take out the Ak-47 with the first volley.

The first double tap hit him high on the chest and knocked him backwards and onto the ground. I moved my aim to the right just as the driver started to move, but he was trapped between the passenger and the fender of the pickup. I shot three aimed shots at him and he was kicked backwards as if hit in the chest or stomach just as the driver of the Suburban turned to his left and made a running dive for the back of his vehicle.

He hit the ground near the rear wheel of the SUV and rolled to the left behind it before I could shift my aim towards him. Stephenson had fired, but she must have missed and hit only the front of the Suburban, because I saw the left headlight explode. I couldn't see where her other shots went when she fired twice more.

The van was disappearing from my peripheral vision on my right. I was trying to see if I could locate the driver of the Suburban behind his vehicle. I could see his shadow on the ground behind it from my position low on the floor in the doorway. He yelled something to the pickup driver and his partner in a language I didn't understand.

He must not have realized that I was in a lower position than the bumper of his vehicle, or he didn't realize where the firing had come from. I knew I still had three shots before I had to insert another magazine, so I shot twice at the shadow on the ground behind the Suburban. He didn't move, as far as I could see, and I didn't know if I had hit him or not, but I had raised dust in front of the shadow with at least one shot. Taking careful aim on the shadow of his body, I shot once more then I hit the eject button with my right thumb. I glanced at the magazine as it hit the floor to confirm that it was empty.

"Watch him. Aim low and put some more shots into that shadow behind the SUV if you see any movement," I said in her direction. "I'm going to see where the van is going."

She shot three times as I was going out the back door. I looked to my left and, ran out of the building, jammed in a loaded magazine and continued to the second row of buildings. I knew the large boxes were in the second and third building to my right so I headed between them, hoping that the van hadn't gotten there yet.

I peeked around the building to my left from a low position as the van made a right turn between the second and third row of buildings and was headed my way. I waited until it was even with the third building about forty yards away from me, counted to five, then I opened fire. The van made a hard left turn when the windshield splintered with the three shots I had sent in at the driver and then I fired three more at the passenger.

There wasn't enough space for the van to complete the turn and it hit the building in the third row just to the right of the door, caving in part of the wall. I saw the flash of gunfire and the sound of an AK-47 and ducked back behind the cover of the corner of the building. There hadn't been any more gunfire from the direction of the Suburban or Agent Stephenson.

She came running out of the building we had been in just as I came around the corner heading for the front doors. I kicked the door hard and heard it breaking, then I kicked it again and it opened inward. She followed me in and I directed her to one of the windows at the back and I went to the window on her right.

"What about the guy behind the SUV?" I asked her as I motioned her back to the window.

"He looked like he was dead," she said.

I checked one of the doors and found that it was loosely being held by the padlock and hasp on the outside. I yanked it hard and the screws pulled loose and I opened the door.

"Take a position on the floor by the door," I told her and went back to the window.

I looked over the lower sill of the window just in time to see the passenger of the van opening the door to get out. I fired at him through the multi framed windows. He had the door open and he rolled to his left across the seat to the other side out of my vision.

"Keep your eyes on the van," I said and turned to look at the stack of boxes.

Quickly, I pushed some of the large cardboard boxes aside to reveal what I suspected would be there. There were stacks of green boxes concealed behind and under the larger cardboard boxes. They seemed to be weapons crates and ammo boxes of various sizes. I saw at a quick glance that some of the one by two by three boxes were labeled "Fragmentation Grenades."

One of the lids seemed to be ajar. I dropped the magazine out of my pistol again and slammed in a new one. After toggling the safety to lower the hammer, I slipped my pistol into the holster on my left hip and I lifted the lid on the crate to check inside. There were smaller heavy cardboard colored boxes resembling the cylindrical boxes that tennis balls are packed into, stacked to the top of the box.

If I could guess as to the size of grenades there would be about four or six to a box. I picked up one of the boxes and it seemed heavy enough so I set it on the floor and pulled it open. The box held four round smooth grenades with pull rings in the spring handles. I had never used a live one and I had no idea how long before it would go off after I pulled the pin. The only grenades I had seen up close had been diffused and emptied of powder and they were of the serrated World War II variety "pineapples."

"Stay here and keep your head down," I said as I headed to the front door.

I went out the front door and turned right and headed around to the side so I could see the van. It had crashed almost directly behind this end of the building we were in and the rear corner of the building gave me some concealment from the van. Glancing around the corner, I couldn't see any movement in the van. They had either gotten out of the van and were now trying to flank us around the buildings, or they were staying inside the cab to use it for cover.

The door on the driver's side was visible from my position so I took aim on it to see if I could get a reaction. I fired three times into the center of the door and ducked back around the corner when I saw the barrel of an automatic rifle come up into view. I hoped that my left arm wasn't completely useless. I pulled the pin on one of the grenades, kept the fuse handle pulled tight with my fingers and lobbed the grenade toward the van in a wide under hand pitch.

I saw the muzzle of the rifle flash at least twice and felt a hot thump on my left thigh before I realized I may have been hit. The grenade hit the ground about two feet from the van and rolled under it. I pulled the pin on another and peeked around the corner and lobbed it in the same direction and ducked back. I saw the flash of the first one light up the building next to me before the sound of the explosion registered in my brain.

I heard the sound of what seemed like shotgun pellets strike the walls of the building to my left and saw dust and small pieces of wood explode off the walls. I hadn't seen where the second one had gone, but I thought it had gone in almost the same direction as the first one. I felt my left leg buckle and I fell to my left and realized when my left shoulder hit the ground that I could be in the line of fire. Quickly I rolled over twice toward the building until I touched the wall and knew I would be behind cover.

It had only been seconds since the first grenade had gone off and just when I was wondering if the second was going to go off I saw the flash on the walls of the building. I heard the sound of the explosion again just as I saw the building peppered with the small fragments as with the first explosion, except that this time I saw smoke and heard a secondary.

The van was still out of my line of sight because I had kept behind the cover of the corner of the building. The sounds of metal coming apart and crashing across the ground was followed by fire and smoke and heat from the van around the corner.

I looked around the corner to see how much fire there was from the explosion and saw a man on fire falling out of the driver's side of the van. The door had flung open and the cab of the van was engulfed in flame. Either the burning man was the driver and the passenger hadn't left the cab of the van or what I had seen was the passenger.

The driver had possibly managed to get out before I shot into the cab from the building. If someone else was out there I was in a bad position where I was now. Quickly I headed back to the front of the building to check on Agent Stephenson and realized that I was dragging my left foot. She was still on the floor near the back door with her hands over her head. I went to her quickly and checked to see if she had been hit.

"Jesus, what did you do?" she yelled at me.

"I did what I had to and cut down the odds. There may still be another one of them out there. I couldn't see the second man near the van and I didn't check the cab to see if anyone was left inside," I said.

"We need to check on your partner then make a thorough search of all the buildings to make sure."

She looked at me suddenly, her eyes wide in surprise as if she had forgotten about him in the excitement and gunfire.

"You're bleeding." She said, looking at my left leg.
As if reacting to her observation my leg started to throb and I looked down to see that my leg was soaked with blood down to my ankle.

"You need to go check on your partner," I said.

She left the building at a run and headed in the direction of the building where we had left him. I stuffed two of the round smooth grenades into my pockets and went back to the box and took out another container of four and put it inside my heavy shirt, then went out to check on the van. I could see as I approached that it was still burning hotly. The cab was fully engulfed and smoke was escaping from the seams of the overhead door in the back. I would have to check later when it cooled off enough to look into the cab.

I was able to hobble back away from the heat of the burning van and went in the front door of the building where we had left the unconscious Kerrington. She was kneeling by his side when I approached them in the kitchen. He moaned when I checked for his heartbeat on his throat but he didn't open his eyes or move.

"He's alive, but he must be weakening by the minute," I told her. "Did you make the call for help?"

"Yes, I did, but I have no idea where they will be coming from or how long they'll take to get here," she answered. "They will more than likely get help from Durango or Farmington, so it may be the local Police.

"I'll make a search of the buildings," I said. "I still have to find out what happened to the other one in the van."

I leaned back against the kitchen counter. I felt a wave of dizziness and nausea hit me. It passed and I looked around at the counters and then opened some of the drawers, looking for a towel or something to wrap around my thigh. After checking several drawers I found one with some light gray and blue towels. I wrapped one of the larger ones around my leg to see if I could tie it, and then cut the pant leg open with my knife.

The bullet that had hit my thigh had passed through, closing in the front of my thigh and leaving a gash where the bullet exited in the back of my leg. It was starting to swell, but was only bleeding from the open wound in the back of my leg. I folded one of the towels in a square and pushed it over the wound through the hole I had just cut. After wrapping the larger towel around the folded towel I tied it securely, but not too tight. It was starting to hurt now and throbbed like it was waking up and coming alive with pain.

A quick search of all the buildings took me about a half hour. There was no one else in the cab of the van and there was only one body near it; the burned body of the one who had to be the passenger. Somewhere out there was the driver. The driver of the

SUV, the pickup driver and the passenger were still where they had fallen. The driver of the SUV had been shot in the body and legs and was lying where I had seen the shadow of his body, almost under the rear bumper.

He must have thought the body of the SUV would give him cover, not realizing that from my position in the building, I had a clear shot at him. I had either hit him directly, bounced the shots into him under the vehicle or Stephenson had actually hit something when she shot.

I circled back and found Agent Stephenson sitting on the floor next to Kerrington. My Colt was lying on the floor beside her. I picked it up and slipped it under my belt and she handed me the extra magazines. From the look on her face I was glad I had picked up my colt before she had. She didn't say anything or look at me before I walked away from her to the front door. I picked up my empty magazines for the Smith 645 on my way through the other building and picked up all the brass I could find. She had fired at least three shots from the other building, so I walked back and checked it before I headed back to check on Kerrington.

"He's going to die if we don't get him out of here," she said.

"Then we need to get him into one of the vehicles and get him to a hospital," I said.

She looked at me as if seeing me for the first time and probably dumbfounded because she hadn't thought of using one of the vehicles to move him. I rigged a stretcher with one of the lids from the ammo crates. It would do to drag him to the SUV. If we hadn't killed him yet by moving him from the shed to this building, he would survive if we got him to a hospital in the next hour.

Dragging my leg and tugging on the jury rigged stretcher, we managed to get it out to the Suburban. I hadn't noticed or it was too far to see when they had stopped where they did, but now I noticed that both vehicles had California license plates. The driver of the SUV had to be moved before we could load the wounded agent into the back. I took his left arm by the wrist and dragged him into the building.

With some difficulty, I was able to drag him over the threshold of the front door. I checked under his shirt for the pistol that I knew he probably had in his belt before I started shooting at him. A leather holster was on his belt, but no pistol. Agent Stephenson must have relieved him of the pistol when I had gone looking for a stretcher.

She helped me with the larger of the other two men and I went back for the last one that had been in the pickup truck. We loaded Kerrington into the back of the SUV then I picked up the Ak-47 and the pickup driver's pistol and took them back to the building as well. I decided not to mention the missing pistol and avoid bringing on a confrontation.

"Ok, you drive," she said.

"No, you drive. I'll walk back to my bike. You need to get him to a hospital and you don't need me for that," I said and started around the Suburban to head down the road.

She hesitated, as if trying to decide whether or not to reach for the pistol I knew she had now, or let me go. She chose instead to open the door of the SUV and stepped in without a word. I limped along for several minutes and wondered why she hadn't started the vehicle to leave.

I heard the engine start just as I reached the woods entrance to the road leading out to the main highway. I kept going, knowing that it wasn't too far to where I had hidden the bike in the brush. The thought of leaving and just getting out the area hadn't entered my mind. I headed up the road to where I had concealed it.

I heard the engine rev up behind me and looked around to see her coming up the road. It looked like she was going to drive by me until I saw that she was headed straight for me on the right side of the road. I looked behind me quickly for a break in the brush that would allow me to get off the road. I felt the brush of the moving air and dust on my back just as I jumped through the bushes and dived for cover.

She fully intended to take me with her, walking or not. If she hit me with the vehicle, she could help me in and then take me to the hospital along with the unconscious Kerrington. She couldn't be trusted and I should have known that she would try something like this.

I got up as quickly as I could and got out into the road just when I heard the vehicle's engine slow down. She was slowing down to look for my bike where I had hidden it and I was sure she intended to damage it so I couldn't get away. She was about forty yards away from me and I was trying to close the distance when the vehicle stopped and she was opening the door. I was about to go down on my right knee when I realized that my left leg was too swollen to bend my leg and I might not be able to get back up.

Her feet were on the ground and she was starting to face in my direction when my two shots kicked dust about two feet away from her on her left side. She seemed to freeze momentarily and seemed uncertain I would shoot again and try to hit her. She hadn't turned to face me but I could see that she had something in her right hand.

She must have felt the shock and heard the clap of the next bullet going past her face. She ducked slightly and raised her hands with the pistol in her right hand so I could see it. I was still aiming in her direction when she let her hands down and turned to her right enough to toss the pistol into the vehicle. She turned and stared at me for what seemed a minute then she turned and got back in and pulled the door closed.

Chapter Thirty One

After watching the vehicle go off in the distance, I looked around for my brass and picked up the three casings. When I reached where she had stopped I looked for the markers I had left in the road. She hadn't stopped in the right place after all. The bike was hidden in the brush about twenty feet further. I found it easily and checked it over for any signs of tampering. It started easily and I headed it out of the brush and entered the road.

There was still another man out there somewhere, either in the warehouse compound or in the woods. I knew that I was taking a chance going back but I didn't know if he had seen me close enough to recognize me and I had already had enough of being followed around by someone wanting to shoot me.

I would have to make certain that anyone connected to this group that Stephenson was investigating would not be following me. I headed back to the compound. I didn't have any choice and knew I was taking a bigger chance of not coming out of this. Surprise would be on the side of the missing passenger or driver of the van that had escaped the wreckage.

I reached the end of the road where it went back to the compound. If I hid the bike here, the least that could happen would be that it would be damaged and I would have to get out of here another way if I could. The bushes were thick here and it couldn't be seen from the road but it would take me too much time to get back to it if I had to run.

The clock was ticking on the amount of time I may have looking for the last member of this party. There would be more agents than I could count descending on this place in a short time if Stephenson had called for help. I chose to take the bike back to the buildings.

It fit through the front door of the building where the SUV had been parked. I got it through the door and maneuvered it around to face the door. I went through and went to the first building in the last row, where we had dragged Kerrington and I had found the first stack of arms. My leg was swollen and I was having a hard time walking, but the bleeding had slowed down enough that I didn't seem to be in any danger of bleeding to death in any short time.

There was no sound or movement I could detect when I approached the front door. I got low on the ground on my hands and knees and peeked around the door frame quickly. I still didn't hear or see anyone in the room. It looked the same as I had left it when I had taken the grenades out of the crate.

I wasn't going to take a chance that the room was clear until I took another look, so I stood up a little and peeked quickly around the door frame and caught movement from behind the stacks of cartons and crates. I dropped to the ground outside the door just as the frame splintered under a burst of gunfire. I rose myself up on one arm just enough to look over the lower frame of the door and aimed in the direction I had seen movement.

He made a dash for the wall in front of him and to my right and ducked his head to dive the remainder of the distance to the wall. He hit the floor face down and was about to roll to bring his rifle into play when I fired. The first two shots hit him in the upper chest just as he started to roll backwards onto his left shoulder.

The impact increased his momentum with a jerk, rolling him away from me onto his back. The rifle clattered to the floor to his right away from me. I fired twice more and saw his body jerk with both impacts, and then I stood up cautiously and stepped over the door jamb into the room.

I approached until I was standing almost over him. He had been hit in the upper middle chest and almost under the ribs on his left side. I walked around him and picked up the Ak-47 and looked at him to confirm that he wasn't breathing. I placed the rifle just outside the door and looked back into the room at the stack of munitions. There had to be a way to dispose of all this ordnance without being blown to bits in the process. This was all military ordnance. The reality that all this had fallen into the hands of clandestine arms dealers and traffickers was mind boggling.

After checking a few more boxes I discovered that the assortment was immense. There had to be ten or fifteen large cases of several types of Ak47 type rifles, AR-15's and many cases of ammunition, more grenades and explosives of several varieties, including plastic and some old TNT, listed on the boxes as U.S.

ARMY, Tri Nitro Toluene and roll after roll of explosive cord and fuse cord.

The fuse cord was of the older type, about one quarter inch in diameter and green, with a black powder core. The explosive cord was mostly yellow on spools of about thirty pounds. I found several types of electrical ignition devices of a type I had only casually seen.

This large array of explosives and arms had to span several generations of military arms, probably dating back thirty or forty years or more. This stash was a collection of many years time connected to someone who had been in the business of arms running for a long time. It must have been taken from a storage depot or several arms storages over a period of time by persons who had access to it.

Fortunately for what I intended to do, there was a lot of the older fuse cord, firing caps and some pull cord igniters to use with it. I didn't bother taking the plastic explosive out of the boxes. I just stacked full boxes where I thought they would set off other explosives and blow up ammunition and firearms. I set them with firing caps on the ends of two rolls of the fuse cord and strung it out to the front door. I was confident that the explosion would destroy all the arms and ordnance in the room and it was certain to be large.

I decided to check the rest of the buildings. First I checked the building that the van had struck, then walked through it and looked at all the buildings in that row. The buildings were essentially empty, so I checked the building next to the one where we had set up to fire at the wrecked van.

There was one more building next to one we had been in, with more arms and ordnance stacked in it. There was enough here to supply a small third world power with enough arms and explosives to invade a country or for terrorists to wreak havoc in the United States for several years. The rest of the buildings were empty except for bunks in some of them and living quarters that may have been used, but not recently.

The last structures I checked were the two sheds; one was where we had found Stephenson's partner, Kerrington. I had seen, but had not made much importance of several sacks of industrial Nitrogen, also called Ammonium Nitrate. I remembered using the stuff to fertilize sugar beets when I was in high school helping my father on the farm we share cropped. Our method of use back then was to place the sacks in the irrigation ditch and puncture them so that the water would run through the holes and dissolve the material and run into the rows of sugar beets.

After loading four of the sacks and two five gallon cans of Diesel in a wheel barrow, I took them to the two buildings where I had found the other contraband. I hadn't been working on setting explosives more than fifteen minutes or so, but every moment was time elapsed; taking me closer to being found here by whoever had stored the arms or the Feds Agent Stephenson had called.

I laid a sack of the Nitrogen on the sides of each of the stacks in the two buildings, cut the sacks in a big X with my knife and filled them with the diesel fuel until it almost ran out, then poured the rest over the stacks of munitions. I went back and got four rolls of the detonation cord.

I left two at the back door of one of the buildings and took two rolls into the other. I placed the two strands of the detonation cord with caps in the ends into the sack of Nitrogen through holes I made with my knife. I unrolled the detonation cord out the back door, and then did the same in the other building. I picked up each of the spools where I had set them and unwound the cord back to the other building where I had set the fuse cord in the C-4.

I had looked in the boxes of TNT to verify that the round foot long metal cans contained the oily smelling round bricks. They looked like large tan colored hockey pucks with a hole in the middle, which I remembered was for the explosive cap. I quickly stacked some of the TNT boxes near the C-4. I didn't have the time to spend exploring all of it.

I wouldn't have time to set all the fuse cords with short fuses and hope to make it back to my bike and get out of the area before all this went off. I set the explosive cord by placing detonation caps on each end of four cords, two for each building. It would create an explosive train from one building to the other.

If the cord worked as it was designed to, it would set an explosive train traveling from the exploded C-4 to the Ammonium Nitrate in the other two buildings at a speed of twenty thousand feet per second. It would be virtually a simultaneous explosion. Another 15 minutes of time had gone by. I was running out of time.

Taking a chance that the ancient ring pull igniters would work to set off the powder fuse cord, I set each cord with one of them. I knew the old fuse cord was still usable after I had cut a piece a foot long and lighted it to see how fast it would burn. At about four feet per minute the one hundred or so feet of cord I had laid out would give me the time I estimated I would need. I laid the fuse cord out the front door where I would be exiting and strung it out so it wouldn't overlap.

Just to be sure the cords wouldn't be removed from the sacks of Nitrogen and the C-4, I booby trapped each one with the four hand grenades from the box I had stuffed in my shirt. By pulling the pins on them and placing them on top the sacks of nitrogen and the C-4 in each of the buildings and wedging them in with an ammo box lid, they would be set off if any of the lids were moved. Whoever moved the lids might hesitate in surprise just long enough after seeing more than one grenade, to run out of time.

Just by some afterthought, I thought to take another box of the Grenades with me along with two Claymore mines, some electrical igniters and a roll of fine double strand wire. I took one last look and estimated by the length of the strands of fuse cord that I would have about twenty or twenty five minutes to get some distance down the road. If luck would have it and Murphy wasn't watching, I could be at least twenty miles down the road in the direction of Durango.

I pulled the cord igniters and saw the puff of smoke from each of them ignite the fuse cord and watched as it blistered with heat as it started down the length of the fuse. I picked up the Ak-47 and backed away, then limped back to my bike as quickly as I could, continually looking to my right and left and used up another couple minutes of my time.

My bike started easily and I reached the road leading to the highway and had gone about a hundred feet when I heard a muffled explosion. It was loud but not loud enough or large enough this close to the buildings that it could be the pile of explosives I had rigged. The worry set in then that the other man in the van was still alive and had set off one of the booby traps. Had the grenade set off any of the high explosives that I had rigged, it would have knocked me off the bike, or worse at this distance. I decided that I couldn't worry about it any further now by going back to check.

I was heading south and every minute was getting me closer to Durango. I checked the odometer and saw that I had been traveling down the road about twenty miles. With the time I had used getting back to my bike and the five minutes I used up to get back to the highway, there was still some time before the main charge would go off, if it was going to. I was getting concerned that whoever had set off the grenade trap had pulled the fuses and none of it would go off.

An exploded grenade may or may not set off high order explosives as they do in the movies. Whoever had set it off had either jumped clear and was now dismantling my rig or he had been hit by some of the ten thousand fragments of piano wire from the grenade. Just when I was about to acknowledge that Murphy's Law had in fact been in effect and had interfered with my half planned fireworks; I felt rather than heard a shock wave.

It felt like something moved through the trees shaking each one all the way to the roots and shaking the ground with it. It took me about five seconds to make a right turn onto a dirt road and stop. I got off the bike and was standing beside it when I saw the flash above the trees then heard the huge explosion about fifteen seconds later.

If he had set off and survived my grenade trap and was on foot, there was no way he could escape that fireball. The explosion was big enough that I could be sure that everything had to have been destroyed. I did what I had to and had gotten away clean except for the gunshot in my leg that was alive now with a deep burning pain.

Highway 550 would take me to Farmington where I could either continue south through Gallup, New Mexico and Albuquerque on Interstate 40, or I could head west directly to Holbrook. Agent Stephenson must have made contact with a different group than she had the year before. Some of the same riders that were with last years group may have certainly been at this rally, but it could only be coincidence. It was more than a certainty that I would be seen in this area by anyone from this new group but they should not be any more interested in me than they would any other rider.

I didn't know who Agent Stephenson had contacted at Green River or who it was that had cuffed her around and possibly tried to kill her. She didn't tell me anything I didn't need to know; except where she thought her partner was being held. I knew only that she was investigating the connection between some of the bikers and a terrorist group operating in the area of Farmington.

It was about four hours after I had gone through Farmington and was nearing Holbrook, when I started to burn up with fever. The wind on my face and the cooling evening helped but it didn't make me feel any better. It felt like I was in the open door of a burning furnace and my face and upper chest felt like I had been sunburned. I reached down with my left hand to check the towel I had tied around my thigh. It felt hot and numb except for the burning in my whole thigh.

I had stopped twice for a few minutes, but I had been traveling well over five hours. Even though I had traveled at high speeds because of the absence of traffic on the road, it had still taken me longer than I had estimated to get there. It took another twenty minutes to find the road to the Holt ranch and another ten minutes to get in sight of the ranch house.

It was late evening and getting dusky when I pulled into the main yard through the old cattle guard. I felt really light headed now and barely remembered to kick out the stand and lean to the left so I wouldn't fall to the right with the bike on my leg.

It was a lot darker than I had thought it was when I got into the yard and I couldn't understand why I couldn't see any more. It felt like I had walked into the outside wall of the house and I was stuck against it. It felt like I was still trying to walk to the house, but I couldn't see it in the dark anymore and the burning in my head wasn't allowing me to figure out why I couldn't get away from the wall.

The burning in my head subsided, but I still couldn't see anything. It was then that I finally realized that I must be unconscious, then everything stopped and it felt like I was floating in the dark. I seemed to wake and found myself in a dimly lighted room looking at a ceiling I didn't recognize.

After blinking several times I looked to the side and realized that I was on a bed, but I couldn't think clearly enough to realize where. It was a strange sensation that I remembered feeling when I was a child and had a fever. The walls seemed to touch me and it felt like I was scraping my fingers in the ceiling, but my hands were at my sides.

The burning in my leg was gone and it was replaced by a steady pain. I reached down with my left hand and felt the bandage on my leg. My head didn't burn anymore, but the room spun and I closed my eyes until it stopped, then everything faded and I fell asleep. I woke again feeling something on my face and forehead. It felt hot and heavy and made my breathing difficult. I wanted to reach up and lift it off. Anne must have been in the room looking down at me from the side of the bed, but she seemed to be standing at the top of a hill far away from me.

I woke again and my head seemed clearer and the room was cool. My leg wasn't hot anymore. The burning sensation had been replaced by a steady throbbing pain keeping rhythm with my heartbeat. I would have preferred to lie still and not have to move my leg, but my bladder seemed about to burst. I managed to move to the side of the bed and after some effort put my feet over the side to the floor. Standing up was another experience altogether. I managed to get on my feet but I wasn't sure that my left leg would hold me up.

The house was quiet and seemed deserted when I walked towards the bathroom. My leg was sore but it didn't restrict my walking. I didn't even take notice that I wasn't wearing anything but the bandage around my left thigh. I had just found one of my bags in the bedroom, when I felt more than heard the front door vibrate.

I remembered the sound from childhood. We lived in a house that had been built by my father. It was built of frame and plank on the floor and the walls. The front doors; there were two, would vibrate when there was traffic on the road in front of the house. I remembered it when I felt the vibration from the front door and I knew that someone had driven into the yard. I tried to slip on my jeans, but couldn't, so I gave up and walked over to my bags to look for my pistols.

I found my Smith 645 close to the top of my bag when I reached into it, then limped over to the window. The curtains were drawn, but there was enough space between the two sides of the curtain and the window frame to see outside. My heartbeat slowed down when I saw that it was the SUV that Anne had been driving. I walked back to the bathroom so that she wouldn't find me undressed and in need of a shower. She opened the front door just as I came out of the bathroom door to the hallway between the kitchen and the bedrooms, trying to hold up the towel with one hand.

"Well, you're up. How do you feel?" she asked as she walked up to me.

"I'll know more about how I feel when I can figure out how long I was out cold," I said.

"It has been two days. You got here Monday, two days ago in the late afternoon. This is Wednesday afternoon," she said.

"What did you have to do to stop the infection in my leg?" I asked.

"I got some antibiotics. You were not in the best of shape. Fortunately, it wasn't too bad. It was infected some, but more inflamed than anything else. It just had to be cleaned and disinfected. You may not have awakened if it had been worse," she said.

"Well, that's twice then. I almost got in trouble with the first one that I got near Farmington. I should count my blessings that I didn't take more than one bullet," I said.

"You still don't look too good," she said. "You're a little gray right now. You had better sit down before you fall."

She helped me to a chair at the kitchen table. I didn't know how weak I was until I sat, and then I got a little dizzy and started to get nauseous. It passed then I was able to talk again.

"Has anyone been here looking for me?" I asked.

"Who would be looking for you?" she asked, looking worried.

"I don't know. I stopped here on the way out of the state last year. An agent, Kathleen Stephenson, came here looking for me," I went on.

"She seemed to be suspicious about Rebecca disappearing out of the biker's camp. She intimated that she was investigating a missing girl, although she admitted that no reports had been made."

"Why would anyone have called the FBI? No one was reported missing. Hal reported it, but they wouldn't make a report and investigation until she had been missing twenty four hours," she said.

"No one made a report. She had been working inside the biker camp and saw Rebecca there. According to what she told me, she was there when I took Rebecca out of their camp," I said. "Whether or not she saw me, is something else altogether."

"Do you think she saw you there?" she asked.

"Maybe, maybe not. She seemed to think someone had kidnapped a young girl, and that would have been Rebecca she was referring to. Then she followed me here when she saw me, but I think she was just curious," I said.

"Then there was a report made to someone other than the Marshall in town," she said.

"I thought that too at first, but it turned out that she was working inside one of the groups. I thought I had seen the last of her until she found me in Green River and sort of enlisted me to help her find her partner. I couldn't get rid of her and she pressured me into taking her to a biker's camp west of Green River," I said.

"What happened?" she asked.

"I took her to a complex past Durango where a bunch of arms were stored," I said. "She lost contact with her partner and found out he was there. We got into a shootout with an armed group of men who were probably there to pick up some of the cache."

I went to on to tell her about Stephenson trying to run me down and then the destruction of the cache.

"Why would she be looking for you in Green River?" she asked.

"Probably just coincidence again; she just happened to see me and remembered me from her contact here at the ranch and hinted that she may have seen me at another biker's camp," I said. "It was just a way to pressure me into helping her."

"Were you at another camp?" she asked.

"Yes. I went to their camp and contacted the leader of the group that had been pursuing you and Rebecca. I made him a deal," I said. "I told him that I wouldn't shoot up half his camp if he called off the rest of them that were still trying to catch up with you and Rebecca."

"Did you really believe he would keep the deal?" she asked.

"I doubted it at the time. My understanding is that they were all headed back to their home clubs," I said. "I believed at the time that he would want to keep their activities from being known or interfered with. He certainly wouldn't want to arouse the interest of the authorities."

"Then I am still in danger from any of the biker clubs," she said.

"Not any more than you would be from any number of outlaws anywhere," I said. "The men who were pursuing you and Rebecca did it out of revenge. They're no longer a threat."

"But now, some of the same outlaw bikers are back," she said. "Does that mean that they will come here?"

"I don't think so. This was just a rest stop for them and coincidence that you became their target. I believe that the last of the group that was helping the one called Brooks is no longer a threat. The leader of the club believed me when I told him I could make trouble," I said. "Getting a bunch of his associates killed for reasons outside of their normal activities isn't something he would want in addition to the usual conflicts over their illegal activities."

"Part of it must have been the illegal arms you destroyed," she said.

"I can't overlook that possibility. Agent Stephenson didn't give me any information about any of it and I wouldn't have understood anyway. I've been out of the loop of Police information for a long time. The only thing she would tell me is that part of it involved terrorist activities and Arms trafficking and that the leader I made contact with last year may be part of it," I said.

"What about the people who the guns were for?" she asked. "Will they come after you?"

"The only one who knows who I am and my connection to the warehouse full of guns is Agent Stephenson," I said. "She tried awful hard to take me with her. For what, I don't know. She didn't need me after she located her friend."

"Then why would she want you now?" she asked.

"She surely would know about the explosion and would want to find out what I know about it," I said.

She walked over to me when I got faint again and started to put my head down.

"You need some more rest," she said. "There's plenty of time to worry about any of this later."

Chapter Thirty Two

Anne had stored the bike in a shed attached to one of the equipment barns behind the house. What I could see of it didn't appear to have been tampered with and seemed ready to go if I chose to leave right away. Just to be sure, I started it and let it idle for a couple of minutes until the smoke buildup in the shed started to get thick.

"What are you going to do?" she asked.

"There are a number of ways to get out of this mess, but most of them require me to disappear, change residence and register the bike in another state. I don't like any of them," I said

"You're going to go back aren't you?" she asked solemnly.

"There isn't any choice. I didn't know at the time I went into their camp a year ago what was going on. If Stephenson saw me and thought I was part of the arms traffic when I was there, that would be a reason for finding me again. It was coincidence that I happened to stop at Green River when she was watching the bike traffic a year later. I don't think she was there looking for me," I said.

Anne looked faint and held on to the door frame for balance. I walked over to her and held on to her left arm to hold her up.

"They're not going to come here," I said. "There is no reason for the FBI to start a search for missing bikers that haven't been reported missing and there's nothing that they know of to tie them to the ranch. You and I are the only ones who know how many of them are missing besides the bikers and they're not going to report it."

"Where are you going to meet them?" she asked.

"I'll meet them in Flagstaff," I said.

"They could arrest you and try to connect you to the arms traffic," she said.

"Agent Stephenson was trying to connect me to them and since I destroyed all the evidence, she may want to pick me up and get whatever information she thinks I have," I said. "If they're looking for me, I may as well get it over with and beat her to the punch. It won't take much conversation for them to figure out that what little I know will prove that I'm not involved any more than what Agent Stephenson got me into."

I waited most of the day for the return call. Just about what I expected of the Feds. They would take it as another crank call, made by someone who wanted some excitement out of life by getting picked up and grilled by some agent for weeks. Right, just the excitement I wanted out of life.

"Is there any other way to do this?" she asked.

"I don't need the contact with the Feds any more than I need a shot in my other leg," I said.

"That sounds like whatever experience you have had with the FBI has been negative" she said.

"I was investigated for excessive force" I answered.

"Was it?" she asked, interested.

"Of course it was excessive force. In 1970 any arrest made west of the bridge on the south side, had to be "Excessive Force" involved. If it wasn't, then you hadn't stopped the fight that you were sent there for, you didn't make an arrest or you had gotten the shit beat out of you and they had all gotten away with it," I said.

"What happened after you were investigated?" she asked.

"I never knew and I didn't ask after the charges were dropped, whether the investigation had been initiated by one of my supervisors, or because of a complaint by the one of the people who was arrested that night," I answered. "I was almost certain it would go to court if I didn't have the right answers, but I was younger then and careless."

Thinking back to that time, I wondered how we managed to get through the fights without getting hurt. Not every one had Mace then. No one had stun guns yet and Tasers weren't invented yet. I carried a twenty six inch long custom made, second growth Hickory "Billy Club" that looked as efficient as it was. It finally got down to whether my Baton was legal and I was going to be charged by the agent who had been sent to investigate me.

"Is this Police Baton illegal?" I had asked the agent who was questioning me, as I presented the equipment in question to him.

"No." he answered. "There is no Federal law prohibiting the use of Police Batons."

"Is there any restriction on the design of Police Batons?" I asked.

"No there isn't," he answered.

"So if I used the baton, which is legal, what is it you're investigating?" I had asked him.

"There is a question as to whether you used excessive force of any kind," he said.

"So what is excessive force? What defines the use of excessive force or the force necessary to make the arrest?" I asked.

"Some of the subjects were injured," he said.

"There is always the chance of injury in a difficult arrest," I said. "What is excessive force, exactly?"

"There is a difference whether they were injured accidentally or if it was done deliberately," he said.

"Then, what you are looking for is intent. The answer is no, I didn't intentionally injure anyone in the arrest. The only thing intentional was the arrest, not the injury," I said.

"So did you intentionally injure any of them?" Anne asked. She hesitated then said, "I suppose it doesn't really matter if someone is attacking you."

"When you're in a fight as a police officer, you can't afford to lose," I answered. "It becomes a matter of a fine line whether it was excessive or the force necessary. The downside of it is that the threat of being charged is always there and it causes enough hesitation that you can get hurt doing the job, or fail to do it at all."

It was true. We had no Police issue batons in 1970. That didn't take place until about six years later, when we were all issued batons of a standard size and weight, both of which made the baton about as useless as the "Yawara" sticks that everyone discovered some years later.

The 26 inch batons became a little more useful after some practice and methods of use which I taught at our Police Academy. What no one understood then and now, is that there are still no Federal restrictions on the design and weight of Police Batons. Those restrictions are imposed by the individual Police Departments.

It brought my thoughts back to the present when I decided that I would try to contact an agent I had as an instructor at an FBI sponsored training. Mike Omura, a diminutive, but extremely physically fit Japanese Hawaii FBI agent, taught the special course those many years ago. He must have long since retired, but I had no one else I could call, so I called the Los Angeles office of the FBI and identified myself and asked for him. He had to have been retired for some fifteen or twenty years by now, the same as me, or even longer, because they only had to work twenty years, and no age restrictions on retirement. I was very surprised when he was the one who returned the call.

"I don't remember you, but if you say you attended one of my classes, then you must have the right man," he said.

I had no idea that I would be contacted at all, because it had been at least twenty years that I had last talked to Mike and there was no special reason that he would remember me. I was just another face in the class, from a small to medium size police department.

"You must have found out by now about the explosion in Durango," I said. "So, at least we both know what I'm talking about."

There was a long silence on the line, probably while he digested what I had just said.

"Where are you now? I guess I should be asking where we can meet," he said.

"Thanks for asking. You already know where I'm calling from," I said. "There's a small airport in Flagstaff. I can meet you there and I'll do whatever you want me to do."

Calling the FBI was the best choice I could make, but I wasn't going to be surprised if I found myself in the custody of Homeland Security. I would have taken an easier way out if there had been one I could see at the time, but at least that part of it was over for now.

I didn't hear from Agent Stephenson so there was no one to tell me anything about Kerrington. I suppose he made it, otherwise I would have been charged for some responsibility in his death, whether or not it was my fault and I would have been picked up by now.

That's the way it is when you interfere with a Police operation, especially with a Federal operation. The blame has to go somewhere and I was the only outsider involved, except of course the Bikers and the Terrorists. I destroyed whatever case they might have had and any chance of finding the Arms dealers and who they were selling to, but destroying the dangerous munitions was the only thing I could think to do at the time.

Chapter Thirty Three

Mike Omura hadn't changed in the 20 years since I had seen him. Small, compact and not an inch of extra weight on him; he was older, with more lines on his face, but otherwise seemingly ageless. His was a face from my past that made a great impression. He had a personality that was easygoing, yet without a doubt competent. He had mentioned lightly that he had dabbled some in the martial arts, studying in Hawaii with one of the less public but prominent instructors of the time.

I had no difficulty recognizing Mike when he walked through the gate carrying a medium sized duffle bag and looking discretely in all directions, yet careful and watchful even after several years of retirement. Watching him as he walked to the exit doors of the small airport lobby, I remembered why I had to make a real effort to lose the behavior and attitude of an active police officer after I retired.

He seemed to be only looking around casually, yet it was a measured observance of everyone and everything within his view. It was recognizable to me, because I had spent my whole life being observant everywhere I went. So it was that he recognized me easily when he became of aware of me watching him.

I waited until he was within a few feet of the doors and casually walked in his direction to meet him and turned to walk out a few steps ahead. I looked around only once and this confirmed to him that I had recognized him and he was walking in the same direction I was. I reached the dually I had taken the liberty of borrowing from the ranch and looked around again at him just as he tossed the bag into the back. He waited until I had driven out of the parking lot and turned into the highway before he said anything.

"You should be under arrest," he said.

"Am I?" I asked

"Jesus, there has to be at least ten federal violations you committed when you blew up at least ten acres of landscape" he said.

"I believed I had no choice. It was a lot of arms and explosives. I didn't want them in the wrong hands," I said.

"How did you get into this operation?" he asked.

"I was shanghaied into it, as you well know," I said.

"That isn't the way I understand it," he said. "You made contact with one of the biker groups that are moving arms and ammunition into the state and it's just about to turn into a matter of national security."

"Yes, I made contact with them. Several times as a matter of fact, but it had nothing to do with illegal arms," I said.

"Then what the hell were you doing?" he asked.

"I was trying to get away from them," I said.

"When did you contact them?" he asked.

"More than a year ago," I said.

"How did you get involved with them?" he asked.

"I wasn't involved with them. They busted into my camp when I was camped out near Joseph City about a year ago. I stopped them from kidnapping a woman near where I was camped and they came after me to try to get even. They shot at me a couple of times, but I managed to get away from them." I said.

"Agent Stephenson was investigating their operations. She became aware that they had picked up a young woman near Holbrook. Inquiries were made, but there was no report of any attempted kidnapping," he said.

"There wasn't one as far as I know. The woman went with them willingly, but they didn't allow her to leave when she wanted to," I said.

"Why would they go after you if she went with them of her own accord?" he asked.

"She did, but her older sister did not. It's her they were trying to kidnap," I said.

"This is a bit confusing," he said. "You'll have to explain it to me so I can understand why you got involved."

I told him about my first contact with the bikers when they came into my camp and how I had found Anne in the arroyo. I recounted the shooting and the fight, but I didn't mention that I had shot back and that one of them had been killed in the incident. I told him about Anne enlisting my help in getting Rebecca out of their rally and helping them get home afterward.

"So you were shot at in the encounter at Holbrook. Did you return fire and were any of them hit?" he asked.

"I don't think so. The one I shot at got away," I lied. "However, I took a hit in the leg at the arms cache at Durango more recently and barely made it back."

"You were in their camp in Durango," he said. "How did that come about?"

"I went there because I knew what club they were riding with to try to see if I could convince the honcho of that group to call off his boys. After I explained that some of my friends would warm up their camp with some well placed sniper fire, he agreed to call them off," I said.

"That part is a little hard to believe," he said. "I can't believe he backed down that easily and let you out of his camp alive. That had to have been a pretty good bluff."

"It wasn't a bluff and I really had the drop on him. He knew it because I tied up his sentries and I had some friends covering the camp from a good vantage point. They would have done just what I promised him if he didn't agree," I said.

"I just don't buy him going along with it. He could just have killed you if you threatened his operation," he said.

"He didn't know who I was and may not have suspected that I was on a bike," I said. "All he knew was that I had him covered and believed I would carry out my threat and shoot up their camp. He had no reason to believe I knew anything about their operation."

"Did you know then that they were running Arms?" he asked.

"No, I knew nothing of their operations. I just took it for granted that being outlaws, they had at least some amount of illegal operations going, drugs or stolen merchandise of some kind. The one I roughed up told me they had been headed for a meeting with other biker groups from New Mexico and Texas to settle some problems of territory. He said they didn't want anything to interfere with that. The incident with the two women wasn't anything their leaders had sanctioned," I said. "As far as I knew, he called them off and I had no further incidents with them."

"You must have convinced him you could hurt him and their operations and he took it to heart," he said. "What happened that Stephenson would report that you took a shot at her?"

"That was probably a cover story because the cache was blown up," I said.

"So you had nothing to do with the arms?" he asked.

"Come on, you didn't come here to investigate my part in a gun running operation," I said. "You know by now that I was dragged into this by one of your agents."

I explained how Agent Stephenson had shanghaied me into taking her to the rally near Green River, then later sewing her up after she stumbled into my room.

"We didn't get that story," he said. "Our information was that she had followed one of the bikers into the storage complex. She was able to rescue her partner where he was being kept in one of the buildings and got shot at while trying to escape. Two of them were shot and she barely escaped after you shot at her while she was leaving in one of their vans."

"So now she's saying that I was part of the group that shot at her. This keeps getting better all the time. There were five of them. Two arrived in an old truck, two, maybe three, in a van and one in the SUV. She shot one, I shot three of them, and one of them almost got away," I said.

"All right, it just doesn't add up. One of our agents is working inside a motorcycle group and her partner is inside another one and he gets made and almost killed. She said she got shot at by you while trying to escape with her partner in one of the vans from the complex and now she's missing," he said. "So, just how do you fit into all this?"

"The whole thing is a lot more complicated than that, but the simple part of it is, she got me into it. She followed me to a friend's ranch in Holbrook a year ago and started asking questions about things I knew nothing about. At the time, I knew nothing about her involvement in an investigation into the biker groups. She said she was investigating a possible kidnapping by one of the biker groups, which coincidentally was the sister of the woman they tried to kidnap out of my camp," I said.

"That was a year ago," I went on. "I came back to the ranch after I got a call notifying me of the death of my friend Hal Holt. Agent Stephenson was investigating the same bunch of bikers in the area of Green River and Farmington about the time I was traveling through the Four Corners area. It had to be coincidence that she happened to be watching the highway when I reached Green River. She recognized me from her first contact with me in Holbrook and decided that I was her ticket back into the rally that was going on near there."

"If you were in Holbrook because of the death of your friend Holt, what were you doing in Green River?" he asked.

"I was headed back to Montana to pick up my rig," I said. It didn't take much more to recount the events leading to the explosion at the storage complex near Farmington, getting shot and ending up at the Holt ranch.

"Whatever group it was that Stephenson was investigating at Green River could still in the area," he said.

"Someone at that camp worked Stephenson over pretty good, but I don't know if they tried to kill her or she just pissed them off and they roughed her up," I said. "She must have established a connection between the group she was investigating and the cached arms that I blew up."

"Why would she try to connect them to you?" he asked."

"Probably to cover her screw up," I said. "When she saw me again, she must have thought it was more than coincidence and also because she wanted to use me to get back into their camp."

"Stephenson should have called it in when she had the location of the arms storage," he said. "She had no reason to get a civilian involved."

"You mean me," I said. "She claimed she didn't want to blow the operation by calling in the authorities. She claimed that a large movement of police in the area would have alerted them and they would have moved everything out of the area. That part I can believe, what with cell phones and long range FM point to point radios."

"How are you going to be able to help us?" he asked. "Agent Stephenson is missing."

"I'm not sure, I just may be recognized if I go into their camp," I said.

"We have to take that chance," he said. "You have to get close enough to identify their leader and possibly locate Agent Stephenson. We have him as James Evan Roland. If he's in the area, we may be able to follow him and identify some of his contacts. If it's still an open rally and they're covering their meetings with a lot of outsiders, they may not take it as unusual if another bike comes into their camp."

"I can go back to the camp I took her to at Green River. I wasn't there very long, and they could recognize me with or without my bike, but I can see if she's there without alerting them to a Police presence," I answered.

"What about you?" I asked. "Are you going in or are you just going to work surveillance on the traffic from the rally?"

"I've never worked undercover," he said. "I'll be your liaison with the teams that will be handling the operation."

"I guess I don't have any choice," I said. "The Best Western is east of here on Highway 40. I'll take you there for now and you can get your operation going and I'll meet you in Green River in the morning. That's the soonest I can get there on my bike."

"So why did you decide to turn yourself in?" he asked.

"I'm over my head in this. I don't know anything about terrorist operations and I don't have any business in any of this. I'm out of the loop since I retired and I don't want to get arrested." I said.

"That still doesn't tell me why," he said.

"I'm a cop, retired or not. I served my country for more than forty years. This is my country," I said.

He looked at me carefully as if measuring me for the first time since I picked him up at the airport, and then he nodded.

"Where are we going to meet?" he asked.

"The Green River Inn, it's easy to find and it's not too noticeable. I don't have to tell you to come alone. Find an old truck, some old jeans, a plaid shirt and an old Stetson style hat, not a cowboy hat. You can pass for an Indian with the right old beat down clothes and your natural California tan," I said. "See you there."

Anne was standing on the wide step in front of the ranch house when I drove the dually into the yard. She would never know if I would have left again without a word had she not been there when I arrived. She watched me while I parked the dually and I walked up the steps of the landing. She didn't move or speak until I was close enough to touch her.

"What happens now?" she asked worriedly.

"I'm headed for Green River to meet with the FBI. They want me to locate one of the rallies and set up surveillance with them," I said. "Agent Stephenson is missing. She either was identified as an agent or she has cut herself off. They haven't heard from her."

"You're going to put yourself in danger from every one of those men who are in this area. There are probably still several of them that will mistake me as Rebecca if they see me, and now every one of them is going to know you as well," she said.

"I put a lot of men in jail over the 23 years that I was an active police officer and I got threats from almost every one of them, but I never had one try to carry out a threat, that I know of," I said.

"Why would that make any difference?" she asked.

"You and I were alone each time they found us. It's one thing to go after a woman and a companion and quite another to go after a police officer and his companion," I said. "Somehow even though cops are attacked all of the time by criminals they're pursuing or investigating, it isn't common that they would actively pursue a police officer. Any identified group will resist arrest and shoot when confronted, but they aren't likely to open fire on all cops or actively hunt a known police officer, active or retired."

"I don't understand why that makes a difference. They don't seem to have any reluctance to break the law and risk being arrested," she said.

"It isn't a matter of fear of being investigated or arrested," I said. "It's a matter of numbers and the odds of winning. They aren't suicide terrorists. If they declare open war against any Police agency it's just a matter of time before they lose."

"But what about the men they were supplying with those arms?" she asked. "They are probably terrorists and they are going to know who you are."

"That's why I made the decision to call the FBI. If there were more of them than I saw at their storage complex, they'll know me and come after me anywhere they see me again. They're not bikers and they won't have any reservations about taking on any number of Police agencies. Terrorists are in it to kill as many in this country as they can and to die trying to get it done," I said.

"When do you have to leave?" she asked.

"As early as possible tomorrow morning, it's a good four to five hours ride to get to Green River," I said.

Chapter Thirty Four

Reluctant as I was to get any further involved in a conflict that involved several motorcycle gangs, terrorists and their suppliers, I knew it was something I couldn't avoid. I left shortly after midnight, riding into a very cool night, with an emptiness growing deep within me that this could very well be a one way trip in more ways than one. Early spring in Arizona is cold enough in the desert night, but heading north into the mountains is a bit colder. I would try to avoid the colder route until at least after I headed north from Flagstaff.

Trying a different route out of Flagstaff might give me a little more time before I started seeing any bikers on the road. I hoped that most of them had reached their rally points and were moving on the highways a lot less. I took route 89 from Flagstaff then I-70 to U.S. 50, and then I could come into Green River from the West.

If most of the bikers headed for this rally point were from Colorado, Kansas or New Mexico, they would be coming in from the East on U.S. 50 or Interstate40. I wasn't going to avoid all of them, but fewer of them should be on the road to the west of where I was headed. They hadn't caused any problems with the authorities so far, so they didn't have any reason to change their meeting locations in Green River, Durango and Farmington.

The road to the location of the rally where I had taken Agent Stephenson wasn't difficult to see when I approached it. I almost had taken the choice to go in and look it over and confirm whether the rally was still there or at least some remnants of it. I thought better of it when I considered that I would be going in alone in broad daylight.

I was far enough from the turnoff that I probably wasn't seen by the riders I saw turn into the road from Hwy 50. Slowing down as I approached it, I hoped that I would see the riders continuing to the rally and not find that they had slowed down to see who it was, approaching from the west. I got only a glimpse of them when they rounded a turn in the road in the distance when I went by the intersection.

It was still early predawn morning when I reached Green River and headed to the motel where I had stayed before. I hoped that retired Agent Omura was the only one watching for me when I pulled into the lot and headed for the unit I had reserved. It didn't take long to walk back to the office, get the keys and walk back to get the bike into the room. Mike Omura came to the room thirty minutes later.

"I got a room in the back row," he said.

"I wondered when I pulled into the lot whether or not you were here or had set up to watch for me," I said.

"Did you check out the meeting place on the way here?" he asked.

"I had a thought to do just that, but had second thoughts when I saw some riders on the road heading in," I said. "That confirms that there is something still going on there, but the place that Evan is likely to be found is at the camp the other side of Durango."

"We got some Intel from Kerrington, who by the way is recovering nicely," Mike said.

"Well, that's good to hear. He was in pretty bad shape," I said. "Did he get any permanent damage from the beating or from being staked out?"

"Unfortunately he will have some problems with his liver from the dehydration, but he's lucky to be alive. Who knows, with time, he may recover completely," Mike said. "He got in with a group of bikers, who happened to join with one of the Colorado groups. They gave him the Intel on the arms cache."

"Was he able to confirm that Evan's group was part of the arms traffic?" I asked.

"He wasn't sure who was in charge," he answered. "He did say that one James Evan Roland was in direct contact with some of the groups moving the arms. They've been moving the contraband in trailers, vans and campers. He got in with the help of one of the so called Free Riders, who is still with them. His contact was also one of his informants."

"He could be the one that Stephenson contacted here at Green River before she recruited me to take her to the rally," I said.

"They either made her or she just got on the wrong side of someone at that location before she limped back here to find me."

"Did she tell you she had a contact?" Mike asked.

"She didn't tell me anything when I took her there or when she made it back. All she would tell me was that Kerrington was at the complex the other side of Durango," I said.

"She may have not known about the arms at the time," Mike said. "She may have gone only to rescue Kerrington."

"That could be true. She said she was investigating the arms traffic, but didn't mention that there would be a cache," I said. "That's why she didn't call out the troops. She wanted to find Kerrington and locate the cache of arms, if there was one, before they moved it. If there is another one, it may have been moved by now anyway because of the loss of the one past Farmington."

"There's more," Mike said. "Kerrington confirmed that, but they have to be located and confirmed so surveillance can be set up on them."

It was near noon when Mike Omura went back to his room to make some more phone calls and set up surveillance and chase teams. The logistics of setting up a tail for suspected traffic looks easy when they do it in the movies, but it's a much more difficult proposition in the actual execution. If there is a lot of traffic coming and going on any given street or highway, it is possible; but nearly or absolutely impossible on an open road, with or without traffic. Any traffic on the road becomes suspect to someone looking for someone on his tail.

Early evening came a lot faster than I had imagined and now it was time to leave. I reached the turnoff just after dark and headed into the camp location where I had dropped off Stephenson. As far as I knew, I was flying alone on this one. I knew no one on the inside and there may be several who might know me, but they were all certain to know that I was a complete stranger. Having them mistake me for just another curious bike enthusiast was Hail Mary thinking. I was likely to make it into the rally and get completely ignored or they would be looking for the opportunity to check me out and find out what I was after.

I looked across the road into the clearing at the trucks and campers parked around the edge of the clearing and motorcycles parked almost everywhere. The vendor stands were still there and there were a lot of trucks with camper shells of the windowless type that are used as transports for food or other vended goods, parked on the left side of the road. I parked my bike behind one of the vans then walked back around and looked around the camp and the traffic that seemed to begin after I rolled in. I stopped at one of these short of reaching the main gathering and got a bottle of beer.

Shock and a swallow of beer that stuck in my throat brought me out of my wandering thoughts when I saw Agent Stephenson in the distance. She didn't appear to have seen me yet and I wasn't going to contact her or give her any recognition even if she saw me and walked over to me.

I recalled a conversation with a former narcotics officer who was explaining to me why he never gave recognition to officers not in uniform, if he was in uniform himself.

He had said, "I never know if they're undercover or just off duty, so I don't make them known if I'm in uniform and I never make myself known to other officers when I'm out of uniform, unless it's necessary."

I didn't know where to go or how to look nonchalant about being here, so I walked along the line of vans away from where I had left the bike. I hadn't walked more than thirty feet toward the camp still holding my beer bottle in my right hand when I felt rather than saw someone moving behind and to the left of me.

There were other riders walking around the vendor stands and some of the vans, some talking to each other and others just looking around just as I was. I looked around without completely facing in the direction where I had seen movement behind me, trying to look as if I was just casually looking around. When I did I saw what it was that had drawn my attention. He was dressed like a rider, a little scruffy in a jean jacket over his worn leather coat and his jeans tucked into his boots. He was motioning to me. I looked around to my right to make sure he meant me, and then I turned to meet him.

"Darla wants to talk to you," he said.

"Who is Darla?" I asked even though I knew when he approached me that Darla had to be Stephenson and she must have pointed me out to him. He must have thought I was looking for a password or a recognition signal when I asked.

"Who the fuck you think?" he whispered forcefully. "She's my contact."

"All right, show me where," I said.

"Walk along this side of the road behind the trucks and other shit parked along here. You'll see her," he said.

I hadn't gone quite halfway to the end of the line of stands and vehicles when something hit me from behind and I couldn't see or feel anything. I didn't know that I had fallen and was dragged and dropped into the tent I woke up in. It was dark, but I could see light outside the flap of the tent door and I could hear all the same activity I was hearing when I had reached the camp. I tried not to move or otherwise give away that I was awake when I saw the tent flap move from the corner of my vision. Quickly, I checked my left side to see if my pistol had been taken. It was still there.

"Don't make any noise," I heard a voice say. I recognized it as the voice of the man who had approached me to meet with Stephenson.

He stepped into the tent and I sat up, and then felt the left side of my head just above my ear for the raised lump I knew would be there.

"Did anyone move my bike?" I asked him in a whisper.

"No not yet. I don't think they know where it is right now," he said.

"Where's Darla?" I asked. "And who are you?"

"I'm Charlie," he said. "I only saw her when she told me to come over to you."

"Well, it's clear that I have to get out of this camp. I may not have another chance," I said.

"Well, let's go" he said. "I'll get back to my bike and try to get out of here before one of them tries to stop me."

We got a few steps in the direction of the road where I had left my bike behind one of the vans when I heard gunshots behind us. I looked behind me and saw Charlie had fallen with the first two shots. I dived to my left and went between two of the trucks.

After a few steps I had second thoughts and drew my pistol and went back between the trucks to the side away from the road. Charlie was down on the ground in the near darkness about thirty feet away and two men had just walked up to him. I hadn't decided whether or not to shoot when I saw that one of them had just leveled a pistol to aim at him where he lay motionless.

I fired at them, trying to point at one then the other with each shot, shifting back to make sure I would hit them both in the shortest amount of time. The one on the left dived to his left when I shifted my aim to shoot the one at the right and fired. I shifted to the left again and saw that he was gone, so I shifted back to the one on the right to shoot one more time and saw that he was gone too. I closed the distance quickly to get to where Charlie was lying. I couldn't see any more movement or anyone coming in our direction, so I reached down to check on him.

I turned him over on his back and he moaned and said, "They hit me in the back and legs."

I looked to my left and decided that all I could do was drag him into the brush and hide him for the time being. Stephenson was moving from the direction I had left my bike when I had reached the edge of the clearing behind the parked vehicles.

"Take his right arm and help me," I told her.

With both of us dragging him we got him into the brush and hopefully out of sight.

"We'll have to leave him here for now," I said. "If we can get out of here without being shot ourselves, we can get him some help."

"You can't leave me here to die," he said.

"Help me drag him to my bike," I told Stephenson. "I'll get him out of here and get some help."

"You can't leave!" she said forcefully keeping her voice low.

Chapter Thirty Five

I turned away and started dragging him to the parked vans before she could say any more. There was a commotion from the direction of the two men I had shot at. I looked back in that direction to check and didn't see anyone in the shadows of darkness behind the parked vehicles. I kept moving even after I heard the sound of engines starting from the direction of the bonfires where the main gathering seemed to be. I got Charlie to the bike and struggled to get his left leg over the seat.

"It's not far to get to the road and some help," I told him. "You have to hang on."

The bike started easily and I got moving, staying behind the cover of the parked vehicles and concessions until I had gone about thirty feet and turned left to make my way to the road. Stephenson appeared in front of me just as I reached the road from between the two parked vans.

"Hide for now, and then start walking out. I can't get you both out now," I told her.

I accelerated quickly without turning on the lights, hoping I could continue in the darkness a little farther before the road was no longer visible in the fading light from the camp. I delayed turning the headlight switch on as long as I could then turned it on and accelerated to sixty miles per hour. I reached the highway ten minutes later.

The bike bounced on the edge of the pavement when I left the dirt road and I managed to make the left turn without losing control. I flipped the lights off almost as soon as I straightened out to continue east, went a little farther then stopped and kicked out the kick stand and leaned hard to the left to get my leg over the tank. I turned the switch one more notch and shut down the engine.

I had no sooner gotten both feet on the pavement when I saw the lights of three motorcycles turning onto the highway. They were about sixty yards away when I went down on my right knee to get into a shooting position. They must have seen me just as I started to put pressure on the trigger to fire because I saw the middle headlight bob down as if he had just seen me and hit the brakes.

I aimed just over the headlight and fired two shots at the center one first. The middle headlight jerked suddenly toward the ditch on his right and the beam shifted crazily in the darkness like someone playing with a flashlight. I shifted to the left and fired twice more and shifted quickly to fire at the one on my right. I had fired six times, shifting my aim to hit each of them.

I heard the crash and saw the light of the one that had been on the leader's right, go straight up more than four feet, as if the bike had hit a steep ramp and crash into the ditch to my left about thirty feet away. The headlight of the bike that had been on the leader's left jerked to the left and seemed to disappear in the ditch to my right. I didn't wait to see where the riders landed. I ejected my magazine and loaded another, slamming it in and toggled the hammer release and turned to walk back to my bike.

It started easily and I released the clutch almost too quickly, causing it to jerk forward and lug down the engine slightly before it caught and started to gain RPM. I traveled east for about a mile and started looking for the road to the right where I expected to find Agent Omura. He hadn't told me the make of the vehicles he and the surveillance crew would be using, but I recognized the dark sedan as a large model Ford of the type popular with Police agencies, when I made the turn onto the dirt road. Mike was waiting on the driver's side of the car when I pulled up in front of it.

"Was that gunfire I heard in the distance?" he asked.

"Yes. Three bikes came out of the camp headed after me," I said.

"Where are they now?" he asked.

"They're down on the road." I said.

He just looked at me for a moment and looked at Charlie slumped against my back behind me.

"Did you find agent Stephenson?" he asked.

"She's still back at the camp," I said. "She may even be walking out this way."

"Who is this?" he asked.

"This is Charlie," I answered. "He's Stephenson's contact. He helped me get out of camp after I got cold cocked, then he took a couple of hits in the legs."

Mike helped me get him off the bike and onto the ground. I got my flashlight out of my bag and looked at the wounds in his legs. They were bleeding, but not fast, so he hadn't been hit on any arteries.

"How are you doing Charlie?" I asked him.

"Bad," he said. "I don't feel well, like I'm going to pass out and I'm getting cold."

"Hang on. We'll get you wrapped and see if we can get you out of here," I said.

"Did they make Stephenson?" Mike asked.

"I don't know. I couldn't get them both out," I said. "She may have stayed right where I left her or she may be walking out. I may be able to get her out if I go part way back and park, then go in on foot."

The three bikes were still down when I went by them on the way back to the camp. One of them was down in the ditch to my left and the bike that had apparently gone down in front of him was in the east bound lane about thirty feet further with a rider lying next to it. He looked as though his right leg was still under the bike and he didn't seem to be moving. I didn't have time to check on him or check the location of the other riders.

I made the turn onto the road easily and slowed down when I saw someone in the glare of my headlights about fifty yards ahead. When I was certain it was Stephenson, I increased speed to get to her quickly. She stepped to the side of the road as I approached on her left and turned behind her and stopped, then pushed with my feet and backed enough so I could make the turn to the left to head back to the highway. I stopped just long enough for her to get her leg over and settle onto the seat when I released the clutch and jerked forward.

The bikes were still down when I approached them and stopped short of reaching the rider who was still lying in the road. I kicked out the stand and shut down the engine and stepped off as soon as the bike settled to the left. Stephenson had not uttered a word and didn't move to get off the seat. Just as well, she probably wasn't armed anyway and certainly didn't have her own flashlight.

He had been hit on the left shoulder and didn't seem to have any other bullet wounds. He had a gash on the left side of his head and was breathing with a rattle. He must have gotten some internal injuries from the bike going over him. I walked past him to find the bike in the ditch and found the rider first.

His bike was about twenty feet farther and he had been shot through at least once in the upper chest judging by the visible exit wound in the middle of his back. He was still breathing. I found the third rider trapped completely under his bike. I moved the bike by picking it up by the handle bars with a great deal of difficulty, flipping it over away from me onto its left side.

He had no visible wounds. From the position of his head in relation to his shoulders, the impact and the roll of the bike onto him had broken his neck. I walked back to the one on the road and opened his jacket and saw that the shoulder wound wasn't bleeding much. I removed his scarf anyway and pushed it under his jacket over the wound. I saw the headlights of at least two vehicles coming this way from the east. It could be Mike and some of his team. They stopped short of reaching me and I recognized Mike as he stepped past the headlights.

"Two are still alive," I told him. "The one over there has a broken neck."

He turned to face two men walking into the light of the headlights.

"Pick them up and get them to the hospital." he said.

Stephenson hadn't moved from the seat. She stared ahead like she was in shock and didn't talk when I got on and started it and headed back to the road where the other vehicles were. I turned off the highway and rolled past several official dark Suburban vehicles parked on the right side of the road. Mike approached me just as I stopped and had kicked out the kick stand. Stephenson got off after I did and walked away to the Suburban behind me.

"How's Charlie?" I asked Mike.

"He'll be fine. One of the guys took him to the hospital." he said.

"I didn't go all the way back to the camp," I told him. "Stephenson was headed out already."

No sooner had I told him, when she came walking back to where Mike and I were standing.

"What did you find out about Roland and who is Charlie?" he asked her.

If looks could kill in the dark, I would have fallen with the first sight she had of me when Mike directed his question to her.

"He's been riding with the Wings. I rode with him to Evan's camp a year ago," she said, looking at Mike as if for approval to explain further. "He told me where to find Agent Kerrington."

"Is he part of the same group?" I asked.

"No, he's a Free Rider who was being considered as a prospect for the Wings," she answered. "He thought it was just another outlaw gang. He knew they were running guns, but he wasn't aware that it was such large scale and that they were going to be delivered to a terrorist group."

"How did you turn him," Mike asked.

"He's on Probation on a narcotics sentence and an illegal arms violation. He could go to jail," she said.

"The surveillance is useless now. They must have made Agent Stephenson and you. We'll send a team in there and investigate the whole camp," he said.

"You'll do better if you wait until morning," I said. "If the road is watched, they'll scatter like rats. You'll have a better chance of making contact with more of them in full daylight so they can't get off without being seen."

"How many roads are in there?" he asked. "There isn't anywhere they can go, except back to the main highway."

"There could be several ways out the other side of their camp that lead back out to the highway miles in either direction," said Stephenson.

"Charlie's on his way to Green River with the other wounded. We can debrief them there and find out more about the camp and any others in the area," Mike said.

"Why are you telling me this? I would have thought that your teams would take it from here," I said.

"That would be the best course if it was possible, but with Charlie out of it, we need you to take Agent Stephenson back into their camp and locate Roland," he said.

"I can't see that being of any use," I said. "If it turns out to be a closed meeting, I'll be made instantly. If it isn't there's still not much chance we'll be able to find out anything from them."

"I may have another contact at the other camp where Roland may be," Stephenson said. "One of the women that was driving one of the campers knows a couple of riders from Colorado Springs. She was hauling supplies to the camps and riding support for the two of them," she continued, directing her conversation to Mike. "They will know if any movement of the arms has been made. They may not tell my contact, but she would know something if they've been traveling out of the camp for any length of time."

"I don't like it," I said. "But I take it you're not going to give me a lot of other options."

"You're not compelled to continue with this operation," Mike said. "But we have no other options. Without Agent Stephenson's contacts, the operation is dead in the water. We need that Intel from inside, whatever small it may be, without alerting the camp and have them go underground with the operation and whatever arms and contacts they have."

Mike walked away to talk to one of the other agents. Stephenson watched him walk away. She approached me and standing close she looked at me in the dim light as if pleading that I not mention any of her actions in trying to run me down with the SUV to keep me with her.

"I'm sorry I didn't trust you before," Stephenson said, directing her comments to me.

While I was thinking that it was a lame way to cover the fact she had shanghaied me into the operation then tried to run me down, not to mention about to disable my bike to keep me there. I decided she had her reasons for her actions.

"I'm ready to go anytime. We may be able to make Durango in a couple of hours, three at the most," I said.

Mike's operation was well equipped, including extra gasoline in one of the SUV's, which I took advantage of and topped off my tank before getting ready to leave. Stephenson swung her leg over and got on behind me and held on with her arms over my shoulders.

"Thanks for not letting out what happened," she said.

"I'll keep it in mind," I said as I released the clutch and headed out.

Chapter Thirty Six

Three hours later we were nearly in Durango. The turnoff was about another half hour to an hour further out on highway 160. The smaller towns along the old routes from Colorado to New Mexico are hardly visited during most of the year. The less traveled highways appear on detailed road maps, but not on the maps most people get from the internet or from travel clubs, unless they specify they are going to one of those towns.

I had traveled these roads years ago when going back and forth from Colorado to California on leave from the Navy. I had taken the ride on the old narrow gauge railway from Durango to Silverton as well as the ride from San Luis to Chama.

Twenty minutes later, we were headed for the camp where Evan and his group had been the year before. It was nearly midnight when I saw the road to my right where I had left the bike before going on foot to the camp. I turned into the road and continued to where it ended, stopped and let the bike roll back and turned so I was ready to go the other way.

"Why are you stopping here?" she asked.

"We're walking in from here. I want to look over the camp before we go in, if at all. I want to make sure of the layout so I can see if I would be able to get back out," I told her.

"It's fifteen minutes through the woods from here. We have to stay in the woods on this side of the road, then cross the highway," I said.

Mike answered when I called and I gave him the location of the camp and where I had left my bike. He didn't sound enthusiastic about us walking in almost a half mile to get to the camp, but I was at the location and it had to be my decision.

"What are we going to be able to do on foot?" Stephenson asked me.

"Just what I told Mike we were going to do. We're going to look over the camp and confirm that Roland is there," I said. "You didn't really think we could just ride into their camp and fit right in did you?"

"Well, I've been in several of their camps," she said. "There are a lot of free riders that come into these camps."

"Yeah, and it would be my luck that this particular one would be a closed camp, and my ass would be grass before I shut down the engine," I said.

I didn't go on to confirm that I had been here before, because she already suspected that it was me that had visited Evan a year ago. She had seen me talking to him, although I hadn't seen anyone stirring when I caught him at the door of his camper, but not clearly enough to be certain it was me. She had started to put things together when she had seen me later, riding solo in the area of Holbrook and thought she could pressure me into making some admissions. However, had she seen Anne, she would have put two and two together and known that it was me that got Rebecca out of their camp. That and any talk of missing bikers may have led her to investigate their disappearances and made an effort to tie them to me.

I suspected from the size and number of these rallies, that there were a lot of club riders coming and going all the time. One or two of them or more not returning, wouldn't be unusual and no one from any of these outlaw gangs was going to report any of them missing to any police agency. I knew that some of the hard corps groups didn't confide in their women. They didn't allow women to ride on their own and only allowed them into their closed rallies as guests of their members.

Stephenson should have known after investigating these clubs that she couldn't just show up at a closed camp with an unaffiliated "Free Rider," as she described. It took about twenty minutes to reach the edge of the rock lookout where I had disabled the sentry a year ago. I put my right hand on Agent Stephenson's left shoulder and put my left hand over her mouth.

"No noise, no talking; stay here and watch the path. I'm going up that rock and see how many sentries are up there," I whispered in her ear. "Remember, I don't trust you Stephenson. You make a wrong move or do anything to give me away and you'll be here on your own."

She was certain to know that she couldn't enter the camp on foot without being suspicious and knew that I couldn't have ridden in under any circumstances. It was too late at night to show up without a known rider and hope to find any of her contacts here. She may have made it in with Charlie and probably had planned to, but Charlie was out of it.

I held our position on the ground just short of the lookout point. I would have been seen had I not waited a few more minutes. There were sentries located on both sides of the rock, with the path leading to the top clearly in their view. I wouldn't have seen either one if the one to our right hadn't moved to make himself comfortable.

I pushed Stephenson down closer to the ground and backed up quietly and very slowly made my way to the first sentry. Western movies always portray cowboys knocking each other out by hitting someone on the head with their pistol barrel and in action movies with the barrel of their automatic. It doesn't always work.

It's more than likely to cause the guy getting hit to moan or make a noise when he's hit, damage the pistol and may or may not put him out. If I could get the right position behind him I would strike at the notch between the neck and shoulder muscles. It would put him out or at least stun him long enough for me to use a pressure hold around his neck to put him out.

I waited about five minutes before he relaxed and sat on the ground facing away from me. I took a deep breath before I got close to him and didn't take a chance he would hear me breathe before I hit him. I raised my right arm high across to my left and hit him with my right wrist right in the notch at the left side of his neck, penetrating to the suprascapular nerve.

He jerked upward as if he had bounced lightly on his butt and I went to my right knee behind him reaching around over his shoulder with my right arm to trap his neck in the notch of my arm. I tightened my arm and counted to ten then rolled him to the right to get him face down on the ground. I had no electrical ties, which would be the ideal and he had no bandana to gag him with, but he had a belt on.

I removed his belt and cut it into four strips by holding my knife blade upward in my right hand and guiding the belt through my fingers. I used one of the strips to tie his hands and the rest of it to tie his ankles after pulling off his boots. I used one of his socks to gag him and tied my bandana around his neck to keep it in his mouth.

I put his other sock part way into my left front pocket. He wouldn't be out too long, but he wouldn't be able to move or make any real noise, so I made my way back to where I had left Agent Stephenson. She hadn't moved. I clicked my tongue as quietly as I could, hoping only she would hear me, so she wouldn't be startled when I reached her.

"I got the first one," I whispered close to her ear. "There's another one off to the left."

There was just enough light from the camp fire to light up the face of the other sentry. He didn't seem to be making any effort to conceal himself. Either he was confident no one would try to sneak in, or he had more help that I hadn't located yet. I was able to get close enough behind him and had enough of a clearance from the bushes that I could try to put him out another way. I slipped the extra sock over my right hand. I clicked my tongue, almost like the sound of a cricket or bean bug when I got close enough. He turned his head to the left to check on the curious noise just as I side stepped to the left to add force to a right hand punch to the left side of his neck.

The sock over my fist had the effect I wanted. It didn't allow my fist to make a slapping sound against the flesh on his neck. I pulled him up by his left shoulder and struck him twice more on his left temple to make sure. My knuckles weren't as solid as they had been twenty years ago.

I had conditioned my knuckles by slamming my fists into the floor doing pushups and striking the Makiwara on a daily basis in the days when I was a hard rock Karate instructor, but that seemed like another lifetime ago. I had definitely put him out and even possibly given him a concussion, but my wrist and the smaller knuckles were starting to ache already. I tied him up with the belt strips and stuck the extra sock in his mouth and tied it in with his own belt.

Stephenson hadn't moved, so it was easy to find her and lead her up the path to the top of the rock lookout. I stopped and pushed her down on the path about halfway up and continued the rest of the way alone. I reached the end of the path where it reached the cleft in the rocks short of the lookout point.

Five minutes went by before I saw an opportunity to move in on the sentry. I may not have seen him if not for the cigarette he was smoking. He was facing away from me, but I clearly saw the red glow on the rock in front of him as he drew on it. Just when I thought I had it made and had gotten close enough, something alerted him that made him turn around to face me.

I had been carrying my pistol in my hand, thinking I could hit him with it if I didn't get a good position to punch him or slip a choke hold on him. It was just as well. He turned and I did what I always considered to be a bad idea. I swung my Smith 645 in an arc and struck him on the left side of his neck just under his ear just as he saw me.

He fell like he had been dropped five feet and struck his head against a rock to his right with a thud. I waited for what seemed several minutes to see if he was going to breathe. He gasped lightly and began to breathe very softly. As a precaution, I stripped his belt in half with my knife and tied his hands and ankles.

I heard the rustle of clothing behind me and dropped quickly, turned to my left and stepped out with my right foot to get myself out of the line of attack from behind me. I went down on my right knee with my left leg stuck out to where I had been standing. Someone tripped over it and fell face down. I rolled to my left and on top of the form on the surface of the rock.

"It's me!" she said and I recognized the voice of Agent Stephenson. "I thought you were in trouble."

"Cover me from here. I need to talk to Evan," I told her quietly.

"I can barely see from here. What am I going to be able to do?" she said.

"I can see his truck and camper from here, so you'll be able to see me clearly enough to see me signal you," I said.

"What do I do when you signal me?" she asked.

"I will only signal you if I'm in trouble, so start shooting at anyone close to me. That'll give me time to get into the bushes, unless you miss. If you miss, they'll think it's their lookouts shooting at me and I'll be toast," I said.

Chapter Thirty Seven

It took me almost a half hour, but it could have been more because I didn't have a way of checking the time, except by guessing at the passage of time to get to his camper. For all I knew, it could be two or three o'clock in the morning. I had no idea what I was going to do, except maybe confirm that it was him. Everything seemed the same.

The truck seemed the right color and the camper design was the same, but he could as well have bought another and handed this one down the line to one of his members. If he was asleep, there was no way to make contact. I looked over the assorted group near the main fire almost in the center of the clearing, but I wasn't able to recognize any of the men as James Evan Roland.

The last time I had come into their camp, I was limited by time and the approaching morning light to make contact with him. I was a little more desperate then too and fully intended to shoot him if I couldn't make some kind of agreement with him. Thinking back to that time, I wondered that he had agreed at all. Either he hadn't meant to keep the agreement and was setting me up or he felt nearly certain that I would carry out the threat.

He didn't know who I was, except that I had been able to get into his camp and got the drop on him. It proved to me what an experienced officer told me many years ago. "Even someone without any real experience or training can pull off the unexpected and get the drop on you if you don't watch your back all the time."

Murphy was on my side so far. For having no real experience in covert exercises, I had still been able to get past their defenses. I recognized Evan when he left his place near the main fire. He had been sitting with his back to me and I had somehow missed seeing him on my way in.

He walked in the direction of his camper near the edge of the clearing where I was set up to watch for him over the hood of his truck. Two men walked with him, looking to either side as they walked with him. If they accompanied him all the way to the door of his camper or waited until he got inside, I was cooked. I'd never get to him.

It was still working for me; they stopped thirty feet short of following him all the way to his truck and turned around to return in the direction of the fire. In four steps to the back of his truck, I was in position at the right side of the camper and the rear fender of his truck. He had turned the door handle before I made my move. The unplanned timing was perfect. His head was turned to look over his shoulder to the left, looking away from where I was. I took one step and placed the muzzle of my pistol on the right side of his neck. He flinched visibly, but he didn't move.

"They'll never hear it," I said.
"I thought we were done man" he said, very quietly.
"You remember me do you?" I asked.
"Hey man, I can't cover every idiot who may decide to go after you and that woman," he said.

A slight shiver almost went through me. He hadn't intended to keep his part of the deal and more than likely, he may have sanctioned the actions of the men who came after us. It was more than sheer luck that one of his men hadn't found Anne and the Holt ranch while I was back in Alaska. But it convinced me that I didn't have to have any reservations about carrying out the empty threat I had made, although I wasn't sure I could right at this moment. The revelation that he had knowledge that the search had not ended would temper how I would handle him now.

"I came here to talk only and reason with you about who you're dealing with. You never intended to keep your end of the agreement to call off your men," I said.
"You're not a brother," he said. "We don't deal with outsiders, unless we get the better deal. So what you think you can do now? Kill me?"
"You'll stay alive only as long as I can get out of this camp. If you come with me without a struggle, I have no reason to kill you. If anyone sees us leaving, you're dead," I said.
"How do you figure you can get me out?" he said.
"Quietly," I said. "Either willingly, or I can drag you out unconscious or dead."

I slipped the guitar string wire loop I had brought along as insurance, also known as a garrote, over his head.

"If you don't do exactly as I tell you, I'll separate your head faster than you can take a breath. Now back out with me out of the clearing into the bushes," I told him.

He complied, even though I thought any second he would bolt and test my resolve to tighten the garrote and possibly kill him.

"Trust me, it'll cut your throat like a razor if you make even the slightest move and you won't even make a sound," I said quietly.

It took what I estimated to be twenty minutes to make it back to the path behind the lookout point. We moved slightly faster than I had moved to make it to his camper, but we managed to keep it quiet. I began to think that Stephenson wasn't as dumb or as uncooperative as I had thought when I caught her movement behind the lookout point.

"Stay behind us, watch my back and don't make any noise. Keep it quiet and don't brush against the bushes or trees," I told her in a hushed whisper.

We got to the edge of the brush near the highway and crossed it easily and got into the trees on the other side. Stephenson crossed after I was across the road and into the trees. I kept Evan from looking around.

Then as if he had just realized the Garrote was still around his neck he asked, "Who the fuck are you?"

"No one special, I just need your company for a while," I said evenly.

"Now what man?" he asked.

He was clearly afraid now and he was beginning to believe that I meant to kill him, but the evenness of his voice told me that this was one cold dude. He just didn't want to die yet.

"Don't look around, just sit on the ground and don't move," I said.

I looked around just as Agent Stephenson walked within a few feet of us from behind. It was barely light enough to see her, and not light enough to see her features. I reached out with my left hand

and tugged on the bandana she had tied around her head and motioned for her to blindfold him with it. If he hadn't seen her yet, I didn't intend for him to see her just now. Then I motioned for her to stay back. I reached into my pocket for my phone and hit the preset button for the number Mike had given me for his cell phone.

"First road on the right at twenty five miles," I told Mike when he answered. "Bring your truck."

"Ok tell me about the arms cache that blew up," I told Evan. "Remember; if I don't like your answers no one will find you for at least a few months if at all. There are bears up here."

"You don't have a lot of time," I told him when he didn't respond.

"I a'int afraid to die," he said, but sounding unconvincing.

"Oh, I may kill you, but not just yet," I said.

"Why you want to do this man?" he asked. "I a'int done nothing to you."

"You broke our deal and you're supplying arms to terrorists. Probably the same ones or their friends who blew up the Trade Center buildings," I said.

"Nothing to me man," he said. "I'm just a rider."

"No you're an outlaw biker who's dealing arms to terrorists. It's easy for you to separate yourself from a few thousand people dying in a collapsed building while you and your buddies ride your bikes and enjoy the profits, but me, I don't want them to blow up this country," I said.

"So, are you the cops, or what?" he asked.

"We're not talking about who I am," I said. "We're talking about what you know."

With that, I drew the hammer back on my Colt and put it on his knee cap.

"Last chance," I said. "Like I said, knees then elbows."

"They gonna hear the shots," he said.

"Won't matter, you won't have any knees, then I'll take your head off and leave you dead," I said.

"You don't have to waste me man. This is no way for me to check out," he said with his voice shaking slightly. "Ok. I'll tell you where the other stash is at," he said.

"No, you'll show me where it is," I said. "I'm taking you along for the ride. If it isn't there or there's someone guarding it, you die first. Come on, get up, we're walking."

With the wire Garrote in my left hand, I holstered my pistol and started pushing him ahead of me. We stayed in the trees just out of sight of the highway, in case of any traffic or any of his friends had found the disabled guards and were starting a search. We reached the road where I parked my bike in about twenty minutes.

We didn't have long to wait until I saw headlights point into the road and heard the sound of the truck coming into the clearing. As a precaution, I hadn't walked directly into the clearing. I recognized the old truck Mike had obtained somewhere for the occasion, with a dark Suburban following him in.

"Meet Evan James Roland," I said when Mike and two men from the Suburban approached us. "He's willing to show us where the guns are."

"So what is this, a hijacking?" Roland asked.

"You can say that," I said. "It won't matter to you if there are no guns there or if we have any trouble getting to them. Give me a couple of those piggin' strings, will you?" I said to Mike.

I had Roland facing away from the truck when I saw Mike make his way back to it. I saw that Agent Stephenson walked with him. So far, Roland hadn't seen her. She stayed behind the truck and Mike walked back with some electrical ties in his hand.

"Do the honors, will you?" I said even as Mike was already making a move to put a couple of ties on Roland's wrists behind his back.

With that, I loosened the wire garrote and removed it from his neck. I walked to the truck with Mike to where Agent Stephenson was waiting.

"We'll know when we get there, if there's someone there you know," I said.

"One of my contacts may be there," said Agent Stephenson.

"Who is he?" I asked her.

"He's Jordan Manning, also known as Butch," she answered. "He's one of the Heads."

"Then how come you weren't told where the arms are?" I asked her.

"He didn't know at the time I asked him. He said he would let me know when he found out," she answered.

"You'll be with the caravan and I'll need you when we get there," Mike said. "I do know that it is far from over and you may be needed in what you've been doing; staying inside and tracking more of these dealers."

I walked back and checked the scarf over Roland's eyes and told him, "You don't need to see until we get close to where you're taking us."

He didn't balk or resist when I took him to the passenger door of the truck.

"It's your show now," I told him. "You know how it's going to be if it doesn't pay off. Now where are we going?"

"Head north on 550 from Durango; it's at an old mine site into the mountains," Evan answered.

"Is there anyone there guarding it?" I asked him.

"There's riders from the Heads there," he said. "Our part was to deliver some of the stuff to them. They was supposed to guard it and make delivery to the buyers."

Mike came around the front of the truck to stand beside Roland.

"So whose stuff is it; yours or the Heads?" Mike asked him.

"What's the difference?" Roland asked. "I'm gonna give it to you, what you care whose it is?"

I looked at Mike and he said, "I knew it sounded too easy."

With that he grabbed Roland by the arm. "We need to know who's there."

When he didn't answer, I opened the door and guided him onto the seat and pulled up one of the old safety belts to latch it over his thighs. Agent Stephenson watched while Mike and I rolled my bike into the back of the truck with the ramp I had told him to bring along. I tied it down while Mike got in from the driver's side and started the truck. It took thirty minutes to get to Durango and it was another thirty minutes past when I removed the scarf from Roland's eyes.

"All right, we need accurate directions from here on. We don't want to miss it and we don't want to alert anyone," I said. "Do you know the men that are here and are you going to be able to talk to them so there won't be a problem getting in?"

"Should be three or four of the heads guarding it," he said. "But I don't know em. I only know the ones I made the deal with."

"Is that it?" I asked. "You son of a bitch, you think we came all the way here and went through the trouble of getting you out of your camp to get shot?"

"I don' know what they'll do," he said. "I wasn't supposed to come here without one of their boys. That wasn't the deal."

"So what's the deal?" I asked. "What was your part in this?"

"They put the deal together. My boys was just supposed to get all the stuff together and deliver it," he said.

"Like what?" I asked him.

"We had a lot of the small stuff, Ak's, guns and ammo. We was just the transportation. I don' know what else is there and I don' know where it's going," he said.

"Where are the buyers? Where are they coming from?" I asked.

"Some of them was coming from California, others from back east.
I don' know any of them. Like I said, they put the deal together. I di'nt know the buyers or where they're from," he went on.

He identified the road on the left that we were approaching as the road to an old mine complex. We stopped at a wide place in the road which almost resembled a pull out from the road. I replaced the scarf over his eyes and got out of the truck.

"How far in is it from here?" I asked Roland.

"Bout quarter mile." He said. "The road starts up a hill then bears to the left. The buildings are up near the side of the mountain."

Mike opened his door and stepped out of the truck and I got out on the other side. I walked around to his side. One SUV with four agents in one and two more with two agents in each of them pulled in behind us. Two of them helped me unload the bike.

"We should wait until it starts getting light," I told Mike. "It's only a couple of hours until morning."

"I agree," Mike said. "We're not prepared for an assault. It may not be necessary if only a few men are here. We may be able to convince them to give it up without a fight."

"Don't count on it," I told him. "I had to dodge gunfire each time I crossed them."

Morning came soon enough and the sky was starting to show some light when I headed over to my bike. No one asked any questions when Agent Stephenson walked over to me and put her leg over the seat and I started it. I didn't protest either, although it hadn't been my first thought to go in this way. I watched while two teams of four men each started walking up the road, four men on either side of the road, all carrying Bushmasters, Mac'10's or Uzi's.

"What are you carrying Stephenson?" I asked her and turned my head slightly for her to hear.

"Kathleen," she answered. "Standard Glock."

"Not much firepower," I said. "They'll more than likely have Ak's or Sks rifles with a lot of rounds. So we're on a first name basis now?"

"I can get an Uzi or a Mac'10," she said.

"Get an AR-15 or a bushmaster. It'll have range and firepower," I told her. "Get me a Mac'10 with three magazines."

"All the Mac'10's have silencers. It'll be two long to carry," she said.

"Get one, silencer and all," I said.

She got off and walked over to one of the SUV's and came back with a Bushmaster and a Mac'10 with a sling attached. I put the sling over my head and slipped the Mac'10 under my jacket, concealed enough not to be seen easily, even with the twelve inch silencer attached. I asked Mike for a roll of black vinyl tape, which he was able to find in the truck.

It was tight, but I slipped the butt of one of the magazines, now taped in tandem to the other two, under my belt. We headed up the road slowly just as the agents headed into the woods on either side of the road. I hoped they would have cover close to the buildings to be effective if we got in trouble on the way in. I cleared the hill and entered a flat area of the road where it widened and I could see the old buildings about two hundred feet ahead.

There were several buildings in the process of caving in with the roofs falling in and shacks which were in better shape around the edges of the clearing. Farther in behind them were two large buildings which could have at one time covered separators and classifiers for the rocks, sand and earth which was moved in with heavy equipment to wash the gold and separate it.

It would be in those large buildings where any large cache of arms would be found. There were certain to be smaller structures inside which had been used as offices or sleeping rooms. I continued toward the buildings until I saw one man emerge from one of the smaller structures to the right and closer to this edge of the clearing. He was carrying a Sks in port arms position.

"I don't know him," she said.

"Get off and talk to him as soon as I stop and shut down," I told her.

She stepped off to the right side and cleared her left leg off the seat, and then I kicked out the stand and leaned to the left. She didn't carry the Bushmaster with her. She had hung it on the left side by the sling over the sissy bar and the small pack I had tied to it. It wouldn't be visible from the right side of the bike at this distance; neither would the Mac'10 under my jacket.

She walked away slowly and he started towards her. He was about a hundred fifty feet away when I stepped off the bike and pushed the magazine into the Mac'10 until it locked in, then I pulled the bolt back. I left the safety off and stayed behind the small cover my bike gave me to conceal the Mac'10 from his view as long as I could.

I waited until he covered almost half the distance then stepped off to the left, pointed the muzzle of the Mac'10 at him and started in his direction. He pointed the Sks at Stephenson and fired just as she dived to her right. The Mac'10's bolt clattered as the silenced rounds kicked up dust in front of him. He shifted to point at me and was kicked back by the next burst of my more carefully aimed fire. I walked over to Stephenson to check on her, but she was already on her feet.

"Get the Bushmaster. Anyone else will be well out of pistol range," I told her.

I waited until she walked back. Knowing that the magazine was probably nearly empty, I released the magazine lock as I walked, and turned the bundle of three magazines to insert one of the others. Machine pistols in the movies fire with a continuous wall of flame from small magazines, but in reality a thirty round magazine of the type that is used in M-10's and M-11 automatics is gone in seconds.

A two second burst at over 800 rounds per minute is more than half the magazine. I had fired two short bursts. I untied the small pack from the back of the sissy bar and put the strap over my head and flipped the bag around to my back. It contained the four grenades, the two Claymores, a spool of wire and igniters I had kept from the stash of arms I had blown up. The bag was still bulky with the weight of the two Claymore mines in the bottom of it.

"Whoever is still in those buildings can see us easier now," I told Agent Stephenson. "We have to get behind these smaller buildings."

I had no sooner said it than three more men came around one of the small sheds to the left of the larger buildings, two from the left side and one from the right. I went on my right knee and aimed and fired at the two on the left. I saw dust rise in front of them and held the trigger down and raised my aim into them and emptied the magazine.

The one on the right got off a burst that sent dust to my right between me and Stephenson. There was a clatter of fully automatic fire from my left and he fell away in a hail of ricochets and dust around him. I looked around behind us and saw some of the agents emerging into the clearing from the left of our position. One of them approached me, and then three more positioned themselves behind the building where Agent Stephenson had already taken cover.

"How many more are there in those buildings?" he asked.

"Unknown," I said. "The only one I saw is the one on the ground over there, until the other three started firing. There wasn't supposed to be more than three or four."

Just as I answered him I heard the sound of engines coming from the direction of the highway. Mike was coming up the road into the clearing. Roland was still in the truck and still blindfolded and one of the agents had gone back to bring up one of the SUV's. It didn't feel safe to leave the bike in the middle of the clearing, so I put my leg over the seat and started it.

I headed it straight to the buildings, bearing to the left behind the small building opposite from where Agent Stephenson and the other agents were holding position. I continued around the building and found a flat spot where I could safely position the bike on the kickstand and keep it concealed from the road. Mike drove the truck behind the building and parked next to me. The SUV pulled up beside the old truck. Mike got out and approached me just as I had kicked out the kick stand.

"Is there anyone watching the road?" I asked Mike.

"No, why?" he asked.

"I don't know, but I have a feeling from what Roland told us, that we may have company," I said.

"Ok," he said. "We'll take it from here. We have to search these buildings and find whatever arms are located here."

"What do you want me to do?" I asked.

"We'll just wait it out while the boys make the search," he said. "In the meantime, let's walk Roland over and see if he knows any of them."

If Roland knew any of them, he wasn't giving it away. Half an hour later one of the agents emerged from the nearest of the large buildings and approached our location. They found four motorcycles with California license plates registered to Knuckleheads Inc. in a cabin behind the large building.

The names on the driver's licenses of the dead guards weren't anyone known or with a record of any kind. They had found the same variety of guns, ammunition and explosives that I found at the other location on Highway 550, including RPG's and Rocket Launchers, but in a larger quantity. According to Mike, it was going to take a couple of large trucks to start moving the cache out of here.

"I don't know how much of a case we have," Mike said. "We have
Roland and the arms are more or less tied to him by his own admission, but it's not likely he'll be any more cooperative."

"Talk to him again," I told Mike. "He may be having a change of heart."

"Another team took their camp in Green River and they're searching all the vehicles right now. They found more arms in some of the campers and trailers, but nothing to tie the arms to anyone outside that. No terrorists and no buyers," Mike said.

"Well, there's nothing more for me then. You have as much of a case as you're ever going to have with or without me and you have Roland and probably most of his crew, so I can head out of here," I said.

"Which way are you going?" Mike asked.

"I'll take 160 back to Flagstaff, then head east to Holbrook. You have my cell number," I said.

"All right, I guess there's no point in holding you any longer right now. If you're needed, we know where to find you" he said.

"Yeah, I know. Where's Stephenson?" I asked Mike.

"She's still in one of the buildings," he said. "She's helping with the inventory."

"Ok, I'm outta here," I said.

Chapter Thirty Eight

Somehow, I wasn't relieved that it seemed to be over for me. There was a nagging foreboding in the back of my mind which caused the hair on my neck to stand up and the middle of my back to heat up. It reminded me of my childhood when I expected to get my ass whipped for something I had done. I knew years ago that I should pay attention to hunches.

There were a lot of bikers that were in on this and they had suppliers who must have had access to stored military arms. This wasn't so much a case of accumulating arms over a couple of decades, it was theft from government storage facilities and went a lot deeper than a couple of biker clubs involvement.

I tried to put it out of my mind, but the last passenger from the van must not have been dead, or there was another one in the van that I couldn't see. The wounded one may have set off the booby trap, but it didn't seem likely. He couldn't have gotten out and been clear of the explosion and escaped with the wounds he had. I saw that two of the SUV's were still parked in the pullout when I reached the Highway.

Traffic was fairly clear until I passed Durango and was headed for Cortez, then it seemed to be picking up. My cell phone began to vibrate and there wasn't a pull out near enough to stop before it stopped ringing.

I pulled over at last and dug it out of my jacket. I didn't recognize the number right away, and then I realized that it was a California prefix. I puzzled over it, wondering why Mike would be calling me before I was even out of the state. I hit the send button on the number displayed and it was ringing through, but it didn't look like I was going to get an answer. Maybe he was busy. Just about when I was going to put it back in my pocket, it rang again.

The voice was loud enough, but so was the background noise. It was a lot of cracking and crashing and was amplified by the telephone until it was all out of proportion and hard to recognize. Through all the noise was a female voice screaming. I listened carefully, trying to hear around the noise and realized that it was Agent Stephenson.

"Slow down! I can't understand a thing you're saying," I said loudly. "Say it again, a little more slowly."

"It's Kathleen Stephenson!" she almost screamed again. "We're under fire. Most of the team is down including Mike. He's unconscious and I don't have any other numbers I can call to get any help here before it's too late."

"Where are you?" I asked.

"In the first of the large buildings; we got out of the line of fire and into the building, but we've got wounded!" she said.

"I'm a half hour out. I don't know what I can do, but I'm on the way," I said.

The most absurd thought of all was that there should be police units at Durango and Farmington, but they would be of no help unless they could organize and deploy in less than a half hour. I was almost too far out to be of any use and I was alone. Whoever had attacked a well armed FBI team had a lot more firepower than I had.

There was a lot less traffic in the northbound lanes until I reached Durango, where I slowed down only until I reached the other side and headed north on Hwy 550 at over ninety miles per hour. I was only a few minutes out now and I still didn't have a clue what I could do when I got there. Maybe I could create a diversion until someone there could alert the other team. They should still be either in Green River or close to it, but at best speed they were almost over two hours away. I slowed down when I recognized the area of the mines and pulled off into the parking pullout where we had stopped on the way in.

Whoever had attacked Mike's team had arrived in vehicles, but there were only the two SUV's from Mike's team parked beside the highway. I turned into the road leading to the old mine and soon saw where they had parked their vehicles. Four vehicles were parked on the road ahead well out of sight of the crest of the hill where the road led to the mine complex.

They were an assortment of SUV's in varying shades of dark blue and grey. I looked to the sides of the road at least two hundred feet from the closest of the vehicles, trying to find a place to conceal my bike. There was a break in the brush on the right side of the road and I took it quickly, not even worrying that it may go nowhere. There was no clearing, just more brush and beyond that trees. It would have to do; at least it was out of sight of the road.

I didn't bother to dig around in my pack. I just untied it and pulled it free, shouldered the strap and started up the hill past the parked vehicles. There was the sound of sporadic gunfire coming from the top of the hill. I was going to have to leave the road and make my way through the woods before I went too much further. I stopped short of the crest in the road and looked around for a good place to set up. I set up quickly and shouldered my bag and headed up the hill, keeping to the shelter of the bushes just off the road.

The buildings had probably been in a wide open area during the time the mines were working full time and probably for years later, while chance prospectors came here to look for cast offs of gold. Many of the large mine operators had taken only the most obvious gold in their diggings in their hurry to get the most gold out in the shortest amount of time.

The trees had grown back into part of the clearing behind the buildings. If whoever had attacked Mike's team hadn't found a way to flank the buildings, I may still be able to get in from behind. It was just like an FBI team to hold their ground instead of taking any route of retreat out of the line of fire, so they were probably all still in the building if they were alive.

I saw movement in the trees and brush opposite my position while I was approaching the back of the buildings while still under cover. They weren't hard to identify in their assortment of colorful sport shirts and loose trousers. Even at this distance, I could see that they could be any nationality, except that they were all dark haired.

I continued in the direction I was taking so it would place me well to the opposite side of the buildings from the clearing. Using the cover of the mounds of tailings and rock and trenches behind the buildings, I made my way to the back of the one where she said they had taken cover.

I entered the building easily through a tear in the sheet metal wall. The inside of the building was not unlike a very large warehouse, but with platforms against some of the walls that had been built in levels on uneven ground. I made my way around some of the large troughs, machinery and conveyor belts on large frames.

"Stephenson!" I yelled out.

I was hoping I could be heard and recognized before what was left of the team took a shot at me.

"Over here!" I heard Stephenson over to my left.

I made my way to her position and saw then that one of the team had been trying to keep an eye on the back of the building, but had missed me when I came in.

"How many of the team members are still on their feet," I asked
Stephenson.

"Just me, Jack Reynolds and Matt Conklin over to the right; the rest of the team made it to the building, but most of them are shot up. I don't know if any of them are still on their feet. Most of us were caught out in the open with the first burst of gunfire. We still have Roland. He got hit on the side and his left arm."

"Where are the arms?" I asked her.

She pointed to her left at a large wall with two large double doors, one set close to the front wall of the building and the other near the back wall. While Agent Reynolds and Agent Conklin held their positions, I walked to the storage area.

"I don't think we have much more time," I told her. "Come on, we have to wire this stuff then get out of here before they decide to rush us. It won't take them too much longer to figure out how to flank the building and hit us from both sides."

"We can't just blow this stuff up!" she said.

"It's either that or they may get their hands on it and we have to get your team out of here," I said.

With her help, I rifled quickly through the stacks of boxes and other materials until I found the explosives. I didn't bother to look any further for any more explosives when I found the C-4 and the detonation caps. Both groups were looking for the same type of explosives, C-4 or Semtex; light and powerful and plenty of detonation cord, but there were also several boxes of old dynamite near the wall. That latter part of the explosives cache must have been found in the old mines offices. I took two spools of the fine double twisted wire, but I couldn't take the time to look for any of the magneto twist type igniters.

I took four of the electrical caps and tied them to the detonation cord to start the explosive train then ran more detonation cord to the C-4 in boxes around the stacks of munitions. After wiring the C-4, I handed the two spools of wire to Agent Stephenson and pointed to the hole in the wall at the back of the building where I had made my way in. I scratched a mark on the side of one of the wire spools and twisted the ends of one set of wires and she started in the direction of the wall stringing it out.

There wasn't any tape handy to tape the electrical firing caps to the Detonation cord, so I held them against the cord and twisted the double stranded wire around them to hold them in place. Then I twisted the wire around one of the boxes so it wouldn't be pulled loose when the wire was strung out. It was a large cache of assorted arms, including some serious RPG's, automatic rifles and ammunition, but mostly explosives, detonation cord and more Claymore mines.

I carried two of the Claymores to the front of the building and wired them so they faced the doors at the front of the building. I tied them in with the double stranded wires leading to one of the spools Stephenson had taken down the hill, the other was tied into the explosives. The strands of detonation cords and fitted caps I had used to tie in the C-4 and Semtex with the other boxes would complete the explosive train.

"Get Mike and let's get moving," I told the closest of the agents. I didn't know who Conklin was and who Reynolds was.

"I'm Jack," he said. "I can carry Mike. Matt can help with the others."

"Get the rest of the team and head out that hole in the wall and bear slightly to your left past the tailings and piles of rock into the brush and turn right and start making your way back to the highway," I said. "We'll follow and string out the wire."

"What about Roland?" Agent Stephenson asked me.

"Where is he?" I asked.

"He's over there where Mike is. He's conscious," she said.

I walked over to Roland where he had been behind the cover of several large metal ore cars, still on tracks, that ran in from the one of the double doors. He was sitting up and was still tied, but the scarf over his eyes was now down on his neck.

"Hey man, untie me. I can't go down like this. I a'int fightin' the whole U.S. government over this shit," he said.

"Don't give me any doubts about what you'll do if I cut you loose," I told him as I cut the electrical ties from his wrists.

He shook his hands to get some of the circulation back into them.

"How bad you hit?" I asked him.

"Hit me on the left side and my left arm," he said. "The arm is numb above the elbow and my ribs hurt."

He was bleeding through his denim jacket, so I tied the bandana around his bicep. The wound on his left side was on the ribs under his arm. Another inch and he would have gotten a lung punctured. It was bleeding, but not a lot. It looked like the bullet went through a little flesh and had broken a rib, or at least bruised it.

"We're moving," I told him.

"Where are the motorcycles?" I asked Stephenson.

"They're in a building behind that hill of rock behind this one," she said.

"Get the rest of the team on their feet and moving, carry anyone who can't walk, but we have to move," I said.

"Kathleen, you lead the way out," I told her. "Keep me in sight. I have to show you how far to string the wire."

I counted heads and saw that three of the agents were wounded badly enough to need help walking.

"I've got two of them," Agent Conklin said and helped two of the wounded agents to their feet. They were still bleeding through the makeshift bandages, but they could walk with help.

"One of you, take four of those Claymores if you can carry them and stay behind me," I said. "Roland is with me."

"Come on," I told Roland. "Find out who needs help walking and get them moving. We're wasting time."

I picked up the Mac-10 Mike may have been carrying and turned to follow them out of the building. We went out the back of the building through the open metal siding walls and headed past the mounds of mine tailings that I had passed on my way in. The bikes were in a metal building next to a bunkhouse in the same direction we were headed down the hill.

"See if there are some cutters or a pair of pliers in the tool kit while I rip the seat off one of these," I told Roland.

"What you gonna do with it?" he asked.

"I want the battery out of it," I told him.

I knew that the front bracket of the seat would give if I gave it a hard yank, which it did. Roland found a pair of pliers and handed them to me. I tried to cut the battery wires off with no success then took hold of the bolt on the ground cable with the pliers and twisted it a couple of times and the bolt came off the lead post it was screwed into. Quickly I removed the bolt from the hot cable and lifted the battery out of the case.

"Help whoever needs help walking and stay ahead of me until we get out, but don't get out of my sight," I told Roland.

Agent Stephenson was out of sight already, but I could see Conklin a few feet behind me, struggling with two of the wounded, just as I reached the crest of the hill where it started on the downward slope. I pointed Roland with the other wounded agent in the right direction heading down the hill through the brush and trees away from the old clearing. One of the agents collapsed just as he made the crest of the hill. I reached out and took him by the arm and started dragging him down the hill. Agent Stephenson was waiting just over the hill.

Chapter Thirty Nine

It had taken me about fifteen minutes to wire the C-4 with several strands of the detonation cord and electric firing caps after I had gotten into the building. It took us a little over ten minutes to reach the position where I had set up earlier. I had set up the first two Claymores just short of the crest of the hill. It had been too quiet and too long without any firing from the trees around the complex. I was hoping that they were just waiting it out until they thought we would let our guard down, then they could make a charge on the building.

"Kathleen, hand me that marked spool of wire," I said.

I heard the clatter of automatic rifle fire and I knew they were ready to make a charge at the building. I had barely cut the wire from the spool and stripped the ends bare when the firing at the buildings paused and I knew they were making their charge. I counted off thirty seconds to give them time to reach the front of the building and start into it, then touched the two strands of wire to the battery and heard the Claymores in the building go off with a loud blast.

"Why did you set up Claymores in front of the doors?" Agent Stephenson asked me.

"I didn't want them to charge inside the building and find we weren't there and remove the wiring from the explosives. That'll keep them from entering the building until I set up the next step," I said.

"So, what now?" she asked.

"Matt, can you set up those Claymores part way down the hill about ten feet apart pointing in this general direction. Set them in an array that will cover the road on both sides and into the brush as well, but so they'll get full coverage of this whole area," I told him.

I reset the wire to the two Claymores I had set earlier, from the rest of the marked spool Agent Stephenson was holding.

"Head down to the bottom of the hill and cut off the wires on that marked roll then bring the roll back to Matt's location. Leave the other roll down there," I told her.

When she started down the hill, I started after her and stopped at Matt's location and waited for her to return with the marked roll. I cut off pieces of wire to wire the four mines together that Agent Conklin had set and attached them to the strands of the roll Stephenson was holding.

"Matt, can you string that wire down to the highway as far as it will reach? Take Roland and the rest of the team and make your way down with Agent Stephenson," I said.

"I don't know if Mike's going to like you blowing away all the evidence," Conklin said.

"I don't think we want them to get hold of any of it and I'm not sure we have control of anything yet," I said.

"How do you think they would use it?" he asked.

"Can you imagine them using any of those RPG's against any of your teams?" I asked.

I waited just a moment and listened for any sign of approach from the direction of the mine buildings, then followed Conklin and Roland down the hill to the highway. Immediately I stripped the wires on the unmarked roll and touched the twisted strands to the battery. It seemed like longer, but one second after I touched the wires to the battery, the ground shook, then I felt the shock wave as it passed over us shaking the tops of the trees.

The explosion of sound that followed was nothing short of horrendous, almost in stages and mixed with the sound of flying wood and metal debris. We were far enough away that none of the debris reached us, but I could see the flame, smoke and flying debris over the crest of the hill. It was worse than I had imagined it to be, shaking the ground almost like an earthquake.

"Watch the road," I told Agent Stephenson and Agent Conklin.

"What's left of them will come boiling down that hill. If any of them make it past the Claymores, drop them with those bushmasters."

"Jesus, we can't just shoot them all!" Agent Stephenson said.

I walked up to her and asked, "Do you think you're going to talk them into surrendering?"

She just stared at me wide eyed when I took the strands of wire from her hand. I didn't take any more time to discuss whether or not to shoot. Conklin was in position looking up the hill. Roland was standing between him and Agent Stephenson.

"Matt, can you and Roland take position on the other side of the road?" I asked. "Kathleen, give Roland your Glock."

"What? Are you crazy?" she yelled.

I looked at Conklin. He didn't say a word. He took his Glock out of his waistband and handed it to Roland.

"You gonna trust me?" he said.

"No, but you better trust us," I told him. "Lie flat on the ground behind the berms on the side of the road until the Claymores go off. I don't have to tell you not to let any of our friends get into the brush."

They no sooner had positioned themselves across the road, Roland out front, when almost a dozen men came over the hill at a trot. I waited to see if any more of them were coming over the hill and let them get past the location of the first two mines. I glanced behind me and saw that Agent Reynolds was coming up the hill through the brush. He walked by me and positioned himself about twenty feet ahead. I waited as long as I could and yelled, "Fire in the hole!"

When I saw Agent Reynolds drop to the ground, I touched the wires to the battery. The first two of the Claymores that I had set at the base of the hill went off, peppering the road and the trees on the opposite side of the road, hitting the group of men from the side and behind. There were still several more on their feet heading down the hill and had just passed their parked vehicles.

"Fire in the hole!" I yelled again and touched the wires on the remainder of the marked roll.

The four Claymores went off simultaneously, blowing the brush back behind them and sending up clouds of dust and rocks in the direction of the hill in a wall of smoke and flame. I tried to see through the dust to see how many of the terrorists were down. Three had gotten through and had stopped in their tracks as if trying to decide which way to go.

"Surrender now or we will open fire!" I yelled.

They raised their Sks rifles to point them in my direction just as Conklin and Roland opened fire. I started firing at the same time Agent Reynolds opened fire. One of them went down from his first volley and another went down from the fire from Roland and Conklin.

The third one almost got into the brush on the side of the wide road when Reynolds emerged from the brush to get a better position to fire at him. His next two shots missed and he went down to one knee to reload. The third man stopped and turned around to get him in his sights when Roland, I and Agent Conklin opened up. He was struck from the opposite side of the road and twisted to his right, then knocked backwards. My next burst hit him in the upper chest and raised dust all around him.

Agent Conklin followed Roland when he stepped out of the brush and started across the road to our position. They walked almost side by side and Roland handed Agent Conklin the Glock he had loaned him. I started down the road and Roland kept pace with me until we reached the SUV's. He put his arms behind him, but Agent Conklin motioned for him to put his wrists out in front and started to place the handcuffs on him. He looked at me and I moved my head side to side to indicate not to.

"You don't have much of a case anymore," I told him. "The evidence is gone, the terrorists are dead and Roland was compelled to take part in killing them."

Reynolds walked up to us and glanced at Conklin and tipped his head to one side, as if to say, "It's no use."

I checked the SUV's until I saw that Mike was in the back of the second one. He was lying on the floor behind the back seat and he was awake.

"How are you doing?" I asked.

"Not good." He said painfully.

"We'll have to get moving right away to get the wounded to Durango," Agent Reynolds said.

"Lead off. I'd like to go by and check on him after the team gets here," I said. "I suppose Stephenson or Conklin will remain here and wait for the other team?"

"Yes, they should be here any minute, but we can't wait," he said.

I still had Mike's Mac-10, but I had used up all the magazines. "If you'll give me a couple more magazines, I'll go with Conklin and check out the site and any survivors, if there's any left up there," I told Agent Reynolds.

"What about Roland?" he asked

"He's with me.?" I said.

"What if there are survivors?" he asked.

"The sooner we get up there, the greater chance we'll have of finding anyone alive," I said.

Agent Stephenson met me when I reached her and Agent Conklin. They seemed to be trying to make a decision whether to start checking on the bodies strewn on the road ahead of us towards the hill or just bypass them and check the buildings at the mine. No one said anything when Roland walked with me past the blasted bodies of the terrorists on our way up the hill.

I held the Mac-10 at port arms and hoped that the shooting war was over. We would be in the open as soon as we crested the highest point of the road into the clearing of the old mining compound. I reached the first of the men lying on the ground and quickly checked for their weapons. There were several Ak'47's on the ground. I picked up the first one I got to, checked the magazine and handed it to Roland.

Most of the large building was gone and the remainder of the wood from the walls was still burning. There were bent scattered scraps of metal and wood covering most of the compound. The smaller building where I had parked the bike the first time next to Mike's truck, was leaning away from the blast, but was still standing. Several of the other small sheds were down, but some of the other buildings were still standing and seemed unaffected by the blast.

The windshield of the old truck was gone but didn't seem otherwise damaged and the SUV was on its side. I checked on Mike's truck and found a chain behind the seat. I attached it to the frame on the upper side and strung it out to Mike's truck. Roland understood what I was doing and got into the cab of the old truck and started it.

"Ok, let her go," I yelled at Roland.

The old truck strained at first and the rear wheels spun.

"Back up, then take up the slack fast when I yell," I told Roland.

I motioned for Agent Conklin to follow me around the SUV, put my hands on the top and waited for him to do the same and I yelled at Roland.

"Hit it, now!" I yelled.

This time the SUV moved off its side and landed on its wheels with a crash and rocked up and down slightly.

"Ok, I guess you have transportation now," I said to Agent Conklin.

"Please take Stephenson with you," I told him before we started back for the SUV.

"What are you going to do here?" he asked.

"There isn't anything more to do. There doesn't seem to be any survivors. They were too close to the blast," I replied.

"One of us needs to stay here and wait for the other teams," he said.

"Then take the SUV and when the wounded are loaded, please send Stephenson in with them," I said.

I could see by her gestures that she wasn't happy with Conklin's order to leave with the wounded. She got into the driver's side of the SUV we had just righted and he got in on the passenger side. He came back shortly, driving the remaining SUV and Roland and I helped him move the bodies we found to a central location. We walked around the area where the agents had fallen and policed up their weapons, then walked around the destroyed building checking for any remnants of the cache.

"It's time I left," I told Agent Reynolds after we had picked up as many of the teams weapons as we could find. "I'd like to get down to see Mike before the other team gets here, or I'll never get out of here."

"All right, Mike knows where to find you," he said.

"Let's go check on the rest of the bikes," I told Roland.

The blast had been well deflected by the mounds of mine tailings and had not visibly damaged the bunkhouse. The motorcycles weren't damaged that I could see. I opened the gas petcock on the first the bike and it started easily. I looked over at Roland and shrugged my shoulders. He just looked at me with a questioning look to see what I was going to do.

"Well, lets get it out of the building," I said.

Fortunately it had a double seat, instead of the more common solo seat of many of the outlaw bikes. I started past the destroyed building, to get to the main clearing which led to the road, with Roland on the seat behind me. It still didn't feel right when I headed across the compound to the road. It would be one hell of a cleanup. I went past a dozen bodies and weapons scattered over the downhill side of the road leading to the highway.

Their vehicles had been in the path of the Claymores and had been damaged extensively. I went through them out of curiosity, but didn't find anything of interest except a lot of 7.62 X 39MM ammunition for the Sks and AK's they had been carrying and several boxes of 9MM, probably for any pistols they had. I picked up two of the Ak-47 forty round capacity magazines that were fully loaded and put them in my jacket pockets. I had returned the Mac-10 to Agent Conklin when we had picked up the team's weapons. Roland still had the Ak-47 I had handed him earlier, so I picked up another one and pulled the bolt back to check the chamber. It was still chambered, so I put it on safety and checked the magazine, which was still full.

Chapter Forty

My bike had been well off the path and out of sight, otherwise Stephenson may have made another attempt at damaging it. I decided I would call Mike later and check on him. I didn't want another confrontation with Agent Stephenson. I set the Ak-47 down and Roland and I had just wrestled my bike around to point it in the direction of the road out of the bushes when I heard the sound of vehicles coming up the highway.

Either I was still paranoid about running into someone else chasing me or it was just natural caution that warned me to stay out of sight. I reached into my pack and felt for the two loose Hand Grenades that I had taken out of the box before I had set up the first Claymores.

For the first time since I had returned, I noticed the lack of sound and the movement of traffic on the highway. Sound would carry through the canyons along the highway and the presence of vehicles along the stretches of pavement between the turns would be heard in the distance. The road from the highway leading to the mine complex was in the middle of one of the long stretches of highway through this canyon.

Had there been traffic of any kind, I would have heard it and looked in that direction out of caution. I had missed the approaching sound of the vehicle probably because of all the noise and activity after the explosion and the fight with the remaining men who had attacked Mike's team. I had almost put my caution aside to step into the road and prepare to leave when I heard the sound of an engine winding down.

I stayed low and approached the edge of the bushes next to the road to watch for any vehicles that may turn in this direction and motioned for Roland to stay under cover. A grey SUV with at least two men in it, that I could see, made the turn into the mine road. The driver gunned the engine after he made the turn and slammed the brakes, just fifty feet short of the bike we had left in the road.

The sound of their shouting at each other in a language I didn't understand sounded like shock at the sight ahead of them beyond the parked vehicles. I pulled the pin on the first grenade and rolled it toward their vehicle. I hadn't been seen yet, so I pulled the pin on the second one and tossed it out toward the vehicle too.

The first one had rolled under the back of the SUV, but I couldn't see if it had landed under the vehicle or had rolled through to the other side. The second one took a bounce and hit the frame just under the passenger door and I could see that it was heard by the passenger because he jerked to look to the right. He opened the door to bail out just as I ducked my head and the first grenade went off under the tank. It sounded almost like two explosions.

The first one a sharp, loud cracking sound followed by the sound of the gas tank exploding in a flaming crash. I looked up to see him blown out of the door. The grenades had gone off with a loud cracking sound, throwing wire shrapnel into the undercarriage of the vehicle like gravel hitting the side of a barrel, tossing the passenger five feet out to the side of the road.

I got up quickly and could see that he was down and not moving. I picked up the Ak-47 and started across the road directly, not wanting to get any closer to the burning vehicle. I got far enough into the road to see that the driver's side door was open and another man was trying to get up off the ground about twenty feet to the side, almost in the bushes.

I pointed the Ak-47 at him and started walking toward him. He looked up to see me when I stopped about fifteen feet away from him. His hair was scorched and his shirt was in rags but he was looking directly at me. He didn't look surprised, but had a look of recognition or comprehension in his eyes and not a shred of fear. I gestured with the rifle, jerking the muzzle up twice.

"Hands up!" I said loudly.

Then I gestured at him again, jerking the rifle to the left to indicate that he walk to me. I walked backward and indicated to him by pointing the rifle to my left for him to go there. He walked to my left and I gestured with my left hand for him to sit on the ground. "Put your hands behind your head." I said and patted my left hand behind my head so he would understand.

I had a feeling that he understood English very well. He knelt down and put his hands behind his head and glared at me. I kept his vehicle between me and the road in case any more of his friends happened to show up. Roland emerged from the bushes and walked to the motorcycle we had brought down from the mine.

I heard a vehicle at the top of the hill and glanced up to see Agent Conklin walk over the crest and stop to look in my direction. I waved for him to come down the hill and he turned around and walked back in the other direction. The SUV appeared presently and started down the hill a couple of minutes later. He maneuvered around the bodies lying in the road and past the parked vehicles to stop about twenty feet away from me.

"This is getting uglier by the minute," he said when he stopped and looked at my prisoner on the ground. "How many more were there?"

"I didn't check the vehicle. One tried to bail out of the passenger side and this one made it out with just a few burns," I answered. "You may want to search him now that we're both here."

He drew his Glock and walked to the prisoner and gestured for him to lie forward on the ground. He patted him down and checked his legs and ankles for any possible weapons.

"There's some ties in the glove compartment," he said, pointing at his SUV. I handed him some ties and he made quick work of binding the prisoner's hands behind his back and then his ankles.

"I wonder why he gave up so easily?" he said.

"I don't know. It could be that he didn't want to die without the chance to take one of us with him. Maybe it wouldn't be any honor for him to die without some kind of weapon to fight his way into paradise," I said.

"Ok, I think I can keep things in control here." He said.

"I'm outta here," I told him. "If I see anything unusual on the way out, besides the other FBI team, I'll head back if I can.

I walked to my bike and tied the Ak-47 sling over the sissy bar and stuck the rifle into my bag and tied it in. The barrel and sights showed clearly out of the bag so I tied a shirt over it and stuffed it down into the bag and retied it. He still had the other Ak-47 and looked down at it in his hands then looked back at me.

"Don't think about it," I said.

I held out my hand and took it from him and threw on the seat of one of the teams SUV's, and then motioned towards the highway. I pulled onto the highway and headed south. Roland followed on the bike we had brought down.

We had gone about three miles when I caught sight of some vehicles coming up the highway in the distance. I dropped into a low part of the highway with the crest of a rise in the distance and looked for somewhere to get off the pavement. There was a widening in the road, almost like a pull out to the right, about a hundred feet ahead. I pulled off the pavement into it with Roland following and went straight in the brush where it started to taper back into the highway and shut down the engine. It was far enough out of sight except for vehicles coming in the same direction we had come from.

There was no mistaking the like colored, dark blue Chevrolet Suburban's and the dark utilities of the passengers that I could see when they went by at a pretty high speed. I waited a couple more minutes and was rewarded with the sight of two light colored utility vans going by at high speed.

It took about thirty minutes to reach Durango, where we stopped a short distance out of town. Roland stopped in front of me and I got off my bike and walked to him. He shut off the engine when I reached him and just looked at me with no emotion on his face.

"You're not out of it," I told him. "They know where to find you and will probably want more details, but I can't see how they could charge you. You weren't at the camp when they made their raid and there's no evidence tying you to any of the munitions that are now gone."

"Well, a few of my boys will be in jail," he said. "They still had some guns and stuff with them."

"Well, they can consider themselves lucky," I said. "They could've been guarding the contraband when we got there, instead of the owner of that bike you're on. It may be a while before you see any of them."

"They may start thinkin' it was me turned 'em in," he said.

"They may find that it's easier to cooperate with the government and get immunity or a reduction. It's a lot better choice then getting treated as a terrorist by Homeland and disappear for a couple of years," I said.

"What about me? You think I can get immunity?" he asked.

"Oh, you'll figure a way out of it," I said. "You can consider yourself quite lucky to come out of it as no more than a witness. This is a national security problem now and it'll take years to sort it out. You may want to reconsider your values and think about becoming a citizen again."

"What do you mean?" he asked.

"You came out of this alive. It's about time you decided which side you're on. If you and a lot of other outlaws, gang bangers and radicals don't change their ways, they won't have a country much less be able to ride around freely," I said.

"What about you man?" he asked. "What's it going to be for you?"

"I don't know," I answered. "I'll be seeing a lot more of the Feds, since they think I have knowledge of some of the terrorist's operations, which I don't. It'll be a long time before they forget about me."

"Am I going to have to be watching my backside for you and any of your boys sometime down the road?" I asked.

"Too much trouble man; I don't need the grief," he said.

"Just remember what side you're on. No hard feelings Roland?" I asked him.

"Naw, I owe you for getting me out of there," he said.

At Cortez, I took 160 to a little place called Teec Nos Pos. I reached the junction to Highway 64 a little over an hour later and stopped for a break. I reflected over the events of the last few days while I sat on my bike looking toward the highway.

It was going to take a lot of time to shake off the dark thoughts of more of the terrorists showing up or some still pissed off biker to show up looking for me. It was less confusing when it was just bikers jumping me and taking shots at me. Now there was the possibility of some terrorist showing up too, although I couldn't see anywhere along the line that any of them had seen me or would have a way of locating me.

Four hours later I was heading into the main yard of the ranch. It was early afternoon and not a cloud in the sky when I rolled the bike close the house and stopped in the shade of one of the trees. Anne's SUV wasn't in sight, but I could see the dually parked around the back.

I took the liberty to clean up and I felt safe enough to lie down and was asleep so quickly that I didn't remember when it was that I had dropped off. I awakened to the sound of the front door opening and swung my feet to the floor. I walked out of the bedroom just as Anne entered the front door.

She was wearing a light blue long sleeved western shirt tucked into her boot cut, barely faded blue jeans. Her light brown blonde hair was loose and flowing around her startled face as she walked across the room slowly. I held her for a long time, the scent of her skin and hair filling my nostrils until she pulled away to arm's length and spoke to me.

"Well, it looks like you made it almost in one piece. Is it over now?" She asked.

"It seems to be," I said. I could feel the fatigue of the last two weeks drawing me down until I felt like I was going to melt to the floor. I didn't think any more about it while she led me to the bedroom and backed me to the bed until I sat on it, then lay back. She pulled off my boots and I was barely aware that she had pulled off her boots and I was barely awake when she lay beside me and cradled my head in her right arm as I faded out.

Other books by Antonio Sandoval:
TIMESTONES,   http://www.amazon.com/dp/B005SBIYDC,
available on Amazon Kindle/ebooks.
SUNSET RUN, available on Amazon.com ebooks and paperback.
TALKING ICE, available on Amazon.com ebooks and paperback.

15525356R00188

Made in the USA
Charleston, SC
08 November 2012